Solace

Bethany Adams

Solace
Return of the Elves
by Bethany Adams

Edited by Jody Wallace at www.jodywallace.com
Cover design by Melissa Stevens of The Illustrated Author Design
Service at www.theillustratedauthor.net
Interior design by Gaynor Smith of Indie Books Gone Wild
at www.ibgw.net
Published in the United States of America

Author's Note: Previously On...

I've done my very best to make each book in my series capable of being read alone, but now that we're on the eighth book, I thought I'd give a brief summary of the previous books. I'll also include a character list and short dictionary in the back. If you're new to the series, only read the rest of this section if you're okay with spoilers!

In SOULBOUND, half-blood Arlyn confronts her elven father, Lyr, after traveling to his world. He's surprised to find that the woman he left on Earth bore him a child, but he welcomes his daughter. But things are far from easy. Not only is Arlyn drawn into a soulbond with her father's friend, Kai, but her arrival prompts Kai's father, Allafon, to hasten his plot against Lyr. Arlyn only has time for a little training with new magic teacher, Selia, before she, Lyr, and Kai are taken captive. In the end, Allafon is defeated, but Lyr is injured, and Arlyn's grandmother almost dies.

SUNDERED continues the story from Lyr's point of view. Though Allafon was defeated, the person behind his actions was not. Banished Prince Kien is creating havoc amongst the fae with poisoned energy, and the Neorans, vassals of the Seelie Sidhe, petition Lyr for aid when their city is overrun by disease and madness. As Lyr struggles to help them, another faction of fae, the Ljósálfar, arrive from Alfheim—brought by Meli, his potential soulbonded. Lyr sends Kai to help evacuate the Neorans, but when he arrives, the inhabitants have been massacred. Eventually, Arlyn and Kai manage to destroy the spell causing the poison, but they are captured by a Seelie lord, Naomh, who turns out to be Kai's true father.

The novella EXILED features Delbin, a young elf who was sent from Moranaia to Earth when he was a teenager in order to escape Allafon. The scout Inona is sent to check on Delbin. Soon after her arrival, Prince Kien tries to recruit Delbin to join his group of half-bloods. Delbin refuses, and he and Inona eventually track down and capture Kien. Kien escapes, but Delbin is allowed to return to Moranaia and becomes the student of Prince Ralan, a powerful seer.

In SEARED, Ralan leaves his daughter Eri on Moranaia and returns to Earth to track down his brother Kien. Plagued by visions foretelling his death, Ralan is nevertheless determined to stop Kien for good. In the process, he meets his soulbonded, Cora, who owns a shop where fae can trade gold or jewels for human clothes. Her friend and employee, Maddy, is kidnapped by Kien's minions, leading Cora to join Ralan in the quest to defeat Kien. With the help of Vek of the Unseelie and his nephew, Fen, Kien is found, although he ultimately escapes to Moranaia. Ralan and Cora confront Kien at the palace. Kien nearly kills Ralan, but Cora manages to save him. The king beheads Kien, but in the process, a mysterious surge of power is released.

Though Kien was defeated, he used his death to release poison into a barrier that withheld magic from Earth. In ABYSS, the dragon Kezari senses that poison through her link to Earth and goes to retrieve her rider, Aris, only to find him being tortured by his potential soulbonded. After she saves him, Aris agrees to accompany the dragon to Braelyn, the estate of Lord Lyr. Aris doesn't know that his wife Selia, who believes him to be dead, accepted a position there a few months before. He struggles to deal with his trauma as he longs to reunite with his wife. Although a mind healer helps, Aris must overcome his darkness in time to prevent the barrier from shattering, releasing a catastrophic amount of energy at once. He, Kezari, Selia, and Kai manage to prevent disaster, but in the process, a direct portal is created between Moranaia and Earth, one that will need guarding in the future.

In AWAKENING, Ralan appoints his sister Dria to be in charge of the new outpost on Earth guarding the portal to Moranaia. In the meantime, the Unseelie prince Vek is tasked by his father to kill the leader of the outpost and claim the power stored there. Beholden to the Moranaians, Vek seeks to find a way out of this order, and while researching, he discovers that the new leader of the outpost is his mate. When the outpost comes under attack, Dria and Vek work together to find the person responsible. They eventually uncover a plot that involves the Unseelie king and the Seelie lord Meren. Dria challenges the king to combat, but Vek's sister Ara ultimately defeats him, becoming the new Unseelie queen. Meren later attempts to kill Vek but is thwarted.

Meren continues to cause trouble in ASCENT. This time, he attempts to manipulate Fen and claim the Seelie throne. However, Fen and his potential mates, Maddy and Anna, stumble into one of Meren's plans to spread poisoned energy and act to diffuse the situation. Eventually, Fen, Maddy, and Anna complete the mate bond and confront Meren. This leads to a fight in the Seelie court, though Meren escapes. Maddy, Fen, and Anna help the Seelie queen by removing a mysterious poison from her blood before returning to the outpost.

Books by Bethany Adams:

Soulbound
Return of the Elves Book 1

Sundered
Return of the Elves Book 2

Exiled
A Return of the Elves Novella Book 3

Seared
Return of the Elves Book 4

Abyss
Return of the Elves Book 5

Awakening
Return of the Elves Book 6

Ascent
Return of the Elves Book 7

Also Available:

The Return of the Elves Collection
Books 1-4

The Return of the Elves Collection
Books 5-7
Includes bonus short story The Sentinels

The Return of the Elves Coloring Book
Volume 1

Notes and Acknowledgements

Before I get into thanks, I have a bit of an author's note. You see, when I first started pondering what Lial's and Lynia's book might entail, I knew there would be some form of illness involved. There are threads of that potential starting several books—and years—back. What I didn't anticipate was writing this book in the middle of a global pandemic. It would be incorrect to say that the last year hasn't colored Solace in some ways, but I do want to make clear that I didn't base the illness in this book on the coronavirus. I did my best to leave out current events and focus entirely on what was needed for my own story in my own fictional universe. I would never want to capitalize on others' pain, so know that if I have done so, it is accidental. Also, please forgive any inaccuracies. I did my best to research a complex subject.

Now, for my thanks. As always, I owe much gratitude to my husband and children. I appreciate your support more than I can say.

Thank you to my critique partners, Shiloh and Catherine. Your advice is invaluable, and this book wouldn't be nearly as awesome without you. Poor Catherine was answering texts at all hours, too. Many thanks!

Of course, I owe much gratitude to my editor, Jody Wallace, my cover artist, Melissa Stevens at The Illustrated Author Design Services, and my formatter, Gaynor Smith. Thank you for sticking with me despite my disordered ways.

Though they might not see this version, many thanks to Stefan Rudnicki, Gabrielle de Cuir, and everyone at Skyboat who works so hard on my audiobooks. I appreciate it!

Thank you to Roxana for compiling so much about Moranaia for me. It was (and will be) such a great help. I hope you love Lial's and

Lynia's story. I know you've been waiting a while.

No "thanks" section is complete without sending my love to my wonderful readers. I treasure every kind message and email. It makes me happy to make you happy!

*To the doctors, nurses, healthcare
professionals, and medical researchers
around the world.
'Thanks' can never be enough.*

MORANAIA

ISLE OF DRAGONS

UNCHARTERED LANDS

THE NORTHERN MOUNTAINS

BRAELM

SOUTHERN MOUNTAINS

ROYAL PALACE

THE PLAINS

⊙ THE CITADEL

⊙ FIORH

SOUTHERN DESERT

Bethany Adams

1

Though the cold seeped through the cloak beneath him, Lial remained seated on the smooth grass, his focus on the small hole at the base of the healing tower. It was a rare sunny day for early winter, and the next ice storm wasn't likely to hit until at least the morrow. No one was in imminent need of treatment. What better time to see if any of the *camahr* would emerge without the draw of food?

It wasn't likely. The *camahr* mother had raised three litters here already, and none of those had shown him more than passing favor. The current litter appeared to like him no better. Although a snout peeked out now and then, none emerged into the dim afternoon light. Perhaps they had already scanned him and identified him as a loner, too accustomed to living by himself to deserve a bond with one of their kind.

They, too, were lone creatures. By late winter, the mother and kits would be gone, parting from each other to wander the forest individually. After that, his chance at a *camahr* companion would disappear for the season. But what was the hurry? If none from this litter chose him, there was always another year, and if the *camahr* mother didn't come back, well…he was accustomed to living alone.

No matter how much he'd begun to long for a partner. A family.

A rustle of cloth and the soft sound of footfalls caught his ear, and Lial scowled at the interruption. However, as soon as he caught sight of the source, his blood froze from a chill deeper than the frigid ground beneath him. Eri. Never before had he met a six-year-old who could bring terror to a person, but she managed it.

Without a word, she plopped down beside him. Her neutral expression brought him no comfort. Nor did the serious glint in her golden eyes, a near replica of her father's. Had she come to share some terrible prophecy? Visions of some catastrophe? No one could ever guess what the child-seer would say.

"I hope you aren't planning on giving up," Eri said.

Lial considered her and her words for a moment. There were multiple things she could be speaking of, and her face gave no indication of her thoughts. "To what are you referring?"

Eri smiled. "The *camahr*, of course."

"Have you foreseen my success?"

Just like that, her smile dropped. "No. I…I didn't mean anything like that. I've seen you over here a few times, but this time, you looked sad. That's all."

"Forgive me, Eri," Lial said, wincing at his blunder. Had he fallen so low that he would question a child? She was far too young to be treated as an official seer, strong gift or no. "I didn't intend to pressure you."

She shrugged. "You didn't. I guess I should get used to people asking. *Onaial* tried to warn me about telling too much, and I didn't listen. I think everyone is afraid of me except him and Cora and Iren."

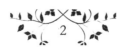

Regret sliced through Lial like the winter wind as he studied the forlorn little girl. He was as guilty as anyone else. Hadn't he tensed in dread at her arrival? She must have noticed, but she'd sat beside him anyway.

It wasn't pleasant to bear such a strong ability as a child. His healing gift had weighed him down so heavily in his youth that he'd almost squandered it out of rebellion, especially when Aralee... *No.* Lial cut that memory off before it could form. He could use his own experiences to help the girl without revisiting the worst of those events.

Eri needed to feel that she belonged, and not because of her gift.

The people of this estate were kinder than those in the royal court where he'd been raised, so she stood a greater chance of finding friends here who liked her for herself. But Eri had only lived at Braelyn for a few months after her father had brought her across the Veil from Earth. Since the only other child living at the main estate was Iren, she would have to travel down into the valley to the village of Telerdai to meet others near her age, and that hadn't been safe until fairly recently.

He would have to remind Ralan of the possibility now that things had calmed.

"You are lonely," Lial finally said.

Eri sighed. "Not as much as you are, but yeah."

Did she think the same about him, then? He frowned. She wasn't wrong, but he hadn't believed anyone noticed. "Do I truly seem so?"

"It's sort of obvious," she answered with a chuckle. "That's why I hope you don't give up on the *camahr*. I would Look to find out if one picks you, but Lady Megelien told me not to examine your futures for a while."

3

What? Lial's hands clenched in his lap as he fought the urge to ask questions. Such as why the goddess of time and seers was warning the child away from visions of his future. What could be worse than the things Lady Megelien had allowed Eri to See already? Just in the last few months, she'd foreseen assassination attempts and her father's possible death. Though those attempts had been foiled and her father saved, none of those events could have been easy for a child to handle.

But the goddess told Eri not to Look at *his* futures? This couldn't be good.

Abruptly, Eri stood, the lack of worry on her face in sharp contrast to the dread her casual statement had brought Lial. She merely smiled at him and then shifted back and forth on her feet as though preparing to run off. "I think Iren's lessons are almost over," she said, "So I'll leave you alone now. You won't give up, though, right?"

"I will endeavor not to," Lial answered, praying the child didn't catch the tightness in his voice. It wasn't her fault that her innocent words had caused him such turmoil. "Go enjoy your play time with Iren."

It could be nothing. It had to be nothing. Perhaps Lady Megelien was giving Eri time to rest after Seeing so much over the last few months. Lial took a deep breath and tried to focus on the hole in the tower wall instead of Eri's words. But it was no use. The twisting in his gut told him the child's words were definitely something.

Maybe part of him had been waiting for this. Ever since he'd detected that strange illness that had infected Fen, Lial had been uneasy, haunted by a nagging whisper of a task unfinished. Could that task be coming due now? If there was some poison that would kill half-bloods, thousands could die. Horribly. He would certainly be called to help treat that.

There could also be a war, of course. Meren, a former Sidhe lord, had all but declared himself an enemy of the Seelie court by claiming the throne should be his, and he was an enemy of Moranaia, too. If he managed to find enough support to attack the Seelie queen, Moranaia would give aid. Yet again, many would die, and Lial would be right there trying to save them.

Lady Megelien might give Eri glimpses of dire events, but She wasn't known to be a cruel goddess. Lial couldn't imagine that she would allow any child to See horrific, mass death on this world or any other. And while his fears might prove wrong, he could not dismiss the chance that Eri had been warned away from his futures for just such a reason.

If his fears proved right, he would need to prepare.

Lial had to find Ralan, who was a seer like his daughter. Lial couldn't presume to second guess the actions of a goddess, but She seemed more likely to hide such possibilities from Eri than to inhibit Ralan's Sight. If the prince did know, he might not tell Lial anything, of course, but he had to try.

His ability to plan depended on it.

Lynia skimmed her gaze up the long spiral staircase that circled its way to the top of the library. At each floor, a small landing led to the walkway and bookshelves lining the walls. There should be ample room there for the lift Selia hoped to install, especially if the landings were widened. But the tables on the lowest level of the tower could be a problem.

"We'll have to shift things around at the bottom," Lynia said.

From her place at the base of the steps, Selia frowned over at Lynia. "Would that be a problem?"

Lynia studied the bare area beside the group of tables, and when she felt the telltale rise of bile up her throat, she ruthlessly swallowed it down. She was here. Alive. Her body might have been broken when she'd landed on those stones, but she was whole now. What better way to show it than to slide a table over the spot, plop herself down with a book, and get on with her research?

"I believe it is an excellent idea," Lynia said. "Although I do hope you aren't installing the lift for me. Aside from the odd ache now and then, my back has fully recovered. I can climb the stairs as I always have."

A hint of pink tinged Selia's tan skin. "It did occur to me when I saw the lift Dria installed in the outpost that such a thing would have been handy during and after your attack."

Lynia grimaced, but she couldn't deny it was true. Norin, Braelyn's former first-in-command, would not have been able to trap her at the top of the tower if there'd been another method for getting up and down. And she couldn't deny that she would have welcomed an easier method to access the books while she was recovering from her terrible injuries after her fall.

"Besides," Selia continued, "Iren and Eri would benefit, as would Arlyn and Cora when they grow heavier with child. I'm surprised no one has built such a thing already."

Another truth. When Lynia had first moved here, she'd been surprised by how little things changed on the estate. She'd asked her bonded, Telien, about the matter, and he'd told her it was tradition. The lord or lady of the estate maintained things as they were rather than alter them. There were even a few furnishings left from when the dragons had burned the original house thousands of years ago.

"Telien, Lyr's father, that is…" Lynia hesitated, searching for the words to explain even though she'd always found it unusual herself.

"Being direct descendants of the prince who founded Braelyn, Telien and his predecessors held a great deal of pride in the history of this place. My birth family is minor nobility up north, so I found the extent of Telien's resistance to changes rather unusual."

Especially since he'd been all-too-willing to experiment with dangerous things—like steel swords. But Lynia didn't want to get into *that*.

"I wish I could say all of the minor nobility are that way." Selia's mouth twisted into an odd sort of grimace-smile. "My father is stiflingly traditional. Though not when it comes to structural modifications to our estate, I suppose. But will Lyr have the same trouble with my idea?"

"I don't know if it's because of the time he spent on Earth, but fortunately, Lyr is more open to such changes than his father was," Lynia said.

Guilt swamped her before the words had finished echoing through the room. Telien's stubbornness might have been one of the biggest issues that had caused discord between her and her bonded, but it felt like betrayal to hint such. Over twenty years had passed since Telien's death. How long before the memories of their disagreements didn't sting her heart with self-recrimination?

If Selia noticed the darkening of Lynia's mood, she was kind enough not to say so. "It is indeed fortunate for me. I would rather not have to convert the brooding tower back to its original stone."

Lynia found herself smiling at the reminder of the observation tower, its nickname earned by one too many moping sessions at the top—usually by Lyr or Kai, but they were far from the only ones. Truly, though, it was an excellent place to think. Or it had been before Selia's husband Aris had taken up residence there. He stayed in Selia's room more and more, but when the dark memories of the years he'd

spent being tortured overcame him, he returned to the tower with its large windows and hatch to the open roof on the top floor.

"It is more beautiful after you transmuted the stone to crystal."

"Thank you," Selia answered.

Lynia let her gaze trail up the floors of bookshelves. "Do you have a design in mind? I'm certain Lyr will want to know what you intend before he approves the plan."

"Something that will blend, I hope." Selia ran her hand across the wooden railing beside the stairs. "The walkways of each floor are stone, but the bannisters are wood. If I can get Maddy to bring Fen during her next visit, I might be able to have him create a stone platform. It would save time on hunting down an earth mage. Most of the ones here are too busy maintaining the cliff sides and other stonework during the ice storms."

Unfortunately, that was true. The month when autumn transitioned to winter was the second-toughest time of year. As the temperature hovered around freezing, rain froze on contact or fell as ice, and only when the cold settled deeper into the land did it transition to snow. Winter-to-spring was worse, although for the same reason. Poor Lial had to be overburdened with all the slips and falls, and they'd only had a couple of minor storms so far.

She should—

Her heart lurched. No, she should not offer to help him. Though—or maybe because—he was temptingly handsome, Lynia did her best to avoid the man. He was in love with her, and she had no idea what to do about it. Pursue the draw she felt toward him or ignore it?

When she'd first learned of his feelings, the answer had seemed obvious—do nothing. They'd never even talked about his interest, which suited her well enough. She still mourned Telien. Regardless

of her attraction to the grumpy healer, another relationship didn't feel right. How could she even contemplate one after having and then losing a soulbond?

And Lial. He was prickly, arrogant, obstinate…and lonely. She'd never guessed how much he bore by himself until she'd seen him break down over Aris's healing. Lial had willingly taken the pain of Aris's tortured memories, and if Lynia hadn't seen the result for herself, she never would have been the wiser. How many other burdens did he keep inside? How much had healing her spine cost him? She could ask, but he was unlikely to tell her.

"Lynia?"

Her face heated at Selia's worried query. "Forgive me. My thoughts wandered. Could you ask Kezari to help you?"

Selia grimaced. "I would rather not. She has been agitated since her last visit to Earth with Aris, and I would prefer not to deal with an antsy dragon."

"Understandable," Lynia said.

The door swished open behind her, and Lynia glanced back in time to see Eri dance through. Odd. It wasn't the right day for the child's lessons in the library, and Ralan handled those as often as not. What could have brought her? The child could be searching for a book to read for pleasure or merely stopping by to say hello. But still, shivers trailed down Lynia's spine as she met Eri's eyes. Gods forfend it be a dire prophecy that brought the child her way.

"Is all well?" Lynia asked.

A hint of sadness tinged the child's smile. "Nothing's wrong. Just looking for Iren. He finished with his lessons not long ago, right?"

The strangeness of the question struck Lynia, for Eri and Iren could find one another by telepathic communication. The child had to know that Iren was working with Kai on sword fighting today, not

history or etiquette lessons here. She and Selia exchanged wary looks before the other woman walked closer.

"Iren should be finishing up in the practice field," Selia said. "Didn't he remind you this morning?"

Eri shrugged. "Guess I forgot."

"I'm sure he wouldn't mind if you met him there," Lynia said, trying to stifle her nervousness.

"Well…" Eri scuffed her foot against the floor and averted her gaze. "I'm sort of not allowed at the practice field. I could maybe ask *Onaial* if I could get close, but I'm not going to interrupt his meeting with Lial to ask. That's too important."

Unease shifted through Lynia. "His meeting with Lial?"

"Yes. My father looked pretty serious, but I couldn't See much." Eri shrugged again. "Thanks for the help. I guess I'll wait for Iren as close as I can get."

With a smile and a wave, Eri darted from the room, leaving Lynia staring after her. Why would Lial be having a serious discussion with Ralan, heir to the throne and a powerful seer? Furthermore, why had Eri decided to come by to "innocently" drop that bit of information?

"Something about that…" Selia said hesitantly.

"Agreed." Lynia closed the door before turning back to her friend. "That encounter was far from normal, even for Eri. I suppose it is up to us to figure out why."

Selia nodded. "You'll speak with Lial?"

"I don't know." Lynia's shoulders slumped. "Part of me feels that it isn't my place. We aren't… Unless it concerns Braelyn, I have no right to question him about his conversations without a deeper relationship between us. The child gave no indication that estate business was involved, but we both know Eri told us of his meeting with Ralan for a reason."

"I suppose if it's important enough, he'll tell you himself," Selia said. "If nothing else, I can see if Iren knows anything."

It was kind of Selia not to pressure her, although she had to be as curious as Lynia. But she needn't have bothered. No matter how much Lynia argued with herself, she knew she would have to talk to Lial before she drove herself mad with all of the possibilities. The question wasn't if.

It was when.

Lial's concern carried him up the steps to the top of the guest tower at a quick pace. He and his cousin Ralan had never been close, but hopefully, there was enough respect between them for Lial to get some answers. Or perhaps not, considering how aggravating his cousin could be. If he wanted to imitate Ralan's typical bad behavior, Lial could blast his questions directly into his cousin's head. But although he wasn't afraid to annoy Ralan, he didn't deem it best to begin such an important discussion with rudeness.

Before he could knock, Ralan swung the portal inward and gestured for him to enter his suite of rooms. So he'd known Lial was coming. Had his cousin known Eri would taunt him with her words, or had Ralan Seen his presence after the fact? Either was possible, and Lial honestly didn't care which. What really mattered was whether Ralan would give him answers.

Lial strode into the living area, a quick scan revealing it to be empty. Ralan closed the door and waved to a couple of chairs beside the window. "Have a seat."

As his cousin settled into his chair like the king he would someday be, Lial lowered into the seat across from him with much less ease. This errand might be important, but that didn't mean it was

pleasant. He didn't really *want* to know about some dire future, yet he had less choice than most people did. Others' survival depended on his knowledge.

"Is Cora at home?" Lial asked. A little bit of procrastination, perhaps, but procrastination with a purpose. If she had just stepped out for a moment, he would rather know before she returned. He didn't want an audience for this.

Ralan's distinctive golden eyes fastened on Lial with unsettling intensity. "She is napping."

"I hope she isn't feeling unwell."

"I would assume a healer would understand how exhausting it is to grow another person," Ralan said, one corner of his mouth curling up. "Stop stalling. Your thoughts don't usually beat upon my mental shields the way they're doing now unless you're sending them on purpose, especially not at a distance. I've sensed you nearing for several minutes, and I would like to know why."

Lial found the words sticking in his throat. Gods, but this was no easy matter. Especially since he and Ralan were hardly friends. They were alike in far too many ways for that. Unfortunately, there was no one else Lial could ask about this.

"Eri dropped by to speak with me a while ago," Lial began. "A little unusual but otherwise unremarkable. Except for one thing."

Ralan let out an exasperated sigh, and some of his regal demeanor faded. "What did she say?"

"That the goddess Megelien has blocked her from examining my future."

"What?" Ralan straightened in his seat. "You mean she doesn't know?"

Lial ground his teeth together. "*I* don't know. I can guess at possibilities, but that's it. So *you* tell *me*. Is some terrible future about

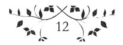

to occur? If that is the reason for her block, I would prefer to hear the truth."

His cousin's gaze grew distant, and Lial braced himself for whatever dire event Ralan was about to foresee. Even so, he wasn't prepared for Ralan's skin to go pale a few moments before the prince blinked. The chill Lial had felt with Eri returned in full force as his cousin stared at him.

"Well," Ralan said.

Just that—then silence.

Lial made a quick catalogue of every unpleasant potion he could slip into the other man's drink. "I feel much relieved by your descriptive explanation."

His stomach sank when Ralan didn't even smirk.

"The strands have…shifted a little since my last check," Ralan said, ignoring the bite to Lial's words. "You don't want to know some of them. Praise be to Megelien that Eri can't See a few of the possibilities. Or even most of them."

Lial hesitated, his lips not wanting to form the words, but he had to ask. "My death? Elan is not strong enough to take my place, especially in an emergency, and while I *am* teaching Maddy to use her healing gift, she lives on Earth with her mates, one of whom is an Unseelie prince. If I will be in need of—"

"Are you more worried about dying or leaving the estate without a healer?" Ralan shook his head. "Never mind. I'm already aware of the answer to that even without using Sight."

"I'm hardly pleased about either option," Lial pointed out.

"Regardless, I imagine you'll be happy to hear that while your death is remotely possible, it isn't likely." Despite the words, Ralan's expression didn't soften. Not precisely reassuring. "That being said…you'll be the one walking into the maelstrom."

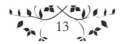

Frustration and fear fought a quick battle inside him before ending in an unpleasant truce. "What maelstrom? I'm usually the one fixing the results of trouble, not causing it."

"I didn't say you would cause the problem," Ralan said. "But if you and Lynia aren't willing to take it on, many will suffer. Worse than what happened with Neor."

Neor? The small Seelie colony had sought Lyr's aid after poisoned energy afflicted many of its citizens with madness. Kai had brought the survivors to a safe spot near the portal for Lial to heal their damaged minds. Men, women, children—few had been spared from the effects. And that hadn't been the worst part. Lord Meren of the Seelie court had sent an army through Neor to try to eliminate the sickened, so Lial had been responsible for healing those types of injuries, too.

"More trouble from Meren?" Lial asked. "Lyr would be a better choice if you must stop another invasion, though I am always willing to help people where I may."

Ralan's chest heaved with the force of his breath. "Meren, yes. Invasion, no. How much has Maddy shared about their conflicts with the bastard?"

"A fair amount, as far as I know. Meren attempted to afflict a young half-blood with the type of poisoned energy that once sickened Fen, and a version of that dark magic kept the Seelie queen unconscious for some time. It was a perversion of a similar spell that Prince Kien used on Earth's energy field."

At that, his cousin grimaced. No doubt Ralan hated to be reminded of his brother, Kien, who'd been banished to Earth for using dark magic—amongst many other horrific things. Kien had used his own death to both crack and poison the wall preventing magic from flowing freely on Earth, but beyond that, his actions had cost Ralan dearly, and more than once.

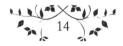

But Ralan's expression blanked quickly. "Yes. Most similar, I would say, to the splinter that lodged in Fen's heart. The one that caused physical sickness in Fen and possibly Maddy."

All at once, Lial understood exactly where this was heading, and his stomach pitched and roiled until he sent a tendril of his healing magic to soothe the turmoil. It seemed that unfinished task *was* coming back to haunt him—the mystery illness. In this case, being right was hardly a comfort. He would almost prefer a war.

Almost.

Clechtan. Healing Fen had been part experiment and part luck. Elves and fae weren't affected by viruses, which didn't survive the rush of magical energy their bodies required to survive. Lial's knowledge of those was more theoretical. Though he knew viruses could cause illness, he'd never been able to study how. He was more familiar with bacteria—but only a little. Bacteria could be tricky since most lifeforms hosted some amount of the organisms to function, but their systems typically expelled the bad kind without trouble.

Because of that, even the extensive training a healer undertook on Moranaia provided little information about the type of sickness experienced by humans. Kien's initial spell had focused on attacking the elves' energy renewal systems—the channels that drew magic into their bodies—but until Fen, there hadn't been any sign the poison could create true illness in elves or fae. Even when Lial had healed Fen, he hadn't been able to identify much about the cause aside from the stain of dark energy.

Running a fair bit of healing energy through Fen seemed to have worked, but Lial's ignorance of the true cause had formed the base of that nagging whisper he hadn't been able to quiet. He'd searched everyone else in the outpost on Earth for similar sickness,

but he'd found no sign of it. But he hadn't forgotten. Apparently, that lingering worry had held just cause.

"Looks like you're getting a clue," Ralan said, but his tone lacked the mocking edge it usually would have borne.

Lial met his cousin's somber gaze. "How bad?"

"Depends on your actions," Ralan answered. "Yours and Lynia's."

2

Once Selia left, Lynia considered returning to her research, but there was no way she would be able to concentrate after her encounter with Eri. She did a quick check of the spell connecting her to the estate and discovered that Lial was no longer with Ralan. Should she rush over to the healing tower or wait for some other time? There was every possibility that the little girl had intended nothing by seeking Lynia out. A coincidence that could end in embarrassment when Lynia spoke to Lial.

It was close enough to dinnertime that she decided to wait. Perhaps he would be there tonight, and she could pull him aside afterward. The possibility was greater than it once had been. As more guests had arrived at the estate, Lial had slowly been drawn in. Now, he joined the formal dinner more often than not. So instead of rushing to the healing tower, she forced herself to make a few notes on Selia's suggestions for the new lift and then returned to her room to freshen up—and maybe pace a little.

The water clock had barely dripped to the proper mark before she was standing outside the dining room door, smoothing her hair and gown. She entered first, but she took her usual place to wait for the others. It didn't take long for the table to be nearly full.

But Lial never appeared.

Lynia struggled to focus on the conversation that swelled around her during the lively meal. At the other end of the long table, her son shared a joke with his bonded, Meli, and his daughter, Arlyn. Kai, Arlyn's bonded, was listening to Aris's account of an expedition he'd once taken to the far reaches of the northern mountains, and Selia compared spell-working techniques with Cora.

Iren and Eri had been caught sneaking back onto the practice field, so both were eating their meals in their rooms. Though Lynia liked both children, their absence was a small relief. Mostly, she didn't want another unusual encounter with the little girl, and Ralan seemed more intent on his conversation with Kezari than on delivering any prophecies.

The conversation, though, was fascinating enough. What could the seer know that might affect the dragons? Of course, it could be nothing. They might be talking about a coming ice storm or the distribution of cave systems in the mountain range. Maybe they were debating the ancient war between elves and dragons. Nothing in Ralan's demeanor indicated that he held some dire knowledge of the future.

But nothing could shake the insistent worry that thrummed through her.

Less than a mark after the meal was over, Lynia grabbed her cloak from the hook beside her door and descended the staircase down into the entryway. She paused to give a slight bow toward the broad trunk of Eradisel, sacred tree of the goddess Dorenal, before heading out the front door and into the night.

Cold whipped around her, and her muscles seized in reaction. A faint ache crept across her back, but Lynia wasn't sure if it was

true pain or a ghost of the grave injury she'd taken a few months ago. Her spine had healed. She'd worked extensively to rebuild her strength. Even so, her body didn't always believe it.

It wasn't a long walk to the healer's tower, especially since the trails were currently clear of ice, but it felt like an eternity. By the time she reached Lial's door, she'd had plenty of opportunity to doubt her errand. She must have misinterpreted Eri's visit. If there was something crucial she needed to know, Lial would have found her. Or Ralan. Maybe even Lyr. Lial would surely be confused by her sudden appearance.

Lynia stared at the warm light gleaming against the wooden door from the mage globe beside the entry. Her hand lifted, her fingers already curled to knock. Should she? He was probably busy with a patient and would be annoyed at her interruption. An annoyed Lial was no pleasure, indeed. Perhaps she should check the estate key to see if he was by himself? She didn't like to use it, but it would tell her where everyone on the estate was located, including here. She could at least answer that question.

A quick look with her magic told her he was alone. No patients. No friends.

No lovers.

Heat rushed through her at the thought, but she did her best to stifle it—only to have her effort wasted when Lial opened the door. Gods of Arneen. The glow from the mage globe poured across his perfectly wrought face and glinted against the tendrils of auburn hair that had escaped the strands gathered at his neck. The thin fabric of his summer-weight tunic draped across his fit form better than a lover would have, and—

Stop staring, she ordered herself.

"Lynia?"

She swallowed down any hint of desire. He could not discover that she found him attractive. What would it gain either of them if he was aware? "Forgive me for the interruption. I suppose you sensed my disordered thoughts."

"I always sense you, Lynia," Lial answered softly. "No matter the state of your thoughts."

Her heart gave an uncomfortable tug, but as she did with her desire, she attempted to ignore it. "I…"

His lips widened slowly into a smile as he opened the door wider. "Come in. I am uncertain why you have come, but I needed to speak to you in any case. I spent most of my dinnertime working out what to say."

Lynia's brows rose at that. "Truly?"

"Yes. Is there a reason you hesitate?" His smile took on a mischievous tilt. "I assure you I am no threat to *you*. I keep the worst of my potions locked away when you're near."

Although she chuckled at the jest, his claim was partially false. He was far too much of a threat. "Only the worst?"

"I do have to keep something close to hand in case Ralan shows up," Lial quipped.

When it came to those two, she was never certain what was friendly taunting and what was true discord. "I suppose so," she said.

Lynia had been to the healing tower many times, especially during her injury, but it took more willpower than usual to force her feet across the threshold. Something felt different. Portentous, though that might have been because she'd spoken with Eri and was already on guard. She tried to shrug the feeling off as easily as she did her cloak once the door had closed behind Lial, but like her desire, it was more stubborn than mere fabric.

More like the clinging, oppressive heat of his workroom, actually.

"You keep it warmer in here than I remember," Lynia said, draping her cloak over her arm and wishing her gown wasn't so heavy. "No wonder you're still in your summer tunic."

His eyebrow lifted. "You're admiring my tunic?"

The teasing lilt to his voice sparked her irritation, and she nurtured that flicker of annoyance like the savior it was. "No. I was merely remarking on the atmosphere. A bit of politeness."

"Of course," he said, any hint of levity leaving his tone. She ignored the twinge in her chest at the loss. "I do keep it warmer in here during the late autumn and winter. I find it helps my work, not to mention the comfort of my patients if they need to disrobe. I can adjust the spell if it's causing you discomfort."

"I am certain it is fine," Lynia said carefully.

And it likely was. The jumble of heat and emotions pouring through her had nothing to do with the temperature spell.

"Is something amiss?" Lial asked. "It is unlike you to be so hesitant."

Lynia sighed and gathered what calm she could. "I fear you will find the errand foolish."

He took a step closer, so near he could touch her if he wished. She swallowed against the sudden tightness in her throat. "I will not," he said. "Unless you've come to tell me you're taking up mountain climbing."

She blinked. "Is there a reason I shouldn't go mountain climbing?"

"*Miaran,*" he cursed beneath his breath. "You know very well the weight of the packs would not be good on your spine."

Though he had a good point, Lynia couldn't resist poking at him. "Is your work so unreliable? Perhaps I should seek out another healer to ensure my back is sound."

"You know my work is among the best, and that is no boast." His lips thinned. "However, parts of the bone were shattered nearly to dust. I do not know how the knit bone would react to so much weight. To explore the mountains in this weather would require—"

Her laugh stopped his words. "Calm yourself. You know very well I have no intention of going climbing. Though according to Arlyn, the scouts have spells that are very effective at lightening the packs."

"But if that were to fail…" Lial's voice trailed off, and she almost laughed again at the long, calming breath he took. "Never mind. It is, as you say, a useless point to debate. What brought you to seek me out this evening if not an ill-advised escapade?"

The reminder of her errand stole her humor. "I had an unusual visit from Eri earlier, and I haven't been able to shake the foreboding it caused."

Lial shoved his fingers through his hair in a gesture that made it all too clear how those tendrils had escaped. "Of course it was Eri. What did she say?"

"No prophecies, if that's what you're worried about." Lynia eyed him with increasing concern. Now that their banter had ceased, she noticed a restless, worried energy pulsing around Lial, one she wasn't accustomed to seeing. "Which is why you might find this silly. She came by looking for Iren, whom she has never had trouble finding before. While she was there, she made a point of mentioning that you'd gone to have an important discussion with Ralan."

"Really?" Lial frowned. "She told me she was going to play with Iren since his lessons were nearly over."

"I knew she was up to something," Lynia grumbled. Beneath his sharp gaze, she shifted her cloak to the other arm and brushed at her

skirt. "I… In truth, it is none of my business. I realize that. But… even though Selia was there, too, Eri clearly directed the comment at me. I was worried there might be a reason for that."

"I regret to say that your fears are correct," Lial said. "Let me show you something."

Lynia stared after him as he hurried to the spiral staircase and began to climb. Was she supposed to follow or wait? She nibbled on her lower lip for a moment before she shrugged and hung her cloak on an empty hook. His living quarters were up there, a place she'd never been invited. As far as she was aware, few were. Perhaps there was a receiving area for guests? There was no reason they couldn't continue their discussion in a sitting room even if he hadn't intended for her to follow.

By the time she reached the first landing, Lial had turned from a table by the window, a book in his hands. Lynia halted, taking in the surprisingly small room. Or perhaps sparsely furnished was more accurate. A couple of chairs were situated beside the table, but otherwise, she only spotted a wardrobe and a rumpled bed.

This was where he lived?

"Forgive the disorder." Lial grimaced. "I wasn't expecting company. Though I suppose we might as well sit for this if you are not too uncomfortable."

His words echoed her thoughts enough that she smiled. "I can manage."

"Good," Lial said, sitting at the same time she did. "I would not wish to make you uneasy."

Lynia blinked in confusion. Although his dinner tray still sat under the window, food half-eaten, and his bed was a mess, the room wasn't in that bad of a state. "It's hardly slovenly. Why would I be bothered by this?"

Lial sat the book down on the table, but his gaze flickered to his bed for a moment. "It is very…personal, I suppose. An intimacy to be in my private rooms. Not a polite, public place for our discussion."

"I see." Lynia sat up straighter until her back ached with tension. "So it is. But I'm not certain why that would make me uncomfortable. We're hardly strangers, and I've seen you far more vulnerable than simply sitting in your bedroom. After Aris…"

His nostrils flared at the reminder of that breakdown, when he'd cried in her arms from the horror of Aris's memories. "I hate that you saw me like that. I never wanted you burdened by what I experience during or after a healing."

They'd never had an actual discussion about his feelings, though he was aware that she knew of his love. Only once, during a dark moment after Lyr's near death, had they touched on the subject. She'd apologized for a comment he'd misinterpreted as a rejection, and he'd said only that he understood. Neither of them had braved more since.

She should give him a solid answer about how she felt, but the truth was, she couldn't decide. She kept wavering. But moments like this, when he held his troubles so close, refusing to show weakness… His words bruised as they trampled across the flickering spark of curiosity in her heart. What better example of why they would never do well together? A man who insisted on hefting the entire world needed only a subordinate, not a companion.

"Add that to the reasons we would never suit," Lynia snapped, only to regret her harsh words when he flinched. She hated being cruel, and blaming him when *she* wasn't ready for any entanglements was partly that. She took in a careful breath to calm her temper. "Sorry."

"There is no reason to be," Lial replied. "My feelings are my own, and you've no obligation to ever return them. I've never asked you

to. But I confess that I am not sure how to handle mere friendship. It would be a pleasure-pain for me and a source of uncertainty for you, always wondering if it was a ploy to earn your affections."

Lynia pursed her lips. He made a valid point. "Would it be?"

"A source of pain? Frankly, yes." His expression hardened. "But I would not use friendship as a trap."

That strange, uncomfortable feeling returned to tug at her heart. Was it guilt? Regret? The annoying glint of curiosity she'd thought trampled? *Clechtan.* Lial didn't deserve uncertainty—he deserved a true answer. *Not* false hope, though that was all she could give for the foreseeable future. She'd felt broken since Telien's death, a branch left to bob and float along the stream after being torn from its tree.

She might never feel secure again.

"Losing a soulbonded…" Lynia began, trying to find a way to explain. "It is a terrible agony. I am not sure I will ever get over it."

His eyes lowered, anguish ghosting through them so quickly she might have imagined it. "I know," he said in a low, rough voice.

Gods, she hated to hurt him. Despite his cranky bluster, Lial was a good man. He might grumble about being summoned, but he always came when he was needed. Always. He'd used more energy than she could calculate healing her back and helping her recover, and that was on top of healing other patients. He'd even traveled to the Moranaian outpost on Earth to heal their injured people. When was the last time she'd seen him rested and happy? She honestly couldn't remember.

And here she was, denying him. Her lack of obligation for his emotions didn't keep that from stinging her own heart.

"I should go," Lynia said.

"No." Lial set his hand on the book he'd placed on the table, reminding her of the reason for her visit. "You can't concern yourself with my feelings. Not with what we must do."

Lynia studied him for some clue to his meaning, but his words gained no clarity. "What do you mean?"

"My discussion with Ralan was…" Lial shuddered. "Not good. Not for any of us. I spent a mark searching through this book, desperate to find answers myself. Hoping I could prove him wrong and do this without having to ask for your help."

Her hands clenched together in her lap. "You're not making sense. Ralan wants you to get help from *me*? I am not a healer."

Lial's fingers tapped against the leather binding as he caught her gaze. "According to my cousin, the two of us working together is the only way to prevent a plague."

His words tumbled through her mind like stones slipping over a cliff and skittering all the way down. It took time to catch them and form them into something that made sense. A plague? Tragic stories of humans suffering such things had reached Braelyn over the centuries, but elves were immune. Why would Ralan be concerned about this one? She could understand Lial helping the humans if it would save lives, but that wouldn't cause an impact to their world.

"Why am I needed? I know even less than you about human illnesses." Her nostrils flared. "I never did help you find enough information to create a tracking stone for Fen's mystery illness, remember?"

Lial slid the book closer to her. "Perhaps not. But look at the page I have marked."

She lifted the heavy tome, only then recognizing it as one she'd given him a couple of months before. Her heart dropped, and the fine hairs on her arms prickled against the long sleeves of her

dress. She'd used her magic to transcribe these words from an older, harder-to-read volume, but she'd only done a detailed study of one part. One terrible part.

Lynia swallowed her nerves and slipped her finger against the bookmark, flipping the tome open and settling it on the table. She didn't want to look. She didn't want to have her fears confirmed, but she had no choice. Eventually, knowledge brought solace. Pain was in the mystery.

So she read.

Before they could stop him, Bleyiak poured every drop of his hatred into the fracture. The Source heaved as it absorbed, and its touch brought perversion instead of renewal. The chants of life became the moans of death. With this darkness, the people suffered, until the great Healer Emereh banished the poison. Such has never been seen before or since, the secrets of that evil lost when the colony was abandoned.

The text continued, but there was no reason to read more. Lynia had discovered this section while searching for a way to defeat Kien. The author of this tome moved on to discuss other failed colonies that had once been associated with Moranaia millennia before.

Because of this, she'd been able to warn Ralan to kill Kien with a steel sword to drain his energy before he could shove poison into Earth's energy fields. The warning hadn't entirely worked; Kien had managed to cast a little through anyway. In fact, Lial had asked for the book to seek answers for the illness afflicting Fen.

"This is about tainted energy, isn't it?" Lynia asked. "It interferes with our ability to renew our bodies and use magic, but it doesn't cause a plague."

Lial's gaze settled on the book. "I am no longer certain. 'Perversion instead of renewal' could refer to such, but Kien's energy poisoning was fixed by a life mage, not a healer. This seems

to indicate something different. It is all I could think of after Ralan's warning."

"I don't suppose you'll tell me what he said?"

"Very little, in truth," Lial muttered. "Iron-cursed seers. Best I can tell, some type of sickness is going to break out amongst the elves. Remember how Fen and Maddy were ill? I'd already been concerned about that, but it came to nothing. Well, now Ralan claims that the affliction mentioned in the text is capable of affecting our kind, but he is uncertain how. He only knows it would devastate full-blooded elves and fae like a plague since we have no immunity. Unless we prevent it."

Lynia huffed. "As I said, I am not—"

"A healer. I know." Lial tapped the edge of the book. "But you found this. I need your research abilities once more. I need you to help me find the answers I'll require."

It might be necessary, but the last thing Lial wanted was to force Lynia into his presence. As he'd told her, forming a deeper friendship would cause more pain despite the pleasure of being near her, and he was uncertain he would survive the inevitable cut. His heart ached, tired of being alone, surrounded by families while he had no one. He should be avoiding Lynia, or he would never get over her enough to move on. As he stared at her pained expression from across the table, he could no longer deny the need for that.

Over and over, he'd read the account of Bleyiak, hoping he could find some clue by himself, but he'd failed. He needed more sources—and the knowledge from them—a task that would take him months, if not years. He couldn't indulge his aching heart at the expense of others, and so he had to suffer the current awkwardness.

Lynia was a chronicler, her magic attuned to the flow of information in a way he'd never seen. If anyone on this world could help him find clues, it would be her. She'd unearthed this tiny account of someone using poisoned magic in a spell, a hint that he would have overlooked. As much as it galled him to admit it, Ralan was right.

"Fine." Lynia's shoulders slumped. "I'm not sure I'll do better than when I sought information for the tracking stone, but I'll try my best. What do you need me to search for?"

The crack in his heart widened at the unhappy resignation in her tone. This was going to be pure torment for them both. Their friendship might even fall to this strain. "I was considering that very issue before your arrival, but I am uncertain. Do you have more information in the library about Bleyiak and the failed colony?"

Lynia's lips pursed. "I do not believe so, but I can have Meli search with her runes to be certain. If there is not, I can contact a few of my associates. Surely the palace records will have more."

"A good first step," Lial said. "If this account does refer to physical illness, a more detailed chronicle might describe the cause and treatment."

An uncomfortable silence fell between them. Avoiding his gaze, Lynia appeared transfixed by her fingers as they trailed across the pages of the book. Gods. If only she would caress him like that. He would pay any price to have the right to tug her from the chair and lead her to his bed. Any price except for his honor, as it was a permission unlikely to ever be granted.

Lial jerked to his feet and strode toward the stairs, not caring about the abruptness of his actions. He had to get her out of here. As it was, her presence would linger, memories taking the place of less solid imagination. At each meal, he would know what she would

look like sitting at his table. He could see the way the mage globes caressed her soft, pale skin.

Miaran.

This was intolerable.

"I have a potion that needs tending," Lial bit out, glancing over at her when she joined him at the top of the staircase. "I almost forgot."

A half-truth, but it was the best he could do. The blend of herbs he had steeping could wait a little longer, but his sanity could not. Of all the times not to have the interruption of a medical emergency, it would be this one. Naturally. When else had the universe ever granted him a reprieve?

Lynia didn't challenge the assertion, though her expression turned dubious. "Very well. I'll begin working on this puzzle and let you know what I discover."

"Thank you." If the tension hadn't grown so strong between them, he would have squeezed her hand in appreciation, but he didn't dare to touch her. "Hopefully, we can end this possible future before it grows probable."

She nodded. "Indeed."

Only when the door closed behind her did Lial let out a long sigh.

Absolute torment.

3

The next morning, Lynia entered the dining room to find it empty of everyone but Lyr. An unusual circumstance these days, although it had been the norm between Telien's death and Arlyn's arrival. At least now, there was none of the somber silence that had reigned during much of those two decades. Her son smiled at her as she took a seat beside him instead of at the end of the table where she sat for formal meals, and there was true happiness in his eyes instead of regret or resignation.

"Good morning, *Laiala*," he said.

"Good morning." Lynia served herself fruit and bread, then grabbed a small container of *klereh* syrup. "Where is Meli today? She's usually here."

Lyr's lips took on a wicked slant. "She went back to sleep."

Ah. No need to ask for details there. His expression gave Lynia more than enough information about what they'd been doing to inspire his bonded to get more rest. "I'm surprised you didn't do the same now that you've caught up on the harvest reports."

"If only that were all that plagued me," Lyr said, frowning. "Unfortunately, I received word that another ice storm is incoming tomorrow."

Her son no doubt thought her wince was for the storm, but his choice of words had her shuddering. *Plagued.* It was a term he'd picked up centuries ago when he'd gone with Kai on scouting missions, before he'd become Myern at his father's death. Lynia had heard it quite a few times without giving it much mind, but now… It took on an entirely new meaning now.

Lynia lowered her hands to her lap, unable to contemplate food—not with the fear rising steadily inside her. She'd tossed and turned most of the night, considering how she would approach this new task and fretting over the awkwardness between her and Lial. In the dark, she'd barely dared contemplate the other implications.

But as she stared at her son, his expression more relaxed than she'd seen it in years, the full import of the problem nearly overwhelmed her. A plague that affected elves and fae. Gods of Arneen. What if Lyr caught it? Meli? Arlyn? Arlyn was pregnant, so that could be two lives gone at once.

Losing Telien had shown her that even their long lives could end abruptly, but illness had never been a threat she'd prepared for. Life was simply…constant, interrupted only by accident or foul deeds. Even her parents were still alive, though they'd placed themselves into a state of dreaming a century before out of boredom and might not wake for another century yet.

No elf lost their entire family at once from something like a plague.

"*Laiala?*" Lyr asked, concern creasing his brow. "What's wrong?"

Was this a secret? Lial hadn't said so, and she hadn't spoken to Ralan. "I…"

Silence stretched between them as she sought—and failed to find—the proper words.

Lyr settled the slice of bread he held on his plate and focused his gaze on her face. With every moment that passed as he peered at her, his demeanor grew more strained until he radiated his tension. Lynia nearly squirmed in her seat as though she was the child rather than the parent.

"Something has happened, and you don't want to tell me about it," Lyr said, his voice steady enough that many would have missed the hurt hidden in his tone. But she heard. "Does it have to do with Lial? If you've decided to pursue a relationship with him, you must know I will not be upset. Father died over two decades ago, and I've no doubt he would want—"

"No, it isn't that," Lynia interrupted, her fingers twisting together in her lap. "My uncertainty about Lial hasn't been resolved, but I wasn't considering that. I simply do not wish to upset the peace of the morning."

"*Miaran,*" Lyr muttered darkly. "That never bodes well. You might as well tell me what has happened."

Lynia slumped back against her seat. She hated to be the one who brought unhappiness to her son. Perhaps selfishly, she'd hoped Lial or Ralan would break this news. But it couldn't wait now. Lyr couldn't abide having a mystery unsolved, a trait he had no doubt gotten from her.

"Lial asked for my help last night," Lynia began. "A comment from Eri prompted him to speak to Ralan, and the news from him was not good."

"I should have known Ralan would be involved. If he wasn't a friend…"

"Although I understand the sentiment, it is hardly his fault," Lynia chided gently, unable to resist correcting her son even after five hundred and fifty years. "His gift cannot be an easy one to bear. And might I remind you that his foresight saved my life?"

Lyr's cheeks tinged pink, and he inclined his head. "True enough. Thank you for the admonition. It was well deserved."

She patted his hand and smiled, though there was no happiness in the motion. "As to the current situation, I'm afraid I only partially understand it. Apparently, Kien's dark magic bears some relation to an unknown illness capable of infecting elves and fae. Lial wants me to help research the connection as well as a way to stop any outbreaks."

"Gods of Arneen," Lyr breathed, the color her chiding had brought now rushing from his face. "How can that be possible? Even low on energy, our bodies bear so much magic that infections are eradicated. Perhaps those with little fae blood are more susceptible, but… Gods, Arlyn. I don't know if her human blood would make this better or worse."

Worry weighed heavy in her heart as she met her son's eyes. "I don't know, either, but I will do my best to find out. According to Ralan, Lial and I might be able to stop this from becoming disastrous. My research combined with Lial's medical skills, we assume."

"What do you need from me?" Lyr asked.

"Nothing directly. I have more than enough contacts in the needed archives." Lynia tapped her finger against the edge of her plate as she considered her son's question. "Although now that I think on it… Is Delbin currently engaged in an official task?"

Lyr frowned. "He and Inona are helping Dria at the outpost. Why?"

"If it is fine with you, I would like to have him gather some research materials for me on Earth. I think he'll be able to find what I need, and Inona can help him bring things through."

"I have no objection, but you will need to verify that with Dria."

"Of course." Food forgotten, Lynia pushed away from the table and stood. "You might want to speak with Arlyn about this if you don't want her to learn about it from someone else. I may need to lean on her knowledge of Earth to formulate a detailed request for Delbin."

Lyr's eyes narrowed. "Must we? In her condition—"

"That is precisely why. She must prepare," Lynia interrupted firmly. "Believe me, I understand the protective impulse. I would guard you from this if it were in my power, but I couldn't even manage to delay alluding to it. I suppose we both must learn to deal with having children grown, hmm?"

"An interesting statement to say to *your* child grown."

Lynia tweaked a lock of his dark brown hair, much as she had when he was little. "You'll just have to take my word as an expert."

His dry chuckle followed her from the room as she headed toward the library. For some reason, their conversation steadied her fear into resolve, though she hadn't gained any new information. Perhaps it was the reminder of all she had to lose—or how much her family had already overcome.

Lial unwound the blood-soaked strip of cloth he'd tied around the scout's leg to stop the bleeding and prodded the muscle to ensure the healing was sound. Pasan's leg twitched, but Lial could tell the motion was purely reflex. Not a single speck of dirt or splinter of wood remained from the sharp stick the man had accidentally impaled his calf on.

"There you go," Lial said, tugging the scout's torn pants leg down. "I don't suppose you want this piece of your tunic as a memento?"

Pasan's nose wrinkled. "No, thank you. I would happily burn it."

"If you wish, though I believe I can find a better use for it."

"Then I am happy for you to do so." The scout stood and balanced for a moment on his toes before bouncing to test his weight. "Thank you, Lial. That hurt like the gods' own fiery brand."

Lial opened the basket beside the bed and tossed the cloth inside for his assistant to sanitize later. On an estate full of scouts and warriors, bandages always came in handy. "Been branded by the gods at some point, have you?"

"No." Pasan chuckled. "Not unless they were the ones who shoved that stick through my leg. But I suppose I wouldn't want to be god-touched in truth."

Eri's troubled, lonely face flashed through Lial's mind. "Nor would I."

"Forgive me for bringing trouble to your morning," the scout said. Then he tugged a ring from his finger. "I would offer this in recompense."

Lial waved his hand. "That is unnecessary. The Myern sees to such things, and doubly so since I'm the healer for both the estate and the army stationed here. You needn't part with your treasure."

"I insist." Expression stubborn, the man held out the ring. "I arrived at the same time as your morning meal, which you haven't been able to eat for tending to me. It was my foolishness that led to the injury and cost you a warm breakfast. Besides, this hardly qualifies as treasure in my eyes. I have other rings I much prefer and so I insist you take it as payment."

After centuries dealing with patients, Lial knew it would be pointless to argue unless he wanted to offend the man. Which he didn't. Pasan was an affable sort, his good humor remaining during his healing. Conceding would be the path of least resistance.

"Then I will accept with thanks," Lial said, holding out his hand for the ring.

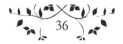

The scout dropped it into his palm with a grin and headed for the door, the ragged end of his torn tunic flapping around him as he exited. Despite the weight of his responsibilities, Lial smiled as he returned to the small table situated beside his workbench to retrieve his breakfast. He dropped the ring beside the plate and lifted the tray from his workbench to carry upstairs.

Another meal alone in his empty room—a thought he quickly shoved aside before taking his usual place at the table.

Lial had scarfed down his entire serving of fruit before he summoned enough interest in Pasan's gift to examine it. He lifted the gold band to the light, his attention going immediately to the stone set in the center of the delicate piece. A yellow-white, nearly a match for Lynia's pale blond hair. Lial forced that thought away, too, and settled the ring on the table where it twinkled at him in the window's glow.

A glimmering taunt.

He'd just taken a bite of syrup-coated bread when the mirror beside his wardrobe chimed. *Miaran.* With a sigh, he popped the other half of the slice in his mouth as he pushed away from the table. It must be time for Maddy's call. Healing Pasan had taken longer than he'd thought. Unless it was Alerielle again? The healer from Oria had been seeking pointers on spine healing of late, curious to learn the techniques he had used to help Lynia. But he'd already shared all he knew.

Lial swallowed his food and brushed away the crumbs before activating the mirror link. It wasn't Alerielle. Instead, Maddy's cheerful face filled the glass, her hair, a lighter red than his, piled atop her head in an unusual knot. She eased back slightly, and half of Fen's face appeared beside hers. The young *Felshreh* prince appeared more relaxed than the last time Lial had seen him, so if there was disaster brewing, it might not involve Fen this time.

"Good day to you, Maddy. Fen," Lial said.

"And Anna," a voice called, though Lial couldn't see the source. Lial smiled. "We need to commission you a larger mirror."

Fen nudged his head gently against Maddy's. "Told you."

"Okay, okay," Maddy said, but there was more amusement than annoyance in her tone. "I'll work on it. But that's not why I called. I wanted to talk to you."

"I hope all is well." Lial studied her face, but like her tone, there was no indication that anything was wrong. "You didn't mention the reason for requesting this communication, and I admit I am curious since you're supposed to be here tomorrow for a lesson."

Maddy sobered. "I know. But there are a couple of things I must ask first."

"Intriguing," Lial said. Also concerning, but he didn't want to add that part. "What is it?"

"I told you about the Seelie queen falling ill with a poison Meren slipped into her water." Maddy glanced at Fen, who nodded. "Well, the queen granted us a gift. She let us take a vial of her blood to study. We've been thinking…"

"Could you examine the blood to see what you can discover about it?" Fen finished for her.

Lial let out a quick breath, and an inexplicable chill rushed along his skin. The timing of Fen's question couldn't be a coincidence. Just yesterday, Lial had contemplated a connection between the plague Ralan had foretold and the Seelie queen's illness. Now Maddy and her mates offered the one thing that might prove that connection.

No coincidence at all.

"I would certainly be willing to study it," Lial said.

"My other question, though." Maddy nibbled at her lower lip until Fen nudged her again. "I want to bring Fen and Anna. The blood is in Fen's charge, and Anna helped us isolate it."

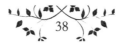

Lial shrugged. "I see no problem with this."

Maddy sagged slightly with relief. "Thank goodness. Oh, but we'll need another place to stay. No offense, but the three of us aren't going to be able to cram together in the bed in my usual room, and I don't want to be separated from my mates."

Lial smiled. "I will speak with Lyr. We'll work it out."

He would need to figure out how to shield her at a greater distance, something that wasn't a problem when she stayed in the room upstairs, but it would be worth it not to have the new trio radiating love and happiness in the room above him every day and night.

Lial barely suppressed a shudder. Any inconvenience would be worth avoiding that.

Lynia tried to avoid mental communication with Lial whenever possible, especially lately. The rich, low tones of his mental voice made her quiver every time, and she was beginning to suspect she'd been lying to herself about the reason. At first, she'd told herself it reminded her of the dark days after Telien had died, when Lial's voice had acted as a tether amidst the painful tumult of a broken soulbond. Then he'd whispered into her mind again to prevent her from slipping away with the pain after she'd shattered her back in the fall.

Some nights, she woke from a deep sleep with the echoes of his murmurs resounding through her mind as though they were still connected. But a quick check of her shields always proved that to be untrue. No, it was memory. Twice, Lial had fought to keep her alive when she wasn't sure she could continue, and it was time to stop pretending that his attention made her unhappy.

Bothered, that's what she was. She just couldn't decide if that was a good or a bad thing.

Lynia set another book on top of the stack on her favorite research table and settled herself into her seat. Time to stop stalling lest the morning slip away. She was going to need Lial's input before she requested those research materials from Delbin, and it would be faster and easier to connect mentally than to track Lial down in person.

She closed her eyes and reached out with her mind, careful to only tap against his awareness so she didn't intrude. Lial hated deep mental links, and after seeing the pain he'd experienced from Aris's healing, she could understand why.

It only took a couple of breaths before he completed the connection. *"Lynia? Is your back—"*

"No," Lynia interrupted sharply. Would he ever think of her as healed? *"It isn't my back. Though I might injure it throttling you if you don't cease making that assumption."*

Shock flowed between them. Then amusement. *"Fair enough. I was merely concerned since you do not contact me this way often."*

Lynia winced. Hadn't she been thinking that very thing? *"Also fair. In this case, I was seeking your input. I plan to ask Delbin to find research materials on the causes of sickness on Earth and bring them here. However, I am uncertain what would be most helpful."*

"I see," Lial answered. *"Have you found anything here yet?"*

She ran her gaze along the stacks of history, anatomy, and healing texts and sighed. *"Nothing directly related to physical illnesses, but there are several topics I want to study to have a stronger grasp of them. It might go faster if you could cull some of the healing texts so I needn't analyze them."*

"Of course. I'll come to the library immediately, before someone else requires my services. I am always happy to lend you aid, Lynia."

Something about the way his mental voice caressed her name sent a shiver running through her, a reaction she desperately tried to ignore. *"Thank you."*

He disconnected their link as quickly as he'd allowed it, and Lynia sagged against the hard back of her seat. That man was going to cause her no end of distraction, and he wasn't doing anything untoward. Gods help her if he actively pursued her. Gods help both of them, really. There was no way they could be a good match, not when they each held their burdens so close.

Ah, but the temptation…

Straightening, Lynia opened her eyes, only to startle at the sight of Meli standing a few paces away. And from the hint of a smirk on the other woman's lips, she'd probably been there for much of Lynia's conversation with Lial. Hopefully, Lynia's expression hadn't been too telling.

"Speaking to Lial?" Meli asked, her soft voice belying her teasing tone.

Lynia groaned. "Not you, too."

"I hope you aren't upset." Meli placed her hand on the table and leaned forward. "I shouldn't have said anything. It's only… I haven't known you long, but I can see a difference in you of late. Even Lyr hopes you'll consider a relationship with Lial at this point."

Lynia lifted a brow. "Even Lyr? I was unaware he had *that* much of an opinion about this, though I suppose that explains why it was on his mind this morning."

Red flushed across the Ljósálfar woman's pale cheeks. "I have overstepped."

"Of course not."

Lynia stood, hoping it would help put Meli at ease if they were at a similar height. The poor woman hadn't received the best treatment

on her home world of Alfheim, and although Meli was adjusting, she sometimes struggled. At least she'd grown comfortable enough to tease Lynia in the first place.

"In fact, I'm glad you're here," Lynia continued. "And in a good enough mood to jest at my expense. I suppose sleeping in was good for you."

Instead of blushing again, Meli grinned. "Very much so."

Lynia almost made a joke of her own at Lyr's expense, but she really should ask her favor before Lial arrived. The more texts she had for him to examine, the better. "I don't suppose you're rested enough to help me out with your runes?"

Meli tugged a small pouch from her tunic pocket and jiggled it. "Tell me what you need, and I'll find it."

The god who'd given Meli those runes might not have intended for her to use them to help Lynia retrieve books in the massive library, but Lynia was grateful all the same. As a Diviner, Meli could use her runes to locate anything lost so long as she had the direction. Now Lynia just had to find the proper questions.

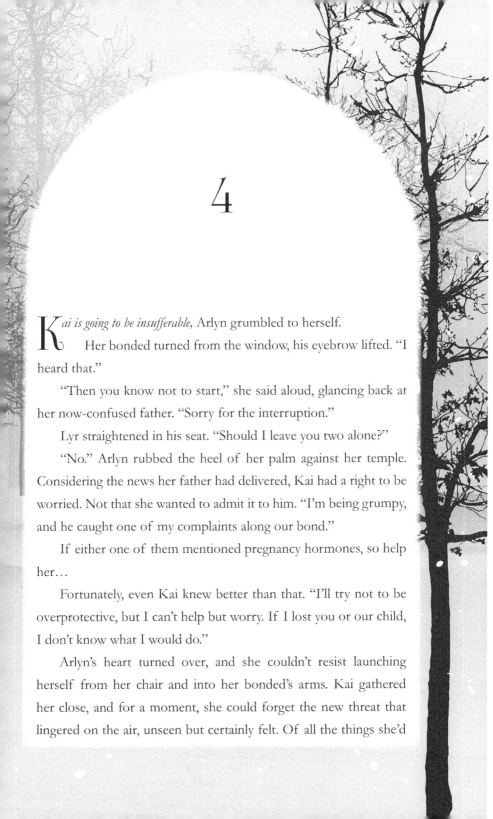

4

Kai is going to be insufferable, Arlyn grumbled to herself.

Her bonded turned from the window, his eyebrow lifted. "I heard that."

"Then you know not to start," she said aloud, glancing back at her now-confused father. "Sorry for the interruption."

Lyr straightened in his seat. "Should I leave you two alone?"

"No." Arlyn rubbed the heel of her palm against her temple. Considering the news her father had delivered, Kai had a right to be worried. Not that she wanted to admit it to him. "I'm being grumpy, and he caught one of my complaints along our bond."

If either one of them mentioned pregnancy hormones, so help her…

Fortunately, even Kai knew better than that. "I'll try not to be overprotective, but I can't help but worry. If I lost you or our child, I don't know what I would do."

Arlyn's heart turned over, and she couldn't resist launching herself from her chair and into her bonded's arms. Kai gathered her close, and for a moment, she could forget the new threat that lingered on the air, unseen but certainly felt. Of all the things she'd worried about since crossing the Veil from Earth to Moranaia, a plague hadn't been one of them.

She lifted up slightly to give Kai a quick kiss before she pulled away. When she turned back to her father, his worried frown hadn't abated. It wasn't her fault, but it still felt like he'd had nothing but trouble since her arrival. The poor man needed a break. She didn't say so, though, as she sat back down beside him.

Silence fell, other than the sound of Kai's footsteps as he crossed the room to stand behind her. Arlyn almost wished Lyr had done this in his study instead of here, a homey room overlooking the gardens that they'd begun to use as a retreat over the last couple of months. Before her arrival, her father had spent most of his time working in his study, and Lynia had stuck to the library or her rooms. But as the months had passed, they'd sought a more comfortable spot to spend time together. Now, at least one member of the family could usually be found here, reading a book on the overstuffed couch by the window or working at one of their hobbies. Arlyn even had a small woodworking bench in the corner.

"I take it there's some kind of plan?" Arlyn uttered, unable to bear the silence any longer.

Lyr sighed. "As much as there can be at this point. According to Ralan, Lial needs your grandmother's assistance with research, and much of what we do depends on what she and Lial discover. Actually, *Laiala* was hoping you might help, too."

"Me?" She glanced over her shoulder at Kai, who leaned against the back of her chair. "Why me?"

"You lived on Earth where sickness is common," Lyr answered. "She's planning to ask Delbin to gather resources and bring them back, so I suppose she wants guidance on what the human world has to offer."

Arlyn furrowed her brows. "What kind of resources?"

"Books? Tools?" Lyr lifted his hands and let them drop. "I'm not certain. I believe she's in the library if you want to speak to her."

Want was a bit too strong—if Arlyn had a choice, she would avoid thinking about the situation entirely. She'd rather be practicing her archery with a quiver full of randomly enchanted arrows—while blindfolded—than to deal with something like this. But she'd faced danger before. She'd survived being shot by an arrow because of her bodyguards' neglect, getting captured by a Seelie lord, and having her energy infected while dispelling Kien's handiwork. If not for the fairies—

Arlyn jerked to her feet at the thought. "The fairies!"

Lyr's head tilted. "Which ones?"

"There are more than…?" She ran her fingers through her hair. "Never mind. Princess Nia, the one who healed me of the energy poisoning. Maybe she could help with this, too."

"That was tainted energy rather than physical illness, but it's worth pursuing. They may have knowledge of other types of illnesses, too," Lyr said.

Her chair jostled as Kai pushed away, and he stepped around to sit in the chair across from her, his attention on Lyr. "I could go out to the fairy pond while Arlyn speaks to Lynia."

"You?" Arlyn couldn't resist giving him a smirk. "Are you sure you can handle that level of diplomacy? The man who accidentally started our bond the first time we met?"

He huffed, but she could feel through their bond that he wasn't truly angry. "I only lose my composure so fully around you, my love. Usually."

Snickering low, Lyr finally stood. "True or not, this plan is sound. It's a beginning, at least. You'll go now?"

"Yes," Kai agreed.

Arlyn rose at the same time as Kai. "And I'll go to the library to consult with *Elnaia* on what she might need from Earth. The more I can help her with her research, the faster we have a solution."

"A good plan," Lyr said with a nod.

They walked together into the hallway and all the way to the study, where Lyr left them. Arlyn slipped her hand into Kai's as they turned toward the library where they would part. Fear thrummed in her veins like an electrical current, but it felt good to be doing… anything, really. Action was better than inertia.

Lial thumbed through yet another ancient tome written by a healer who'd died long before he was born. He'd read this one, of course, as he had the three he'd already discarded. Before settling at Braelyn over four hundred years ago, he'd made it his mission to learn as many healing techniques as he could, even seeking out apprenticeships and assignments in far-flung places during his first thousand years or so of life. These particular books were common enough to have been in almost all of those libraries.

Not that they were useless. There might not be information about viruses, but all contained sections on how elves' bodies processed invading bacteria, which might be of benefit if that turned out to be the cause of the mystery illness. This one even mentioned the humans' robust physical immune systems, an evolution to compensate for their lack of magical regeneration and purification.

Unfortunately, he'd long ago memorized them all.

This one could be helpful for Lynia, however. It didn't rely on significant advanced knowledge of the subject and did a fair enough job of explaining the concepts that with Lynia's research skills, she

would have no trouble comprehending the technical details. She only needed a little time.

The woman in question sat back down across from him and opened the book she'd grabbed from a shelf. Lial fixed his gaze on his own text. He had to stop staring at her like the lovesick fool he'd become. Especially after her bluntness the evening before, when she'd mentioned "all the reasons we would never suit."

Apparently, she kept a list.

The comment haunted him, but he had to honor that she wasn't interested. It wasn't her fault he'd been in love with her since Telien's death. She didn't remember the link they'd shared during her earliest days of grief, and it might not mean the same thing to her if she did.

Lial shook himself free of the memory of those days. He needed to start considering his future plans, or he would remain alone forever. If he didn't remove himself from her presence entirely, he would no longer be able to move on. A few thousand years pining by himself in the healing tower wasn't an appealing future. He'd already spent fourteen hundred years pining the loss of Aralee.

But any plans would have to wait until they stopped this newest disaster.

Carefully, Lial placed a marker against the current page and set the book on the *possibly helpful* pile. "I believe that text will provide a good introduction. How advanced would you like to go?"

Lynia looked up from her book with raised brows. "As far as you can find, of course. Even if I can't actually heal anyone, I can still understand it."

"I didn't mean to imply otherwise," Lial said, biting back a sigh. Ever since her fall, she'd interpreted his concerns and questions as criticism or doubt—at times with good cause, he had to admit. But he wished she would stop assuming the worst. "There isn't anyone in

the kingdom I would rather have researching this, and not because I feel… It's only because I value your skill. However, I don't want to waste time on information you won't need."

Her expression softened. "Sorry. I shouldn't make hasty assumptions. I suppose I have been for the last couple of months or so."

Gods. So often, their thoughts were in accord. Not duplicates of one another but a close parallel. Did she even realize it? They would get on so well together if they could just—

With a muttered curse, Lial pushed back from the table, the echo of chair against floor screeching up through the tower. Lynia blinked up at him in confusion, but he didn't have the words to explain what he was thinking, at least not without sounding like a fool. Iron's curse, but he had to get away from this madness. It was time he found his pride and stopped moping over what would never be.

Before he could think of an excuse for his odd behavior, Arlyn entered, waving over her shoulder at Kai as she closed the library door behind her. If she noticed the tension in the room, she ignored it, but her face was pale enough that she might have been oblivious. Lial frowned. Was she ill? She was between her first and second quarter of pregnancy, and unlike Cora, Arlyn hadn't suffered from the typical stomach complaints.

Lial met Arlyn in the center of the room, his aggravation forgotten. "Are you unwell, Ayala?"

"You must be worried if you've slipped back to using my title," Arlyn answered with a soft laugh. "I'm concerned about the news my father just gave me, but I feel okay."

He waved toward the table. "Sit. I want to scan you and the babe."

Though Arlyn rolled her eyes, she complied. "I counted on Kai being insufferable, but I didn't consider you."

"An oversight, that." Since she'd taken the chair he'd vacated, Lial pulled out the one beside it and settled it close before plopping himself down. "You should know well enough that I don't wager with anyone's health."

Lial almost told her what truly drove him, but he didn't want to scare her. He'd seen more go wrong with pregnancies over his centuries of healing than he wanted to think about. If being thought of as an overbearing annoyance saved her and her child from a preventable complication, then he would happily endure the bad opinion.

Arlyn's lips twisted with frustration, but she closed her eyes and nodded. "Fine."

Between breaths, he swept his healing magic through her, scanning for any hint of trouble. Her heart rate was elevated, at least until she relaxed beneath the calm his gift brought. Lial checked to see if her heart was overburdened from the strain of pumping extra blood, a rare but unfortunate problem. Thankfully, that wasn't the cause.

Stress hormones had increased, though not unduly. If Lyr had told her about Lial's and Lynia's mission, that would account for it, but that would need to be confirmed. The stress wasn't bad enough to affect her son, he found as he checked the baby. No irregularities had developed since his last examination, either. Even so, he ensured her energy was at full capacity and her stress reduced.

Satisfied, Lial drew his power back and waited for Arlyn to open her eyes. "You know," she said, "I was annoyed, but I have to admit that was good for my anxiety."

"I have my uses." Lial smiled. "And I am happy to report that you are both well. He or she…they… Are you certain you don't want to know the child's sex? This is becoming tedious."

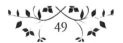

Arlyn laughed and then surprised him by patting his arm. "Nice try, but you know Kai will cave before I do."

Lial shook his head at that—mostly because she was right.

Footsteps drew near, and he glanced over in time to see Meli approaching from the staircase, a book gathered against her chest with one arm and her other extended, light gleaming around her palm. After a few paces, the light winked out, and Meli lowered her arm. Blinking, she crossed to their table and stopped.

"I believe I've found something," Meli said.

Lial peered at the book she set in front of Lynia, but he couldn't make out what the elaborate print said from this angle. Unfortunately, it wasn't likely to be *On Preventing a Plague Amongst Elves and Fae*. This illness was so unprecedented that they'd be lucky to find anything remotely useful.

If only they could be so fortunate.

Lynia managed to drag her gaze away from Lial and Arlyn before he caught her staring. Removing her attention from what she'd seen wasn't nearly as easy. Until today, she'd never seen him treat another person the way he had her after her fall. But then, she wasn't usually near him when he was healing a patient. Even when she'd found him in the garden, struggling beneath the weight of Aris's pain, Lial hadn't been actively working. He'd merely received backlash through the healer's link.

Was the man as overbearing with all of his patients as he was with her and Arlyn? If so, it suggested that he didn't think she was weak. Or useless. Or any of the other negative words that had scratched at the edge of her thoughts during her recovery. Unless he had a low opinion of every patient, and she doubted that.

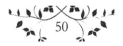

"I sense other books that could help, but they are not nearby," Meli said, snapping Lynia back to the present moment.

Research. Research should be the focus of her attention.

Lynia blinked up at Meli. "Do you know where?"

"Well…" Meli's hand lifted, and she pivoted until she faced roughly west. "The strongest is that way, but I sense that it is far. Thank goodness I've learned to resist the call of the stones, or Freyr knows how far I'd walk before you caught me. Another, fainter trail is that way." Meli angled in a more southerly direction. "And I think there's something over…"

Following Meli's gesture, Lynia looked over her shoulder toward the northeast, but of course, she couldn't see anything except the library wall. "I hope it isn't as far flung as the dragons' isle."

Meli dropped her hand back to her side. "I'm sorry I can't be more accurate."

"I understand, and I appreciate the effort," Lynia said. "It narrows down the possibilities, if nothing else. The one to the west might be the Citadel, and the royal archives could be one of the others. There are also a few estates to the northeast, but only a couple are likely sources."

"That is good." Then Meli grinned. "You'll have to let me know if I need to start walking."

The woman's wry tone had Arlyn chuckling and Lial's lips twitching, but Lynia had to fight back a surge of worry. Meli had once used the runes to find Lyr when he was injured, and they'd taken her over so thoroughly that she really might have walked across a continent, possibly until she'd collapsed. What if that happened again? Lyr would be devastated, and Lynia couldn't stand the thought of being to blame.

Meli's brows drew together. "I wasn't serious."

"I know." Lynia forced herself to smile. "I suppose this situation has me nervous about everything."

Not that she wouldn't keep an eye on Meli next time she helped. Just in case.

Meli's gaze grew distant for a moment before she blinked and focused once more. "Do you need me to search for anything else? Lyr just asked for my help with a report."

"That's fine," Lynia said. "I need to speak with Arlyn, anyway."

Not that she entirely believed Meli's claim. There was a reason she was careful to knock on the study door now.

Lynia waited until Meli had given her farewells and closed the door behind her before she dared to look at Arlyn. As expected, her granddaughter was barely holding in her amusement, and as soon as their eyes met, they both broke into laughter. Arlyn settled her hand against her growing belly as her body shook with it, and the motion had Lynia's humor settling into a perfect moment of joy.

"A report," Arlyn said as her chuckles died down. "Sure. If we weren't talking about my parents, I could pull out a list of jokes about that lie."

Lial's warm laugh had Lynia and Arlyn staring at him, so rare was the sound heard. "I am not so constrained," he said, "But I will resist for both your sakes."

With that laugh, her son was the last thing on Lynia's mind. She was too busy studying the unexpected sight of an amused Lial. With the midmorning sun highlighting his relaxed expression and sparking his auburn hair to embers, it would have been difficult not to. She couldn't deny he was a handsome man. If she didn't have so many burdens, not the least a soul left raw from her broken bond, then maybe…

Thankfully, Arlyn broke that line of thought before Lynia could let herself drift so close to future heartbreak. "Not to bring down

the mood, but *Onaial* said you wanted my help with your research? It's nearing the midday meal, and this baby will give me hell if I miss food."

Lial turned a frown on Arlyn. "You haven't been testing that lack of food often, I hope?"

"Of course I haven't." Arlyn's lips twisted, and she raised her brows at Lial. "Do you really think I'm going to starve my baby? Seriously."

He straightened. "It is my duty to—"

"Stuff it, Lial," Arlyn snapped, making Lynia snort. She didn't entirely understand the slang, but she got enough of the intent to appreciate it. "And don't bother trying to threaten me. You wouldn't do a damned thing to a pregnant woman."

Although Lial scowled, he actually shut up.

Lynia needed to take lessons from her granddaughter on that skill.

It wasn't a long walk to the fairy pond, but Kai rushed along the path regardless. All he wanted to do was curl up with Arlyn in their room, barricaded from the world. But that wasn't reasonable, and even if she would have put up with it, she shouldn't. He knew that. His worries, borne of his own past, weren't her fault or responsibility.

The fact that avoiding a plague was both reasonable and vital didn't silence his protective impulse.

Moranaia is free of illness, Kai reminded himself—repeatedly.

Finally, he reached the border of the fairy lands, and he had something to focus his scattered thoughts on. As he paused at the line of energy shielding the pond, he considered what he should say

and concluded that the unembellished truth would be best. It would make for a quick and hopefully productive meeting. Then he could return to Arlyn.

Light sparked at the center of the pond, and a fairy the size of his head appeared without preamble. Blue hair danced around her iridescent wings and tangled in the folds of her light purple dress as it rippled in the breeze. Princess Nia. Kai hadn't had much reason to come this way until recently, but he would recognize Nia anywhere after she'd saved Arlyn. With luck, she would be willing and able to save many more.

"Enter in peace," Princess Nia said, flying closer.

Unlike during his last visit, she had no attendants, and none appeared as Kai crossed the invisible threshold onto her land. She hovered there, her impassive gaze locked on him as he strode to the edge of the water. This time, the princess didn't shift her size to match his.

So she also anticipated a short meeting.

Kai inclined his head. "Thank you, Princess Niesanelalli. I am honored that you granted me a meeting."

"Relatives of the Myern are usually welcome." The princess studied him for several heartbeats. "And in this case, I admit to curiosity. We aided the Ljósálfar by healing the poison invading their energy fields, yet I sense your distress. Neither our seers nor our healers have revealed to me a new danger."

That was unfortunate, at least for his mission. Any time they'd needed the fairies' aid, Princess Nia had known about it before they had. "I have come with a request from Myern Lyrnis, although he is fully aware that you might not be able to grant it."

"A surprise." The princess frowned. "Thank you for bringing the matter here on his behalf. I will hear his request."

"One of our strongest seers, Prince Ralan, has foreseen the rise of a new illness," Kai explained. "One not of the energy fields but of the body, much like human sickness. It is believed to be related to the energy poisoning spell you cleansed from Alfheim, but this version is capable of infecting elves and fae physically. Lord Lyrnis asks for the help of any healers who might aid in stopping this blight."

Princess Nia canted her head. "True illness affecting either of our kind? Impossible."

Kai wanted to agree, but Ralan was correct far too often for him to believe it. "Perhaps it will be impossible for your people. That I cannot say. However, there is already evidence that this is feasible for mine."

The princess considered him again, and he held her gaze until she nodded. "I will see this matter investigated amongst my own seers. As for the Myern's request, I will need to consult with my healers. If any are willing, then we will grant aid. I will send a call forth when it is decided."

"A mental call?" Kai asked, although he was certain that whatever method she used, it would be unmistakable.

"Yes," Princess Nia confirmed. "I will ensure it reaches you."

Her wings beat faster, and she began to drift backward. A dismissal, then. "I will await your call. Thank you."

"Blessed journey," she said, and then she was gone.

Kai didn't waste time looking around. When the fairies bid you farewell, you left. They weren't necessarily more powerful than elves, but their gifts were different enough that they could be tough to counter. Kai spun away, his steps carrying him toward the estate. Though the princess hadn't agreed to give aid, there was hope. That was better than nothing.

5

Lynia tucked her feet up against the arm of the chair and grabbed a book from the stack on the side table. She'd sent her request to Delbin and eaten a quick midday meal. Now, it was time to research. She'd considered staying at the large table at the base of the library, but she was more likely to be disturbed down there. Less so at the top, which took a fair bit of climbing to reach. The possibility of increased interruptions was certainly a disadvantage to adding the lift, but one she would manage.

Light poured in through the window, highlighting the empty chair across from her. Once, the glow would have gilded Telien's brown hair with streaks of gold as he bent over some epic tale or a stack of reports that couldn't wait. She could almost feel his presence at times, the memory of his laughter or wry comments curling around her body with every breath.

The memories should have made her lonely, but they brought more comfort than pain. They surrounded her, supporting her like the soft, deep chair where she curled. She refused to let that feeling go. Lyr had once asked how she'd gained the courage to return to the library so soon after Norin had ambushed her in this spot, leading to her near-fatal fall, but she hadn't found the words to fully describe her drive then.

She'd come to realize it was a combination of stubbornness and nostalgia.

Not that it was always easy. She startled at times if someone else was using the library and their footsteps drew too near on the stairs. She'd almost thrown a book at Kai once when he'd come up to see if she needed anything, but that had been weeks ago. These days, the knife she wore tucked against her calf was comfort against those anxieties, and years of working in this spot meant she concentrated better here in spite of momentary disturbances.

Speaking of which.

Lynia shook off the memories and focused on the title of the book Meli had found for her. *Import and Export Records for the Years 11,201-11,211, Volume 6.* Such an unusual tome for this task. What in the world could she possibly find in a list of goods traded over twenty-six thousand years ago? Had Meli grabbed the wrong book? It made no sense.

Even so, Lynia opened the cover and skimmed the list of contents, and a hint of clarity hit at the names of each section—this volume contained information concerning trade with then-colonies of Moranaia. But where to begin? The book that mentioned the traitor Bleyiak hadn't given a precise year, and she'd been unable to find another record of the colony.

The initial list was no help in that regard. With a huff, Lynia flipped to the first section and began to skim the endless lists. Colony name, date, trader name, item, cost or item bartered. At first, it was slightly interesting to see the flow of goods so long ago. *Peresten* and *peresten*-forged weapons had brought an even higher price then, and one colony had requested far more meat and timber than was generally offered. Telien's great-grandfather had traded patterned fabrics from that colony in return, and she found herself wondering if it had been used on any of the furnishings still on the estate. No way to know from these records.

Unfortunately, it didn't take long for even that novelty to fade, and the lines blurred together until she almost slammed the book closed in frustration. But she held out. She was on the third colony listed in the book before her patience paid off in the form of a trader name.

Bleyiak.

Had Meli's runes not delivered this text into Lynia's hands, she might have passed the name off as a coincidence. After all, someone else could have borne the same name, and it seemed incongruous that a simple trader could bring on the downfall of an entire colony with a spell. People with that kind of power usually became battle mages or guardians. But whatever the reason, she couldn't dismiss the information as mere happenstance.

The question now was…what did she need to do with it? Bleyiak had signed orders for a variety of foodstuffs, herbs used in both cooking and healing, cloth, paper, a rare ink, and decorative pottery from the Seelie court—none of which screamed *item used to begin a plague*. Of course, the items themselves might have been a catalyst for the man's rage rather than an instrument he'd used, but the dry lines of facts gave no indication of that.

Perhaps the two most useful things here were the name of the colony, Abuiarn, and the year, 11,208. It would be far easier to request information from other archives with these facts. Lynia lifted her small notebook from beside the larger pile and opened it. With a quick burst of magic, she transcribed a copy of the relevant pages into her own records.

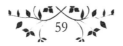

It wasn't much, but it was a beginning. One she owed to Meli, since Lynia wouldn't have thought to grab this particular book. The colonies that had branched from Moranaia in the first few millennia had either disbanded, died out, or separated into their own kingdoms long before Lynia was born, so the lack of records might have driven her to this book eventually.

But with a potential outbreak to deal with, she didn't have time for eventually.

This meeting wasn't going to be easy, but it was necessary if Lial were to begin looking for his replacement.

Pausing outside the study, Lial took a deep breath. The last couple of days had shown him all too clearly that he wouldn't be able to tolerate remaining so close to Lynia now that she knew—and didn't return—his feelings. He valued his friendship with her, but even that would be at risk if he stayed. He'd begun to long for so much greater between them. Home. Family. A deeper connection. It would be pure misery to watch that dream fade as the decades blurred into centuries.

Certainly, there might be times when they would be able to avoid one another, but there was no way to prepare for events that might throw them together. And it didn't have to be something as monumental as researching a plague. Injuries and births. Festivals and formal occasions. Too many things would bring her near.

But never near enough.

As much as Lial loved his position at Braelyn, he couldn't imagine staying in a place that promised so much agony. It had been hard enough attempting to live at the palace after he'd unexpectedly lost his first love. To live each day dreading and hoping to see his

second love? He couldn't do it. Better to spare himself and everyone involved future turmoil by leaving now.

Resolved, Lial knocked on the door of Lyr's study and waited to be invited inside. A more ceremonious beginning than they'd become accustomed to over the years, but it would be a good signal to Lyr that this would be no casual discussion. And as expected, Lyr was standing formally in front of his desk at the far end of the large oval room when Lial entered. Message received.

Crossing between the chairs grouped in the center, Lial stopped a couple of paces away from Lyr, inclined his head, and tapped his chest twice with his closed fist. While Lyr's expression was impassive, his hesitation in responding told well enough of his confusion. It couldn't be helped. With luck, the formality would make this easier, at least as much as it could be.

"Good afternoon, Callian iy'dianore sebarah i Lial Caran nai Braelyn," Lyr said. "I hope you fare well this day."

Ah, his full title. Lyr had decided to really go for it, it seemed. Fortunately, Lial wouldn't have to return the favor as a subordinate. "As well as can be, Myern Lyrnis. Is your family well?"

"I do hope you are aware," Lyr answered, his brows lifting infinitesimally. "Considering you are responsible for healing their ills."

Like Lynia's. Lial wanted to growl at the thought, but it would do no good. The only thing that would help was escaping this intolerable situation. "That is true. It was mere politeness."

"Not one of your finer talents, I'm afraid." Lyr crossed his arms, his demeanor losing its cold, formal edge. "What is this about, Lial?"

"As to the first point, you were the one who rebuffed my inquiry with rudeness," Lial felt compelled to point out. "But the second… I wanted to begin this meeting with the proper tone since my request is likewise serious."

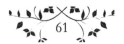

Lyr waved toward the chairs. "Sit. And I suppose I was a bit sharp in my commentary, although the point stands. You've been directly treating both my mother and daughter, after all. They are both well?"

"They are," Lial answered as he lowered himself in the seat across from the one Lyr chose. "But you know I wouldn't give you details without their permission, not unless there was no choice for the safety of all."

"Fine. But again, I must ask." Lyr tapped his fingers against the arm of his chair. "What is this about?"

Although the formality had broken, the moment held no less import. "This request is preliminary, as I have not spoken to Dria or Ralan, but you deserve to hear it first. I would like to transfer to another location, possibly Ralan's new palace or the outpost. Preferably the latter."

Shock crossed Lyr's face, and his fingers ceased their insistent beat. "You want to leave Braelyn? Now?"

"Not now," Lial replied quickly. "I would not leave while the threat of illness lingers over us. This is obviously not the ideal time for a change like that. However, once that problem is overcome, I would like to arrange the transfer. As it could take months to find the best person, I thought I should make the request now."

"But why? You've been here since my training years, and you've told me more than once that you enjoy what you do." Lyr's eyes narrowed. "If you do not feel fairly compensated after the increased workload our new arrivals have brought, I would be happy to—"

"It's not that. I could commission an entire healing compound with the wealth I have stored," Lial interrupted, his frustration building. "Can you really not see what would prompt this? You know how I feel about your mother."

The muscle in Lyr's cheek twitched. "Ah. That."

"Yes, that." Lial fought to keep his emotions in check, but it was a battle hard won. "It has become clear to me that Lynia will never return my feelings, and I find that I do not wish to spend century upon century longing for someone I cannot have. If I am able to shift to the outpost, I could still lend aid here in emergencies should the new healer or healers need my assistance."

Lyr shifted in his seat, a frown creasing his brow. "You're certain of this? You've spoken to her about the matter?"

Lial might not have asked her about her feelings in so many words, but after what she'd said the day before, he didn't have to. Never suit. He closed his eyes for a moment against the memory before meeting his friend's gaze.

"Yes," Lial answered. "Beginning the process now seems best. I would rather leave before awkwardness becomes aversion."

"I had hoped…" Lyr sighed. "It doesn't matter what I'd hoped, I suppose. It is difficult to imagine Braelyn without you goading us into better health, but I understand your reasons. If Meli had decided to stay here but not bond, I would have struggled much the same."

Lial had known his friend would understand, although neither of them was happy with the choice. Braelyn was home. He might be lonely at times, but he'd loved it here from the moment he'd arrived. He had a steady stream of patients thanks to the training fields and scouts, and the estate was less formal than the palace had been.

But there was also his growing longing for a family. It might have been a thousand years, give or take a century, since he'd yearned for such a thing, but the urge was no less strong for the delay in occurrence. He was tired of being alone. He would prefer to have that family with Lynia, of course, but it wasn't meant to be. Only when the hope of that relationship died could he consider another.

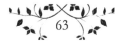

He needed space for his heart to heal if he wanted any chance of moving on.

"Then you give me leave to speak with Dria?" Lial asked.

Lyr frowned, but he nodded. "If that is your wish."

"I wouldn't call it that, but it is my need." Lial stood, ready for relief to fill him at his new course of action. It didn't come. "I'll bid you good day."

"Good day, Lial."

Lial gave Lyr a brief nod and strode out, searching his emotions for that sense of relief. For satisfaction. Regret. Even hope. *Something.* But none of those filled him. Right now…

He felt nothing.

Dinner was a fuller affair than the day before, but it brought Lynia discomfort instead of happiness. The complicated balance of family members, rank, and preference placed Lial at her right hand and Kezari at her left, and since Lynia was at the opposite end of the long table from Lyr, no one was really across from her. Even that wouldn't usually be a problem, but the dragon woman was in a quiet, withdrawn mood, leaving Lynia to converse with Lial or no one at all.

Iren and then Eri were beside Lial, and Aris and Selia sat next to Kezari. Although Lynia could hear their conversation and sometimes respond, distance made deeper discussions nearly impossible. Not for the first time, she contemplated a redesign of the table. This worked well for formal occasions, but those here most nights were beyond such strictures. They could convert another room to more intimate dining, but that would be a shame. This room jutted out into the gardens, floor-to-ceiling windows seating them amidst nature.

"The sliced *daeri* is excellent," Kezari said, "But you seem uninterested. Is your portion lacking in some way?"

Lynia blinked down at her plate. She'd been too distracted to give it much heed, but the contents weren't particularly inspiring. "I have never been overly fond of meat."

Kezari tilted her head. "What else would you eat?"

"A great many vegetables," Lynia answered, chuckling. She speared a piece of *nesel* and lifted it. "See? Had we been serving ourselves from platters tonight, I would have left the *daeri* for others, but I suppose I'll have to eat it. I won't dishonor its sacrifice."

"I would be happy to honor its sacrifice for you if you do not wish to consume it," Kezari said, her eyes taking on a draconian gleam.

Lial's fork cracked against his plate as he set it down with a snap, and the rest of the table went silent. "You should not neglect protein while your muscles regain their strength. I do hope you have been balancing the types of vegetables you are choosing."

"I am certain that after four thousand, two hundred and twelve years, I am capable of eating properly, Lial." Her fingers tightened around the wooden handle of her fork until she was sure the engravings would leave indentions in her skin, but mindful of their audience, she managed to keep her tone on the right side of politeness. "Although I thank you for your concern."

The others stared down at them in varying degrees of amusement. Then Ralan outright laughed until Cora nudged him with her elbow, and Selia made a point of beginning a conversation with Lyr about the changes she wanted to make to the library. Though a few grins were hidden behind cups, discussions resumed without too much focus remaining on them.

"Why do you always do this?" Lynia hissed beneath her breath, hoping to avoid further scrutiny.

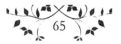

His light blue eyes flashed with anger, but he kept his own voice low. "Why do you react poorly to my concern?"

Lynia huffed out a sigh. "I am capable of taking care of myself. Did I ask for a healer's advice?"

"And I no longer rate as anything but the estate's annoying healer." Lial returned his attention to his plate, the loss of his gaze leaving her oddly bereft. "I will attempt to remember."

Iron's curse. No matter her intent, Lynia couldn't seem to avoid hurting him. She longed for the days of easier friendship, although truth be told, that had been before Telien's death. The strain had grown over the last few years, and she wasn't sure if knowing that his feelings were to blame was better or worse than remaining ignorant.

"Cousin," Ralan said, leaning forward so he could speak to Lial. "Have you decided when you're going to approach Dria? I imagine you would prefer her to me."

Lynia frowned at the unusual comment, and her confusion only grew when Lial glared down at Lyr. The table went silent again. "I wanted to pursue this matter myself, Lyr. Our meeting was not intended to hand over responsibility for—"

"He didn't tell me," Ralan interrupted with an absent wave of his hand. "Seer, remember? Your timing affects the future strands, as does your ultimate decision. The when and where will greatly alter your ideal replacement for one thing, and it could change who Cora and I pick as the healer of the new palace as well. I would like to narrow down the strands."

Suddenly, Ralan's meaning became clear. "Replacement?" Lynia asked. "Surely you aren't leaving in the middle of a crisis."

Lial's expression went blank in a way she hadn't seen outside of difficult healing sessions. "I would not do so."

Relief filled her, but it was short-lived.

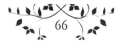

"My plan is not yet set, but my intention is to wait until our current dilemma is solved before transferring to another location," Lial said without meeting her eyes. "The outpost is my hope."

The silence grew heavy, the tone a darker one. Lial had served as Braelyn's healer for over four hundred years, and he'd grown to be an indispensable force. The very idea of him leaving was so unbelievable that most could only stare at him in shock. Except for Ralan and Eri. The former stared at Lial with a suspicious amount of satisfaction, and the latter gaped at her father with wide eyes.

For once, it wasn't the father chiding the daughter for dropping hints at the future.

"But what about us?" Arlyn asked from the other end of the table. She rubbed her hand in anxious circles across her belly. "Will you leave before the baby is born? What if something goes wrong?"

"I doubt any move would be so quick," Lial answered. "It could take months or even years to arrange properly. But regardless, I would not transfer so far away that I could not see to the health of my current patients until they are comfortable with my replacement. I give my word."

Lynia's stomach twisted in on itself in sick dread, and she dropped her fork with a hollow thud, the *nesel* she'd speared no longer appealing. His feelings weren't her fault—no one owned responsibility for another's emotions—but she couldn't help but feel responsible anyway. Had her indecision increased his pain? Was it being forced to work with her so intensely? She'd never wanted to cause havoc within his heart.

What was she going to do without him pestering her?

Though she hated bad manners, Lynia pushed away from the table and jerked to her feet. It was the best of her choices, for if she were to stay, she would no doubt be unable to hold her tongue

concerning this matter. She would never make it through the rest of dinner without losing her composure.

"Please forgive me," Lynia forced out, though her throat wanted to close on the words. "I must return to my research. Please honor my portion of *daeri*, Kezari."

Lynia didn't wait for acknowledgement or to see if the dragon scooped up the meat. Instead, she fixed her gaze straight ahead and avoided everyone's eyes, especially Lial's, as she strode as calmly as she could manage from the room. Everyone knew it was an escape.

But she would escape with her composure intact.

6

Lial found Lynia in the library, of course.

It hadn't taken him long to follow, but he'd had to stop for a moment to reign in his desire to throttle Ralan. His cousin was no child like Eri to let such things slip, and he had no right to meddle in Lial's life. Lynia had found out about his departure in the worst possible way. It was inexcusable.

Lial braced his fist against the wall, his heart in the room on the other side. Maybe he should leave her alone. Considering the friendship they'd built over the centuries, she was no doubt annoyed that he hadn't told her about his decision first, but that didn't mean she was truly hurt. If he left it at this, her anger would fade by the time he saw her again. To go in there now would be to invite another rejection.

But there was another possibility, however slim. One he barely dared contemplate—she cared, and more deeply than one felt for a friend. It was highly unusual for her to break etiquette, but she'd dismissed herself before eating with a thinly veiled excuse. That implied strong emotions, and it was why he'd followed.

He had to talk to her.

Finally, he straightened and opened the library door. Had it only been a few marks ago that he'd sat here helping Lynia search through texts and make a list for Delbin? The table where they'd worked was empty now, but he could sense her presence in the room. Closing the door behind him, Lial scanned the floors of bookshelves rising ever upward.

There. Fourth level, not far from the landing to the staircase that spiraled around the room.

If Lynia detected his energy or heard his footsteps as he crossed to the base of the steps, she gave no indication. Instead, she tugged another book from the shelf and added it to the stack balanced precariously against her torso. Lial's heartbeat quickened with concern at the weight she held, and he rushed up the stairs. If she fell descending the steps while trying to carry that much, he might not be able to heal her spine again.

When he reached her, she shot him an annoyed glance. "Do not dare imply I'm too weak to handle a few books."

His jaw clenched as he counted. "Eight large tomes aren't exactly a few."

"Did you come here to ruin the remainder of my evening?" Lynia demanded. "Or have you decided to make your way around the estate, annoying the general populace?"

"Neither." He took a deep breath. "You were upset, and I wanted to see why."

Both of her brows winged up. "Honestly?"

Before he could answer, Lynia shoved half of the books at him. He took them quickly, concern hastening his motions as her hold on the rest of the stack wavered, but she managed to right them. Then she settled the remaining books more securely against her chest and marched past him. Lial trailed behind her down the stairs, her pace

rapid and steady for someone who'd been using a cane a couple of months before. Only when she'd settled her burden on her favorite research table did she turn to glare at him.

"I realize we have grown more distant since Telien's death, and I know you are guarding your heart." Lynia crossed her arms. "But why did you not think to warn me that you were seeking another post? Earlier today, we spent a couple of marks together, some of that time alone. Did you leave this room and go straight to Lyr without a word to me about it?"

Lial dropped his books on the table beside hers. "That time together was what I needed to fully decide."

She flinched. "I see."

"It was the pleasure of it, not the pain," he snapped. "More than that, it was pride. For both of us. I will not become a pathetic ghost haunting your steps, and you do not deserve to be confronted with my turmoil on a constant basis."

"But to leave? We have done well enough avoiding one another lately."

Her shoulders curled inward, and her hands dug into her waist. His actions had caused her true pain. Lial wanted to peel her fingers away from their death grip and pull her close. But he couldn't.

"Until this crisis drew us together." He let out a deep breath. "This will be difficult to manage in so many ways, and I fear I will be unable to bear more once this is through. Distance will bring relief to us both. I don't want you feeling guilty for your own emotions. You owe your love to no one, including me. Especially me."

"You count your worth too low," Lynia murmured, "If you believe my struggle is because of something you lack."

He found his lips curling upward. "I do not, though I could repeat the same to you."

"I don't like this turn of events," Lynia said, pushing her shoulders back. "Not at all."

"Nor do I." Lial raked his fingers through his hair. "But although I was content in my tower for some time, lately I find myself considering a family. Even if you weren't hurting from Telien's death, I doubt you would be—"

"That is low," Lynia said, her arms dropping to her sides. "It isn't my fault that I don't conceive easily. That has never been a secret, yet you still claim to love me."

His brows lowered, first in confusion for her misunderstanding and then in anger. "You believe I would reject you because it might take a while to have children? Gods of Arneen, Lynia. I was going to say that I doubted you have interest in such a thing with *me*, not that…" He sucked in a breath, a futile attempt at cooling his temper. "Do you truly think I would taunt you with such a thing? I didn't realize your opinion of me was *that* low."

Her hand drifted to her throat, and she took a step back until the table stopped her. "I assumed…"

"I'm a healer, one with a great many favors owed." Lial settled his hand on the edge of the table and leaned close as though confiding a secret. And in a way, he was. "If you were mine… If you wanted children, I have no doubt I could give them to you whenever you wished."

Her eyes went wide at his blunt words, and her lips parted on a gasp. The brush of her breath across his face sent a spear of heat straight through him. Ill-timed desire, as always. But Lynia didn't shove him away as he expected. Her hand softened against her throat, her fingers trailing against the delicate skin there, exactly where he would love to trace his mouth.

He needed to step back. Thanks to his temper, he'd already said

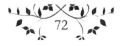

more than he'd intended. Why wasn't she yelling at him? Had he shocked her that much? This time, he had surely gone too far.

Lial struggled to gather the scattered fragments of his composure. And he nearly succeeded—until her tongue darted out to trace her lower lip. Until he caught the hint of desire sparking in her gaze.

Then he made the unbelievably stupid mistake of kissing her.

Before Lynia gleaned his intentions, Lial's mouth captured hers, the bite of their argument echoing between them. But not for long. Within a heartbeat, he gentled the kiss until his lips took hers with reverent sweetness. Rough she could have denied—a mistake brought on by anger—but not this. It was as though every brush of his mouth held his heart.

The kiss deepened, and he feasted. But he didn't hold. She could free herself with the push of a finger, but in that moment, she didn't want to. The heat stoked by his earlier words surged to life until she wanted to wrap herself around him and take the kiss even further.

If only she dared.

He nipped her lower lip as though he'd heard, and finally, he touched her. Not with the heat she might have expected, though. He skimmed his knuckle down her cheek and along her jaw, so tenderly he might have been tending a wound. But she wasn't soothed. She'd felt the calming rush of his magic before, and that was the opposite of what she wanted.

Before Lynia could process that thought, Lial pulled back. The haunting blue of his eyes sucked her in, though she couldn't begin to untangle the emotions surging within. Then he backed up another step and ran his hand through his fall of auburn hair, the motion

breaking their shared gaze. That didn't help her find the path—apparently, she couldn't untangle her own feelings any better than she could his.

Lynia expected him to apologize; despite his gruffness, he wasn't rude when it mattered. But he rarely lied, either, so she wasn't entirely surprised when he spoke. "I should not have done that, but I cannot claim regret. I hope I didn't cause you distress."

"You would have known instantly if I had been unwilling, if that's what concerns you." Lynia twined her fingers together to stop their trembling. "Although I have to admit to confusion since you claimed to be leaving Braelyn to avoid such a possibility."

His nostrils flared. "That was a perfect example of why I must leave. I didn't have a plan, Lyni. My heart called, and I listened. It grows increasingly difficult to resist doing so."

For two decades, Lynia had feared that she would never enjoy another kiss, any future moment ruined by comparisons with Telien, but she'd been wrong. She hadn't thought about anyone but Lial when his lips had been on hers. Still, that was a long way from a relationship.

"I'm not certain how to move on," Lynia tried to explain. "From Telien, that is. Most of the time, I don't feel so raw, but then it hits and… I don't know how to explain."

"I comprehend this more than you realize." Lial stared absently at the books on the table. "More than anyone realizes."

Before Lynia could ask what he meant, Lial spun away and strode toward the door. "Wait!" she called.

He paused, half-turning to meet her gaze. "Yes?"

"I…" There was so much she could say, but none of the questions roaring in her mind felt right. Not without inviting further intimacy. "The books. The ones I handed you earlier. They're medical

texts written within the probable correct date range. I meant for you to take them with you."

Lial blinked, but his expression was too closed to interpret as he returned to gather up the books he'd placed on the table. "Thank you."

As soon as the door closed behind him, Lynia sank into the nearest chair. He'd just hinted at a deep trauma—possibly even a broken bond—and she'd rattled off information about the research she'd found. Gods help her, but he always wrecked her equilibrium. Perhaps if this latest encounter hadn't rattled her so deeply, she might have thought of a way to ask what he meant. Not that she should. It wouldn't be right to question him about something like that while rejecting any chance at closeness.

Lynia drew in a shaky breath. She had a feeling sleep would be difficult to come by tonight.

Lyr settled deeper into his favorite seat by the window, one he'd taken to using when in the family room. His book sat forgotten in his lap, but he had a better source of amusement at the moment— Kai attempting to teach Arlyn to play the *ehrehp*. His daughter might be able to pull a bow string, but she hadn't managed anything more than discordant groans from the stringed instrument.

"This is close enough to the harp that I shouldn't be this bad," Arlyn complained. "I could at least get a decent sound out of Mallory's when she let me try."

Kai smiled and lifted the *ehrehp* into his lap. "You're plucking too harshly at the strings."

Though Lyr's friend-turned-bondson was no *omree*, he played a serviceable rendition of a popular tune. Arlyn scowled at Kai's

fingers so fiercely that Lyr couldn't hold in the snort of laughter, which earned him a glare from his daughter. Ah, well. It might save the instrument—or Kai—from being incinerated by her gaze if nothing else.

"Shall I search for a music teacher, *tieln?*" Lyr asked.

She was in no way soothed by the fatherly endearment. "Don't 'beloved' me when you're over there laughing at this, and no, I don't want lessons. The bards I met at the autumn festival were obnoxious. Ridiculously full of themselves, for the most part."

Lyr grinned at the assessment, for she wasn't wrong. Not that all of the *omree* were so difficult, but one in particular had been. "You mean Kerel Liere nai Ebaia? It's only because she wanted to impress Ralan. Little did she know that severe formality is the worst way to do it."

The door swung open. "You've got that right."

It wasn't fair, but Lyr couldn't keep his smile from dropping as the man himself took the seat beside him. What was it now? Assassins? A punishing blizzard? An invasion force from another world? He struggled to keep his thoughts from his face, but Ralan's upraised eyebrow told him he'd failed.

"I suspect I'm a happier man because of your strong mental shields," Ralan said. "Relax. I'm not here to speak of doom. Though I suppose my gift does aid in scheming."

Kai's fingers went still with a jarring screech. "Scheming? Ah, hell."

"In a good way." Ralan flicked his hand toward Kai. "Leave if you want."

Lyr relaxed at the mischievous glint in the prince's eyes. This was not how Ralan acted when he was delivering a prophecy. "I assume this is an informal affair since you approached me here instead of my study."

Ralan shrugged. "There's a formal proposal involved, but we can worry about that later."

Kai settled the *ehrehp* on its stand, but neither he nor Arlyn stood. It seemed they were curious to hear this, too. What had gotten into Ralan? First, he'd interfered with Lial and Lynia at dinner, and now this unusual interruption.

"Very well," Lyr said. "On with it."

"Despite what he may think, I like my cousin." Ralan smirked. "Not that you should tell him I said so. Regardless, I have no desire to have him working at the new palace, and the outpost is not the best place for his particular skills. He would go mad from how quiet it is there, at least at the moment."

Lyr grimaced at the blunt assessment, however accurate. "Without those two options, his choices will be far removed from here."

"Thus my plan." Ralan leaned forward. "One that isn't entirely altruistic, I might add. Braelyn guards one of the main portals to the Veil and the new palace shields a direct gate to Earth not far away. It is time to consider constructing a healer's enclave in case of trouble."

Curious that Ralan should say so after Lial's quip about being able to afford that very thing, but Lyr wasn't going to ask if Ralan had gleaned the idea through the future strands. "Between Braelyn and the palace, you mean?"

"Yes." The amusement drained from Ralan's expression. "I knew one would probably be needed in several years for futures you don't want to know about, but I have no certainty of the timing for those events as yet. There's no reason we can't go ahead and build it, though."

"Wait." Arlyn leaned forward. "What is a healer's enclave?"

Ralan smiled. "You might consider it a kind of teaching hospital, except the healers live there. This wouldn't be as large as the one at my

father's palace, but I think it would be a benefit to the area. I've been hoping I could get Lial to be the head healer of the enclave. Thanks to his stubbornness, the futures haven't been favorable until now."

Lyr's heart pinched at the thought. "It is difficult to imagine Braelyn without him."

"You wouldn't be." A satisfied gleam sparked in Ralan's eyes. "Without him, that is. Being so close, he'll never be able to resist butting in here, which will keep him in contact with Lynia. It's an ideal situation. If he leads the enclave, Lial won't be tending to a major estate by himself, so if he and Lynia do form a relationship, he won't be stretched thin by work and family. If they don't, he at least won't be so stressed. Not that we could ever remove him from such stress without this kind of scheme."

Arlyn frowned. "What part of all this is a scheme? It seems fairly straightforward to me."

"The part where we don't tell Lial," Ralan replied. "I plan to stall for time when he asks me about a position at the palace, and I'll see if Dria will do the same if he asks about the outpost. He already knows we can't do anything until we see what happens with this mystery illness. If he and Lynia fail to stop it... Well, I choose to remain optimistic."

Lyr couldn't help but notice that Ralan didn't *look* particularly optimistic. "Should I ask—"

"No," Ralan interrupted. "I know you want to be prepared as Myern, but you don't need any details for that. Trust me. In case of failure, be ready to set up quarantine areas like the one Lial used to help the energy-poisoned Neorans, and give Lial and Lynia what they need when they request it."

At least one of Ralan's motives for messing with Lial became clear—distraction. Lyr hadn't seen the seer's eyes so bleak since he'd

had to confront his brother, Kien. In that moment, he knew without doubt that Ralan was correct. Lyr didn't need to know the horrible possible futures that the prince foresaw.

"How do you sleep?" Arlyn murmured.

"There are nights when I don't," Ralan answered honestly. Despite his stark words, he smiled, even at a frowning Kai. "So. How about we try to ensure my stubborn cousin doesn't lose his chance at happiness while we wait? I tried to recruit Cora, but she told me to mind my own business after my dinner interruption."

Kai shook his head. "She's probably right."

Part of Lyr agreed. His mother and Lial were more than old enough to make up their own minds. At the same time, he understood all too well what was behind his mother's reluctance. He'd felt the pain of losing a soulbond and then finding love again. Though he'd never completed the link with Arlyn's mother, it was close enough.

More than anything, he wanted his mother to be happy.

"I will not lie if asked," Lyr said. "But I see no harm in trying so long as there's no coercion. The enclave is a good idea, and if Lial doesn't want to lead it, we can always find someone else."

Arlyn nodded. "You should have seen the way Lynia was staring at Lial right after he finished giving me a quick check up earlier, and yes, Kai, everything was fine. You know how Lial is."

Ralan laughed, interrupting whatever Kai was about to say despite Arlyn's reassurance. "We'll plan a healer's enclave and see what else we can manage."

"Very well," Lyr said.

Then Ralan stood, smirked again, and bid them farewell as quickly as he'd entered. Lyr stared after his friend even after the door had closed. Certainly an unusual conversation. "And I thought Arlyn's attempts to play the *ehrehp* were…interesting."

This time, his daughter chuckled. "Yeah, my notes weren't as discordant as that. Ralan acting as a matchmaker while hoping to stop a plague… Who would have thought? You know there's more to it than what he says, though."

"Undoubtedly."

Kai still frowned down at Arlyn. "Did Lial find anything—"

"Come on," she said, rolling her eyes. "You can ask for all the details in our room. Even though the baby and I are fine. As I told you."

Soon, Lyr was left alone with his circling thoughts, waiting to dump worry on his head once more. Though he wanted to lose himself in the latest tale by his favorite *onraiee*, he couldn't focus on the book. He needed to begin planning, and not just for this new healer's enclave. Ralan had said he would need isolation areas if his mother and Lial failed, but the time to prepare for that wouldn't be after the failure.

The time to act was now.

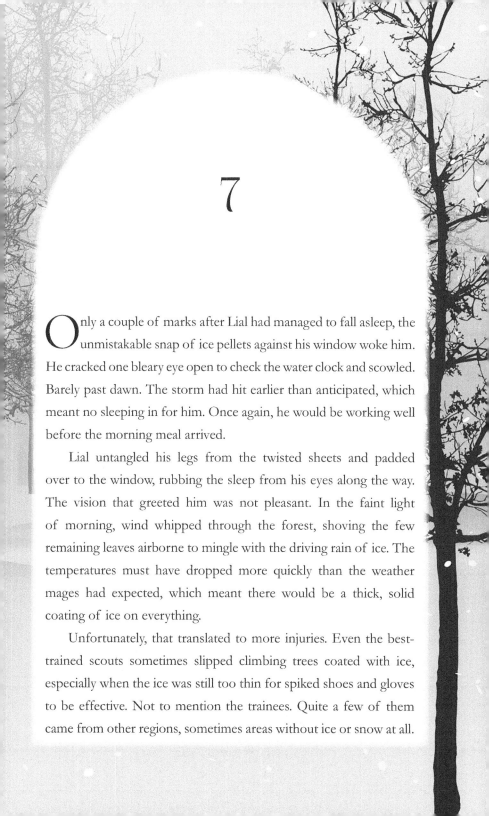

7

Only a couple of marks after Lial had managed to fall asleep, the unmistakable snap of ice pellets against his window woke him. He cracked one bleary eye open to check the water clock and scowled. Barely past dawn. The storm had hit earlier than anticipated, which meant no sleeping in for him. Once again, he would be working well before the morning meal arrived.

Lial untangled his legs from the twisted sheets and padded over to the window, rubbing the sleep from his eyes along the way. The vision that greeted him was not pleasant. In the faint light of morning, wind whipped through the forest, shoving the few remaining leaves airborne to mingle with the driving rain of ice. The temperatures must have dropped more quickly than the weather mages had expected, which meant there would be a thick, solid coating of ice on everything.

Unfortunately, that translated to more injuries. Even the best-trained scouts sometimes slipped climbing trees coated with ice, especially when the ice was still too thin for spiked shoes and gloves to be effective. Not to mention the trainees. Quite a few of them came from other regions, sometimes areas without ice or snow at all.

The first winter storm was always…an adjustment.

Lial chose a muddy brown tunic and pants from his wardrobe and shrugged into them at a healer's speed. He'd ruined far too many clothes during his apprenticeship to waste time considering more than color, and he had a feeling he would need something that blended with both mud and blood. Slipping and sliding in the forest brought its fair share of both. In any case, he'd always found it more reassuring to the patient not to see their blood standing out in sharp relief on the healer's clothing.

Before he descended the stairs, he gathered the notes he'd made during the deep marks of the night when he'd been unable to sleep. He hadn't examined all of the books Lynia had given him, but he'd made a good start. He'd already written down some of his conclusions as well as a few additional resources the books had referenced.

If he hurried, he could slip into the library and leave his observations beside Lynia's research for her to examine later while he was swamped with injuries to treat. He scribbled out a quick comment to that effect on the top of the first page, slipped the bundle into a waterproof envelope, and rushed out of the healer's tower like the storm itself.

The path to the estate was already beginning to freeze over, so Lial slowed his steps once he left the grass. Hopefully, the mages had finished augmenting the protective spells on the cliff walls yesterday. The icy rain was falling fast enough to flood the stream, and the rocks had been weakened by the last storm. He had enough problems already—an avalanche was one more disaster than he wanted to deal with at the moment.

With luck, the weather's ferocity would keep most inside, so Lial would only have to worry about the *sonal* out guarding the estate.

Fortunately, he hadn't received any urgent mental calls by the time he pushed through the entrance closest to the library. Lynia rarely worked before the morning meal, so he could complete the errand quickly and be back to his tower before he was needed.

Except for one miscalculation—these weren't usual times, and Lynia wasn't sticking to routine. Lial sensed her presence before he opened the door, and he cursed to himself as he entered the library. He didn't have time for her to take him to task for kissing her, and the restless, heated marks he'd spent trying to sleep hadn't given him the best disposition even without the storm. He wouldn't be able to apologize regardless, for he still didn't regret his actions.

Everything he loved might turn to ash, but at least he would know the taste of her lips.

Lynia glanced up from her book in surprise as he approached. "Lial."

The sleepy rasp of her voice had him shoving down thoughts better left alone.

"I didn't think you would be up yet." His fingers tightened around the envelope until the paper crinkled its protest. "The ice arrived early, so I thought I would leave my notes for you to examine. If you need the books themselves, you have leave to retrieve them from my room while I'm working. I'll be waist-deep in bruised arses and twisted ankles, most of which could be resolved with simple rest. I'll be lucky if there's nothing more dire."

She chuckled softly. "That's quite the mental image."

"I suppose it is," Lial said, a reluctant smile crossing his lips. Then he held out the envelope. "Here. I've added some references that might be worth pursuing, but I don't know if we have them in our library. I'll fit in what research I can amidst the chaos. I hope you realize I'm not trying to shirk our task."

Lynia took the packet from his hands and set it aside without taking her gaze from his. "Caring for current injuries is important, too. Accidents don't stop when we wish it."

His fingers itched to trace along the frown marring her brow, but he didn't dare go that far. He might have no remorse for the kiss, but he had no illusions about it, either. "Would that I could halt it all. But alas."

"We should…" Her throat worked, her expression turning hesitant. "I suppose we should talk about earlier. What happened before you left."

It was his turn to frown. "Before I left? Have you been here all night?"

"Yes, and no lectures," Lynia said. "My back feels fine. I'm well. You'll not annoy me out of discussing this."

That hadn't been his intention, but it would have been an admirable result. "For once, I wasn't thinking about your back. It's never good to drain your energy in a crisis, but you know that limit well enough. Better than Kai or Lyr, that's for certain."

"Or you." She lifted an eyebrow, but he didn't refute her. No point in arguing when she was correct. "Now, about last night—"

"I told you I had no regret." Lial straightened his spine. "I still don't. I expect nothing beyond that moment."

Lynia stood, her hands rubbing absently at her lower back as she stared at him. It took everything in him not to scan her with his magic and then to take away the ache she barely seemed to notice. But if he said anything about her injury now, he would be the one needing a healer.

"What were you hinting at when you said you understood?" she surprised him by asking. "About my struggle to move on, that is."

Lial froze. He almost never alluded to his past, but he'd found himself risking that slight admission last night. He should have known better than to do so with Lynia, whose greatest strength was analyzing information. Had he wanted her to ask, or had he fooled himself into believing she wouldn't bother?

"It is…not well known," Lial hedged. "I doubt even Ralan is aware since it happened before he was born."

Lynia crossed her arms. "There's no need to evade if you don't want to tell me. You don't owe me your secrets. But that's the first time you've said anything like that in over four hundred years. I couldn't help but wonder."

Part of him wanted to confess everything, but the other portion held tight to his shame. His abilities were well-known and respected, his youth lost to memory behind a thousand years of solid service to his gift. What she asked for was buried so deep he wasn't even certain he could pull it free well enough to make sense.

"I…"

Naturally, Elan chose that moment to contact him. *"I got to the tower at the same time as a scout with a broken elbow. Where are you?"*

"Returning shortly," Lial sent back before cutting the connection. "What is it?" Lynia asked.

"Elan." Lial let out a long sigh. "First broken elbow of the day."

Her arms uncurled, and she shoved gently at his shoulder. "Better than arses. Go ahead. We can talk later, if you're willing."

"I'll try to explain, but I make no promises to clarity." Lial met her eyes. "I've never told anyone. But I'll tell you."

Before she could answer, he hurried toward the door. He didn't have time to see how she took those words. Elan didn't have the skill to fix a broken elbow, and Lial would rather not see the wound begin to heal incorrectly because he delayed. Rebreaking bones was

one of his least favorite tasks, along with cutting iron out of Lyr and discussing his unfortunate youth.

"Lial," she called when he reached the door, much as she had the night before.

He paused. "Yes?"

"You might want to pull your hair back before you reach your patient." Her eyes glinted with mischief, but she was kind enough not to laugh. "It's tangled enough without adding in caked blood."

"Thanks," he muttered, mentally cursing the existence of this day.

A suspicious, chuckle-like sound carried through the door he'd closed, but Lial ignored it as he rushed for the back door, his fingers already tugging through his hair. He didn't typically care about his appearance beyond surface presentability, but even he balked at being caught in such a hurry that he hadn't bothered to comb his hair.

Not to mention she was right—blood and tangles were a nightmare combination.

Lynia managed to wait until Lial was gone before opening the envelope he'd given her. A surge of excitement brought a smile to her lips as she smoothed the paper on the desk and caught sight of his bold-but-hurried handwriting. What was wrong with her? It was hardly a love letter, but she had to admit her heart reacted like it was.

She traced her finger over the scrawl. *Leaving this information for you. Will examine the other two books soon.* Though she'd stayed up working, she hadn't expected him to do the same. Not because he wasn't diligent—he had to replenish his energy to heal effectively. That he'd been able to provide so many notes already was a gift.

Once Lynia had skimmed the pages, she had to admit that this was better than a gift. It wasn't just information. It was respect. He'd trusted her to read the books on healing he'd suggested yesterday and had clearly expected her to understand them. His analysis might have been more detailed had it been written to another full healer, but it wasn't overly simplified, either. She opened her notebook and began to take notes as she studied his report and compared it to what she'd learned.

Current theory held that most elves and fae had some form of immune system, but it focused on distinguishing good bacteria from bad since viruses didn't survive against their magic input. Augmented by magic, that immune system was effective enough that bad bacteria was cleared before the body showed a physical response. Viruses were dismissed as inconsequential in most healers' texts, if they were mentioned at all.

It was tempting to assume that their mystery illness would come from an unidentified bacterium, one their bodies hadn't learned to identify, but Lynia hesitated to do so. For one thing, their immune systems had the ability to clear bacteria—a process familiar to Moranaian healers. A virus, though…that would be truly unknown. And since Lial hadn't learned about viral infections, it would require research to defeat it.

Especially considering the curious thread Lial had noted in the two books written in Bleyiak's time. A couple of off-world healers had started studying viruses in local animals. The books from Braelyn's library didn't contain those analyses, but they referred to them. There was also an unusual amount of research on mineral and plant toxicity for the time, at least according to Lial.

Until she had more information, she wouldn't rule out any possibility.

Lynia slid out the list she'd started and wrote down the titles Lial had suggested she search for. Then she frowned. He hadn't thought to include the name of the *onraiee* or healer who had penned either of the references mentioned in the books she'd given him. There weren't likely to be many books with these exact titles, but it was possible. She would have more success sourcing them from other libraries with the author's name, and she could also request similar tomes by the same person. It looked like she'd have to grab the original books from his workshop to find the rest of the information.

She stuck a placeholder in her book and stood. Her back twinged in protest of the mark or two she'd spent hunched over her research after Lial's departure, and she huffed out a breath before rubbing out the kinks. Then she did a series of stretches until the ache had eased.

She'd recently stopped doing her exercises, and that had apparently been a mistake. Not that she would admit it to anyone, especially not Lial. They might pity her. Or scold her, in Lial's case. But truth be told, she was happy to be alive despite the fact that her back might never fully recover. She could bear the inconvenience more than she could being treated like a child.

To protect her aching muscles from the cold during the walk to the healing tower, Lynia retrieved her waterproof cloak from her room. She had just slung it over her shoulders and stepped out the front door when the ground shook beneath her feet and a roaring sound filled her ears. Her feet slid against the icy threshold, but she managed to grab the edge of the door in time to avoid disaster. All she could do then was hold on and hope for the best.

Though the shaking ended quickly, she wasn't reassured. The last time she'd felt such a thing, part of the cliff wall had collapsed. But hadn't the mages increased their augmentation spells? She skimmed her gaze along the ledge that bordered the clearing in front of the estate, but there wasn't any sign of damage… Was that dust drifting from the southern end of the valley? The freezing rain and sleet stifled it quickly, but she could swear it to be so.

Her throat closed around her gasp. The healing tower was in that direction. Without another thought, Lynia released the door and picked her way along the icy path as quickly as she could, barely even noticing when her son reached her side.

"It is outside the bounds of the main estate," Lyr said. "If you search along the greater estate key, you will see."

Lynia grimaced. The greater key was part of the shielding maintained by the estate's ruling family, and it covered the more distant regions surrounding the main house. She accessed it even more rarely than the main key. "I should have thought to do that."

"You're worried about Lial."

"And anyone seeking aid at the healer's tower," she insisted, though they both knew that wasn't the full truth. "Is everyone accounted for?"

Lyr gave a sharp nod. "In our family, yes, though if not for Ralan, I wouldn't know about Kai. He's waiting beside the portal for Maddy and her mates to come through, and his mental range is poor. Thank the gods for Ralan's boost. But I worry about the mage working on that section of the cliff. I can tell he's alive through the greater estate key, but I won't know his condition until the nearby scouts reach him."

"Let us pray for no injuries," Lynia said.

"Indeed." Lyr's sidelong glance made her tense, and the question that followed clarified why. "I don't suppose you've given thought to why you're sliding along the icy path to the healer's tower in the middle of a crisis?"

Lynia tipped her chin up. She was not going to be lectured by her own child, grown or not. "I was already on my way to retrieve a couple of books. And couldn't I ask the same of you? You could organize a rescue from your study the same way you do other duties."

Instead of arguing, Lyr merely smiled. "I suppose we're both exceedingly hands-on today, hmm? But at least I won't have to suffer Lial yelling at me for risking injury. He'll be too focused on yelling at you."

Gods, but wasn't that the truth? Lynia groaned and considered turning back, but they'd already reached the tower. With a parting smirk, Lyr headed along the path leading farther down the valley, and for the first time in a couple of centuries, she found herself regretting her current inability to send her son to his room.

And devoutly wishing she'd kept to her own.

8

Lial had just sent his patient out the door with an admonition not to show off on an icy practice field when the ground started shifting beneath his feet. With one hand, he gripped his workbench to remain steady, and with the other, he snatched up a vial about to roll over the edge. Glass jars tinkled against each other in their baskets. Those wouldn't break, but he cast a wary eye and a stream of magic toward the distilling apparatus on the far side of the table.

Fortunately, the tremors didn't last long. Less luckily, Elan groaned softly from somewhere behind him. Lial tucked the vial into the correct basket and spun around to find his assistant, who sat on the corner of the bed with his head tipped against the wall.

"Where are you hurt?" Lial asked as he rushed over.

"It's nothing major," Elan answered quickly. "My head cracked against the stone when I slipped, but it wasn't hard enough for real damage. Hurts, though."

"Ah, *clechtan*," Lial muttered. "I'll check regardless and heal what I find. There will be others to treat, I'm sure, and I'll not have you trying to do your job through pain."

They'd only been working together for a handful of decades, but Elan knew better than to argue. Sitting beside his assistant, Lial sent his energy into the wound. A minor contusion, of course—he hadn't doubted Elan's analysis. But head wounds could surprise even the savviest of healers, and he wasn't going to leave anything to chance.

Lial was almost finished when the door opened, and the scent of flowers and Lynia whipped through with the breeze. His power stuttered with his surprise, but he recovered so quickly that Elan didn't appear to notice. Not that Lial cared if he did. He was too busy trying to figure out why Lynia was here. What would drive her to cross the grounds in the middle of an ice storm after gods-knew-what disaster?

He wrenched his mind away from Lynia and focused on Elan's injury. It was important to ensure that no brain tissue was damaged from the impact, and a slight swelling had to be resolved. His assistant deserved his attention. But even with his renewed focus, it took longer than it should have to complete the task.

"Was it worse than I thought?" Elan asked with a frown as Lial's power winked out.

"No," Lial assured him. "The delay was my fault entirely."

"I would hazard to say it was mine." Lynia gazed down at him with a wry smile, but her expression shifted to concern when she looked at Elan. "Are you well? Was there damage here during the rockslide?"

As he rose to his feet, Lial lifted his brows. "That's what that was?"

"Farther along the ridge, part of the cliffside collapsed into the valley, or so Lyr told me when I saw him on the path. He's heading that way now."

"Why are you…" Lial shook his head. The last thing he wanted was to make her angry. "I won't chide you, since I have done far too much of that lately. Do you need something?"

"I was coming for the books before the quake." Frowning, she placed her hand on his arm. "Were *you* hurt? When I saw the direction of the dust, I worried about the tower, but Lyr said it was outside the estate boundaries."

At least she had some care for him, if only as a friend. Lial offered her the best smile he could manage. "I'm well. Thank you for worrying about me."

"Ah. Yes." Lynia lowered her hand and sidled toward the slim spiral staircase. "I'll retrieve the books and get out of your way. Though it seems strange to sit back doing research amidst this newest crisis."

"It is vital in another way. Unlike a rockslide, there aren't countless mages, scouts, and warriors to make short work of it all."

A quick grin crossed her face. "I could count them through the estate key, but I see your point."

Lial stared after her as she climbed the staircase and disappeared. He rarely let anyone into his private domain when he wasn't there, although Maddy passed through on the climb to her floor. With most people, he would hurry after them and demand they leave, but the thought of Lynia alone in his quarters didn't bother him. No, he would rather invite her to stay for much longer—and under entirely different circumstances.

"Has something changed between you and Lady Lynia?" Elan asked, and Lial's skin heated when he realized he'd forgotten the other man's presence.

"No," Lial said. "She still has no interest in me."

Elan's forehead furrowed. "Are you sure you haven't done something to change her mind? I've never seen Lady Lynia look so…light. Almost teasing."

"I brought her research this morning." Lial shrugged and returned to his workbench, hoping Elan would drop whatever madness he had in his head. "That always brings her joy."

"Ah, research," Elan replied, the lilt to his tone suggesting more than simple acknowledgement.

Lial didn't bother trying to decipher it. His assistant was young, barely out of training and full of an enthusiasm Lial hadn't felt for centuries. Elan and Maddy would no doubt be obnoxious together once she settled into her lessons, and that didn't even account for the madness that Fen and Anna would also bring.

Suddenly, he felt far too old.

Before he could linger on the feeling, Lyr's energy nudged against his, and Lial opened a mental connection. *"Yes?"*

"There's a mage trapped within the rubble. He's unconscious, and none of us have the skill to scan him for injuries."

"I'll meet you there," Lial answered at once.

"Kezari is flying back from a hunt to assist with the cliff wall, and Selia's heading over, too. When Maddy and her mates reach the tower, have Fen and Anna join you."

Lial frowned. *"They aren't yet here."*

"I sensed a surge from the transportation gate. They should be soon."

"Very well."

Lial disconnected the link as he bent to grab the bag he kept on hand for such emergencies and then caught Elan's eyes. "Grab the carrying board. We may need it."

In the gloomy weather, Lial's room was little more than shadow when Lynia stepped off the staircase, but with a quick nudge of her magic, the mage globes flooded the area with light. She paused to shake out the folds of her cloak after holding the fabric tight to her body for the climb. Unfortunately, the distraction wasn't enough to keep her gaze from shooting straight toward his bed where the sheets and blankets twisted in snarled tangles. It appeared his night hadn't been particularly restful, either.

Lynia forced her attention to the table where he'd likely left the books. As expected, there was one stack on the far edge and two other books beside a pile of papers. Those were probably the ones he'd reviewed, so when she reached the table, she picked up the nearest of those and read the title.

An Account of Tebid Ored: The Trials of Rrelen.

That was the first one. It wasn't a book she would have selected without Meli's help since it referred mostly to the abandoned colony of Rrelen. She'd falsely assumed that the trials in question had been the challenges that had led to the colony's downfall, but that hadn't been the case. Nor had she properly anticipated the contents of the other title, *The Animals of Rrelen.*

Too bad she hadn't had a chance to read every book in the library, even after so long. When Telien had been alive, she'd spent a great deal of her time researching estate matters, which hadn't included colonies that had failed millennia before. No matter how long she lived, there never was enough time to study everything she wished.

With a wistful sigh, Lynia picked up the second book and tucked them both into a large pocket in her cloak. She was about to leave when the glint of light against metal caught her eye. A ring. Unable to resist her curiosity, she lifted the delicate piece of jewelry so she could study it better.

Gold with a pale, yellow stone, the band thin enough that it appeared more of a woman's style. Had Lial—No. She quashed the worry of him entertaining another woman in his rooms, at least not in a romantic way. She'd known him too long to consider that he would profess love to her while sleeping with another. He would wait until he left Braelyn for that.

A thought that stung more than it should have.

Wincing, Lynia returned the ring to its place and hurried toward the steps as though he'd seen her intrusion. She wanted so badly to ask, but it wasn't her business. They weren't in a relationship. Truly, she would have no right to complain if he *had* taken a lover. And though she didn't believe so, it would be better not to find out otherwise.

Lynia reached the base of the steps as the door opened, and Maddy entered with a man and a woman who were likely her mates. Lial hurried over, his magic flaring around Maddy. Confused, Lynia halted, not certain why the healer was scanning the newcomers. Until it hit her—he must be checking for signs of the mystery illness.

When he finished with Maddy, the young, red-haired woman stepped aside for Lial to continue with her blood elf mate. Fen, Lynia believed. A half-human-half-*Felshreh* prince and current heir to the Unseelie throne. Then after Fen, there was…Anna? If Lynia recalled correctly, Anna possessed some kind of water talent.

"You're clear," Lial said. If the trio was confused, they didn't say so as the healer returned to his workbench and began lining up baskets along the center. "Maddy, you'll stay here. Elan, Fen, and Anna come with me."

That drew a reaction from Maddy. "What? Why am I staying here? Where is everyone going?"

"To a rescue." Lial turned, and at the sight of Lynia, he waved her forward. "You read more than what I marked in those healing texts, correct?"

Gods above, but he knew her well. "Of course."

Lial smiled. "Good. You remain with Maddy. If anyone comes in with bruises or scrapes, you can patch them up. These vials are labeled clearly, and I've no doubt you'll remember their appropriate uses."

Lynia's lips parted on a gasp, but Lial didn't seem to register her surprise. He was too busy directing Elan, Fen, and a bewildered-looking Anna out the door. An entire mark could have passed in the silence that descended as the door closed behind them, but she and Maddy probably only stared at each other for a few drips of time. Not that that wasn't enough to read the young woman's doubt.

Was it Maddy's apprehension about her own ability to handle the situation or misgivings about Lynia's helpfulness? Lynia didn't begrudge Maddy either. The young woman had been dropped into the situation with no clue what was happening, and they didn't know anything about each other save the basics learned from polite dinner exchanges.

"An interesting turn of events," Lynia offered.

Maddy nodded, winced, and attempted an awkward curtsey. "Yes, Lady Lynia."

By the Nine Gods, but Lynia was tired of the stilted, nervous look the young woman wore. Was she truly so fearsome? So often, people first saw her as remote and overly formal when the truth was simpler—she was quiet. Every time a new person arrived on the estate, she had to deal with that false impression, and it wasn't helped by the fact that she *did* appreciate politeness.

But not to the point of impracticality.

"Please call me Lynia," she said, removing her cloak and hanging it by the door. No point in wearing the heavy thing if she was going to be helping here for what could be several marks. "I hope you're more prepared for our unexpected task than I am."

Maddy relaxed slightly and joined Lynia in hanging up her own cloak. "Well, you're one healing text ahead of me, at least when it comes to Moranaian books. I've been trying to look over an anatomy textbook I borrowed from a friend, but it's for humans. Anything useful in yours?"

"It was beginner information, so there were plenty of examples of bandaging wounds and using salves." Lynia inspected the baskets Lial had left on his workbench. A tag was affixed to each, and the vials inside were likewise labeled with the herbal components and usage of each blend. "This looks like a good many of them. *Lehreh, tobahn, maiseh.* A solid combination for treating deep bruises."

Once again, Maddy joined her. "You remember all of that?"

Lynia smiled at the incredulous question. "My magic lends itself to research. I remember most things I study with my gift, whether I want to or not."

"I would say that sounds fabulous, but…" The Sidhe woman's nose wrinkled. "I think we've all read things we'd rather forget."

"I learned to skim before using my magic for just that reason," Lynia replied.

Maddy seemed to consider her for a moment, and Lynia tried not to wonder if the other woman found her lacking. "You've known Lial for a while, right?"

Gods, what did Maddy know? Lynia prayed this wasn't about to get embarrassing. "Yes. Why?"

"I don't always understand what he's thinking. Why would he have left us to stand in for him?"

Lynia held back a relieved sigh. "Because he trusts us to handle small problems. I don't know how much you learned on the way over about what's going on, but part of the cliff wall up the valley collapsed, trapping a mage. Lial would take his usual assistant in an emergency to avoid surprises, and Lyr probably asked him to bring Fen because of his earth magic. I am less certain about your other mate, though."

"Anna recently unlocked her water magic, but I'm not sure why that would help."

Lynia frowned. "I believe the stream runs near the area where the collapse happened. I suppose we will have to see."

"And hope no one else gets hurt," Maddy muttered.

Lynia chuckled at the wry comment, for it mirrored her own feelings. With any luck, neither of them would have their skills tested.

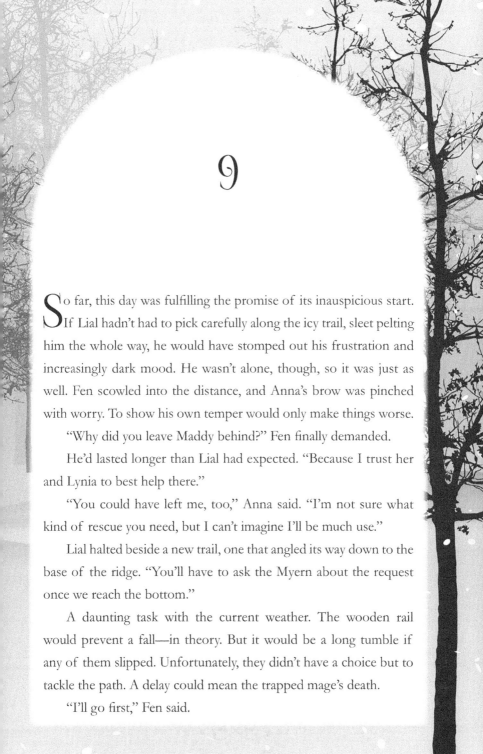

9

So far, this day was fulfilling the promise of its inauspicious start. If Lial hadn't had to pick carefully along the icy trail, sleet pelting him the whole way, he would have stomped out his frustration and increasingly dark mood. He wasn't alone, though, so it was just as well. Fen scowled into the distance, and Anna's brow was pinched with worry. To show his own temper would only make things worse.

"Why did you leave Maddy behind?" Fen finally demanded.

He'd lasted longer than Lial had expected. "Because I trust her and Lynia to best help there."

"You could have left me, too," Anna said. "I'm not sure what kind of rescue you need, but I can't imagine I'll be much use."

Lial halted beside a new trail, one that angled its way down to the base of the ridge. "You'll have to ask the Myern about the request once we reach the bottom."

A daunting task with the current weather. The wooden rail would prevent a fall—in theory. But it would be a long tumble if any of them slipped. Unfortunately, they didn't have a choice but to tackle the path. A delay could mean the trapped mage's death.

"I'll go first," Fen said.

Lial's brows drew together. "I would not put you at the most risk."

Instead of deferring, the young blood elf grinned. "I'm at the least risk, actually. I can connect with the ground here, and it won't let me fall. If you trip, you won't roll past me."

Fen surprised Lial by being correct. With each step the Unseelie prince took, the soil seemed to shift to meet his feet, the ice crackling away. Anna followed behind him and then Lial and Elan. In less time than Lial would have thought possible, they reached the bottom of the narrow valley.

The ancient trees on the undamaged side of the valley rose high enough to provide some cover over them, lessening the force of the sleet. The downside of their protection was the dust cloud that hadn't dissipated as well as it would have without their shelter. The lingering powder mixing with the cool fog along the valley floor coated Lial's lungs with every breath. He should have brought a piece of cloth so he could cover his nose and mouth.

An arrow's arc away, a few people already worked to dislodge the tumbled stones, but their forms were partially obscured by the haze. Fen did something with his earth magic, clearing the remainder of the dust from the air. A bit of the fog rolled away with it, revealing Lyr and a pair of scouts. Lial had to smile at the show of Fen's skill—the young man had grown more confident since their last encounter.

When they reached the others, the magnitude of the problem revealed itself. A large portion of the ridge to their right had fallen, boulders and crumbled stone spilling across the valley floor. Worse, the stream cascaded from the ridge in this very spot. Between the water half-tumbling-half-freezing down the rocks and the sleet pelting through the branches overhead, neither the scouts nor Lyr appeared to be making much progress in shifting the debris.

The injured mage's green robes were visible at the far edge of the rubble, and Lial could make out the man's dust-covered hair where it tangled around his upper shoulders. Otherwise, the angle made it difficult to identify how deeply the mage was buried. Not auspicious, though at least his head and neck hadn't been crushed.

Lyr stepped away from the scouts. "Fen! Anna! I could use your help."

Fen hastened toward Lyr at once, but the woman stared in shock. "Me?"

"I'm told you work with water," Lyr called. "And we have a serious water problem."

Lial tried to think of something he could say to encourage her, but there was no need. Anna squared her shoulders and caught up with Fen, who held out his hand for her before continuing. Good— she was brave. Maddy had mentioned that Anna was half-Gwragedd Annwn, a race of water fae, but Anna had not known of that fact until magic had flooded the human world once more. She would need that courage to adapt to such a big change.

With Elan trailing, Lial followed the pair until he reached Lyr. He kept his gaze locked on the trapped mage as Fen and Anna acted together to move the rubble. As soon as possible, he would run over to assess the damage. Though he wasn't the best at scanning for detailed wounds at a distance, Lial could detect a weakening pulse from the man.

Anna was in the process of diverting the stream when air gusted against Lial's back. He glanced over his shoulder in time to see Kezari land in a flurry of wingbeats, her scales glinting gold in the morning light. Aris and Selia slid from the dragon's shoulders, and the dragon shifted to her elven form. Together the three hurried over.

"I will tend the cliff face," Kezari said, marching past as though the shower of rain and ice didn't bother her.

It probably didn't. The dragon ran so hot that the sleet melted before it landed on her golden hair or summery dress. Lial scowled and tucked his cloak tighter. There were definitely benefits to being a dragon.

Selia joined Fen and Anna, casting a shield over the area that prevented the sleet from falling through. Then the mage switched between helping Anna control the stream and levitating away the rocks that Fen eased to the side with his magic. Any moment, it would be Lial's turn to leap into action. He tapped his fingers against his hip to the beat of the mage's slowing pulse.

If they didn't hurry, he would have to brave darting in before the stones were cleared.

"I've never seen Selia work in a crisis," Lyr said, glancing around Lial to Aris, who had stopped beside him. "Did she do this often before becoming a teacher?"

Aris smiled softly. "And during. You'd be surprised by the number of student disasters she's had to fix."

Lial wouldn't be, but it wasn't something he wanted to dwell on. Especially now. If he didn't get over there soon, it would be his failure, not a student's.

As the last of the large stones was removed from the man's torso, Lial detected the first stutter in the mage's pulse. He darted forward, Elan close at his heels. Lyr tried to call him back, but there could be no more delay. The thready thrum scratched at Lial's mind until it was all he could hear.

Ignoring the rocks floating by his head, he knelt beside the fallen mage. The man was crumpled on his stomach, his lower legs still pinned. A problem for Fen and Selia to solve. Lial sank into a healing trance, and the world went blue around him as he shifted his sight to his senses instead of his eyes.

Five broken ribs. Fractures and contusions to several other ribs as well as to the spine. Two skull fractures with accompanying concussion. One arm nearly crushed and the other broken in several places. And a gaping wound in the stomach leaking blood.

Miaran.

"We have to get him shifted to his back on the carry board," Lial said. "Now."

Elan lowered the board to the ground beside the mage as the final stones were cleared. Normally, Lial would have added his magic to help in levitating the patient, but he would need every bit of energy he possessed to have any chance of saving the man.

But as the mage was shifted to his back, his eyes popped open, and he tried to move the hand that hadn't been shattered. Blood tinged his lips as he tried to move them. "No…accident," the mage finally whispered.

Only then did Lial notice the object slipping from the man's hand—a knife.

A steel one, at that.

Miaran, indeed.

Lynia held back a sigh as she lifted another vial from the basket and returned to her red-faced patient. Lial had not been joking about bruised arses—or hips, which was close enough. This was the third vial she'd given out in a ridiculously short span of time, and like the previous two, the recipient appeared both embarrassed and annoyed.

People truly had become spoiled by Lial, for they were taken aback that their slight ills wouldn't be cured on the spot. But Maddy didn't know the proper technique for healing bruises, and Lynia had no compunction about giving them a vial and telling them to let time

and ointment fix the problem. In this case, being the Myernere had its benefits—none dared to complain.

"I never pictured elves being so clumsy," Maddy muttered when they were alone once more. "As far as I know, the Sidhe aren't, but I admit my experiences there are limited since I was raised on Earth."

Lynia smiled as she settled into the chair near the treatment bed. "Ah, the tales humans have of us. I've read a few Lyr brought back for me. I suppose in some ways they are accurate, but in the end, we're just people."

"There are remarkably few stories about elves slipping on icy trails and bruising their asses," Maddy said with a grin of her own. "Thousands of years of life. Still can't walk on ice."

Lynia couldn't help but chuckle. "In fairness, many trainees at Braelyn come from regions that don't get the weather we do. Either it's farther north where it's cold enough to get snow the entire winter instead of periods of ice or it's an area that's too warm for either. And though Braelyn tends to look fairly uninhabited, there are thousands of *sonal* and warriors in the area, many who journeyed here to train. They'll get the trick of it eventually. Injuries will be far fewer by the time the snows come."

Her nose wrinkling, Maddy hopped onto the stool beside the workbench. "Well, now I feel bad."

"Oh, don't," Lynia said in reassurance. "They should take more care, and I'm bothered by how often they come here for minor ills. Many of these complaints would heal fine without help. I can't believe Lial hasn't chased them away."

"On my last visit, he told me he likes to stay busy because…" Maddy's words trailed off, and pink tinged her cheeks. "Never mind."

Lynia averted her gaze. "He's avoiding me."

"He didn't say that…exactly."

Did everyone know what was going on between them? Lynia sighed and met the other woman's eyes once more. "Because of me, I'm afraid you'll be shifting your lessons to another location. He's planning to move to the outpost or to Ralan's new palace."

Maddy's lips firmed, and she shook her head. "It is *not* because of you. If he's made you feel obligated—"

"No, no," Lynia insisted. "He hasn't, but I can't stifle my guilt over it."

"Well, stop. If he's going to flounce out of here because you don't return his feelings, then let him flounce."

Lynia blinked, her forehead wrinkling in confusion. "Flounce out?"

"You know. Leaving in a snit." Maddy stood, flicked her long red hair over her shoulder, and strutted toward the door with a haughty, pained—truly long-suffering—expression on her face. "A flounce."

The nine gods themselves couldn't keep Lynia from laughing, her hands going to her sides from the force of it. *Clechtan*, but Lial did flounce sometimes. Perhaps not quite so dramatically, but the flavor was the same.

When she could breathe again, she grinned at Maddy. "Apt."

"It's probably bad form to mock my mentor," Maddy said, though the smile she returned held no hint of repentance. "I'd say Fen was a bad influence, but that was all me."

"I like you, Maddy," Lynia said. "And I—"

Lial's energy crashed against hers so suddenly that she established a connection without second thought. *"What...?"*

"This is bad. I'm not sure I can save him. If anyone is in there with minor injuries now, send them out," Lial sent. *"And move to the staircase. Selia is going to transport us shortly."*

107

He cut off the link abruptly. Lynia shook her head to clear it and then shot to her feet. "Go to the stairs or stay by the door."

Maddy frowned. "What? Why?"

"Lial contacted me. They are transporting in."

As she reached the staircase, Lynia shuddered. If Lial said it was bad, then she didn't want to imagine what they were about to see.

Lial pressed a clean cloth against the mage's wound even as Elan grabbed his right shoulder and Selia his left. "What's your name?"

The mage's eyelids flickered, but he didn't open them. "Caeleth."

Lial barely caught the whispered answer before Selia's magic flared, painting the world white for a handful of heartbeats before the healing tower resolved around them. She let go of his shoulder at once and flickered out of view, but he couldn't spare the time to wonder where she'd gone. Blood had already begun to drip onto the floor beneath the carrying board, and Caeleth had slipped into unconsciousness.

"The stone table," Lial said, and Elan nodded.

As Elan levitated the board to the flat stone table beside the staircase, Lial shrugged his cloak to the floor. This was going to be tricky work. That stab to the gut had sliced through intestines, spilling toxins into the man's body, and the damage to the spine would be a challenge to heal, even if it wasn't as severe as Lynia's.

He wouldn't have energy left when this was through.

Lial sat on the stool at the head of the table as Elan took the other stool at the side. Already, Elan had the needle and thread ready, waiting for Lial to sedate the mage. Lial placed his hands on each side of Caeleth's head, closed his eyes, and released himself into his work.

There was so much damage that only experience allowed him to act without hesitation. A touch of healing magic to ease the swelling around the patient's brain. The swift command to sleep. More power to numb any affected nerves. Which was practically all of them. Then he sent his magic toward the knife wound to staunch the blood while Elan stitched.

It would be Lyr's job to figure out who'd stabbed the man with a steel blade. Right now, Lial had to coax the patient to heal despite the mage's allergy to iron. Fortunately, dealing with Kai's and Lyr's injuries involving the metal had taught him a few tricks. As he held the relevant arteries clamped with his magic and Elan stitched, Lial used another stream of power to work as many iron remnants free as he could. Those he gathered in his palm until he could wipe them on a piece of silk.

"Maddy," he said. "Gather bandages. Then observe."

He had to trust that she complied. Elan was struggling to stitch the more difficult areas, and there was a fair chance Lial would have to take over. This attack had been meant to kill. The assailant had slid the blade upward beneath the ribs, slicing part of the mage's intestines, shredding one side of the gallbladder, and piercing the liver. Between this and all his other wounds, Lial wouldn't have stood a chance of healing the man without magic. Had Caeleth's allergy to iron been worse, he'd be dead.

"This section of the wound is beyond my sewing skills," Elan finally admitted.

Without comment, Lial shifted his stool to the other side so he could take the needle. "Begin work on his legs."

Lial's concentration was too split now to continue drawing out the iron, and he could no longer coax the mage's body to regenerate. All of his power went to controlling the man's blood flow and lungs

while he bent over the wound to stitch. Gods, what a mess. Elan had done a good job repairing the intestines and liver, but he'd been right to have Lial work on the gallbladder.

Time suspended as Lial worked, doing his best to restore the organ to its original function. It wasn't vital to life, but it wasn't his nature to shirk any possibility for success. He continued even when his reserves dwindled and his muscles grew stiff with fatigue. Blood coated his hands and sweat rolled down his back by the time he made the final stitch.

Only then did the force of his exhaustion hit. Unfortunately, he wasn't done. Because of the iron, he couldn't heal the wound entirely, so it would have to be bandaged. Lial lowered his hands to the channels carved into the side of the table, and with a touch of magic, he sent the mage's blood rolling from his hands downward, where it would flow to a reservoir at the end of the table. He still had Caeleth's concussions and broken bones to repair.

Even so, he let his power flicker out so he could take a moment to breathe. On the other side of the table, Maddy stared at the now-closed wound on the mage's abdomen with wide eyes, and at the end, Elan used his gift to repair abrasions and straighten bones in the man's legs. Lial blinked, and a cup appeared in front of his face. He followed the holder's arm upward to find Lynia peering down at him.

"Here," she said. "Sip."

Lynia tipped the cup against his lips, and he swallowed the offering gratefully until she withdrew. Then she wiped his damp brow with a cloth and stepped back, a concerned frown on her face—not the disgust or upset he expected. Was she not disturbed by the bloody mess? Despite the cleansing spell, his upper arms and clothes would be flecked with it. Possibly even the brow she'd just wiped.

He refused to look at the cloth she held to find out.

"I'll get the tincture that speeds healing before you bandage the wound," Lynia said, turning toward his workbench and the line of baskets he *hadn't* pulled out earlier.

If he wasn't already in love with her, he would be so now.

The door opened, and Aris strode through. The life mage's attention centered on Caeleth before his gaze shifted to Lial.

"I'll provide energy," Aris said softly.

"A welcome gift."

Lial's reserves were nearly gone, and unlike the average person, a life mage's energy was compatible with any elf. Otherwise, Lial would have to use his own power to convert natural energy for personal use or find a relative close enough in magic to provide some aid. Like Ralan, his seer cousin who *could* have been here to help. Of all the times not to show up unannounced.

Aris settled his hands on both Lial and Caeleth, and Lial lowered his shields enough to accept the gift. A life mage bore the power of life, but they weren't necessarily healers. Creation didn't always relate well to fixing, and although Aris had once cured Selia of an injury, that had only been possible while connected to the heart of Earth's energy field.

The magic he sent coursing through Lial pulsed like the core of Moranaia. It was leaves unfurling and trees stretching their branches into the sky. The power of a million lives throbbed in Lial's blood, and for the barest drip of time, he could sense the beating heart of the world around them.

Then it was gone.

"I hope that helps," Aris said, lowering his hands. "And it does not count as the boon I owe you. I haven't forgotten."

"I thank you," Lial replied. "For this and the boon."

Aris inclined his head, and after a glance at the stitches across Caeleth's abdomen, he sidled back. "I would rather not…"

Having accidentally experienced some of Aris's memories, Lial understood. This type of scene had to remind him of the torture he'd endured during his imprisonment in the past. "Would you see Fen and Anna here when their task is complete?"

Relief crossed Aris's face. "Of course."

Lial flexed his fingers and returned to work as the door closed behind the life mage. His reserves weren't fully restored, but he could do this. The worst was over—he hoped.

10

Lynia scanned the row of labeled baskets until she found the one she wanted and grabbed a vial. Tincture of *ereth, tobahn, maiseh,* and *turek.* Together, these herbs promoted rapid healing, reduced swelling, and helped with bruising. Swiftly, she returned to Lial with the tincture, and just in time. Elan had the patient levitated, and Maddy held out a roll of bandages.

When Lial opened his hand next to Lynia, she placed the vial in his palm. He read the label and nodded before turning to his task. She didn't watch him spread the tincture on the wound—she was too busy staring at his face as he focused on his work. She'd been around when he healed serious wounds before, but never when she wasn't focused on the patient. She cared about the mage's life, of course, but he wasn't family.

Gods, Lial was incredible when he healed. He'd stitched the wound so quickly the motions were difficult to follow, his fingers more nimble than any tailor's. All the while growing paler as lines bracketed his tense mouth and created furrows between his eyes. He had that same intense frown now as he bandaged the wound and waited for Elan to lower the patient once more.

How could he give of himself so absolutely, time and time again? Lynia couldn't look away from his face even once the blue glow of his magic highlighted it an eerie color. He circled the table, pouring his very life into the task. He had to be burning through the energy Aris had given him, but she had no doubt that without that infusion, Lial would have carried on until he was nothing but a husk. And he would stir himself to help anyone else injured today, regardless of the cost.

As though summoned by her thoughts, someone knocked on the door. Lial didn't appear to notice, but Maddy frowned at the entrance as though she couldn't decide what to do. "I'll get it," Lynia whispered.

Maddy nodded, and Lynia walked over to answer. A young scout stood on the other side of the door, his hand raised to knock again. Lynia skimmed the man for signs of injury but didn't see anything obvious.

"May I help you?" she asked.

The scout extended his other hand, revealing a gash across his palm. "I slipped on the practice field and cut my hand on a rock. I'm hoping the healer can help."

Lynia lifted a brow. "You were on the practice field during an ice storm?"

Wincing, the scout tucked the hood of his cloak more securely around his head as if reminded of the pelting ice. "It was empty, and I thought I should work on being outside in bad conditions."

"Which I am certain your commanding officer did not approve," Lynia said sternly, eyeing the cut while she spoke. It wasn't too deep. Uncomfortable, but nothing that wouldn't heal on its own. "Wait here."

Lynia grabbed a tincture and returned to the scout, plopping the vial into his free hand with relish. She refused to have Lial expend

more energy because a trainee couldn't use common sense. He could deal with a sore hand while waiting for the ice to thaw.

The scout frowned down at the vial. "What is this?"

"Put a little bit on the cut and keep your hand wrapped. It will aid in healing," she replied.

"But—"

"Do you have a complaint for me, trainee?" Lynia asked. At her words, awareness of her identity washed across his face. "I will be happy to mention it to the Myern at the midday meal."

A flush turned his cold-pinkened cheeks to deep red. "Of course not."

Lynia smiled. "Good. I would hate to think you're disturbing an important healing for a minor matter after your lapse in judgement."

"Ah. Yes. Or no. I…" The scout's throat bobbed. "Thank you for your help, Myernere."

Her smile spread into a wicked grin as the trainee fled. Sometimes, her reserved reputation came in handy, though she didn't use it as often as she had when she was the Myerna. But today, she was happy to employ her haughtiest expressions if it kept Lial from draining himself over foolish complaints.

If the man needed a guardian, she would be one.

Anger roiled in Lyr's gut and climbed up his throat as he stared down at the silk-wrapped dagger in his hand. He'd never thought to see that hilt again, but here it was. The same design at the crux of his life's worst moments. But how? Allafon was dead, as was Kien. Even if the assassins both men had employed hadn't been defeated, why would they strike out at a lone mage working in the valley?

Selia approached, a frown on her brow. "I helped Anna redo the spells stabilizing the stream, and Fen and Kezari are making sure the sinkhole at the base hasn't become obstructed. I'm afraid the water won't fall down the wall in the same pattern, but it should drain into the water table all the same."

"Thank you, Selia." Lyr scanned the area, now clear of the debris and almost back to the way it had looked before. A few of his best *tayn* were searching up and down the valley, but so far, they'd found nothing. "You unraveled the spell on the invisibility cloaks used by Allafon's assassin. Do you sense that same magic at play here?"

Her frown deepened. "No. Not a hint of it. In fact, the only magic I sense belongs to us or to Caeleth."

"Do you know him?" Lyr asked. "Caeleth?"

"Not well."

Lyr turned the blade in his hands. "Any idea why someone would have come out here to stab him?"

"He is from a prominent family on the Taian branch," Selia answered, her gaze slipping to the knife. "One that might cause trouble if he were murdered here. I hope Lial manages to save him. But I suspect that's not what you're worried about. Not with that hilt."

"You suspect correctly." He wrapped the silk around the knife until it was completely covered and slipped the bundle into the pocket of his cloak. "The way this happened baffles me. Is there a reason behind it, or was it merely an opportunity taken?"

Selia pulled her cloak tighter. "Possibly the latter. Mages don't typically handle this type of task alone, but Caeleth was out here working on the ridge by himself. If he survives, we'll have to find out why."

A muffled curse sounded from the path, and Lyr glanced over in time to see Aris catch his balance against the railing. Selia chuckled, but her amusement was hidden by the time her husband reached them. Granted, humor was difficult to maintain considering the life mage's pale, drawn face beneath the shadow of his cloak.

"What's wrong?" Selia asked, brushing a strand of her husband's brown and green hair from his brow. "Did something bad happen with the healing?"

Miaran, Lyr hoped not. A plague, a mystery assassin, and a murdered Taian mage would be a sad and terrible start to the month. He didn't know Caeleth personally, but they'd met a couple of weeks ago when the mages had arrived to help reinforce the spells protecting the estate and lands from the harsh winter storms. Caeleth had been a pleasant, capable sort, and his death would be a grave loss, one Lyr would be responsible for.

"It wasn't complete when I left, but it appeared to be proceeding well." Aris sighed. "There was so much blood. I…I offered energy, but I couldn't stay."

"Ah, love," Selia whispered.

Lyr averted his gaze as Selia wrapped her arms around Aris's waist. Despite his sessions with a mind healer, the man struggled. Not even magic could erase the trauma of being tortured by one's potential soulbonded and then having to kill her. Centuries might not be sufficient, much less three months.

As soon as the ridgeline was finished, Kezari, Fen, and Anna returned, and together, they worked their way up the pathway to the top. All save Kezari, who'd shifted to dragon form to see if she could find the assassin's trail. She'd caught a scent, one that hopefully wouldn't prove useless. If Lyr needed anything, it was a solid break.

As soon as the mage was settled into the recovery bed, Lial dropped into the chair beside him and tilted his head against the wall. Even after the infusion of life magic, he was tired, but what had he expected after a night with little sleep and the morning's broken elbow to heal? Now he had to gather himself for the next deluge of disasters.

The scent of summer flowers and old books hit his nose before Lynia's hand settled on his shoulder. Her scent aside, he didn't have to look to know it was her. Her energy was as familiar as his own after so many years, especially the last couple of decades. He could find her anywhere.

"Go sleep," Lynia said.

He cracked his eyes open. "Can't. You've seen how busy it gets."

"Some of your patients should learn to take care of themselves," Lynia grumbled, her voice fierce enough to surprise a smile out of him despite his exhaustion. "I would be happy to hand them a vial and send them off as I did that trainee earlier."

Lial lifted an eyebrow. "What trainee?"

"You were too busy to notice." Her fingers tightened on his shoulder. "He had a cut on his palm, of all things. Hardly fatal. In any case, the ice is getting thick enough for spiked boots, so you should see fewer cases. Go to bed."

He straightened, and Lynia dropped her arm, though she didn't look less fierce. Dizziness spun through his head with a flourish, but he summoned his own glare. "You know I will not abandon my duty. Maddy doesn't have enough training to tend to patients, and Elan is nearly as exhausted as I am. If someone needs more aid than a tincture can provide—"

"Then someone can wake you," Lynia interrupted.

"I have other tasks," Lial said, scrambling to pull said tasks from his muddled brain. "I need to secure the feeding box beside the *camahr*'s hole, replenish the tinctures—"

Lynia cupped his chin in her palm and leaned close, the abrupt action surprising him into silence. "You are not one of the Nine Gods of Arneen, Lial. Your energy isn't unlimited, nor is your life. There are three capable people in this room who can do those things, but only you will be able to heal anyone else who might get stabbed. Is it wise to continue to drain yourself on simple tasks with a mysterious assailant on the loose? Think about that."

For a moment, her eyes held him enraptured, the concern and resolve almost his undoing. He wanted to kiss her, audience or not, but he wouldn't. If such a thing were to happen, it would be her choice. Her move.

"Are you listening to me, Lial?"

Gods. Lial blinked, his mind replaying the argument she'd made—and she was right. He'd told Elan much the same earlier. "Fine, but only for a couple of marks. And only if you promise to wake me if anyone needs help."

Letting go of his chin, Lynia straightened, and he suddenly wished that he'd drawn out the argument to keep her close. "I promise. *If* you'll hold up your end of the bargain."

Well, then. It seemed he was taking a nap.

During a break in the incessant sleet and freezing rain, Lynia shrugged her cloak around her shoulders and lifted the bowl of shredded meat from the counter. As Lial had mentioned, she'd found the food in a jar he kept in the enspelled cold box beneath the workbench. She grinned at the thought of it. Lial, the fierce healer

who'd threatened more than one injured patient into compliance, had a large jar labeled *camahr food* tucked amidst his temperature-sensitive potion components.

Maddy followed behind her with a wooden cover designed to go over the bowl to protect it from the weather. It was scratched in spots and weathered smooth in others—old, and not likely something used indoors. How long had Lial been caring for *camahr* at the base of the healing tower? Lynia pondered this new facet of his personality as she picked her way carefully around to the back of the tower.

"There," Maddy said, pointing to a hole at the bottom.

Fortunately, the spells that heated the tower kept the stone and the ground near the base from freezing over, but that wouldn't stop the *camahr* from becoming trapped if the ice built high enough. It already reached the first knuckle of her forefinger, and the weather mages estimated more after this brief reprieve. Lial was right to provide a shelter for the bowl.

Maddy tried to place the broad, arched box against the wall, but the ice was already too thick for it to settle. "Damn."

"I'll fix it," Lynia said, waiting for Maddy to move it once more.

When the spot was clear, she set the bowl of food beside the hole. Then she knelt carefully and lowered her hands to the ice where the box needed to rest. Most of her magic lent itself to research and archiving, but like many of her kind, she could summon a small amount of fire. Enough to light a campfire and—apparently—provide a space for a *camahr* food shelter.

Fortunately, the box provided ample cover. Once Maddy had it in place, Lynia could barely make out the bowl near the hole at the back. At least until a tiny globe of blue light hovered in the darkness. She bent lower, bracing her hand on the cold ice so she could see the young *camahr* creep over to the dish, the tip of its tail glowing as the kit lowered it over the food.

"Adorable," Lynia breathed. Its tall ears swiveled her way.

The *camahr* froze, its eyes pinned on her almost curiously. Then a large paw darted out of the hole, drawing the kit back in, and Lynia chuckled in sympathy with the unseen mother. "I have one just that bold," she said before easing to her feet.

Maddy quirked a brow. "What?"

"One of the kits crept out, but the mother drew it to safety." Lynia smiled. "Reminded me of raising Lyr. I've wanted to do that a time or two during his adulthood, for that matter."

"Is Lyr your only child?" Maddy asked. Then she winced. "That's a rude question. Forget I said that."

It *was* direct, but Lynia found she didn't mind. "He is. I've always wanted more children, but I wasn't so blessed before Telien's death. The Dianore line has never been a fertile one, which is part of why Arlyn was such a surprise. Lyr was only able to stay with her mother for a month before Telien's death drew him back."

"So if you remarried…" Maddy's voice trailed off, hesitation as clear at the freckles on the young woman's face.

"I might have more success, yes." Lynia stared down at the wooden box as a pellet of sleet bounced off the top. Weather reprieve almost over. "But it has only been twenty-two years. How could I dishonor Telien's memory by moving on so soon? He was my soulbonded."

"Hold on," Maddy said, her shocked tone drawing Lynia's gaze. "You've been mourning for twenty-two years, and you're not sure it's been long enough?"

Lynia nibbled on her lower lip. "Is that surprising? We were bonded for more than two millennia."

"I get that, but…" Maddy shook her head, her eyes wide. "That's almost as long as I've been alive. Maybe longer if you calculate the time difference between our worlds. I don't know if it's because I grew up with humans, but that…that doesn't seem like an honor to his memory."

The comment had Lynia stiffening. "A cruel statement."

"I didn't mean it to be." Maddy waved her hand toward the valley. "Somewhere down there, I have two mates. If something happens to me, I hope they are happy together. If two of us are lost, I would want the other one to eventually find love again. It wouldn't be the same, but love never is. My feelings for Fen and Anna are equal, yet it's different for each one. I guess I just meant that clinging to grief isn't an honor your lost mate would likely want."

Lynia flinched at the impact of those words. Telien had adored her. He'd never been able to tolerate when she was sad or in pain. But death wasn't something they'd talked about. They'd both assumed one wouldn't be able to survive the pain of losing the other. She almost hadn't, but Lial's whispers had coaxed her, reminding her of her son and all she would leave behind. Still, while she knew Telien wouldn't want her unhappy, it seemed a stretch to believe he would approve of her finding another.

"I'm so getting sent back to Earth," Maddy muttered.

Lynia let out a long sigh and then settled her hand on the other woman's shoulder. "Not by me. I appreciate your candor, though I admit it is unusual. Even more so that I don't mind. You're easy to talk to. Perhaps it is odd, but I believe we'll get along nicely."

Maddy's lips twitched. "Why odd?"

Another drop of sleet fell. Then another. Lynia started back toward the tower's entrance, waiting until Maddy was beside her to answer. "I do not easily make friends. I admit I would not expect such from a young Seelie Sidhe from Earth. Someone as old as I am surely can't be of much interest."

Maddy chuckled. "Nah. The older a person is, the more stories they have to tell. I'm probably the boring one."

That was a first. Lynia was well accustomed to being considered "the boring one" in most settings. When she smiled again, it was a true one "I suppose we shall see."

11

"Wake up, Sleeping Beauty."

At the sound of the sardonic voice, Lial's eyes shot open, awareness hitting in a snap. He sat up to glare at Fen, who sat at the table staring. "If I'm supposed to understand that, I'm afraid I must disappoint. I have no idea what you're talking about. How long have you been lurking in my bedroom?"

"Only a few minutes. I was supposed to get you up when the water in your clock hit the next line." Fen shook his head. "Didn't expect you to wake up that fast, though."

"A healer learns to react quickly."

Lial glanced at the clock and frowned. They'd given him more than two marks, but perhaps Lynia had accounted for the time he'd taken to clean off in the washroom beside Maddy's bedroom upstairs. Hopefully, disaster didn't await him below. His reserves were far from replenished despite the nap.

"You'll have to teach Maddy that trick. She'd stumble around half-asleep all morning without her coffee."

Lial lifted his brows. "I would think you and Anna would be better at rousing your mate."

"Oof," Fen said, rubbing his palm against his chest. "You old guys are brutal. Is there some kind of club for that? Because you and Vek could be high ranking members."

"I suppose all skills grow more refined with age." Lial allowed himself a moment to relish Fen's wince before he swung his legs over the side of the bed. "Now tell me. How many patients will I find waiting below?"

Fen grinned. "None but the one you already had. But you'll want to see your workroom for yourself."

Despite the man's humor, dread curled through Lial. He finger-combed his hair and bound it at his nape, then straightened the clean clothes he'd donned before falling into bed. Only when he'd taken a few steps toward the stairs did he see the ring Fen twisted absently between his fingers.

"Like the ring?"

A flush reddened Fen's face, and he dropped the ring on the table with a clatter. "I wasn't stealing it."

"I didn't say you were. Liking does not mean taking," Lial replied evenly.

"Sorry. With my history…" Fen sighed. "I'm sure you can imagine. Anyway, I was only admiring the stone. It's not from Earth, but I bet I could still enchant it. Though honestly, it doesn't seem like your style."

Lial shrugged. "It isn't. I don't wear rings. Even with magic, they can be difficult to keep clean when dealing with wounds. That was a gift from a patient, but I'm not sure what to do with it. Perhaps Maddy or Anna would like it?"

"Or Lynia." Fen's wicked grin returned, a comeuppance for Lial's jesting. "I thought it might be a gift for her."

Unfortunately, Lial's scowl didn't erase the other man's smug

expression. Cursed Unseelie. "One she wouldn't accept, as anyone here could tell you. Are we going below or not?"

Fen showed no signs of repentance—not that Lial expected anything else. "Lead the way, Doctor Oblivious."

Lial ground his teeth together to avoid asking if that was another Earth reference, though the intention seemed clear enough. Instead, he ignored Fen and started down the staircase. Oblivious, indeed. He'd been the one rejected, hadn't he? He should know better than anyone the full details of the situation.

Voices caught his ear, and he slowed his descent. Then he caught sight of the three women gathered in front of his workbench and stopped entirely, halfway down. Was Lynia putting something in the distiller? *Ereth* berries? Then she bent low over the table to peer at one of his recipe books, and his chest tightened painfully.

She looked so perfect working there.

"Here," Anna said, bracing her hand on Maddy's waist as she leaned over to give Lynia a large vial of water. "Best I can tell, this is the purified stuff."

Lynia's forehead furrowed. "Are you certain enough for me to try it? We're low on this tincture, and I don't want to mess up the batch."

"I think she's right," Maddy added. "My magic can't find any impurities. We could call Fen down here to analyze it for minerals or something, but I think bacteria is what we need to worry about. Though I don't see why that would matter since our bodies will clear anything like that."

"I'm uncertain myself, but one doesn't ignore directions when creating a potion." Lynia tapped the page beneath her hand with a resolute expression that had Lial smiling. "This says the proper components are vital."

Fen reached the step behind him and spoke in a low, amused tone. "Told you that you wouldn't want to miss this."

Part of Lial wanted to march over and take control of the distillation, much as he would with anyone in his working space. Maybe it was his exhaustion, but he couldn't bring himself to do so. It was a rare pleasure to watch Lynia handle one of his tasks so competently, from analyzing the water to weighing and measuring ingredients as thoroughly as he himself would have. There was only one thing she couldn't provide.

As the potion began to bubble in its flask, Lial finally advanced. "There is one thing I add that the book doesn't mention."

Lynia jumped, and when she turned to face him, guilt suffused her expression. "You did say the tinctures would need replenishing, and I'm afraid I've handed out far more than you usually do."

"Relax, Lyni," Lial said, offering a reassuring smile. "You've done well. The recipe doesn't mention the healing energy I infuse to make the tincture more potent."

Lial expected her to back away, but instead, Lynia leaned closer in curiosity. Their shoulders brushed as he wrapped his hand around the base of the flask, and his heart gave an uncomfortable tug. He did his best to ignore it, focusing his attention on sending a tendril of healing magic into the potion. As blue light flared through the liquid and then dispersed, Lynia trembled slightly beside him.

He shifted to face her. "What's wrong?"

"Wrong?" she asked, her tone suspiciously high. She smiled slightly, but there was no humor in the gaze she lifted to his. "I was merely watching you work. I'm not sure why you think something is amiss."

Lial frowned. "You shivered. Are you cold? Perhaps I adjusted the heating spell too much before I fell asleep."

A flush blotched her pale skin. "I didn't even notice. But I'm not uncomfortable."

"I can readjust—"

"No, no," Lynia interrupted, almost colliding with Maddy as she took a step back. "I've been happy to help, but I should go. Now that you've rested, it's time for me to return to my research. We have more than one problem to deal with, after all."

There had to be something wrong, for her behavior was quite unusual. But considering how annoyed she'd been with him over his constant concern for her spine, Lial hesitated to push the issue. He knew very well he'd been overprotective and had acted accordingly. He needed to demonstrate the respect for her he'd always felt.

"Then I'll offer thanks for your aid today."

Lynia appeared taken aback by his easy acquiescence, but she recovered her aplomb swiftly. "You're welcome."

Bemused, Lial stared after her as she gathered her cloak and departed. Though he wanted to call out a warning for her to be careful on the ice, he resisted. She'd lived here for many centuries before he'd arrived. If anyone knew how to navigate the icy season, it was Lynia. She would be fine.

Truly.

"She did a great job helping," Maddy said as Lial turned to the baskets lining his workbench. "You should consider hiring her when you're shorthanded."

He counted the vials he had left and lifted a brow. "It seems you two sent quite a few people away with nothing but a tincture."

Maddy shrugged. "They deserved it, though. Lynia shut down their nonsense with a vengeance."

Lial scowled at Maddy. "Deserved it?"

"Elves heal as quickly as the Sidhe, right?" she asked, continuing at his sharp nod. "Then they can stop being big babies about cuts and bruises. You've been letting people take advantage of you. No wonder you're always so low on energy."

"You're here for training, not to stand in judgment," Lial snapped.

Mostly because she was right.

Maddy grinned. "I'm observing, not judging."

Before Lial could answer, Anna slung her arm over her mate's shoulder and tugged her close. "Try not to insult our host, my love."

Lial expected Maddy to argue more, but her matter-of-fact response surprised him. "I wasn't. I like Lial and don't want to see him burned out. That's all."

Liked? That wasn't a word often applied to him due to his disposition. Mostly, he was tolerated by all but a few, and he tended to annoy those he considered friends with his worry—and subsequent bossiness. The more he cared, the more he fretted. The more he commanded. He couldn't help himself.

"Thank you, Maddy," he said softly.

"You're welcome," she answered. "I hope your thanks mean you'll consider what I said. Lynia's seriously good at moving people along. I thought a couple of them were going to wet themselves."

He chuckled at that image. "She helped Telien rule this place, and she still wields influence when she wishes."

Maddy's lips turned down. "Why isn't she in charge now? Is this a patriarchy?"

"No." Lial shoved the last basket back into its spot. "But leadership passes through bloodline unless the next in line is unfit. When Lyr dies, gods forfend, Braelyn will be ruled by Arlyn, not Meli. And after Arlyn, the title will pass to her first child, not Kai.

With such long lifespans, it is simplest. No one wants hundreds of years of power struggles, though I suppose they happen sometimes regardless."

As Maddy considered his words, Lial glanced across the room at his patient. The spells he used to monitor the mage's condition held steady, but Caeleth's mental activity was higher than it should have been. He was attempting to wake. *Clechtan.* Lial reinforced the sleeping spell and then peered at the other inhabitants of the room.

There were far too many people in here, and for the first time in a while, Lial wished for a larger space. Separate patient rooms would be beneficial for rest, and chambers for multiple healers and their mates would keep everyone from gathering in one spot. He'd already needed Lyr to find an available guest tower for Maddy, Anna, and Fen, one that was close enough for Lial to keep watch over his student's unstable gift.

As much as he could, at any rate. For his own peace of mind, he didn't dare connect his shielding too closely to the happy triad. He had no desire to torment himself with emotions and desires he couldn't possibly entertain.

"Elan," Lial said softly, wary of disturbing his patient. "Would you show my guests to their new rooms while I examine Caeleth? I fear our talking is causing unrest."

With a nod, his assistant and the other three exited after waves and whispered farewells. Silence enveloped him, totally normal and yet suddenly strange. Solitary though he was, he'd started to become accustomed to having others around.

His gaze fell on the flask at the base of the distiller, and he smiled at the memory of Lynia measuring out ingredients. If there wasn't so much between them, he might have given Maddy's suggestion serious thought. Lynia would be an excellent assistant when it came

to tinctures, but having her here constantly would be…difficult. It was better to continue handling most things himself.

Sighing, Lial went to check on his patient.

After her third reading of the same line, Meli gave up on the report she'd been trying to study. Not only was her own mind disordered with worry, but Lyr's pacing and grumbling gave her no chance to find ease. Not that she blamed him. By Freyr, this situation boded ill for them all, especially in light of the illness that could break loose at any moment. She half-expected Loki to return.

Lyr rounded the desk again, his focus on the two knives arranged side-by-side on its surface. A haunted, angry expression lined his face, and her heart chilled at the thought of what another assassin here could mean. When Kien had sent people after Lyr, her bonded had nearly died tracking the one who'd tried to kill him. Would he risk himself like that once more?

Suddenly, Lyr's head shot up, his eyes meeting hers. "I would not."

Meli's face heated. "I didn't mean to disturb you with my thoughts. I had no idea I'd sent them."

"You could never disturb me." Some of the hardness left his expression. "And something tells me this dilemma will not be solved with rash action. Not that I should have attempted to solve our troubles with Kien that way, either."

Meli set the stack of reports on the side table and walked over to her bonded. Curious, she studied the two daggers on the desk. They were nearly the same size, and each held an engraving on the pommel—leaves vined around a circle with two swords crossed

through. But something seemed off between the two. She bent close, trying to figure out what was bothering her.

"The leaves aren't the same," Meli murmured absently. "And the swords are angled differently."

"What?" Lyr's cheek brushed against hers as he leaned down beside her, his breath heating her skin with his soft curse. "You're right. I was too angry to notice, but these were not pressed by the same mold. I lent the one that injured Kai to *Laiala* for research, or I would check it, too. I'll have to retrieve it later. Too bad the king still has the sword used to kill my father, since Ralan didn't think to bring it back."

Meli couldn't resist kissing his cheek before she straightened. "Why and how would someone copy the design?"

"I don't know." Lyr tugged her into his arms, his body relaxing against hers when she gave him a comforting hug. "I sense Kezari and Aris approaching. Perhaps they will have information."

She leaned back so she could smile up at her bonded. "I suppose it's time for us to act like proper nobility, then."

He didn't return her smile. "Does the formality bother you so much?"

"No." Meli rubbed her hands up and down his back, hoping to soothe his worry. "It's different, but I'm getting used to it."

Lyr brushed a soft kiss against her lips. "Good. I would not have you unhappy."

She gave his back one last pat and pulled away. Together, they rounded the desk to take their places in front of it, Meli standing at his left hand. Only a few heartbeats passed before the door opened, and the dragon woman marched in, Aris trailing behind. Kezari halted in front of them and waited for her companion, but unlike Aris, she didn't tap her chest and incline her head. If Meli sometimes

worried that there were too many social rules she didn't comprehend on this world, well…the dragon made her feel like an expert.

The difference being that Meli actually cared. Kezari might shift into an elven form when she interacted with them, but she gave Moranaian traditions little heed.

"Welcome, Aris. Kezari," Lyr said.

As Lyr and Aris exchanged a shortened version of the typical pleasantries, Meli studied the dragon's face. Her nostrils were flared, and her skin was a deeper gold than usual in this form. Thankfully, her scales hadn't started to appear. With Kezari this agitated, that probably meant that the news wouldn't be good.

"This day is *not* well," Kezari finally snapped. "And you both know the state of each other's families. We see each other daily. Multiple times."

Meli felt Lyr's amusement through their bond and had to hold back her grin. Nothing showed on Lyr's face as he answered. "True enough. I suppose you may give your report."

"I did try," Aris said, giving his dragon friend an annoyed glance. "But this one is short of patience on the best of days. Especially after a fruitless hunt. The trail ended at the lesser barracks in the western woods. We think."

"I thought the scent led to the village, but after that, a similar smell circled around the north edge of the shields." Kezari's nose twitched as though she was still on the trail. "Unfortunately, I can't be certain. There was a shift in scent in the village. Several new tones added."

"A traitor, then. Possibly." Lyr glanced over his shoulder at the knives. "It could be someone attempting to mimic our past troublemakers. You weren't able to find the exact person within the barracks?"

Kezari scowled. "I am a dragon, not a *cofol*. My nose is more attuned to *daeri* than elves. There were far too many for me to identify one."

"I was unable to pick out the intruder's life essence," Aris offered. "They could be using something to hide or muffle their magic and smell. I'm not sure we can find them, not if they are clever enough to disguise any hint of wrongdoing."

An idea hit Meli so abruptly she sucked in a harsh breath. Oh, Lyr wasn't going to like it. She didn't like it. Less than half a mark after worrying that he would put himself in harm's way, she was considering the same for herself. But it would be expedient, and if she and Lyr didn't go alone, it might resemble something safe.

Meli braced herself for an argument. "I'll use my runes."

12

L ial had already finished his assessment of Caeleth and returned
to refilling vials with fresh tinctures when the door opened and
Ralan entered. Unannounced, as usual. Lial sealed the vial he held
and placed the stopper in the flask before scowling at his cousin.
Instead of greeting Ralan, he waved a hand toward the staircase and
then strode over to make the climb, leaving the prince to follow or
not.

He wasn't going to risk his patient being disturbed again, even if
it meant taking one more person up to his private quarters.

"You look like the painting of King Aneratiern after he stumbled
out of the Veil. Pale, exhausted, and sick of everyone," Ralan quipped
as Lial plopped into one of the chairs beside the table.

"Thankfully, I haven't had to lead a colony's worth of people
through the mists for a hundred years like our ancestors. I can't
imagine how he and Queen Aniamorialia held any semblance of
patience by the time they reached Moranaia," Lial said. Then he
glared at Ralan. "Of course, I would feel less like the beleaguered
man if I'd had some warning of this newest threat, but it appears
you only show up when it is inconvenient."

Brows drawn together in consternation, Ralan sat in the chair across from Lial. "I was asleep, and the goddess did not see fit to wake me. Do you think I sit in my tower searching every possible future strand related to you and everyone else on the estate? I assure you that I do not."

"You have given warning often these last few months," Lial said without rancor. "But you're correct. I am not being fair."

Ralan pinched the bridge of his nose, the arrogance dropping away. "This is one of the reasons I stopped using my gift when I was on Earth and hesitated to pick it back up when I returned. If I interfere, bad outcomes can be avoided, but then my help is expected for everything. If I don't interfere, terrible things might happen as the cost of my peace. Please respect that aside from averting disasters, my help is a gift of energy and time. I am not obliged to ease life for everyone."

A hint of shame tightened Lial's throat. With Ralan's sometimes-overconfident attitude, Lial rarely gave thought to the toll the prince's ability took. In truth, it didn't sound much different from the life of the healer. Hadn't he been lectured by young Maddy just a mark or two ago about how he allowed others to take advantage? He and Ralan truly were more alike than was comfortable for either of them.

"My apologies for the presumption," Lial offered.

Ralan dropped his hand to the table, and a slight smile eased his annoyed expression. "To be fair, I probably would have interfered with this situation had I noticed the strand. Take extra care with Caeleth. He's the son of the second duke on the Taian branch, and the Rekel tends to be…overly exuberant in his leadership. Caeleth's death could cause decades of trouble for Lyr. Maybe centuries."

Instinctively, Lial checked his link with the mage to verify the man's current status. Healing well, if slowly. "Is he still at risk?"

"Let's just say the assassin's next moves are a muddled mess of possible futures. This was not well planned, and it shows in the lack of clear paths. Caeleth needs to be guarded."

"As though I don't have enough to worry about," Lial muttered. "I'll speak with Lyr. But if you know who the assassin is, why not tell Lyr yourself?"

"I *don't* know." Ralan's frown returned. "In the strands I've seen so far, no one has referred to him by name. Believe it or not, I'm not personally acquainted with every person on Moranaia. I'll provide Lyr a description and keep searching the strands, but I also have a daughter and pregnant soulbonded to worry about, something you don't have to—"

Ralan's words cut off abruptly, but not before they'd made their strike. An old, familiar pain twisted in Lial's gut, the ache stronger than it had been in a while. Perhaps it was the dual loss—the soulbonded who'd died when he'd been barely an adult and Lynia, who'd made it clear she wasn't interested. Yes, Ralan had a family to occupy his time. But it was possible Lial would never have that joy.

"Forgive me, cousin," Ralan said. "I wasn't thinking about Aralee. I should not have said that."

"It happened before you were born, so I'm surprised you know about her at all," Lial bit out, rising to his feet. "It isn't something I talk about. Please leave. You've delivered your warning, and I will see Caeleth guarded."

"Lial—"

"Go."

Whether Ralan had gained some common sense or the futures told him that staying would be futile, the prince left as silently as he'd come. But the pain lingered.

It always did.

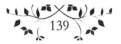

Though she still trembled after her encounter with Lial at his workbench, Lynia stood tall and took a deep breath. Appearing calm was a feat worthy of a midwinter play, for not even her quick luncheon and hasty note-gathering had erased the desire that had heated her body when Lial's energy had brushed against hers as he'd imbued that potion. A galling admission, but it was true. She couldn't even define why.

Perhaps it was best not to.

Her own pale reflection stared back at her in the library's inactive communication mirror as she triggered the spell keyed to Caraden's mirror at the archives. They were old friends, though more distant than they once had been. If circumstances were less rushed, Lynia would be eager to hear of the current happenings in the palace archives where she'd once studied. It had been a year or two since they'd spoken, after all. Lynia had done far less research in the two decades since Telien's death, and like most, her fellow archivists had left her alone to grieve and heal.

The mirror flared, and Caraden smiled out at her. "Good day to you, Myerna Lynia. I do hope you are doing well."

Myerna? Lynia's return smile wobbled. "It is Myernere now, if you'll recall."

"Oh. Yes." Caraden's expression went neutral, likely to hide her discomfort. "Please forgive the slip. It has been a while since we've spoken."

Hah. They'd spoken several times since Telien's death, and Caraden had never made such a mistake. An acquaintance might forget a title, but a friend? Titles were such an important part of identity that Caraden might as well have called her a stranger.

Researchers catalogued facts they considered important.

Caraden had discarded that one.

"It is no matter," Lynia replied, though that was far from the truth. She simply refused to let the hurt show. "I and my family are currently in good health. How is life in the palace archives?"

Caraden relaxed, any hint of awkwardness already gone. "Oh, it is splendid. I've had Parak and Maesen here for a visit this week. We've been comparing theories on the initial cause of the Dragon Wars."

That tidbit twisted the knife.

Lynia, Caraden, Parak, and Maesen had all trained together in the archives centuries ago, and they'd gathered together for research many times since. Had they drifted farther apart than she'd realized? It seemed the other three had formed their own friend group while Lynia had mourned Telien. She tried not to let it bother her, but it still stung.

Lynia offered another, weaker smile. "Do give them my greetings."

"Of course," Caraden said in a cheerful tone that belied the hurt in Lynia's heart. "Is there a bit of research I can help you with? I imagine that is why you've called."

Lynia nodded stiffly. "Naturally."

There wouldn't be any other reason, right? she thought wryly. *Like centuries of friendship.*

"I'll be happy to send you any books or records I can, provided copies are fine. Some tomes are too ancient to lend," Caraden said.

Did she believe that bonding with a Myern had rendered Lynia insensible? Anyone who'd trained in the archives knew that. But she had a plague to stop, and insulting the head of the palace archives wouldn't aid her cause. With that in mind, Lynia bit down on her sharp retort and forced another smile to her lips.

"Any format is acceptable," Lynia said. "I need any books you can spare about the colony of Abuiarn, particularly between the year 11,200 and the colony's end. I am also searching for other books by or about Riere iy'felak maean pel sebarah i Tebid Ored nai Stasa. He wrote my reference text, *An Account of Tebid Ored: The Trials of Rrelen*, or so it is claimed. If he had the aid of an *onraiee* to compile the work, they are unnamed."

Caraden's brows rose. "Obscure indeed. I only vaguely remember learning of that colony. As for Tebid Ored, are you certain he is a real person? A healer mage from the Rieren branch is…unusual."

"I cannot be positive, no," Lynia replied, struggling to hold on to her temper. "But that was the name given for the work. I'm afraid it is difficult to analyze the provenance of the man or his claim without more sources contemporary to his time. I would be happy to send you a list of my own references if that would help you locate these works."

A light laugh slipped from Caraden's lips, and she waved her hand. "No, no. I will find everything I can and send it. The task shouldn't take more than a month."

"But could you manage days?" Lynia asked. "A few marks, if possible. I'm afraid my task is urgent."

"I can't imagine what would be so urgent about an old colony long disbanded and a man who might not have been real," Caraden retorted, for the first time frowning.

Lynia nearly groaned. She hadn't expected Caraden to be so difficult—but then, she hadn't expected Caraden to call her by a title she hadn't used for twenty years, either. Unfortunately, Lynia couldn't give the reason for the haste.

But maybe she didn't have to.

"I am undertaking this research at the direction of Prince Ralan, and I am told the information is needed quickly." As the other woman's eyes widened, Lynia offered her own verbal blow. "I assumed it would be acceptable to make the request directly to you without involving the prince, but I can have him contact you through the palace channels if you would prefer."

"Of course that isn't necessary," Caraden hastened to say. "I should have assumed that was the situation with the prince building the new palace so near to Braelyn. I'll have Parak and Maesen help me, and we'll send the results through as soon as possible."

"Thank you." Lynia took a deep, relieved breath. "You have my gratitude, and I am certain you'll have Prince Ralan's as well."

If Ralan ever found out about this at all, he was unlikely to care about an archivist merely doing her job, but by the gleam in Caraden's eyes, the other woman didn't realize that. "It would be my pleasure to give aid. I will get to work now."

Blessedly, Caraden's newfound vigor meant that their connection ended without more useless pleasantries. As soon as the image reflected the library behind Lynia again, she allowed her shoulders to slump. That had been an unexpectedly terrible conversation. Had she mistaken her friends' lack of contact as support when it had really been anger? Not at first, of course, but perhaps they'd grown weary of her perpetual unhappiness.

It was a sad fact that not everyone stood beside a person in their darkest moments.

Not that she didn't bear some blame. She'd been less grieved the last several years, but she couldn't remember the last time she'd seen any of the three in person. Probably before Telien had died. As usual, it was her own reserved nature likely to blame. The more she hurt, the less she reached out.

At the sound of rustling fabric, Lynia turned toward the door. Cora and Selia stood on the landing in front of the steps down. From the way Selia frowned at the mirror, Lynia suspected they'd been there for at least part of the conversation with Caraden, but they hadn't discussed anything sensitive. Unless, of course, Cora took offense at the way Lynia had leveraged Ralan's name, true though the claim had been.

"I'm sorry to interrupt," Selia said. "And even sorrier you had to talk to Caraden."

Lynia stared at the mage in surprise. "You've met?"

"Unfortunately. She gives me a difficult time whenever I need a text for one of my students." Selia's nose wrinkled. "At least I'm able to obtain most texts from the Citadel."

"A-plus use of name-dropping," Cora added. "Though she seems to seriously overestimate Ralan's concern for the archives."

Lynia shook her head, confused about the first point despite agreeing with the second. "A…what?"

Cora grinned. "A plus. It's the grade you get on Earth when you've shown mastery of a subject. And name-dropping is about how it sounds. You use an important person's name to get what you need."

The exchange returned some of Lynia's good humor. "I see. It helps that in this case, the claim is accurate. Ralan is the one who got me and Lial started on this project, after all."

"Hey, truthful name-dropping is the best kind." Cora took the steps down and continued over to Lynia, Selia following a heartbeat later. "I hope you don't mind the intrusion. Selia was telling me about the lift she wants to create, and I wondered if some of my techniques might help. I wanted to see the space before our meeting with Lyr."

"We're going to work on the outer estate shielding," Selia said before Lynia could ask. "Do you want to come?"

Her breath tangled in her throat for a moment before she could clear it enough to answer. "Me?"

Selia smiled. "You've been linked to the estate shields longer than any of us, Lyr included. Even if you don't have the right type of magic to alter the protections, you can provide valuable insight. Truth be told, I should have asked you sooner."

"I…"

Lynia had been planning to scour her books again, but there really wasn't much she could do until Caraden sent her more sources or Lial gave her notes on the other books. Although she did need to contact the other two possible places Meli had indicated, she had to clear her head after talking with Caraden, anyway. Helping guard the estate would certainly qualify.

"I would love to."

Kai had barely started reading when the mirror chimed. With a worried glance toward the bed where Arlyn napped, he rushed over to the desk and activated the mirror hanging on the wall. Caolte's face resolved on the surface, and Kai lifted his fingers to his lips to indicate silence. Though his uncle frowned, he nodded in understanding.

"Keep it quiet and brief," Kai whispered. "Arlyn's asleep."

Hopefully, Caolte wouldn't ask questions. Taking time to explain the exhaustion she experienced during pregnancy would only add to the amount he had to speak, and that would risk waking her. It had been difficult enough to convince her to nap despite the newest bit of turmoil on the estate, but she'd barely been able to keep her eyes open after the midday meal.

"Both I can do," Caolte replied softly. "We have a problem."

Kai eyed his uncle for some sign of the severity. Only a few sparks sprang from Caolte's short red hair, and though his pale face might be whiter than usual, nothing in the background was on fire. Unlike the last time there'd been trouble.

"What's wrong?"

"Your father. He's not regenerating." A couple more sparks danced above Caolte's head. "When I checked him, he was shivering."

Fear as cold as the sleet outside rolled through Kai. "Meren did something."

"I have not sensed him," Caolte said.

"Perhaps he set some trap in the spell he used on Naomh. My father," Kai added awkwardly, still not accustomed to considering the Sidhe lord as such. "What do you need?"

Caolte's jaw clenched. "You said your healer might be willing to try a few techniques to speed Naomh's healing, but I have heard nothing on that score. It's been weeks."

There was so much about the reason for the delay that Kai couldn't share, not the least of which was a possible plague. That thought sent another chill through him. Hadn't Lyr said that the Seelie queen had been infected with some type of illness by Meren? A half-blood on Earth had also become sick with poisoned energy after speaking with Meren. Had the *drec* done something similar to Naomh when he'd stabbed him while escaping the Seelie palace?

One thing was for certain—Kai wasn't sharing that suspicion with Caolte yet. The man would burn the entire place down in his anger. The wall behind Caolte already sported fewer tapestries than it had on Kai's last visit.

"We have had some difficulties here, but I will speak to him," Kai said.

"Thank you."

Then Caolte cut the link, keeping to his word about being brief.

Unfortunately, it was a wasted effort. The bedcovers rustled, and Arlyn's voice cut through the silence. "Time to head to the study."

Kai groaned. "I should have hauled the mirror to another room."

"I'm fine." Arlyn stood, smoothing the wrinkles from her clothes and patting her belly. "We only needed half a mark. Let's go."

He had to admit she looked significantly less tired. Besides, she would know better than anyone what she was capable of, a point she'd had to make embarrassingly often. Impending fatherhood had tightened his nerves to the point of ridiculousness.

"Thank you for the support, love."

Arlyn slipped her hand into his. "Every time."

13

It was a little surreal being part of a crisis-solving meeting after so many years, and this time with her son in charge, besides. As she'd walked toward the study, Lynia had worried that it might bother her to be an active participant without Telien, though recently she'd begun to wish Lyr would stop handling her feelings quite so carefully. Even during the series of troubles that had befallen the estate lately, her son had preferred to ask for her help in private rather than request that she attend formal meetings.

A nod to her grief that had begun to chafe rather than relieve.

Now, Lynia knew that both her worry and Lyr's care had been for nothing. Her son might resemble his father in many ways, but his method of working with others wasn't one of them. For most problems, Telien had merely asked a few questions and then handed out orders, but events like the current one would have been debated around the massive table in the war council room. Not so for Lyr. Instead, the five of them—Lyr, Meli, Lynia, Cora, and Selia—sat in the chairs in the middle of the study, the clatter of ice against the windows an oddly comforting contrast to their words.

"When Meli uses her runes, I'm going with her," Lyr said.

"How soon do you think you could enhance the shields on the outer lands? It would be good to have extra protections in place before we attempt to track the assassin."

"It depends on how difficult it is for me to access them," Cora answered, a frown marring her brow. "My magic is bound to Moranaia's energy, so I shouldn't have trouble doing my part once connected to your specific shields."

The magical protections around the estate were maintained by the Dianore family—being keyed to the full shields was a rare honor. Full access allowed the ability to discern the location of anyone on the estate, a serious trust that should never be used casually. But they wouldn't need to grant Cora that level of connection for her to add extra shields. It would only require a bit of time.

Something Lyr had little of.

Lyr's shoulders sagged. "Yet another task to add to my list, but it must be done."

"I'll help," Lynia offered. At his startled glance, she sniffed. "I'm as bound to the estate shields as you are, and if Cora and Selia can do their work in the library, I won't be away from my research for long."

"*Laiala,*" he began softly, "Are you sure you're ready to—"

"Yes, I am." Lynia pinned him with her best mother's glare. "I appreciate the care you have taken with my feelings after your father's death, but it is past time for me to stop hiding myself away. I am alive, and as a certain young Sidhe recently reminded me, I do Telien no honor by living as though I'm already dead."

A hint of pain shadowed Lyr's eyes, but it was tempered by understanding. He, too, had grappled with such loss, not only of his father but also Arlyn's mother. "I will do my best to remember your preference, and I would be grateful for your help with this task."

Lynia relaxed. "Good. Then if it's fine with Selia and Cora, we can begin after this meeting. I'm waiting for new resources, anyway. That will leave time for you and Meli to prepare. And have fun warning Lial about this little jaunt. He will surely be pleased that you're putting yourself at risk again."

Lynia wasn't exactly happy about it herself, but she understood the necessity. Catching the assassin off guard might be their best chance at success, and none of them were safe in the meantime. At least now, her son was preparing for the confrontation instead of thinking he could handle the task on his own.

The door opened, and Kai strode in with Arlyn, their expressions heralding more trouble. A suspicion confirmed by Kai's first words. "There's a problem."

Lyr let out a groan. "Of course there is. What now?"

"Caolte contacted me a moment ago," Kai said, stopping with Arlyn in the gap between Selia's and Cora's chairs. "My father isn't healing, and there may be something else wrong. Apparently, he's shivering."

Several of the others bore varying degrees of confused expressions, no doubt uncertain of the significance. But Lynia's thoughts went immediately to one of the texts she'd read. Shivering could be caused by the body's shock if a wound hadn't been properly repaired or, of course, by being cold. In humans, it was a sign of sickness. Would a Sidhe man react the same if he'd managed to be infected by some type of illness?

"He is in a deep, restorative sleep, correct?" Meli asked, continuing at Kai's nod. "Perhaps the room is cold. It is unusual to show that kind of physical response, I think, but not unheard of."

Selia's brows lowered. "Is there a reason your uncle is concerned about shivering?"

"Aside from the fact that Caolte worries about Naomh like a father rather than a brother?" Kai snorted. "He didn't explicitly say why, but I imagine it isn't normal. For one thing, no one is cold around Caolte. He puts off too much heat even when his hair isn't sparking with his inner fire."

"It is a symptom of sickness," Lynia interjected before the conversation went astray. "I read about it during my research."

Arlyn nodded. "Yep. Maybe he has a fever."

Selia's frown didn't lift. "He's a Seelie Sidhe lord. How could he be ill?"

The mage didn't know about the plague.

Lynia was so accustomed to Selia's presence during every other disaster that she hadn't considered the mage's current lack of knowledge. But from the understanding now clear on the others' faces, Lynia had to assume they'd found out about the possible plague. Lyr must have told Meli, Arlyn, and Kai, and Cora would have found out from Ralan. Was it supposed to be a secret from the others in their household?

"I'll consult Lial," Lyr said. Then he turned to her. "You can explain the situation to Selia before the three of you work on the shields, though I prefer that the details not go beyond Aris and Kezari from there."

Lynia stood with the others. "What if Lial needs my help? I'm also working with him on said situation."

"The timing of this in general will be…difficult," Lyr answered. "We have to find our assassin before anyone else is hurt, and we'll need Lial nearby in case something goes wrong. But if Naomh is the beginning of an outbreak, that must be addressed. I suppose I'll have to see what Lial suggests to fully answer your question."

"I can do my part quickly," Cora said, her gaze finding Selia and then Lynia. "Shall we go ahead and get started?"

Lynia nodded, and although Selia still appeared confused, she inclined her head, too. "Very well."

"If you'll watch what I do," Lial said to Maddy, "then you can see the method for coaxing a body's natural regeneration. This is helpful when your patient has been wounded by an iron or steel weapon and is unable to heal at their natural speed."

His student studied Caeleth, still unconscious on the treatment bed. "If the presence of iron interferes with the patient's magic, then how can you use magic to help?"

Lial smiled. "I am not allergic, so it does not impede me. It is different for an iron-allergic patient. When their natural magic is obstructed by the allergy, their bodies heal at a drastically slower rate than normal, barely faster than a human's. Thus, I use my own power to speed their body's natural process."

"I don't get why you can't just use your healing gift to fix the problem if the iron doesn't bother you," Maddy replied.

"Because it is never *just* fixing a problem." Lial gestured toward Caeleth's exposed abdomen, the stitches standing out in stark relief. "A healer is not entirely an external force. Instead, we must merge with the patient's natural energy and use it along with our own to repair the wound. Though that synergy is difficult to describe, it is the essence of healing."

Her eyebrows drew together. "So when you send magic into an injury, your magic isn't doing the repair? That's not how it has seemed before."

Lial shrugged. "With my magic, wounds are knit at an unnatural

rate that couldn't be achieved without my help, even if the patient were provided extra energy. In the case of an iron allergy, you are directing the patient's magic toward something repugnant, and thus you get resistance. That resistance makes the entire process clearer. As I said, it is difficult to describe. You would do better to observe."

"So…" Maddy nibbled on her lower lip for a moment before her expression cleared. "You're going to use your magic to try to get him to heal at elven speed despite the remnants of iron. Anything quicker than that, like the way I've seen you repair gashes and broken bones, would be impossible because of the iron."

Lial nodded. "Exactly. Let's connect so you can see the process."

As soon as she agreed, Lial established a mental link. Not one so deep that she could discern his thoughts, of course, but she would have no trouble "watching" his magic with her own senses. Then he closed his eyes, hovered his hands over Caeleth's abdomen, and sent his energy and awareness into his patient.

First, Lial observed. The stitches all held firm, and a few of the places where he'd been able to remove the iron fragments had begun to knit together on their own. But the area where he'd taken over for Elan was still a raw mess barely held together by thread. If Caeleth wasn't unconscious, he would have busted the stitches open with the slightest movement.

Lial ensured that his patient was numb and unaware before shifting his energy into the worst section. He surrounded the area with his power and directed Caeleth's organs to heal to their original state, following the stitches as a guide. As he expected, his patient's body resisted the unnatural command to approach the iron.

With calm resolve, Lial poured more power in, implacably herding the man's energy where it was needed. It took patience and an unfortunate amount of magic, but by the time Lial finally withdrew, Caeleth's wound was more solidly knit. Not enough to allow him to wake, but it was a start.

Lial swayed on his feet before he adapted to the wave of exhaustion. He'd long ago learned to work with this level of tired, so his smile for Maddy was laced with wry humor. "Don't worry. I won't collapse on you."

"I don't know how," she muttered. "No offense to your patient, but is that small amount of progress worth that kind of energy expenditure?"

"Absolutely. I will repeat that process many times over the next couple of days, and it will grow easier as his body expels the iron like any contaminant. Each treatment gets him closer to a full recovery."

Maddy stared down at Caeleth. "That makes sense if you can manage it. I hope you can get some sleep."

"Learning to stitch wounds is a great help. Many Moranaian healers don't, their pride resting on their magic in the absence of iron." Lial sighed. He'd learned the folly of that attitude at a far-too-early age. "My knowledge of the technique is why Telien invited me to be the main healer here four centuries ago."

"Because Braelyn guards the portal to Earth?"

"Not primarily. He was fascinated with how his iron allergy worked and experimented with ways to overcome it. Needless to say, the Dianore family has always been…different." As though summoned, Lyr's mental presence nudged the outside edge of Lial's awareness. "Speaking of which, it seems Lyr needs something. If you'll forgive the rudeness."

Lial opened the connection as Maddy nodded. *"Yes?"*

"I need you to come to my study," Lyr said without preamble. *"Kai received word that something is wrong with Naomh."*

He scowled, even though Lyr couldn't see. *"I do not have time to deal with the Seelie lord."*

"Caolte said something about Naomh shivering."

"Miaran," Lial cursed vehemently. *"That symptom does not bode well right now."*

"My mother said the same."

Despite his annoyance, Lial's lips curved. Lynia truly had studied those books. *"I will be there momentarily."*

When he focused on Maddy again, she was staring at him with concern. "Bad news?"

"Possibly," Lial answered, allowing himself one long, tired exhale. "I must meet with Lyr. If you would have Fen and Anna come over from your guest tower to help protect Caeleth, you'll have my appreciation."

Maddy's gaze darted to the door. "Isn't there already a guard outside?"

"I have it under great authority that Caeleth needs to be well-shielded until the assassin is captured." Lial gathered his cloak and strapped a pair of spiked metal soles to the bottom of his boots since the ice was now thick enough not to crack. "A certain prince-shaped authority."

She nodded. "Got it. Fen and Anna incoming."

With a quick thanks, Lial exited the tower and picked his way carefully along the trail. Though the spikes gave him traction, they also required a slower gait. A speed that gave him more than enough time to consider all that could be wrong with Lord Naomh.

None of them good.

Lynia rubbed the heel of her palm against her lower back and dropped into her customary chair at the top of the library tower.

Selia sat across from her—Telien's favorite spot—and Cora pulled the other seat from its place beside the window. To her surprise, Lynia found their presence in her sanctuary comfortable instead of intruding.

The topic of discussion notwithstanding.

"I was worried when Aris traveled to the outpost after Fen's mysterious sickness, but that didn't appear to spread to others," Selia said. "I still find the entire concept difficult to fathom."

Lynia grimaced. "As do I. The way the colony of Abuiarn was dismissed during my childhood studies, I never would have guessed it would somehow be involved in an elven plague."

"Abuiarn?" Selia asked, her voice rising in surprise. "I learned a little about that place. As I recall, a mage released a terrible spell there. It has been some centuries since I heard the tale, though."

"*Before they could stop him, Bleyiak poured every drop of his hatred into the fracture. The Source heaved as it absorbed, and its touch brought perversion instead of renewal,*" Lynia quoted. "That's one of the few clues I have. But your familiarity with the place suggests that Meli's runes *were* pointing toward the Citadel. I'll contact their library next."

Selia tucked a lock of dark golden hair behind her ear. "I don't recall that exact passage, but it sounds right. Abuiarn is among the many cautionary tales we discuss during training."

"That mention of pouring his energy into the Source…" Cora began, a thoughtful expression crossing her face. "Even if there was a fracture, energy doesn't typically work that way. The core of magic usually has too much push, so it would repel a spell like that. Without the right kind of connection, anyway. That passage you read doesn't mention that his magic is bound to the place the way a Galaren's would be, but that kind of link would make it easier to fracture and infect the core. He could have come from my home planet."

Lynia studied the princess, who'd fled her home world of Galare to live on Earth for a few centuries before meeting Ralan. The fae of Galare could only draw energy from places where they were bound. Could Bleyiak have been from that world?

"Galarens can do that?" Selia asked, alarm lifting her tone.

Cora shrugged. "In theory, but it's not something I've heard taught. It would still be difficult to shove magic into a planet's energy field, though. You could perhaps inject something that works its way through the way Kien introduced poison into Earth's magic. Maybe that's what the author meant by the hatred being absorbed? But I don't think infections transmit that way, so I'm not sure it's relevant. There certainly aren't plagues on Galare."

The speculation on Bleyiak's origin was fascinating, but it might not ultimately help. Lynia made a mental note of it anyway. One never knew which tidbits could come in handy.

"Hopefully, more sources will bring clarity," Lynia said. "I originally found that snippet when researching Kien's poisoned energy spell. I'd hoped that if Ralan killed his brother quickly, it might prevent further disaster, but I now find the passage an eerie echo of the crack Kien made in Earth's energy field."

"The one Aris and Kezari healed and transmuted," Selia murmured.

To fix the wound Kien had made in Earth's energy—and the wall established in ancient times by the Unseelie and the dragons to hold back the bulk of the planet's magic—Aris and his allies had converted the breach into a direct portal between Earth and Moranaia that bypassed the Veil. Lynia sighed. There were so many pieces of that situation that could be related, and she didn't have an accounting of all of it.

"After we work on the shields, I would love to hear more about

that," Lynia said. "The details may be important. Hopefully, I'll also have a chance to speak to Fen and Maddy about the illness they experienced."

Selia nodded. "I would be happy to help, and I'm sure they would be, too."

Though Lynia itched to grab her note-taking book and quiz Selia, she couldn't do so yet. Instead, she accessed her link with the shielding so she could connect Selia and Cora. Time to work on their physical safety. After all, none of them could stop a plague if they were dead.

14

Of all the emergencies Lial had been called to address, a shiver had to be among the strangest. In normal times, he would have laughed at the very idea, but now the slightest oddity could be momentous. Prudence had become his greatest companion—maybe his only companion.

But he wasn't the only one worried. A frowning Lyr leaned against the edge of his desk, and Kai had already circled the study three times since their conversation had begun. Even Arlyn perched on the edge of her seat, the restless swinging of her crossed leg catching his attention out of the corner of his eye.

"I do not like the idea of leaving Moranaia while you and Meli undertake a dangerous mission," Lial said to Lyr. "But I cannot neglect the possibility that this is related to our other crisis."

"Do you think it will take that long to examine Naomh?" Lyr asked.

Lial rubbed a tired hand across his mouth. "No. But when you traveled there to find Kai and Arlyn, two days passed here. I cannot risk that kind of absence."

"That's not typical," Kai said, halting his restless pacing long enough to interject. "The Veil was a turbulent mess then, and a lot of time was lost both when Meli had to use her runes to find the path and when I had to guide everyone back while keeping Arlyn stable. Time is a little different there, but I can get you back with only a mark or two lost."

"Hmm." Lial considered his options. Risk testing the containment zone established near the portal here on Moranaia—with possibly disastrous results—or lose a few marks of time while an assassin was on the loose? Neither choice was good, but in the end, the latter won out. "It would probably be safest to go there. When will you and Meli act?"

"Likely at some point before dawn when all is quiet," Lyr replied. "She's talking to Kezari right now, so that might change. But night seems a better time than day, when more of the estate is up and about."

Lial glanced at the water clock. It wasn't much past the thirteenth mark, which left a solid seventeen before the dawn. "Let's go, Kai. We should be back in time for the mission."

"Wait," Arlyn said, shooting to her feet and drawing all eyes her way. "Won't that risk Kai getting infected? Will he have to be quarantined?"

Kai muttered a sharp oath, and Lial's brows drew down as he considered the problem. "I can't cure this infection yet, but I can detect it. I can ensure he doesn't bring illness back."

"Which won't help him or me if you can't heal him," Arlyn argued.

"It should be safe enough if he remains beside the gate and away from others," Lial said. "But you are correct. There are no guarantees. Having a soulbonded, much less a pregnant one, makes him a poor choice for this task."

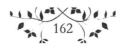

Straightening, Lyr shoved himself away from his desk. "Kai, do any other *sonal* know the way?"

Kai lifted a shoulder. "Not that I'm aware of, and it would take a long time to ask around. Maybe Caolte could bring you through. He's desperate enough to leave Naomh for a brief time."

"And if he's infected?" Lial asked.

This time, it was Lyr who cursed.

"Hey, could you stay inside the Veil and sort of push Lial through?" Arlyn gave a quick grin. "I mean, we've all wanted to push Lial a time or two, so here's your chance."

Despite the situation, the comment startled a laugh out of Lial. He knew better than anyone how his moods came across—after all, no small bit of it was intentional. And he obviously did a good job, based on Arlyn's widened eyes and Kai's considering frown. They must not have expected him to take her jest with good humor.

Only Lyr wasn't fooled, his lips twitching with a suppressed smile.

"A good idea, if harmful to my ego," Lial said. "Then, after I see who is infected there, we can arrange for my return."

Lyr sobered. "And if you catch this illness?"

"It is unlikely anyone will if Caolte hasn't despite their close contact, but I have no bonded or wife to miss me if I must isolate there." Would Lynia—No. Not something Lial wanted to think about. "While it will take some time to find my replacement at Braelyn, Ralan could order someone over from the palace in an emergency. I will be cautious, however."

"Caolte would be the first to show signs, and he appeared to be in good health," Kai said, his expression clearing. "So you're probably right. Send a bit of warning when you're done, and I can be there to grab you when you step through."

"So long as you're certain to be careful, then it's settled," Lyr said, gesturing toward the door. "Go find out if Naomh is indeed ill while we work on our plans here."

Lial almost said he would stop by the library to tell Lynia, but he hesitated. What would be the point? She might go looking for him since they were working together on the research, but Lyr would tell her what had happened if she did. He wouldn't have any new information to give her until his return, in any case. The way she'd fled the healing tower earlier suggested she'd had enough of his presence for the day. Or the decade.

"If your mother asks, tell her where I've gone." At Lyr's nod, Lial turned toward the door. "I'll grab my bag from the tower and give Elan and Maddy a few instructions. Then we can go."

As he and Kai headed toward the healing tower, Lial tried not to worry that leaving was a mistake. Most of the warriors had settled into a solid routine now that the surprise of the ice storm had faded, but there could still be injuries. And that wasn't counting the menace of the lurking assassin. So much could go wrong, and he wouldn't be here to help.

A hint of panic tightened his throat, but Lial breathed through his nose until it faded. Mostly. This was the right thing to do. Stopping a plague was the best thing he could do to protect those he cared for, and he would just have to hope that none of the other possibilities occurred.

He could only do his best.

It was only a couple of marks until sunset by the time Lynia had a moment to herself again. Selia and Cora had completed their changes to both the inner and outer estate shielding, and then afterward, they'd stayed to give her more details about Earth's energy poisoning. Lynia might have invited them to stay longer, but she'd drained her energy reserves writing down the pertinent details with her magic

Truthfully, she hadn't used her power this much in centuries, especially not after missing a night's sleep. Her muscles were stiff with exhaustion, and her thoughts muddled together in a blur. But despite how much she needed a nap, she refused to leave the library. She needed to know the moment Caraden had those books available.

She could only hope Caraden hadn't lied about acting in haste. Lynia wouldn't have worried about that before their earlier conversation, but now she didn't know what to think. She hadn't expected such a casual, thoughtless rejection, either. Perhaps professionalism and ambition would motivate Caraden where their former friendship had not.

And it *was* former, whether Caraden realized that or not. It might have been carelessness on the woman's part—but Lynia deserved better. She would hardly beg to remain where she wasn't wanted. Though it stung, the pain of knowing the truth was better than the hurt of fake companionship.

Some days, she found research far preferable to people.

While she waited, Lynia flipped through her notes, stopping on the list of supplies Bleyiak had ordered for Abuiarn. Much of it was innocuous, even the herbs, and yet… She listed the five herbs on a separate piece of paper and pulled over the stack of healing books she hadn't yet read. Unfortunately, a quick search though those texts revealed little of use. These were more technical and magic-based books, eschewing potions and herb work.

Grabbing her list, Lynia climbed the stairs to the fourth level where many of the books on healing were catalogued. She trailed

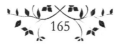

her fingers along the smooth railing as she circled to the other side, beyond the shelf holding the tomes she'd already studied. She was almost above the door to the tower by the time she reached the section on herbs.

She began with general knowledge books, gathering two before moving on to herbs used for healing. She took two more on the basics of that, one intermediate source, and an advanced tome that might need to wait for Lial if the first texts proved insufficient at explaining the complexities. This hunch might prove pointless, as often happened during research, but she had little else to study until Caraden provided more useful resources.

Her back muscles twinged when she hefted the stack, but she ignored the discomfort as she started toward the steps. She'd come to accept that she would always have such aches and pains. It didn't bother her beyond the moment. If it was the cost of being alive, she would willingly pay it again and again.

An interesting change, that. For years after Telien's death, she'd wavered often in her desire to carry on. But despite missing her soulbonded, Lynia found she wanted to live. She wanted to see her first great-grandchild and any children Lyr and Meli might have. She wanted to enjoy being with her family as it grew, and if she were lucky, she might even—

Lynia halted at the top of the stairs as the weight of her idle thought hit.

She might even find out if she could have more children of her own.

When had that long-vanquished hope begun to resurface? Pondering, Lynia descended the stairs. She'd told Maddy that her trouble conceiving might have been Telien's fault, but she wasn't certain. The healer before Lial hadn't found anything wrong with either of them, and she'd never thought to ask Lial for a second opinion. She'd convinced herself to be happy with one child centuries ago. So why the thought now?

Lynia had a suspicion as to the cause   and he had dark red hair and a mercurial disposition.

No, no, no.

She tried to concentrate on each step down rather than the mad fantasy that had wormed its way into her mind, but it was a wasted effort. Maybe it was her exhaustion letting the treacherous temptation slip through. Hadn't she already resolved that they wouldn't suit? There was too much about his life he wouldn't share and too much of hers she might never get over. He was planning to relocate, for Arneen's sake.

Of course, this madness could be partially his fault. Perhaps his wicked words had crept into her thoughts. *If you were mine… If you wanted children, I have no doubt I could give them to you.* Lynia shivered at the memory of those gruff words, and she could no longer deny the heat that suffused her body each time she remembered them.

Dear gods, she was in trouble.

Lynia lowered the books to the table she'd claimed for her research, but instead of getting to work, she stared blankly at the stack as her heart raced. She desired Lial. Her response to their kiss hadn't been an anomaly, but she hadn't wanted to admit it. Not even earlier, when the brush of his energy in his workroom had burned through her like flame. How long had she felt this way without acknowledging it? How long had she been covering it up with irritation and arguments?

Surely not while Telien was alive. Gods. That would be—

"Are you okay?"

Her gaze shot to the door where Arlyn stood, her brow creased in concern, and a different kind of heat crept up Lynia's neck. "Yes. Yes, of course."

"Really?" Arlyn asked as she closed the door and ambled over. "Because you look flushed."

Lynia dropped into her seat and started sorting books, careful not to meet her granddaughter's eyes until her cheeks had cooled somewhat. "I was startled."

"Hmm." Arlyn pulled out the chair on the other side of the table and sat. "But what about before I spoke? Because you looked like you were either going to faint or vomit."

Clechtan, but Arlyn was too perceptive. "Maybe I was."

"Lial, right?"

Lynia groaned. "The entire estate must be laughing about this."

Arlyn leaned forward. "Not really. I mean, sure, it's a little amusing to poke fun at Lial in particular, but we want you both to be happy regardless of how you end up."

Understandable, as Lynia herself had been delighted to watch the others pair up. She'd even given advice here or there. Peering at her granddaughter, she rubbed her finger against a slight gouge in the smooth tabletop, a comforting habit after days in this spot. Did she dare confess her latest thoughts, or would Arlyn find that too awkward? They had grown to be friends over the last few months, but there were some things family didn't want to know.

"Spill it," Arlyn said. Then winced. "By which I mean, go ahead and say what you're thinking. I won't be offended."

Lynia's lips tilted upward at the thought of how transparent she must be. "I realized the depth of my attraction to Lial, and I don't know what to do about it."

"I…" Arlyn's nose wrinkled. "I'm going to pretend you're not my grandmother for a moment when I say this. Sorry. So. Why don't you just sleep with him? Unless you actually do feel like throwing up at the thought, but that doesn't sound like the case."

An excellent question with a sadly clear answer. "I've already rejected him, and he deserves better than my indecision."

"Are you going to remain celibate for however many millennia you'll live?"

Lynia shuddered. "I hope not."

"So you're not upset about the desire so much as…what?" Arlyn asked.

"I don't know how long I've felt it," Lynia answered in a rush, a hint of guilt surging through her. "Almost certainly since my injury, though I buried it under annoyance. But what if it was there while Telien was alive? Maybe I have been disloyal without realizing. In a worse way. So much worse."

"Well, damn," Arlyn said, her emerald green eyes taking on the serious look her father's sometimes held. "That's heavy. I doubt you were lusting after Lial then, though. You probably noticed he was attractive like anyone with a pulse would, but I don't think you'd have waited twenty years to act on it if you'd felt that way even with your soulbonded alive."

Lynia slumped against the back of her seat. "Maybe."

"There's a saying where I'm from. Don't borrow trouble." Arlyn propped her elbow on the table and settled her chin against her hand. "In this case, I'd say don't go hunting for it retroactively, either."

Surprisingly, Lynia found herself chuckling. "A good point."

Arlyn grinned. "I thought so."

Her granddaughter's words had given her much to consider, but she was too tired to sort out such complicated emotions now.

Instead, she straightened in her seat and resolved to return to her task, creating lists of herb uses—boring and requiring no thought.

"What brought you to the library, anyway?" Lynia slid her notebook closer. "Surely it wasn't my abysmal ineptness with relationships."

"I thought I would see if I could help with anything. I need something to occupy my time while Kai's gone on this mission."

Mission? That was unusual. "Where is Kai?"

Arlyn's brows drew down. "Didn't *Onaial* tell you?"

"Your father hasn't said anything to me," Lynia answered, her alarm growing. "Did something happen?"

"Ah. Not exactly." Arlyn dropped her arm and leaned back. "Kai took Lial to check on Naomh. But you were there when he learned about that."

It shouldn't have hurt, for as Lynia had acknowledged to herself more than once, she had no right to expect anything from Lial besides his help with research. He didn't have to tell her where he went or when, and he hadn't ever done so. But it did hurt—far too much.

"I see." Lynia swallowed down the pain and forced herself to smile. "Then let's hope Lial finds something useful. I don't suppose you'd be willing to help me track down and catalogue information about herbs?"

Arlyn eyed her, clearly not convinced by Lynia's false cheer. But she nodded and grabbed a blank piece of paper. "Sure."

Lynia split the introductory books into two piles and read off the names Arlyn should look for. Then she opened the first of her own books with a snap and set to work. She would not think about how Lial had left for a mission without a word to her.

No, she wouldn't consider it at all.

15

Despite Arlyn's joke about shoving him through, Lial's entry into Naomh's small realm was smooth, and since Lyr had warned Caolte of his arrival, Lial was escorted to the mansion in the center of the cavern with respect. Fortunate, that. Lial had been so ready to get the task over with that he hadn't considered the implications of entering a Seelie lord's home dimension without a known ally present.

The place was a marvel, but Lial was too tired to appreciate it. He could find out later how a single crystal at the top of the cavern allowed so many trees to grow around the large house. A greater concern at the moment? The unstable energy that met his tentative mental probe. He hesitated to connect enough to draw in more power, and that would be a hindrance if Naomh required serious healing.

An uneasy pall hung over everything. Tree branches drooped, and the grass held an almost-wilted look. As he was led through the house, the guards peered at him with dull gazes, no question or comment disturbing the tomb-like quiet of the place. Since Naomh was connected to the estate, Lial made note of every unusual occurrence. They were likely to be related.

Instead of taking him to an office or receiving room as expected, the guard escorted Lial down an endless spiral staircase to a large, empty room and then left without a word. The elaborate space was beautifully designed, the floor painted to look like a gentle stream and the walls carved with scenes of Sidhe nobles at court. Mage globes hung from the ceiling, though one was curiously absent near the center. Based on the crack in the stone, it must have broken.

Was this a ballroom? Considering how long they'd spent descending the stairs and the lack of windows along the walls, the room was probably underground. Why would the guard have led him here? Tension knotted Lial's shoulders, and he reinforced his shielding. The Sidhe lords were allies, but it paid to be cautious.

A door on the far side opened, and Caolte entered, his dark red hair so tousled that Lial thought it was aflame—which wasn't outside the realm of possibility. But although Caolte's face was pinched with worry, Lial relaxed slightly at the absence of that dire sign. Perhaps Naomh's condition had improved.

"This is a curious location for a greeting," Lial said when the other man neared.

"Consider it an honor that you are allowed to see it," Caolte retorted. "My brother's resting place is deeply guarded and difficult to find. Do not betray this trust."

Lial inclined his head. "My only interest is in healing the injured. I give my word that I will not reveal Lord Naomh's location, unless, of course, I must share the information with allies in order to save his life. I will not promise to let someone die to maintain secrecy."

Caolte's lips pinched, but he gave a nod in return. "Let us hope that is unnecessary, as Naomh would not be pleased."

Though Lial was tempted to ask if Caolte did anything outside of his brother's command, he resisted the impulse. For whatever reason, Caolte had long ago established himself as Naomh's protector, and that was unlikely to change. Alienating the man would only cause trouble for Kai.

"Shall we?" Lial asked.

Without a word, Caolte spun on his heel and strode toward the door where he'd entered. Lial followed, careful to note each odd turn and random passage they traversed. Great gods, who had designed this place? There were living quarters here, but their arrangement made no sense. Bedrooms placed between kitchens and food storage—and the latter adjoined with a bathing chamber. An office with an open relieving room in the corner. He spied stairwells leading to nothing but the ceiling and corridors that held no doors. Unless the entrances were hidden?

He was hardly going to attempt to find out.

Eventually, the unusual living quarters gave way to empty rooms, and a few floors lower, Lial glanced through an open door to see manacles and chains attached to the wall. An involuntary shiver traced down his spine. He trusted Lyr and Kai implicitly, and they both had accepted Caolte's word on Lial's safety. Still, he couldn't help but feel concerned about being led to the dungeon in the bowels of a high-ranking Seelie lord's private domain.

"I am not foolish enough to detain a healer," Caolte said, his voice ringing with amusement.

Lial tore his gaze away from the chains and met the other man's eyes. "Good to know."

"We only need to descend a few floors lower."

It was a good thing Lial was accustomed to physical activity. Between traversing the estate to treat injuries and check on patients and traveling into the valley to help in the village, he spent more time walking than anything else. Despite that advantage, his calves stung

by the time they reached the proper floor.

Lial waited a couple of paces behind Caolte as the other man placed his hand on a closed door, magic swirling around him until the heat of it licked uncomfortably at Lial's skin. Whatever spell Caolte wrought, the door finally clicked open, and Lial followed him into a small, spare room. Dirt squished beneath his boots as he examined the prone form stretched out on a stone slab in the center.

Vines twined up the rock and surrounded the Sidhe lord resting there. But the plants didn't appear to restrict. Curious, Lial stretched out his senses, cautiously examining the energy swirling around and through Naomh. The plants seemed to be exuding power, but despite that, the other man didn't react to their magic. If they were meant to provide energy, they were failing. Naomh's energy stores read dangerously low.

"You were there when he was injured, correct?" Lial asked.

Caolte's jaw clenched, and he nodded. "Yes. Did Kai not give you my account?"

"Do I look like the lord of the estate?" Lial circled the stone slab, searching for any clue as to why Naomh wasn't pulling in energy. "I have heard some details here and there, but I am not privy to every report. In any case, I would prefer to hear the story in your own words."

"I'm afraid there aren't many details, considering how quickly it happened." Caolte knelt beside the low stone platform. "Meren used his magic to draw water from the nearby fountain and formed it into some kind of mist that he forced into Naomh's lungs. While Naomh struggled to free himself, Meren stabbed him with an iron blade and disappeared."

This time, Lial skimmed Naomh with his gaze rather than magic. Pale skin and lips, eyes sunken, the shape of his bones showing in stark relief as though he'd lost weight and muscle tone. A long robe covered Naomh's body, but his chest rose and fell steadily beneath the fabric. Lial needed to examine the wound, too, but he would have to scan him for infection before he physically touched him.

Closing his eyes, Lial extended his hands over Naomh and sent out his power for a closer look. It didn't take long to find the first hint of a problem. Though the man's brain and vital organs were clear, darkness tinged the blood pumping through his veins. Was there an origin point? His first thought was the wound in Naomh's stomach, but a quick check showed no increase in the amount of infection there.

He shifted to the lungs, only to withdraw from the area immediately. Well, then. There was the source. And there'd been more trouble there than just the darkness pumping through Naomh's blood—that was akin to what Lial had seen in Fen's blood a few weeks back. The stuff attached to Naomh's lungs was different.

Tentatively, Lial eased his energy closer. He had no name for the substance attacking the cells, but he could tell immediately that it wasn't bacterial. Was this what a virus looked like? He'd thought a virus would resemble a cellular organism, similar to bacteria, but no—not if this was it. These little particles had genetic material but weren't alive—at least as best he could tell without closer examination.

He itched to delve into the mysterious particles so he could uncover their secrets. Virus or something else, he needed knowledge. Too bad he couldn't risk it. With the infection taking over Naomh's lungs so virulently, Lial dared not experiment unless the man's life was in danger. Since this illness was exactly the type of thing fae bodies naturally flushed with magic, there had to be a reason Naomh's body was not doing so. The wrong action could make things worse.

Was his body not clearing the illness because of his low energy? Upon closer examination, Lial could see that Naomh was absorbing energy from the plants, but the power drained away as soon as it was gathered. Because…Ah, there. His connection to this realm sucked out the bulk of it, and the iron still in the man's wound repelled the rest. His body might purge the infection if some of his magic was restored.

Otherwise, the sickness could overcome him.

Lial drew back into himself and opened his eyes, focusing on Caolte. "This is bad."

"Explain," Caolte snapped.

"He has an infection," Lial said. "An illness, much like one a human might get."

Caolte shot to his feet, his hair taking on a suspicious glow that heralded danger. "That is impossible."

"I would have thought so, too. However, Ralan recently warned us of a plague that may be unleashed." Lial's gaze flicked down to Naomh's still form. His breathing was steady despite the virus, but for the first time since Lial's arrival, a long shiver shook the Sidhe man's body. "I don't know what Meren has been playing with, but I would wager he forced more than water into your brother's lungs."

"*Ruya*," Caolte snarled. "It is difficult to know. Meren didn't work with Kien, not exactly, but he paid far too much attention to the poison Kien released into the energy fields. Is it a form of that?"

Lial considered the question carefully. The darkness in Naomh's blood was similar to Kien's handiwork, but it was unclear if it was connected to this infection. "I don't know for certain. All I can tell at this point is that Kien's energy poisoning invades a person's magic system while this illness harms their physical body."

A single spark danced above Caolte's head. "Then heal his body."

"I would if I knew how," Lial admitted, as much as he hated to. "But I lack the knowledge to defeat something like this. Lady Lynia and I are researching that now."

Caolte's eyes flashed. "That is unacceptable."

"I see." Lial lifted a brow. "So you prefer I experiment on your brother? While there are a couple of things I'll try to keep him stable, attempting to treat an infection with no knowledge could make the situation worse. Perhaps you would be happy to risk the illness replicating throughout his body instead of merely the lungs, hmm?"

"No." Caolte closed his eyes for a moment, visibly gathering in his anger until the glow faded from his hair. "Forgive my ill temper. I feel my failure to protect Naomh keenly, but pain and anger will not resolve the results of that mistake."

Such a curious man. Caolte and Naomh shared a Seelie Sidhe father, but Caolte's mother had been Unseelie where Naomh's had not. How had Naomh's younger half-brother come to be his most dedicated bodyguard? It was surely a fascinating story, but it was one that would have to wait.

"It is no matter. I am hardly the master of pleasant discourse," Lial replied. "As to treatment…I believe your brother's low energy is partly to blame for the infection's persistence. He is losing too much power to maintaining this realm."

Caolte frowned. "I have some ability to connect to this place, but I cannot take on the bulk of it. Not with my current level of access."

"Then we must wake him enough to pass the responsibility to you."

Immediately, Caolte shook his head, his hand slashing down in a gesture of denial. "Absolutely not. Kai is his heir, not me."

"Kai is not here, and I do not think you'll coax him to be." Lial studied the other man. Why was he so uneasy with the suggestion? "He will not risk infection with his bonded carrying their first child."

"That is not my role," Caolte insisted.

There had to be more to this, something to do with the way Caolte protected Naomh. Unfortunately, Lial had neither the time nor the energy to care. "I do not want to see my friend's father die, but I will be unable to stall this while said father's energy is pouring like water into an underhill realm. It is unstable enough here that I can't draw in power to attempt any kind of healing. Is your brother's life worth less than whatever role you think you have?"

Caolte paled. "It is Kai's birthright."

"Once Naomh has been healed, you can pass the stewardship back," Lial retorted. "And if I fail, you can grant the realm to Kai. Though I must insist you decide now. There is much afoot on Moranaia, and I dare not stay here long. Truly, removing this source of harm is the best way to protect him."

For a few moments, Lial thought Caolte would still decline, but after staring down at his brother for what could have been an eternity, he nodded. "I am uncertain how to manage this. He was near death when I placed him into the dreaming."

"We must both feed him energy until the transfer spell." Lial held back a sigh at the level of exhaustion this would bring, but it couldn't be helped. "Then I will take over if you are too distracted."

"Didn't you say you couldn't connect to the magic here?" Caolte asked uncertainly.

Lial shrugged. "I will manage."

Another shiver wracked Naomh's body, the force of it seeming to spur Caolte to action. He sat on the floor beside his brother while Lial lowered himself down on the other side. Lial gestured for the

other man to go first. Once he'd made note of how Caolte's energy affected Naomh, Lial closed his eyes and poured his own power in as well.

As Caolte began the process of waking, Lial monitored and maintained Naomh's systems. No small task. The Sidhe lord's body was weak from the flakes of iron that had been cauterized into the wound in his stomach, not to mention the effort required for the wound to heal. That Meren had done so much damage—and with cold iron, besides—spoke to a hate Lial found difficult to fathom.

Finally, Naomh stirred to awareness, and Lial rushed to stop the adrenaline that would accelerate his heart rate. Ruthlessly, he forced calm to cloud Naomh's mind instead. "Convince him," Lial whispered aloud.

Sweat beaded on his brow as he waited for the results of a mental conversation he could sense but not hear, and his limbs grew heavy as he poured energy into a rapidly crashing Naomh. They had to succeed soon. Lial was near his limits, and if he lost control, he would be unable to keep his patient still and relaxed.

A new power surged in the room, one that both did and did not emanate from Naomh. Lial's stomach lurched as the man's energy levels plummeted even further, and he could no longer attempt to examine what happened between the brothers as Caolte stopped contributing power. Instead, Lial blocked out all thoughts of exhaustion and poured himself into the task.

Endless marks later—surely—Caolte began to give Naomh energy once more, and though no words passed between them, Caolte forced Naomh back into the dreaming as quickly as possible. As soon as the Sidhe lord was stable, Lial stopped providing energy and withdrew. Only to be confronted with the crushing weight of the magic he'd done.

Too weak to consider dignity, Lial flopped back against the dirt floor without opening his eyes. Gods, he hurt. Every muscle seized and throbbed from the effort. For a moment, he considered sleeping then and there, but of course, he couldn't. He had to find the strength to return to Moranaia in case Lyr, Meli, or anyone else was injured by an assassin.

Today was definitely not his favorite day.

It was nearing dinner, but Lynia detected her son in his study anyway. She could have a word with him there. Almost reluctantly, she closed her notebook and stood, straightening the growing stack of books before leaving the library. Caraden had updated her a short time ago, promising a delivery of texts within the next few marks, and Lynia had contacted her acquaintance at the Citadel's library for more from there, too. Now was as good a time as any to rest.

Perhaps sleep would dull the worry.

She knocked on Lyr's door and entered at his call. As his mother, she hadn't always stuck to such formalities, but she'd discovered it was prudent since he'd bonded with Meli. Knocking had become the norm after the second time Lynia had stumbled across her bond-daughter attempting to coax Lyr away from his desk rather…creatively. A noble goal when Lyr was over-working, but not something Lynia wanted to witness.

This evening, he was alone.

Lyr glanced up from the stack of papers on his desk. "How goes the research?"

"Well enough overall, although progress feels slower than it actually is." Instead of standing awkwardly in front of his desk like a supplicant, Lynia circled to the side, leaned her hip against the edge

of the wood, and crossed her arms. "I'm waiting on more books from the palace archives and the Citadel."

His gaze shifted to the water clock and then back. "Is all well? You wouldn't usually seek me out so close to dinner without good cause. Not that I'm not happy to speak to you at any time, *Laiala*."

"There's no crisis," Lynia said, smiling. "At least not anything new. I was up working all night, and I've done a great deal today. I didn't want you to worry when I skip dinner. I plan to eat in my room and take a nap."

Instead of returning her smile, he studied her intently. Her son never had been easy for her to fool. "Why do I get the feeling there's more you want to say?"

"Because you're far too perceptive of my moods." Lynia straightened, dropping her arms to her sides. "If I sleep longer than I intend, promise you'll wake me before you and Meli search for the assassin."

He pushed back from his desk. "*Laiala*—"

"No shielding me." She closed the distance between them. "I'm not asking to go with you. I'm no warrior. But I was asleep when your father was murdered, and the pain of waking to that… Promise me, or I won't be able to rest at all."

Lyr's expression softened, and he stood, pulling her close for a hug. "You have my word we won't begin without telling you. We're intending to wait until the twenty-seventh mark at the earliest. You'll have ten marks to eat and rest—and we'll do the same."

Relief had her lowering her forehead to her son's shoulder for a moment before she drew away. "Why so long?"

"The answer will not bring you ease." At the arch of her brow, he sighed. "I want to give Lial plenty of time to return, and I suspect he'll need his own rest, besides. I doubt he'll restrain himself while

helping Naomh, no matter the situation here. It isn't in him to give up."

Lynia tried to hide how right Lyr was about the unhappiness the news brought, but the twist of her son's lips showed that she'd failed. This time, she was the one heaving a sigh. "I'd say he's been known to give up a time or two."

Lyr didn't pretend not to understand. "Isn't that what you want?"

"I wish I knew," she confessed.

"That's a different answer than you would have given a few days before."

"Yes." Lynia pressed her palm to the bridge of her nose. "My thoughts are a mess."

Finally, Lyr gave her a soft smile, one of understanding. "I remember that state all too well. Maybe rest will help? Exhausting yourself will not bring clarity."

She shook her head. "Now who sounds like the parent?"

"I gained such knowledge from you," Lyr said, patting her shoulder. "So you're truly listening to yourself."

"Indeed?" With a laugh, Lynia spun away and rounded the desk. "Then I suppose I'd better listen. Please give my regards to the others at dinner."

Despite the initial seriousness of their conversation, Lynia found her heart a little lighter as she made her way to her room. She downed a quick meal from the tray one of their helpers had left in her room and changed into a sleeping dress before collapsing into bed. If she kept her thoughts away from all that worried her, she might even manage to sleep.

16

A light flickered in the darkness.

Lynia ran toward it, something inside her longing for that bright spark. She could see nothing else. She didn't want to. Soon, it was a towering plume of gold, so close she could almost touch. But when it resolved into the figure of a man, she skidded to a halt. This could be dangerous. It could—

She gasped when the figure turned.

Telien.

The area brightened until she could see the gray fog drifting between them. Around them. Through him. Her chest closed in until she could barely breathe, and a strangled moan slipped through her lips. What was going on?

His beloved face was twisted into a pained frown. "Why are you doing this to me?"

"I…" Her body went cold. "What am I doing?"

"You keep me bound."

He held out his hands, and she saw the twist of spectral rope holding his wrists together. Confused, she shook her head. "I haven't done this. Our bond was love, not restriction. And you're…you're gone. From my world, at least."

"It is not love that keeps me." Telien lowered his arms. "Love frees."

Lynia pressed her palms against her sternum in a vain attempt to calm her frantic heart. "I've heard bound souls never fully part. Even in death. I don't know what to do."

She blinked, and Telien's form was a step closer. He looked just as she remembered, from the echo of his long brown hair dancing around the ghostly outline of his favorite tunic to the intensity of his blue-green eyes. But rarely had he been so stern, at least in her presence.

"Our souls may always hold remnants of the other's, but we are not one person. We are two." His expression softened. "I will always love you, my Lynia, but I cannot move on while you bind yourself in such pain. In truth, you hold us both. Let go. It is time."

She lifted a hand, but she was too afraid to make contact lest he disappear. "It does not feel right to find happiness without you."

"I do not want a sad half life for you," Telien said. "Is that what you want for me?"

His light grew closer, so bright she had to close her eyes. She felt the barest brush of warmth against her forehead, and a sob caught in her throat as his essence surrounded her. But it was only for a moment.

His voice whispered around her. "I want your joy."

Lynia reached out again, but he was gone.

With a cry, Lynia jerked upright. Darkness surrounded her, but it wasn't the same. Dim moonlight trickled through the window, casting a silver glow through the gloom. No bright tower of light. No Telien. Her breath hitched, and pain stabbed through her stomach, worse than the knife wound Norin had inflicted before the fall.

So much worse.

Lynia pulled her knees up and curled her arms around them, burying her face in the darkened vee. Had her dream held truth?

Could that have actually been Telien? She'd never dreamed of him so clearly before, not like that.

And he'd been angry at her.

Tears trickled down her face to land with a plop against her legs. Surely, it was her imagination. *Please, Bera, let it be my imagination.* But if the goddess had an answer for her grief, Lynia couldn't hear it. Like so many of the years after Telien's death, there was nothing but cold silence.

She could ask Eradisel, but She was the sacred tree of Dorenal, Goddess of portals and the Veil, not of the afterlife. If he had been stuck in the mists of the Veil— Lynia straightened as the memory of her dream rolled through her mind. They'd been surrounded in fog. Could there be a connection?

Resolved, Lynia stood and darted toward the door.

Eradisel would know.

Though his head spun with exhaustion, Lial checked Caolte as thoroughly as he'd examined Naomh. A feat that had taken no small amount of time in the convincing. If he'd been less tired, he might have been insulted by Caolte's doubts, but he merely insisted the other man cooperate if he wished for healing aid in the future. He had to ensure that the illness hadn't spread.

Not that he didn't understand Caolte's reticence—especially after the examination. The half-Seelie-half-Unseelie man had… interesting blood. Powerful, with a hint of something ancient that Lial hadn't encountered in all of his studies. But like so much else in this place, it was a mystery for another day.

Fortunately, Lial detected no sign of the infection in Caolte or anyone else in the house. There were apparently others who lived

in the surrounding forest, but after considering the problem, Lial decided to check them on his next visit. As well as Naomh was guarded, if Caolte didn't have the illness, it was unlikely any of the others would. It was a risk, but as low on energy as Lial was, it was one he would have to take.

By the time he stepped through the portal into the Veil and halted just on the edge, the ache in his body was bone-deep. But even now, he wasn't finished. Before Kai returned to guide him back, Lial needed to scan himself. He'd considered doing so before crossing through the portal, but he wanted no risk of the results being muddled.

Not to mention his lack of energy.

The Veil wasn't the best place for him to draw in more. Since he didn't have the gift of the guide, the power here largely ignored his call, but it was better than the questionable flow of power in Naomh's realm. Thankfully, Lial was able to glean enough magic from the swirling mists to scan himself without falling on his face. Only when he was certain he'd carried no hint of sickness did he breathe a sigh of relief.

Gods help him if Lyr didn't give him time for a little sleep.

Lynia padded down the stairs and headed straight toward the wall-sized tree trunk on the far side of the entryway. She ignored the guards standing beside the empty stone arch of the transportation gate, though they had to think her wild appearance was odd. She never descended in her sleeping gown, much less with her hair a tangled mess.

They would just have to wonder.

Once she reached the sacred tree, Lynia slipped into the narrow room built around the trunk, creating a sort of hallway encircling the tree. Peace surrounded her, a gift from Eradisel, but Lynia didn't

stop to commune with the tree. Not here. She waited until she'd reached the altar on the far side, where she lowered to her knees and lit the soft gray mage globes.

Lynia sat back on her heels, closed her eyes, and extended her hand. Then she took a deep breath and settled her palm against the smooth bark. Instantly, Eradisel wrapped around her, the tree's consciousness connecting with Lynia's thoughts.

The tree couldn't speak as such, but the images She sent somehow resolved into words. *"You are distressed."*

"I dreamed of Telien."

A pause. *"Show me."*

Lynia did her best to replay the dream as it had happened, although the memory was already beginning to fade. A new grief, that. Another loss among many.

"I must know if it was him," Lynia said when she was through. *"It looked like the Veil. But that's impossible, isn't it?"*

"Telien has not passed through the Veil," Eradisel answered. *"Not tonight or any other since his death."*

Lynia's head lowered until her chin nearly touched her chest. *"Can you sense Bera's realm? Perhaps I shouldn't ask, but I... I need to know if it was real. I need to know if he hates me."*

"I do not sense hate in your dream memory."

It wasn't a full answer, but Lynia suspected it was the best she would receive from the sacred tree. It wasn't for her to know what Eradisel could see. *"He said I bound him here when he wanted to leave. If love frees, then why wouldn't he have moved on?"*

"More hopes pass through my realm than you can fathom." Warmth brushed across Lynia's cheek. *"But the holders can't always see them."*

It was an odd statement even without the visual that came with the word-thoughts, and Lynia only caught the barest peek of faceless

people slipping through the mists of the Veil. Each one possessed hopes and dreams that they—and Lynia—couldn't identify, but from the certain knowledge that coated Eradisel's words, she could. The sacred tree discerned the essence of everything that entered her realm.

Lynia gasped in awe at the hint of power, though the glimpse was gone in a heartbeat.

But how was it related to her dream?

"It does not matter if the dream was real," Eradisel sent, answering the question Lynia hadn't purposefully asked. *"The core of the message rings true. Whether yours or his, the truth* is. *Do not deny this gift, though it be unasked for. Ask yourself instead if it is a hope unrealized."*

What? She didn't hope for Telien to be upset with her. It was the opposite.

"I would never wish to cause him pain."

"Think on his words, and you will see," Eradisel replied.

Then the tree's consciousness withdrew, leaving only a trace of her comforting energy to surround Lynia. But now, there was no peace. Not with that command still ringing through Lynia's head. She dropped her hand to her lap and stared at the mage globe glowing softly on the altar. If only she could illuminate herself so neatly.

Love frees.

I cannot move on while you bind yourself in such pain.

You hold us both.

I do not want a sad half life for you.

Is that what you want for me?

I want your joy.

Let go.

Over and over, his words echoed through her mind until she bit back a sob. Was she keeping him from true peace with her mourning? But she couldn't quite call it that now, could she? She

wasn't immobilized with grief. If she were honest, she wasn't clinging to their love to the exclusion of all else, though their bond would always be with her.

Love freed, but fear bound.

Tears dropped onto her hands, and her shoulders shook. She was a liar. She wasn't unable to love another—she was scared to. Afraid of not being good enough, a shell of her former self. Afraid of the pain of another loss. And afraid most of all of what would happen after her own death. Would Telien be waiting there, angry that she'd moved on with another?

Gods, how foolish. Lynia didn't know the nature of the afterlife, but she knew Telien. She could find him after a thousand other partners, and his love would remain the same. Even if she wed again. Even if she somehow managed to find a second soulbonded. He would welcome anyone she loved, because love freed.

And she would do the same for him. If he were reborn into another life, she would pray it was a happy one. She would gladly accept anything that brought his spirit peace and joy, even if it wasn't her.

She had to let him go.

Whether the dream had been her own creation or not, it was time. If there was the slightest chance her own fears kept him bound—them bound—she owed it to them both to release him into happiness. That was the heart of their love, and that could never be diminished.

"I want your joy, too," Lynia whispered.

Then she lowered her forehead to the altar and sobbed.

Lial had absorbed more energy once they'd emerged on Moranaia, but it had done little to ease his exhaustion. His reserves

were too low to convert enough natural magic to resolve the worst of his energy drain. By the time he and Kai stepped through the front doors so Lial could report to Lyr, he more than welcomed the brush of magic from Eradisel.

They'd only taken a couple of steps before the sound of harsh, muffled sobs reached his ears. Lial froze, Kai halting beside him, and scanned the area. Then he felt Lynia's energy on the other side of the sacred tree, and his heart squeezed at the pain she emanated.

"That sounds like—"

Lial lifted a hand, silencing Kai's words. "Tell Lyr what I told you. He'll have to wait for an official report."

"But I should—"

"Let me check on her," Lial said softly.

Kai studied him for a moment before nodding. "Fine. I'll talk to Lyr."

Lial didn't wait to see if the other man followed through. Instead, he rushed across the entryway and darted between the tree trunk and the wall. He barely noticed the tree that usually awed him—Lynia's pain drew him like a starved cell needing nourishment. Though she might not let him comfort her, he couldn't stop himself from trying.

When he neared the altar, his heart shattered to see her bent over the stone, her body shaking with the force of her sobs. In that moment, it didn't matter why she was upset or if he could solve the problem. He would not leave her in such pain alone.

"Lynia," he said as he dropped to his knees by her side.

She straightened so abruptly she almost hit her head against his chin. Not that he would have cared if she had. He was too busy dying inside from the agony twisting her face. "Lial?"

Without a word, he held out his arms, and she collapsed against him. Carefully, he sat down in the narrow space, leaning against the

wall and gathering her trembling form into his lap. She nestled her face in the vee between his neck and shoulder, her quiet sobs soaking his tunic in moments.

Lial lowered his forehead to settle against the top of her head and rubbed her back, letting her cry out her pain. She'd once done the same for him when he'd lived through Aris's terrible memories, and she'd never asked why. He could do the same for her.

Even if it took a lifetime.

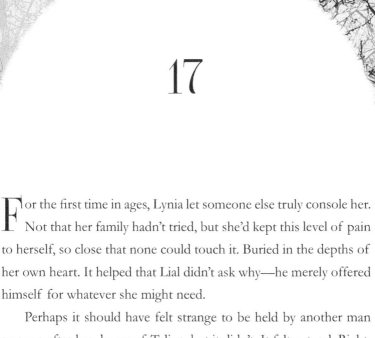

17

For the first time in ages, Lynia let someone else truly console her. Not that her family hadn't tried, but she'd kept this level of pain to herself, so close that none could touch it. Buried in the depths of her own heart. It helped that Lial didn't ask why—he merely offered himself for whatever she might need.

Perhaps it should have felt strange to be held by another man so soon after her dream of Telien, but it didn't. It felt natural. Right. Her tears slowed as Lial's warmth surrounded her, his hand never faltering in its soothing circles against her back. They could have done this before. A thousand times be—

A memory solidified, one long-buried, and she shoved herself up enough to look into his eyes. "You comforted me like this after Telien died."

"When your bond was first broken, yes," Lial answered softly. "I didn't think you remembered."

"I hadn't until now, at least not that you held me." She shivered as she recalled the darkness she'd swam in then. More than once, she'd almost been lost to it. Lial had helped her through, whispering into her mind. Holding her much like this. "Did you… Did you have feelings for me then?"

His lips curved upward, though his eyes were sad. "I'm not sure. I think my love was born in those dark days trying to keep you alive, but I didn't realize it for years."

"An odd time to develop feelings. I was so shattered."

"It…" His voice trailed off. "I would prefer to speak of this when our privacy is guaranteed."

For the first time, Lynia realized how exposed they were. No one would intentionally disturb someone communing with Eradisel, but this spot was hardly sealed away from the world. She winced. No doubt the guards had heard her crying as Lial obviously had.

"We can speak in my room," she said. "Unless you need to get back to the healing tower, though privacy isn't likely there."

Lial snorted. "Not with Maddy, Fen, and Anna taking turns watching Caeleth. I've been informed my patient is resting well, but I'm sure one of those three would find a way to bother us if we attempt discussion in my chamber."

"My room it is, then."

She settled her hand against his chest to push herself to her feet, but Lial surprised her by standing, still holding her in his arms. He shifted her weight and started around Eradisel's massive trunk, and for a moment, she was too surprised to protest. Then she shoved at his chest.

"What are you doing?" Lynia demanded. "I can walk."

Lial gave a quick grin. "Taking care of you while you'll let me. It's a rarity."

Though she huffed, Lynia dropped her head to his shoulder and did as he wanted—she let him. Not because she was weak. Really, it was the opposite. For so long, she'd felt too fragile to get close, too worried she would shatter at the slightest kind touch. It was no small part of why she'd been so annoyed by his fretting after her injury.

Lial carried her through the entryway and up the spiral stairs to the family's private chambers, no doubt giving the guards a week's worth of gossip in the process. Fortunately, the upstairs hallway was empty and the other doors closed. She would rather not deal with teasing at the moment, no matter how well-intentioned.

Once he'd pushed through her bedroom door and closed it behind them, Lial lowered her to her feet. "Thank you," he murmured.

Lynia smiled. "I'm the one who should say that."

"It's always my pleasure to carry you," Lial said. "But in this case, I am uncertain how far."

Her cheeks warmed. "I wasn't suggesting we come up here for *that.*"

"I didn't think you were." His lips pursed in a curious blend of amusement and exasperation, Lial gestured toward the chair beside her bed. "You only have two chairs up here, and they aren't close to one another."

"Oh." Lynia hadn't been embarrassed when he'd held her while she wept, but this moment more than made up for the lack. "Umm."

Chuckling, Lial tapped his finger against her chin. "You needn't fear, Lyni. I'm too tired to tease you. Truthfully, I'd be too tired to make love to you if that *had* been your intent."

Her body went hot from his words, and this time, it wasn't a blush. But his comment also had her really seeing him for the first time since he'd found her, and alarm shoved away her desire. Gods, he looked awful. Dark circles hollowed his eyes, his shoulders slumped, and if she weren't mistaken, he wavered on his feet slightly.

"I can't believe you carried me up the stairs in this condition," she snapped, her brows lowering. "You look less able to walk than I am."

Lial shrugged. "It was worth it."

She grabbed his hand and tugged. "Come on. We can talk on my bed, and then you can nap. Lyr promised to wake me before the mission, so you can rest until then, too."

"I'm not sure…" Lial pulled his hand free as they reached the bed. "I did not intend…"

Lynia pushed at his cloak until it dropped to the floor with a thud. "Can't you be near a woman without ravishing her?"

He scowled. "Of course I can."

"Good," Lynia said, smiling sweetly. "And I promise to guard your virtue."

"That's not a fear," he grumbled.

Lynia couldn't help it—she laughed. Despite it all, the vexation and affront on his face were beyond amusing. "Lial. If I ever decide to share my body with you, it won't be at a time like this. I'm being practical. Besides, we both need solace, not sex."

He sat on the edge of her bed and tugged off his boots. "Those can go together. But not tonight."

She nodded. "Not tonight."

As soon as Lial had settled against the pillows, Lynia took a bracing breath and stretched out beside him. Her bravado hadn't been entirely feigned, but she didn't give voice to her nervousness, either. Not that she was afraid Lial would take advantage of her. It was more what she sensed was coming.

Lynia tucked her head against his shoulder and draped her arm over his waist. "Why would you have fallen for me at my worst? I don't understand it."

He remained silent for a moment. "At first, it was…affinity, perhaps. I have felt that pain."

She tilted her head up enough to look at him, but his gaze was fixed on the ceiling. "You've never mentioned being bonded."

"I doubt many would remember," Lial said tightly. "I do not speak of it. I didn't even realize Ralan knew until recently."

Lynia ran her hand soothingly along his waist. "You don't have to tell me."

"I'm not sure why, but I want to," Lial replied, finally glancing at her. "Or perhaps I do know."

Swallowing hard, she rested her cheek against his chest once more. Was she ready to hear this? She'd once told him that their lack of sharing troubles made a relationship impossible. With his words, there would be one more obstacle to that removed. Could she let herself go wherever that led them?

Love frees.

"Whenever you're ready," Lynia whispered.

"Ready" wasn't precisely apt, but it was the closest he was likely to get. In a way, his exhaustion helped, for it echoed the weight that always burdened him at the thought of his lost soulbond. But perhaps releasing the words aloud would free him, if only a little.

"Her name was Aralee," Lial began, closing his eyes. "We met at court when her parents brought her on her twentieth birthday. I was only nineteen myself."

Lynia's hand stilled against his side. "So young."

"One thousand, four hundred and sixty-one years ago last spring." He sighed. "These days, I can barely remember what she

looked like. A flash of her smile or the glint of light on her dark hair. She deserves better, but time passes as it will."

Lial could practically feel Lynia's curiosity, but she didn't ask what happened. For that, he was grateful. It was difficult enough to pry each word from the vault of his heart. "Her family was from a distant branch far down the Rieren line. Barely nobility. The king is my mother's uncle, so I'd grown up at court. I understood it far too well."

"Some there can be cruel," Lynia said softly. "I did not enjoy my visits to court with Telien."

"Yes. But other nobles weren't precisely the problem." Lial curled his fingers in Lynia's hair where it tangled against her back. "She and her family were there for months before Aralee and I bonded, but we did so in secret. See, Aralee had great potential as a sculptor. She'd already learned to imbue wards into her creations despite her lack of formal training. Her parents hoped to apprentice her to one of the king's own artisans and from there raise the status of the whole family. At first, they were overjoyed to learn that Aralee and I were potential soulbonded. It was widely believed that I would become the primary palace healer after my training, and they saw that as yet another favorable connection at court."

"What about your family?" Lynia shifted against him. "If you ended up bonding in secret, I imagine they objected?"

His lips curved into a self-deprecating smile. "Oh, yes. Not to Aralee herself. I was…not the best student. I did want to be a healer, but I wasn't in any rush, being only nineteen. Despite the strength of my gift, my skills and knowledge were only average. It was my power and family connections alone that had many believing I would someday rise to primary healer. However, when Aralee arrived, my interest in studying lessened to nearly nothing. My parents urged me not to start the bonding process until Aralee and I had both completed our training."

"That isn't uncommon," Lynia pointed out. "Telien and I didn't bond for a couple of years, and we were not so young."

"Yes, well, if you think I am difficult to dissuade *now* when I'm certain I'm right, imagine me with the brashness of youth." The smile slipped from his face. "I wish I'd heeded my parents' advice, but not because of my social status. It might have saved us much grief had we not been so hasty."

He felt Lynia's gaze on him like a caress. "You don't know that."

"Perhaps not for certain, but I can imagine," Lial said, meeting her eyes. "When Aralee's parents learned that mine objected, they began to put a great deal of pressure on us both. They knew very well how precarious my position was. Born to the royal family, but not close enough for a chance to inherit the throne. I would either find a role at the palace or join one of the lower branches. Many of my cousins chose to renounce their royal titles and become part of the House they married or bonded into."

Lial paused as the remembered ache echoed through him. "I began to lean toward doing the latter. In spite of my parents' hopes for me, I had no desire to be the palace healer. I lacked the patience for life at court. Aralee felt much the same about her own training. She wanted to find someone closer to her home to apprentice with, not suffer through court intrigue. So a few weeks after we'd bonded, she told her parents that she and I would return to their estate. Only…her father refused to allow me to join their House. I would have to remain at court or find some other House to take me in."

"*Drec*," Lynia muttered.

Lial released a bitter huff of laughter. "And you haven't heard the worst of it. Her father told Aralee that my parents threatened

to see me exiled if I refused to use my gift in service to the king. In fairness, I had my share of arguments with them, but neither my mother nor my father would have said such a thing. Aralee knew there'd been disagreements, so she believed the lie."

Silence fell heavy around them as he sought the strength to finish the tale. Nervously, he twisted a strand of Lynia's hair around his finger, then let it unravel. He'd repeated the action three times before he felt her hand against his cheek.

"You can stop here if you need to," Lynia said.

"Though I appreciate the kindness, you deserve to hear the rest." Lial took a deep breath. He might as well begin—delaying the healing spell never cured the wound. "You've been to the palace, so you're aware of how hard it is to find privacy. But there was a little grove I'd discovered a few years before. Our favorite spot. It had a tiny waterfall that shielded an entrance to one of the many cave systems in that part of the mountains. That's where I found her."

Only once since that day had Lial forced himself to slip down the path to the grove. He'd sat beside the small pond beneath the waterfall and tried to imprint every happy memory he could into his mind. It hadn't worked—after so long, it was all a blur of color and laughter.

He couldn't imagine ever going back.

"What happened?" Lynia whispered.

"Nothing good." Lial's hand fisted gently in Lynia's hair, the strands grounding him amidst the pain. "She'd waited until I was training to confront her father about our relationship again. In fact, her pain drew me from a healing trance. I followed her only moments after, but it took time to discern exactly where she'd gone. When I reached the grove, she was half dead already."

That wretched discovery he couldn't forget, no matter how much he tried.

Lynia gasped. "Did her parents…?"

"They didn't kill her." His jaw clenched. "At least not directly. Her father held firm to his lies, and her mother reinforced them. Aralee believed our bond would see me exiled unless I chose a miserable life at court, a place she hated, too. We'd heard that broken bonds were painful, but in her note, she said…She assumed I would recover rapidly and then escape the pressures of our families. Believing she brought me nothing but misery, she downed an entire vial of *deonel* she'd pilfered from one of the healers."

Lynia's hair tugged from his grip as she lifted up to her elbow. "What? That herb is poisonous. Why would anyone make such a tincture? That certainly wasn't in the book you use."

"For good reason," he snapped, only to wince. "Sorry, Lyni. It isn't your fault. I did exclude the *deonel* tincture in that book. In miniscule doses, it eases muscle aches. An entire vial leads to organ failure and rapid death unless treated immediately with the antidote. But I knew little about herb work then. It wasn't a popular field of study, and as I said, I wasn't particularly studious."

"You're certain she drank the potion voluntarily?" Lynia asked, her eyes glistening with unshed tears. "I can't imagine doing such a thing while bonded. To risk the other half of your soul like that… Gods, that's horrible."

"I'm certain. She whispered into my mind just before she…" Lial swallowed against the lump in his throat, and his eyes pinched closed. "I tried to save her. I thought my magic would be enough, but I was wrong. If I'd been more adept, I would've known to pull some of the *nesel* growing beside the river to feed her. It would have helped long enough for one of the palace healers to reach us with the antidote."

Aralee's whispered apology had wrecked him even as the echo of the poison had scoured his own veins along with hers. He tried

to give voice to that mark of time—the desperation, the failure, the pleading and tears, all consumed in the end by the agony of the severed bond—but it was impossible.

"The pain of her death… Well, you know. Weeks later when I finally emerged from my insensible state, I vowed to learn all the healing techniques I could, even methods others ignored. Especially herb work. But I couldn't remain at court after that. Though my parents weren't precisely to blame, our relationship never quite recovered. I renounced my royal title and found an apprenticeship at a lower estate. My cousin Kehda is the one who kept me from madness after the bond was broken, and she more than deserves to be the palace healer. She's training my younger sister now, in fact, but I can't tolerate being at the palace long enough to get to know her as well as I would like. Our family has never been the same."

At the feel of Lynia's lips against his cheek, his eyes popped open. What would he see when he looked at her? Pity? Disgust? The soft kiss didn't imply the latter, but it didn't stop him from worrying. However, when he dared to meet her gaze, he found only commiseration.

"You're not to blame," she said softly, her fingers tracing away the tears he hadn't noticed shedding. "You couldn't have anticipated Aralee's actions."

"I know. And yet…" Lial shook his head. "Aralee might be alive if I'd been a better student. That thought drove me to pursue a variety of apprenticeships during my training and challenging places to work after that."

Lynia's lips thinned into a line. "You were nineteen. Younger than Maddy, who you've just started teaching."

"I didn't say I could have saved her alone." Lial huffed. "But it's difficult not to consider what might have happened had I bothered

to read my text on toxins and their treatments. I have worked to avoid such lapses ever since."

Even as he protested, something released inside of him. He relaxed into the mattress as a measure of pain and tension eased its weight from his heart. The sadness wasn't gone, but the grief had lessened in the sharing.

Lynia propped her forearms on his chest, and the way she studied him made him want to squirm. "So that's it."

"What?"

"That's why you worry over us all so excessively and why you pour so much of yourself into healing, no matter the cost." Her smile was soft and almost sad. "I suppose I'll have to stop hassling you so much for going to extremes."

He dared to settle his hands gently around her waist. "I do not. I am merely…thorough."

Her brows lifted. "As you say."

"I have few complaints these days," Lial quipped. But the circles under her eyes had him frowning. "You need more sleep."

"I'm not sure I can," Lynia said, averting her gaze.

"I should leave."

"No." Her sigh warmed the fabric of his shirt. "It isn't you. I… dreamed of Telien. That's why I was so upset."

His heart slammed hard, though he had no right to be bothered by her confession. Especially not after his own. "A bad one, I assume."

Lynia slid back over to nestle against his shoulder. "He was upset with me for holding him back when he would rather move on."

He'd counted Telien as a friend, but Lial had the sudden, uncomfortable urge to throttle a dead man. "That's—"

"There's truth to it," she interrupted. "Whether it was his spirit or my imagination. When you found me downstairs, I was thinking

about how it's time to release the past, and though my tears were part pain, they were also part relief. Your consolation helped immensely. Thank you."

A tendril of peace curled through him. With Lynia warm against his side, both of their pain now lessened, his eyelids grew heavy, and he let his eyes close. Either her bed was nicer than his, or his reserves had finally given out, for it took great effort to speak.

"Lyni?"

"Yes?"

"How long can we sleep?"

Her arm settled against his waist. "Two or three marks, I think."

"Good."

And for the first time in ages, Lial drifted to sleep with a smile.

18

As he'd promised, Lyr knocked on his mother's door on the way to meet the guards he'd picked to accompany Meli and him on their mission. He hated to wake her, but he understood why she wouldn't want to be asleep during the dangerous task. Fortunately, she was a light sleeper, so it shouldn't take long. He exchanged a smile with Meli and waited patiently.

When he heard no noise on the other side, he lifted his hand to knock again, but the door opened abruptly. Lyr could only stare at the sight of his mother. Her hair was a tousled mess around her wrinkled sleeping gown—both an oddity. At the least, she usually grabbed a robe on her way to the door, but her hair was typically braided, too.

Perhaps the most perplexing, though, was when she lifted her fingers to her lips and made a shushing noise. "Don't wake him."

Lyr blinked. "Wake who?"

Lynia gestured toward the room behind her, and Lyr glanced over her shoulder with a frown. *Is she imagining things?* Of course, his eyes answered the question before his brain processed what he saw. No, she wasn't, unless he was also hallucinating Lial's presence in her bed.

Though Lyr had long ago begun to hope they would stop avoiding their feelings, it was still a shock to see Lial there. In his mother's bed. Sleeping. Right there. "Ah…"

Lynia shooed him back, but Meli had to grab his wrist and tug him out of the way before his mother could slip from the room and close the door behind her. Still, he could only stare at his mother's increasingly annoyed face. He was happy for them. Truly. He just… hadn't been as prepared for the reality as he'd thought.

"We were only talking," Lynia said. "No need to look so appalled."

Lyr cleared his throat. "It is none of my business. Only unexpected."

She and Meli shared disbelieving grins. "We all know you make everything your business whether it should be or not. For your information, I haven't decided about a relationship with Lial, but I did work through some things last night. And I needn't have shared his presence at all, but I want him to sleep as much as possible. Whatever happened in the Seelie realm, Lial returned incredibly drained."

Now that Lyr's shock had cleared, he recalled Kai saying that Lial had needed to help someone and would report later. Apparently, that someone had been Lynia. Lyr frowned. Why wouldn't Kai have told him his mother was upset? He hated the thought of her being in pain without him realizing.

"I do hope you aren't about to say something foolish," Lynia said, probably misinterpreting his frown.

"As do I," Lyr replied. "Though I doubt it's the foolishness you're expecting either way. I am worried that I neglected you last night. If you were upset and needed me, I am sorry."

The annoyance faded from her expression. "I was consulting Eradisel after a bad dream, and Lial happened to find me. Don't stress yourself about it, especially not before a mission like this. Besides, it gave Lial and I a chance to talk. There is no reason for you to feel bad."

"Very well." Lyr pulled his mother into a quick hug and then stepped back. "I'll leave you to guard the healer's beauty rest."

Lynia nudged him. "Go. And stay safe."

He did his best to push the unusual encounter to the back of his mind as he and Meli descended the steps. It would do no good to become distracted, though he would no doubt spend a fair time in thought later. Instead, he focused on Kera, who waited in the entryway with Errin, Meli's primary bodyguard. Other guards had already been stationed along the route they would take to the outer barracks in addition to the usual *sonal*.

Kera tapped her fist to her chest twice and inclined her head. "We are ready, Myern."

"Meli?" Lyr asked his bonded.

Her hands trembled slightly, but Meli smiled at him as she unfurled the cloak draped over her arm and slung it around her shoulders. However, this was no simple bit of fabric. Selia had modified this one, a match for the invisibility cloak she'd crafted for Lyr. Sure enough, as soon as Meli lifted the hood, she disappeared from sight. Lyr only knew she was there because of their bond.

He wore his own cloak, but he kept the hood down so the invisibility spell would remain inactive. That way, it would be easier to communicate with Kera and the others. Not that he imagined he would have cause to raise it. As Myern, all that happened here was his responsibility, and he would not hide in the shadows to confront a betrayer. After the last few months, he had no qualms about killing a traitor if they were foolish enough to resist capture.

"Uncanny magic," Kera said as Meli winked out of sight. "But useful."

"And dangerous," Lyr replied.

He should know. He'd almost died once after he'd been hidden, wounded, beneath one. But these, at least, were made by Selia, not a foreign mage. He could circumvent its power if he needed to.

"I have the trail," Meli said into his mind. *"Still the outer barracks."*

Lyr answered aloud for Kera's benefit. "Then to the outer barracks we go."

Kera led the way out the door, Lyr and Meli following with Errin behind them. Just outside, he helped Meli attach spikes to her shoes—an awkward task since he couldn't see her—and did the same to his own boots. There was a lull in the pelting sleet, but their breaths streamed around them in the frigid air, including a ghostly wisp from his bonded's direction. Lyr tucked a scarf around his mouth and nose, then waited for the others to do the same.

Such a miserable night to creep through the woods.

As they stepped carefully toward the forest at the edge of the clearing, the night enveloped them, obscuring sight. Kera crept ahead of them, her dark skin, hair, and blue-black night armor blending so thoroughly that she could have had her own invisibility cloak. But she kept pace with them, and he was unlikely to get lost on his own lands, in any case.

He was far more uneasy about the way Meli was obscured. If the magic consumed her, it wouldn't be immediately obvious. He couldn't see her facial cues or body language to judge the state of her control. But they were bound, their spirits linked. He could feel her presence despite being unable to see her.

Even if she loses herself to the runes, I can find her. I can stop her.

"This is as simple as helping your mother with a book," Meli sent. *"I'm fine."*

Her words were reassuring, but Lyr didn't relax. His hand went to the hilt of his sword as they followed the iced-over stream around the far edge of the property. Finally, they crossed a bridge and took the path toward the barracks. The warriors stationed here were still in training, many in the early stages. He wasn't sure if it was a good or bad thing that their traitor was housed amongst the beginners rather than the seasoned warriors.

Lyr expected to enter the barracks proper and wander through the bunks until Meli's runes directed her to the proper one, so when Meli circumvented the main entrance to walk around the outside of the building, his grip on his sword hilt tightened. Kera snapped a soft order to the woman standing guard at the front door, and the warrior turned her head away from their small group as they passed.

"Not inside?" he asked Meli.

"I get a clear image of a man at the back exit. Another guard?"

"Likely."

Lyr frowned into the darkness. Usually those already out of training were tasked with standing guard over the barracks, so their traitor was no new recruit. Had they chosen to be stationed here to avoid detection? It would certainly be easier to slip away from a group of beginners in order to cause trouble.

As they neared the back corner of the building, Lyr directed the group to fall into the shadows along the nearby tree line. A quick search of the estate key revealed the usual *sonal* in the trees above, along with the guards assigned by Kera—and one person at the back entrance.

Fenere, one of the guards who'd failed to protect Arlyn from an attack after she'd first arrived.

Fury welled up, but he tamped it down. He'd believed Fenere innocent of anything except inexperience, but he would not

underestimate the *drec* again. Lyr sent Errin a mental command to station himself against the wall at the back corner to be near Meli as they approached. Lyr would need her confirmation that Fenere was the proper target, but he would do his best to minimize her risk.

If her cover was broken for any reason, her bodyguard would be prepared to act.

Careful to advance slowly to keep the ice from cracking beneath the spikes on his shoes, Lyr eased forward beside Meli, their bond allowing him to sense her presence. Then they paused at the corner of the building and merged more deeply until they could see through each other's eyes. He had to blink against the surge of light, the glowing trail that had guided her steps, but it didn't go away. Once his sight adjusted, he crept forward, Meli remaining behind.

The trail appeared to end in darkness not far from where he walked, or so he believed. It was always possible that he wasn't interpreting her magic correctly.

"You're almost there," she sent, confirming his assumption.

Her words came at the same time the person standing beside the door grew clear to Lyr's normal sight. Rage pounded through him like a pulse to see with his eyes what the estate key had confirmed—it was Fenere. Of the three guards who'd failed to protect Arlyn, only Korel had been dismissed for insubordination after he'd made foul statements about Arlyn's human blood, but Fenere and Leral hadn't appeared to be part of that betrayal. An error, it seemed. There must be more to the man's behavior than being assigned a too-difficult task.

Lyr connected with Kera. *"What happened to Leral after his ill-fated stint as a bodyguard?"*

"He decided to apprentice with the Elite as you suggested, Myern."

"Have him brought to my study under full guard," Lyr ordered. *"The assassin is Fenere. Leral may yet be innocent, but care must be taken until that is proved."*

Though he sensed her surprise, Kera asked no questions as she ended their mental link to relay his orders. Lyr continued his advance on Fenere. He didn't bother to cloak himself with the invisibility spell. The man could have detected all of them except Meli with a sweep of his magic, but he didn't appear to be completing that basic task frequently. His lack of skill as a guard apparently hadn't been feigned.

Lyr drew his sword as he neared—Fenere would not have the chance to hurt another.

The soft hiss of metal sliding against sheath finally caught the man's attention. Fenere started to draw his own blade, but once his gaze met Lyr's, he froze. "Myern?"

There was no mistaking the nervous lilt to the man's tone. While Lyr might have dismissed it as normal under the circumstances, the way Fenere sidled carefully away from him told another tale. Was he attempting to escape? Any guard would be surprised to be confronted by their superior in the middle of the night like this, but an innocent one wouldn't consider fleeing.

He sent a quick order to Kera to advance on the man's other side and then separated his inner sight from Meli's. No need for her to experience the fight if things went wrong.

"You know why I'm here," Lyr said levelly, "Or you wouldn't be backing away."

"Of… Of course not, Myern."

Lyr took a step forward, settling the tip of his blade at the hollow of Fenere's throat. "You will come with me without a fight, or you'll be dragged to my study bleeding."

Fenere glanced around the area as though plotting his escape or hoping for a rescue, and Lyr's grip tightened on the hilt of his sword in preparation. But with no rescue forthcoming, cowardice appeared to win against brashness. Fenere held his hands outward, his fingers splayed wide. As Kera melted from the darkness behind the traitor to twist his arms behind his back, Lyr disarmed him.

Only when Fenere was bound with both rope and magic did Lyr brush his thoughts against Meli's. *"Any others?"*

After a brief pause, she answered. *"Not here. There's…something toward the village, I think. It's… No. I was wrong. The magic caught on Caeleth and the rockslide, but there's no thread to anything new."*

"Let's haul our friend to the estate," Lyr said to Kera in a low voice. "I'm afraid we'll need to find someone else to stand guard tonight."

"I will see it done," Kera replied.

By the time they'd marched Fenere to the edge of the clearing, another warrior had emerged from the back door to watch the scene with wide eyes. It was going to be a long walk back, but at least Meli had saved them days of interrogating each person in the barracks. Unfortunately, though, her runes couldn't make the man talk.

And Lyr had a feeling that would be the most difficult task of all.

A gentle nudge woke Lial at once, but it took him longer than usual to process the sight that met his eyes. The ceiling above him was wood, not stone, and carved to resemble drifting clouds. What…? Then memory rushed through him of the night before. He was in Lynia's bed—just not the way he'd typically dreamed of.

Lial turned his head to find Lynia standing beside the bed, her brows drawn together as she stared at him. "You wake quickly. I'm surprised Lyr's knock didn't disturb you when he came to tell me he was leaving."

"Me, too," Lial said, sitting up and sweeping his fingers through his tangled hair. *What a tempting sight I must be,* he thought sardonically. "I confess I haven't been that drained in some time. Thank you for letting me rest here."

A hint of pink tinged her cheeks. "It was pleasant. And I would have let you sleep longer, but Lyr needs your help."

"*Miaran,*" Lial muttered. "How badly is he hurt?"

Lynia's lips pursed, and one eyebrow lifted. "Do you honestly believe I would be waking you calmly if my son was injured? As far as I know, no one was hurt. I think he wants to intimidate the assassin into talking, and you're particularly skilled at gaining cooperation from the recalcitrant."

Lial swung his legs over the side of the bed as he pondered her words. It wasn't a typical request. Perhaps an excuse to get him out of Lynia's room? "Lyr knows very well I wouldn't torture someone. Intentionally, at least."

"The assassin might not realize that," Lynia said, shrugging and then catching the edge of her robe when it nearly slid from her shoulder.

Lial focused on donning his boots, a much less pleasurable task than what he would rather do—kiss the tender spot where Lynia's pulse fluttered at the edge of her sleeping gown. He loved the graceful curve of her neck and the delicate ridge of her collarbone. He could spend marks exploring each rise and indention with his lips and fingers and tongue.

"Are you paying any attention?"

He glanced up to find Lynia glaring down at him, but he could only grin in return. "Forgive me. My mind wandered."

"At a time like this?" she demanded, her fist settling against her hip. "Stand up and tend to your hair while I get the wrinkles out of your clothes."

There was no way he was going to tell her where his mind had gone. She might have softened enough to share comfort with him the night before, but that didn't mean she had any interest in a romantic relationship. So he averted his gaze to get his body under control before rising from the bed. Lynia hovered her hands over his chest and used magic to ease the wrinkles from the fabric.

At her nearness, Lial squeezed his eyes closed and tried to imagine all manner of disagreeable things. Otherwise, his control would slip, and she would have no doubt what he'd been thinking. He pulled the cord from his tousled hair and untangled the knots by touch before retying the mass behind his head. Only when her magic faded did he open his eyes once more.

Lynia studied him curiously. "Are you always this strange in the morning?"

He let out a rough, choked laugh. "Under certain circumstances. Trust me, you don't want to know."

"Hmm. Perhaps I'll discover the reason someday," she said, a teasing, almost flirtatious lilt to her voice and a glint in her eyes. "But not now. Lyr is no doubt growing impatient."

Part of Lial wanted to ask if the hint of innuendo in her words was intentional or his imagination, but he couldn't bring himself to voice the question. He'd put his feelings out there too often to risk that now. If she changed her mind about a relationship, she would have to tell him. He wouldn't pressure her.

"I'll have to return to the healing tower after this," Lial said. "I

have sensed no distress from Caeleth, but his next healing session is long overdue. After that, I'll look at the books you left for me."

Lynia nodded. "I'm going to the library to resume work. Although...did you discover anything while healing Naomh that might help?"

"I'm not sure, but I will give it some thought."

If he had the right, Lial would have kissed her goodbye. But he didn't. Stifling frustration, he bid her farewell and started for the study. It would do no good to linger on what he couldn't have, even if the past night had only strengthened his longing. He should contact Dria later to enquire about a position there. The sooner he broke this cycle of hope and despair, the better. He'd experienced that tumult more than enough his first couple of centuries.

19

Lial connected with Lyr as he neared the study. *"Are you honestly expecting me to help you question someone? You know very well I will not—"*

"Relax, Lial. I might throttle the drec, *but I won't torture him,"* Lyr sent, his exasperation clear. *"I want your report before I seek my rest, but I have this matter to settle first. You don't have to do anything. Though I admit an angry healer might serve to give Fenere pause."*

"I thought you might be trying to get me out of your mother's bed."

"My mother needs neither my protection nor my consent," Lyr replied sharply. *"You are both more than old enough to figure this out for yourselves. But you needn't share details once you do. Please."*

Lial chuckled aloud, drawing a strange look from the guard stationed beside the study door. *"Noted."*

Lial forced a more serious expression to his face as he entered the large, oval room made small by the number of people currently inside. Lyr and Meli stood in front of the desk on the dais. On the floor to the right, four warriors kept watch over Leral, who had his arms secured behind him, and on the left, Kera and Errin held Fenere, also bound. Belore Koranel, the captain of the guard, waited in the center, and the way he straightened from a bow revealed that he hadn't been there much longer than Lial.

"Ah, Lial," Lyr said, as though they hadn't been speaking mentally a moment ago. "Thank you for joining us. I fear I may have need of your aid in the near future."

Lial barely managed not to snort. "As you require, Myern."

"I suppose we shall see." Lyr gestured toward his right. "If you'll wait over there in case your help is needed?"

It took little effort to scowl as he marched to his spot beside the window—all he had to do was make a quick catalogue of all the frustrations awaiting him after this meeting. A plague to stop, a Seelie lord who might be the harbinger of said plague, and a patient still in danger of death. As Lial turned to face the room, he caught sight of Fenere, the supposed assassin, and his annoyance solidified into anger. He wouldn't have an injured mage to deal with if not for that attack.

From the uneasy glances Fenere kept casting Lial's way, Lyr's idea had apparently been a good one.

"Belore Koranel," Lyr said. "I would like to hear the status of these two warriors."

The captain inclined his head. "Leral began apprenticing with the Elite not long after Ayala Arlyn was injured, and Fenere returned to normal duties. Last month, he asked to transfer to helping with the trainees, and I granted the request."

"You did not think to mention these events to me considering their pasts?"

"I'm afraid I did not, Myern," the Belore answered. "Their punishments were complete, so I gave it no more thought."

That was unlikely to go over well, although there was no sign of emotion on Lyr's face as he studied the captain. Perhaps it was because Koranel had worked with Norin, the man responsible for Lynia's brush with death, but something about the captain's demeanor bothered Lial. He had the uneasy stance of a patient denying his worst symptoms. Was he simply nervous during formal inquiries, or was there something more?

"You are aware that a mage working under our protection was gravely injured yesterday?" Lyr asked, pausing long enough for Belore Koranel to nod. "There should have been more *sonal* stationed in that area. Furthermore, Kezari tracked the attacker's scent back to the trainee's barracks, and I have evidence leading me to believe Fenere is the one responsible. Leral's involvement is yet to be determined."

Both of the accused went sickly pale, but their reactions were otherwise subtly different. Eyes wide, Leral took a step back, almost colliding with the guard behind him. Sweat beaded his forehead as he focused his bleak gaze on Lyr. Fenere, on the other hand, couldn't seem to focus on anyone or anything, his gaze flitting around the room at the same restless pace as his shuffling feet.

"Leral," Lyr said, the sharp word making the other man flinch. "I have no evidence to suggest you were involved, but I have grave concerns about anyone connected to the disgraced Korel and now Fenere. What words do you have to share in your defense?"

Leral struggled to drop to his knees despite his bound hands. "I beg you to believe I have no knowledge of this, Myern. I was not friends with Korel or Fenere, merely assigned to guard Ayala Arlyn with them several months ago. Having failed that job, I have trained hard to do better in the future. If Fenere has chosen to pursue a dishonorable path, I want nothing to do with it. We haven't even spoken since that mission."

The man's voice wavered, and his breath came fast. But Lial believed him. This didn't look like fear borne of guilt—this was the

fear of losing everything. Attempted murder would earn a harsh punishment, not the least of which would be a ban from military service. In truth, a calm reaction would have been more suspicious.

Unfortunately for Leral, Lyr didn't appear inclined to render a quick judgement. "Thank you. I will consider your statement."

Leral inclined his head, helplessness suffusing his expression before he dropped his eyes. Poor man. Surely, Lyr was better at reading physical signs than that. But perhaps that was a healer's strength, at least outside of battle. Learning to identify a patient's physiological cues through observation sped up many a healing session.

As such, Lial knew Fenere's words would be a lie before his mouth had even opened. He shifted around with all of the guilt of a child who didn't want to admit their stomachache was caused by excess honey cakes. When Lyr demanded his explanation, he proceeded with as much bravado as deference.

"I was standing guard over the barracks when you confronted me out of nowhere," Fenere said, his tone somehow a mixture of placating and accusatory. "I can't imagine what evidence you might have against me."

For the first time, Meli spoke, only a hint of a tremor to her voice. "My magic revealed it to be so."

Her runes weren't precisely a secret, but they weren't well-known, either. Despite her position as Myerna and her formal introduction some time back, Meli was quiet enough that she was a mystery to many. A benefit, in this case. Fenere sucked in a sharp breath, and his skin went so ashen Lial worried that he might need treatment.

"I wasn't supposed to kill anyone," Fenere said in a rush. "It was a warning. Korel told me to be subtle, but the foolish mage pulled the ridge down around us. I barely made it out of the way in time to avoid injury."

"Korel," Lyr said, his voice cracking across the space like lightning. "Who was supposed to be sent home after he was dismissed from his position."

Fenere nodded. "It was his plan. Naturally, he is most at fault."

"How long have you been plotting with him?" Lyr demanded.

Lial didn't have to look at Lyr to know how furious he was—so he didn't. Instead, Lial focused on Belore Koranel. The man stood straight, his gaze directed toward Lyr and Meli on the dais, but his breathing had sped up. Not a great deal, a slight enough change that even Lial might not have noted it if he hadn't been carefully observing him. But possibly telling.

"I wouldn't say I've been plotting, Myern," Fenere answered. "I don't want to see you overthrown like Korel does. It's just… I do agree with him that there have been too many changes. I can accept that the Ayala has human blood, but her arrival opened the portal to everyone, so to speak. A Galaren, a dragon, and now a bunch of half-humans here to work with the healer. How can we feel safe around a bloodsucking half-*Felshreh*? Even the new Myerna is from the Ljósálfar."

"I recommend that you be careful with your words," Lyr said coldly.

Instead of gauging Fenere's reaction, Lial continued to study Koranel. The Belore's lips twitched, and his eyes glinted with a hint of satisfaction. That wasn't the look of a superior officer whose subordinate was casually discussing the merits of treason.

"Lyr," Lial sent. *"Belore Koranel may be involved. I have no proof, but his body language is suspicious."*

"As is his lack of knowledge of these events. Thank you for the warning."

"And you, Belore Koranel," Lyr said aloud. "Do you have more in common with Korel than a similarity of name? It appears

you were also unaware that Korel remained in the area instead of returning home as ordered. I understand that you inherited this role from Norin some six months back, but I expected better vigilance."

The captain's expression had returned to being impassive, but he inclined his head quickly. "Forgive me, Myern. I will see that Korel is found."

"You didn't answer my question."

Belore Koranel kept his gaze averted. "I have served this House well for several centuries, Myern. I am surprised that my loyalty is in question."

A sick tendril of suspicion twined up Lial's throat. *Koranel knew about Norin's treachery all along.* He might or might not have joined in on the plot, but he hadn't stopped it. And if that were true, Koranel could have prevented Norin from attacking Lynia. The memory of Lynia's broken body crumpled on the library floor flashed through Lial's mind until his hands clenched.

"Norin chose you as his successor long before I took over for my father," Lyr said, his voice deceptively soft. Lial knew him well enough to catch the hard anger beneath. "I saw no reason to punish you for Norin's betrayal since there was no evidence of your involvement, and so I allowed you to become captain as intended."

The Belore nodded. "My family was grateful, milord."

But not him—an omission that was difficult to miss. Lial's certainty of the man's guilt grew until it threatened to choke him.

"Are you prepared to swear a blood oath to remain the Belore of my army?" Lyr asked.

The captain's throat worked. "I am uncertain I wish to do so, Myern."

"As I thought." Lyr turned toward the warriors surrounding Leral. "Release Leral and bind Koranel."

Anger filled Koranel's expression as he stepped forward. "You cannot punish me for rejecting a blood oath, not outside of removing rank."

"I have yet to punish you," Lyr replied as two warriors advanced on the captain, swords drawn. "But your words lead me to suspect your involvement in Norin's misdeeds as well as our current crisis. You will be removed to the holding tower to consider your defense, and I suggest you take the time to do so before you speak to me again. The rank of Belore now passes to Kera."

Lial expected the man to protest, but he spoke not a word as his hands were tied behind his back with enchanted chains designed to prevent him from using magic. How could Lyr stand to delay? Lial wanted to demand answers from the *drec* now, slowly and with many unfortunate potions. After a few days retching up the contents of his stomach, perhaps the traitor would give them the information they needed.

"I will not cooperate with this," the former captain finally snapped.

How much of this man's negligence had Lial been forced to repair—literally? They had to find out, or more damage could be done. The memory of Lynia's blood-covered body haunted the edge of his thoughts, but at the center of his mind was her constant pain. This betrayal might have gone back to Telien's murder, and Lial would have saved her from that loss no matter how it affected his chance of happiness.

"I hope your innocence is certain," Lial found himself saying, "Or I will be happy to help convince you to share what you know."

Stunned silence echoed behind his words, and even Lyr gave him a surprised glance despite having joked about possible intimidation. In truth, Lial shouldn't have broken protocol by speaking, but he

couldn't regret it. Not when Koranel blanched, fear shading his eyes as the warriors beside him gripped his arms. It was a well-known fact that one did not mess with a healer if one wished to remain whole.

"Consider your choices wisely, Koranel," Lyr said. Then he shifted his attention to Kera. "Do you accept the rank of Belore?"

Though her movements were stiff with shock, Kera tapped her fist against her chest twice and bowed. "I do, Myern. I am honored to be found worthy."

"Then Belore Kera, please escort these two to the holding tower and begin a search for Korel," Lyr said. "I would speak to Leral for a moment."

Lial stifled his impatience as the prisoners were led from the room and Lyr commended Leral for his loyalty. The young trainee even offered to take a blood oath before Lyr dismissed him, thankfully without accepting said oath. Lial itched with the desire to flee the room and tend to all that awaited him before he decided to poison Koranel in truth.

But Lyr would not be denied his all-important report.

There were few things that brought Delbin greater enjoyment than spending Ralan's money with abandon, but waiting for his purchases from the comfort of Vek's posh living room in the mountains above Chattanooga was definitely one of them. His feet propped up on the large trunk waiting to be carried to Moranaia, Delbin hit start on the latest video game on Vek's new system. He'd rarely had the chance to game on the road with the carnival. Of course, living in a tent hadn't helped. Sort of tough to have a TV and game system in that kind of setup.

He was halfway through the second level when the doorbell rang. Finally. He'd started to worry that the mission would be delayed since it was already past eight in the evening, a bit late for deliveries. He paused the game and darted to the door. With Meren on the loose, Inona was outside keeping an eye out for trouble, and she wouldn't break her cover to accept a package.

A harried-looking delivery person waited on the other side, a stack of packages at her feet. Delbin winced. Those had to be hella heavy since they all held books. After signing the device she held out, Delbin dug a hundred-dollar bill out of his pocket and handed it over. Ralan wouldn't notice the lack, and it might make her day better.

It took a moment to convince her to take the cash, but once she'd climbed back in her delivery truck, Delbin started carrying the boxes in. As he hefted the last one, Inona rounded the corner. He couldn't help but grin.

"Great timing."

Inona smirked. "I thought so."

"Well, at least help me load all these into the trunk," Delbin said.

Without argument, Inona joined him in opening the boxes and stacking the books carefully inside the partially full trunk. He'd already found a variety of magazines and pop culture books, along with a few on history and medicine. These newest were more specialized, and he had a feeling he didn't want to know why Lynia needed them. Infectious diseases? Medical research equipment? Modern healthcare?

Yep, definitely didn't want to know.

Only the last box of books had another destination—Ralan. These had been the only ones to truly give Delbin pause, but he'd used Ralan's credit card to order them. If a government agency

wanted to know why someone needed weapon schematics, they could try to hunt down Ralan on Moranaia. Books on gunsmithing and such didn't seem to be illegal, but Delbin didn't want to be on a watch list for buying them, either.

Ah, well. That was Ralan's problem.

Delbin tucked those books into a separate tote bag and secured it on the top of the chest before closing the lid. "That's the last of it."

"Then I suppose you should contact Dria to activate the gate to the outpost." Inona tipped her head toward the TV. "If you can pull yourself away from your game."

Smiling, Delbin pulled her close for a quick kiss. "Sure, but I have an errand to run first."

Her brows drew together. "What?"

"A mission of mercy." At her deepening frown, he chuckled. "Come on. You'll see."

After all, Lynia and Ralan weren't the only ones wanting something from Earth.

20

Though it was a mark or so until dawn, Lynia headed back to the library after Lial left. She was too keyed up to sleep, and a large stack of books awaited her, courtesy of the palace archives. Not that Caraden had bothered to contact her personally—one of Braelyn's helpers had notified Lynia of the books' arrival. But Lynia didn't have the time or energy to worry for long about her former friend's rudeness. She was far too thrilled by her newest acquisitions to dwell on those unpleasant thoughts.

At least her erstwhile friends were good researchers. She counted three history books about Abuiarn and five tomes attributed to Tebid Ored. There was also a large text about Rrelen that included an expanded version of *An Account of Tebid Ored: The Trials of Rrelen*. She could copy these for the library here and then sift through them for relevant information.

Lynia gathered a stack of blank books from a lower bookshelf and carried them to the table. It would take power and time to copy the entire contents of each tome, but it would be worth it. Then she wouldn't have to worry about Caraden needing the books back before she was done, and the information would be in her head, besides. Not that that would make it effortless to process. Lists of facts, like the uses of certain herbs, were easy to pull from her memory and use, but detailed texts required a fair amount of note-taking to grasp.

By the time she'd managed to spell-transfer the information to the blank books, a couple of marks had passed, and morning light glinted weakly through the windows despite the intermittent, icy drizzle. Lynia stood and rubbed at her back, stretching slightly to keep the muscles loose. At least the worst of the ice had passed. According to the weather mages, even the trailing drizzles should be gone by the end of the day. Perhaps then, her beleaguered back wouldn't seize up so frequently.

The door opened, and Arlyn and Selia entered, Iren and Eri trailing sullenly behind. Ah, lessons. She'd almost forgotten they were scheduled for bookwork this morning. Even Arlyn's expression looked a touch downcast, as she would be joining the children in Moranaian history lessons. If Delbin were here, the torture session would be complete.

"I'll get us started if you want to help *Elnaia*," Arlyn said to Selia as they neared the tables. "Provided she wants help, that is."

Lynia smiled when both women glanced her way. "I'll rarely refuse anyone willing to sift through texts with me."

"I would be happy to." Selia placed her hand on her son's shoulder and gave him a stern look while Arlyn continued toward their usual table. "And I trust you will listen to Ayala Arlyn. I don't want to hear you whispering with Eri instead of reading your lessons."

The little girl in question smiled up at Selia. "I won't distract him. Lady Lynia needs to get her work done in case she decides to sleep with Lial again."

Lynia's skin burned with her sudden blush, and a choked sound left Arlyn's throat as she spun to stare. Though Iren nudged the girl

with his elbow, Eri's smile only grew, and Selia's mouth gaped as she struggled to find an appropriate response.

"That is not..." Lynia began, but words failed her.

"It was a good idea," Eri said. "You both slept so much better."

Alas, the comment didn't help.

"I must question what the goddess allows children to See these days," Selia murmured.

"It was an innocent moment," Lynia defended. Not that she should have to explain herself. "I'd had a bad dream, he was exhausted, and... Never mind. More to the point, Eri, how did you know what happened if you can't see Lial's future strands?"

Eri shrugged. "You're not Lial."

"And you're scanning my futures to see how I spend my evening?" Gods, Lynia did not envy Ralan and Cora. "Perhaps you need longer history lessons to occupy your time."

"No." Eri's nose wrinkled, and a hint of worry entered her gaze. "I'm sorry if I did something wrong. I wasn't trying to cause a problem."

Lynia's embarrassment faded enough for objectivity to return, and the truth of the child's words crystalized. Poor Eri. She wasn't old enough to understand the implications of what she'd revealed, nor had she learned enough social rules to comprehend staying silent about private matters. It didn't help that she'd spent her first few years on Earth, too ill to leave her house. She'd barely been running around on Moranaia for a handful of months.

Kneeling in front of the girl, Lynia gentled her expression. "Please note that where one chooses to sleep is private and isn't something one discusses around others. Should you someday have a vision about such things, one that you feel is important, you should tell the person what you Saw when no one else is around."

229

Eri nibbled on her lip. "What if it's something like…Iren deciding to go sleep in the woods?"

As Selia sucked in a startled breath, Iren scowled. "Hey, why are you trying to get *me* in trouble? I'm not planning to do anything like that."

"Oh!" Eri cried. "That was only an example. I promise. I don't See much about sleeping, really. But sleeping in the woods doesn't seem private, so what would I do?"

"You don't need to imagine every scenario," Lynia explained with a smile. "If you See something about a child doing something dangerous, you speak to their guardian. A misbehaving adult? Find the closest person in charge, like your parents or Lord Lyr or Lady Meli. But if there is no danger, you speak to the person involved. Alone."

"I'll try to remember," Eri whispered.

Heart twisting, Lynia studied the little girl's face. She was typically a bright, happy child despite the power of her gift, but her behavior had been more erratic of late. Lynia would have to ask one of Eri's parents if they'd noticed. Not that Ralan and Cora neglected the child, of course, but some changes in demeanor were tougher to see up close.

Lynia squeezed Eri's shoulder and stood. "I'm certain you will."

Amusement had mostly replaced discomfiture by the time Lynia and Selia settled across from one another at the library table. To her credit, Selia didn't ask about Eri's revelation, though her eyes gleamed with curiosity. She merely pulled over a stack of blank paper and one of the history books without saying a word.

"It truly was innocent," Lynia muttered. "We fell asleep after talking."

Selia's lips twitched. "I wasn't going to question you, although I confess I wondered."

A few tables down, Arlyn murmured something to the children before marching over to lean her hip against the edge of the table. "If you're spilling, I want to hear."

Did she want to "spill" her thoughts? Despite her difficulties getting close to others, Lynia had befriended both women over the last few months. She'd already shared some of her concerns about Lial, so why not this? So instead of combing through her notes and ignoring her problems, Lynia found herself recounting her dream and much of what had happened after—except for Lial's confessions, of course. She would not dishonor him by breaking his confidence.

"Sounds like your own subconscious is telling you to give Lial a chance," Arlyn said.

Lynia twisted her fingers together. "It…might have been real. I don't know."

"Exactly. It's impossible to know," Arlyn replied with a shrug. "Honestly, if something happened to me, I'm afraid Kai would become a hermit in the woods, making creepy glass structures that scared off the village's children. Or worse, he'd move to his father's weird compound and start adding to the underground maze. I'd be dream-haunting him to cut that shit out for sure."

Selia snorted. "You know he'd be too busy moping for any of that. He would surely kick Aris from the brooding tower."

"Losing a soulbonded is painful," Lynia argued, frowning.

"I don't mean to make light of a broken bond, and I'm sure Selia didn't, either," Arlyn said. On the other side of the table, Selia nodded. "I guess I'm just reinforcing what you already know. Think about what the other person would truly want for you and keep that in your heart."

"Happiness is more than possible without a bond." Selia leaned forward, her voice dropping low. "Iren doesn't know this, but…I

have a potential soulbonded out there. I rejected him because he was a pompous arse. Our souls might have been a match somehow, but our personalities certainly weren't. And I have no regrets in choosing Aris. None at all."

Lynia's mouth dropped open in surprise, both at the revelation itself and the confidence Selia had been willing to share. "I had no idea."

"Many don't." Selia smiled. "And some don't even realize that Aris and I aren't soulbound. Let others wonder, and don't be afraid to find your own definition of happiness."

"Thank you," Lynia said softly, her throat going tight as she absorbed their words.

Fortunately, both women knew her well enough now to leave her to sort out her emotions on her own. Arlyn returned to her studies, and Selia shifted the topic back to the work at hand. A fortuitous switch, as it would take time to work through the tumult the conversation had brought. So Lynia thrust it to the back of her mind, gave Selia her instructions, and buried herself in the history of Abuiarn.

The rest would resurface later—of that she could be certain.

Lial wrote down the last of his observations and folded the single piece of paper in half, sticking it between the pages of the book. The last two tomes Lynia had given him hadn't been nearly as useful as the first two. A few vague mentions of illnesses as observed in other species and a long-winded treatise on the underrated usefulness of potions and tinctures—that was it. Though he tended to agree with the latter point, he wouldn't have minded something more helpful.

Like recipes for a cure.

Pinching the back of his neck, Lial rubbed out the knots as he straightened. The workroom was quiet, only the steady sound of his patient's breathing stirring the air. Maddy and her mates had returned to their tower to rest—with no few jokes at Lial's expense—and Elan was out checking on yesterday's injured. It was a while before Caeleth would need another healing session, and Lial had no other books to check.

If he were lucky, he might have time for a quick nap.

Not upstairs, though. Lial wouldn't press fortune that far. Instead, he headed for the chair beside his patient's bed. Uncomfortable, but it wouldn't be the first or last time he'd slept sitting up. Of course, it couldn't compare to a few marks' rest with Lynia curled against his side. What would?

Lial settled his head in the gap between the chair's back and the wall, then closed his eyes. But he'd only begun to drift into rest when a knock sounded on the door. He heaved a sigh. He'd better get the door before it woke Caeleth.

A quick stretch of his senses as he marched across the room revealed Aris waiting outside, something Lial's eyes confirmed when he opened the door. The midmorning sun lit the green streaks in the mage's hair and sparked against the ocean of ice behind him as Lial squinted, used to the dim lighting of the workroom. Silently, Aris stepped over the threshold and bent to remove the spikes attached to his boots before advancing further.

"Good morn," Lial murmured as he and Aris halted beside the workbench. "Is all well?"

Aris cast a glance toward Caeleth and then shook his head. "Yes and no," he answered softly. "Nothing that needs your immediate aid, so I'll keep this brief. I was wondering if you might summon Tynan for another session."

"The mind healer?" Lial struggled to keep his voice low as concern threaded through him. "Has something else happened?"

Aris sighed. "Not exactly. But Kezari has been unsettled since she detected a dragon on Earth, and combined with other recent events, I've struggled with control. A couple of light mind healing sessions…wouldn't be a bad thing."

Lial didn't miss the way Aris avoided looking at the stone operating table or the slight tremor in his hand as he brushed his hair out of his eyes. Seeing Caeleth's surgery couldn't have helped his memories of trauma. "I'm sorry you caused yourself harm by assisting me."

"An interesting statement from a man who caused himself harm assisting *me*," Aris said wryly. "I have no delusions about what you suffered after experiencing my memories."

"All part of a healer's work." Through his link with Caeleth, Lial sensed his patient's disturbance and softened his voice again. "I'll contact Tynan. And before you go…I've an idea for that boon you offered to me, but you'll likely want time to think it over."

Aris's eyebrow lifted. "That complicated? Or perhaps I might disapprove."

Making the suggestion was tricky on its own, and that was in no small part because Aris was somewhat of a mystery. It wasn't unusual for life mages to be…well…unusual, but not only was Aris an adventurer who'd likely seen more of their world than anyone on the estate, bar Kezari, he'd also been held captive and tortured on a remote island for years—by his potential soulbonded, no less. No matter how easy their discussions, friendship with Aris would not be simple to attain, and that lack made his reactions difficult to guess.

"Lynia and Telien had difficulty conceiving," Lial began.

Aris held up a hand. "I am not going to be present when you two—"

"That is not what I'm suggesting," Lial snapped. "I found a potion that might help, especially with a life mage's energy behind it. If you're willing to do an infusion, I'll distill the tincture. Then she can drink it whenever and with whomever she chooses."

"With whomever... But I thought..." Aris shook his head. "Never mind. None of my business. I'm willing to help with the infusion, but I'm not certain how well it will work. Are you sure you want to use a favor when it might not be successful, especially when it might not benefit you?"

"I'm certain."

"Then send word when you have your potion at the right stage," Aris said.

"Thank you." Lial trailed Aris to the door and waited until the mage had slipped the spikes back on his shoes to speak again. "I'll contact Tynan as soon as possible. Are you having enough trouble that I should monitor your health?"

Aris's lips curved upward in a humorless smile. "Not quite. Hopefully, we can prevent a return to that level of distress."

Indeed. Lial was always willing to establish another healing link with any patient who needed it, but he couldn't say he looked forward to the possibility with Aris. Lial still woke from nightmares full of torture from time to time. But he didn't say that as he bid the life mage farewell and turned back toward his current patient, who'd begun to fight against the spell keeping him asleep.

Lial scanned the wound with his magic and found the organs knitting back together nicely, if not as quickly as he would prefer. Fortunately, there had been enough improvement that he could wake the mage for a short time. An explanation of what had happened

and where he now was might be enough to set Caeleth at ease so he stopped fighting rest.

First, though, Lial ensured the nerves in and near the injured area were numb and then reinforced the spell holding the mage's torso immobile. Any rapid movement could still separate the stitches, and neither of them would be happy if that happened. Five marks' worth of rest hadn't been enough to fill the gaping hole in Lial's depleted energy. Needless to say, performing surgery was far down his list of things he was in the mood to do.

Once the patient was as prepared as possible, Lial slowly released the sleep spell. In less time than many would have required, Caeleth's eyelids popped open, and he jerked his head up as though attempting to sit up. Thank the gods he'd kept the man immobile.

"Calm yourself, Caeleth," Lial said. "You are safe. I'm the primary healer here at Braelyn."

The mage dropped his head to the pillow, his wide eyes on Lial. "Healer."

"Yes." Lial did his best to give a comforting smile, though that wasn't precisely his strong suit. "You were wounded with iron, so I had to stitch up your injury. I'm afraid I've had to place a spell on you to keep you from moving."

Caeleth's breath hissed out. "Gods bless. I thought I paralyzed myself with the rocks."

"Paralyzed yourself?" Fenere's words from earlier echoed in Lial's head. *Then the foolish mage pulled the ridge down on us.* "So you *did* cause the rockfall on purpose?"

"No one knew where I was." Caeleth grimaced. "Thought I should check yesterday's work before the worst of the ice hit, but I didn't wake anyone when I left. When the attacker struck, I used the last of my energy to grab at the stones, hoping to get attention.

Maybe hit the guy with them, too. But I grabbed more than I meant to."

From just those words, lines of strain bracketed the young man's mouth, causing Lial to frown in concern. "I suppose it brought you help. But I need to place you back into a deep sleep, Caeleth. Your body needs to focus on healing. You'll have to allow me to do so instead of fighting against my magic."

His eyes already slipping closed, Caeleth nodded. "Thank you."

There was a depth to the mage's tone that suggested his thanks were for more than sleep. More even than gratitude for allowing him to wake long enough for an explanation—the mage was thanking him for life. Lial swallowed down the uneasy dread that word brought and focused on his magic. Caeleth didn't know he was still in danger.

At least someone here could rest easily.

21

Lynia flipped through the pages one more time, though she technically knew every word thanks to her magic. But neither her recollection nor her eyes revealed the information she sought. Nowhere in the entire history of Abuiarn was there mention of Bleyiak or a healer named Emereh. There was barely even a discussion of the mysterious illness that had led to the colony's downfall.

"I cannot fathom such an incomplete history being included in the palace archive," Lynia grumbled. "It's almost as though this source is *trying* to be vague."

Selia frowned. "If they wanted to prevent others from learning about the spell used, perhaps that was their intention."

"I think the only book mentioning Bleyiak ended up in your stack." Lynia turned her head to examine the spines before freeing the book on the bottom. "Yes, this one."

"I don't understand why you need the physical text if you already transcribed them," Selia said.

Lynia opened the large tome and flipped to the index, noting the page number she would need. "The information may be in my brain, but it can get jumbled, especially when I copy several books at the same time. Besides, there's a certain satisfaction and clarity that comes from reading the physical book."

With a shrug and a smile, Selia resumed her study of a book on Tebid Oren.

Fortunately, this book had the bit of information she thought she remembered. *In the year 11,201, a Lord Bleyiak Oenan arrived on Abuiarn, his status in the land of Gale more than ample to earn his place amongst the lower nobles.* Lynia skimmed several paragraphs detailing the work he'd done to improve his status, a list almost as boring as import and export records. *After a mere six years, Lord Bleyiak had taken charge of trade matters and set his heart upon a daughter of the ruling family.*

"Had to know there would be some kind of thwarted love in here somewhere," Lynia muttered.

Selia chuckled. "I don't know what you're reading, but that's a definite feature in many a disaster."

Recalling the rest of the story made Lynia grimace. "Not true love in this case. It seems Lord Bleyiak attempted to force his favorite princess into bed with him, but she rendered him unconscious with her magic and had him hauled up in front of the court. He was banished, with all his properties and belongings passing to the princess he tried to rape."

"A light punishment," Selia said.

"Probably because he didn't succeed, though I suppose laws might have shifted in more than twenty thousand years."

Selia nodded. "That colony was independent enough for its own ruling family, too."

"I imagine they wished they'd killed him on the spot." Lynia tapped her finger against the page. "The *what* isn't detailed, but his wrath and destruction are. As my other source stated, he shoved some kind of spell into their energy field. A great many—"

240

"Wait," Selia whispered, her gaze shifting to the children a few tables down. "Softly, please. Iren doesn't know the extent of what we're investigating. I doubt Eri does, either, if future possibilities are being hidden from her."

"Ah, thank you. They're being so quiet for Arlyn that I forgot they were there."

Selia's lips twitched. "Iren hopes to impress Arlyn with his studious nature so she'll share the secrets of human space travel. Come to think of it, I should probably be grateful Iren hasn't mentioned his fascination to Aris. Then they'd both leave me here to go circle planets."

Lynia laughed lightly. "Surely not."

"Never fear," Selia said. "I would find a way to go, too."

Before Lynia could return to the woes of Abuiarn, someone knocked at the door, which opened to admit Delbin and Inona. The scout levitated a trunk between her and Delbin, and she followed him to a clear spot beside Lynia's table. Only as Inona settled the trunk on the floor did Lynia spot the unusual paper bag on top.

"Lady Lynia. Lady Selia," Delbin said, his quick bow offset by his mischievous grin. "I hope you are faring well this day."

Lynia narrowed her eyes at him. "Isn't that the exact line from the etiquette book you read on your last visit?"

"Proof that I retained the knowledge, I'd say."

"I suppose that's true," Lynia replied, no longer able to hold back a smile. "Did you find the information I requested?"

Delbin's forehead furrowed. "Yes, and I suspect I don't want to know why you wanted these books in particular."

"What is in the bag?"

"This?" Delbin lifted the paper bag and jiggled it. "This is a gift for Arlyn."

Across the room, Arlyn's head shot up.

"Me?" she called. Then she spotted the bag and shot to her feet. "Oh, gods, I think you're my favorite person right now, Delbin."

"Don't give her that yet," another voice said from the doorway. Lial. Lynia frowned at his annoyed tone and harsh expression as he strode across the room, a couple of books tucked under one arm. "I don't suppose you checked that for harmful bacteria or potential contaminants?"

Lynia blinked in confusion. What—

"I can't scan for bacteria, but I was careful not to include anything with seeds. Hope you don't have to have tomatoes or pickles on your burger, Arlyn. I didn't want to risk bringing an invasive species of plant. There's not even a sesame seed bun."

Earth food. Lynia and Selia shared a shuddering glance. A few weeks ago, their cook had attempted to replicate something called a hamburger, and the result had been…not the best. But unlike Lial, Lynia refused to spoil the excitement Arlyn clearly felt over the treat. After all, she'd had her own share of cravings when she'd carried Lyr. Telien had once taken the gate to her parents' home in the northern mountains to fetch pastries made with a fruit that only grew there.

Maybe one day she would experience such a thing again. If she and Lial… Lynia's face grew heated, and she forced that thought aside before it showed on her face. No matter what Lial said, another pregnancy was unlikely whether she decided to pursue a relationship with him or anyone else. She refused to get her hopes up for such a thing. Better to enjoy Arlyn's experience without fretting over her own life.

Lynia's focus returned to the room in time to see Lial's magic surrounding the bag, and she smiled again at the care he showed.

Though Arlyn didn't exactly seem appreciative—truthfully, she appeared ready to throttle him first and ask for the results later. Not that Lial let her annoyance bother him. He'd surely grown far too used to impatience at this estate.

The light disappeared from the bag, and Lial lowered his arm. "It's clear."

"I didn't realize this was such a big deal," Delbin grumbled as Arlyn snatched the sack from his hand.

Lynia sucked her lips together to hold back her smile, and even Lial's expression had shifted to reluctant amusement. Arlyn pulled out a bundle of colorful paper and unwrapped it to reveal something very different from what their cook had devised. Two pieces of bread surrounded a slab of meat—at least, Lynia thought it was meat. Some kind of red sauce dribbled from one side, and a pale green leaf stuck out around the edges.

Arlyn took a huge bite of the burger and let out a moan that had Lynia giving up on holding in amusement. Her laugh rang out, but Arlyn didn't even glance her way. She didn't offer to let anyone try the burger, either. Lynia hardly blamed her—she would have stabbed anyone who'd tried to take one of those tarts.

"If we weren't both taken, I'd have to marry you, Delbin," Arlyn said on a sigh. "Bless you. And your whole family. Your descendants, too."

Delbin chuckled. "If I'd known I'd be helping my whole bloodline, I would've brought more than one."

Arlyn reached into the bag again and lifted out something that looked like a long piece of toasted nesel. "Fries, too? Probably a good thing I'm not in charge of the treasury. Though I could likely dig out a jewel or some gold or something to reward you."

"Nah, I'm good tormenting Ralan's credit card at the moment."

Though Lynia wasn't sure what Delbin was talking about, the comment made Arlyn laugh, a wicked sound that didn't bode well for Ralan. "That's fraud," Arlyn said.

"He gave me permission," Delbin argued. "But maybe I should insist he get me a card with my name on it. He could pretend to adopt me."

As he and Arlyn continued to argue about the merits of credit cards—whatever those were—Lynia stepped over to the trunk and opened the lid. An involuntary but happy sigh slipped from her lips at the massive stack of books almost overflowing from the top, though another bag took up a portion of the space. But this one was cloth, not paper. Surely not food. If Delbin had put something as potentially messy as food on top of her precious new—

"That's for Ralan," Inona said, lifting the bag from the pile and shrugging the strap over her shoulder. "There were books he wanted, too."

Lynia's fingers itched with the urge to open that bag and see what books a seer might order from Earth, but good sense overcame that desire. If Ralan needed information about another disaster, she didn't want to know about it. At least not before solving the first one.

Instead, she lifted a book from the top of the stack. *Principles of Virology*. Beneath that was a satisfyingly large tome on Earth's history. Well, the first volume of that history. Her heart picked up its pace with excitement as she started arranging books on an empty table. She caught a muttered curse from Lial about her back before he began to help her, but she was too happy to pay attention to his annoyance. Besides, she would be able to arrange and enjoy her new books faster with his aid whether he was helping out of worry or not.

By the time the trunk sat empty, Lynia had several piles, sorted by subject. From basic Earth information like history, fashion, and

modern technologies all the way to detailed texts on diseases and their treatments, the array filled her with satisfaction. Some might not be useful to this particular crisis, but knowledge was never wasted. If nothing else, they could better train scouts about life on modern Earth before they journeyed there.

"What is this?" Lial asked, lifting a thin, shiny book from one of the piles on fashion.

Behind her, she heard stifled laughter, and skimming the words boldly printed across the cover revealed why.

10 Best Ways to Please Your Man.

What's Hot, What's Not.

Best Looks to Heat Him Up This Winter.

Well. The reader certainly wouldn't need an index with the contents splashed on the front for everyone to see. "I presume it is one of the books on human fashion."

"It's a magazine," Arlyn said around a chuckle. "They like to pick headlines that…catch the eye. The clothes are usually an okay representation, but the average person can't really afford most of the brands."

"Probably why the latest collection from Ralan's clothing line is in there." Delbin grinned. "That's why I picked that one. Magazines are mostly opinion except for the odd serious article. Unless it's an academic journal, but I didn't bring any of those. This is the kind of thing a human might pick up while buying food or household goods."

Lynia snatched the magazine from Lial's hand and flipped through the smooth, glossy pages. Fascinating. A great many pictures were printed in full, vibrant color interspersed with segments of text arranged in narrow columns. Here and there, images describing certain goods for sale filled an entire page. One even emanated a sharp, floral scent.

Perfume sample, she read.

Fascinating indeed.

"This will be a trick to copy," Lynia said, already considering the possibilities. "Paintings and engravings are the most difficult, and these pictures use a different technique from any here. I'll have to experiment when I have the time."

"Are you certain the library needs these?" Lial grumbled, his focus on the next magazine in the stack.

How to Tell a Guy to Get Lost.

Lynia laughed as that title leaped out at her, no doubt the cause of Lial's consternation. "Oh, absolutely."

Let him wonder what she found so amusing.

Lial couldn't exactly say why he was in a bad mood, but after helping Lynia unload her new books and dropping off the last bit of research she'd given him, he found his disposition had gone decidedly sour. So he checked the status of the potion he'd started distilling and set Maddy to her current task—scanning Caeleth to better understand his wounds—before climbing the steps to his room. He'd promised Aris he would contact Tynan, and there was no time like the present. His general annoyance with the mind healer would have ruined a better mood, anyway.

It wasn't that Tynan did a poor job at mind-healing. Aris had been tortured terribly, so the fact that he currently lived a relatively normal life spoke to Tynan's skill at repairing mental channels. But the man was too easily distracted. He'd let his attraction to Kezari occupy his thoughts so thoroughly that he'd forgotten the basic courtesy of checking for Lial's healing links before starting therapy. It would take a few decades before Lial forgot the blast of horrific

memories he'd experienced because of that lapse.

Unfortunately, Aris was comfortable with Tynan, and if it would benefit the life mage's recovery, Lial would have to put up with the inept youngling. Unless Tynan wasn't permitted to come after his supervisor had reviewed the full report of the minder healer's previous work here.

It took an obnoxious amount of time, naturally, for Tynan to answer his mirror. Lial was about to give up and try again later when the man's image solidified in the glass. His pale hair stuck up at odd angles as though he'd been tugging at it, and his robes had wrinkled so deeply the embroidered flowers looked trampled. Had something terrible happened at the temple where the healer priest lived?

"Lial," Tynan said, a hint of breathlessness in his voice. "Please forgive my untidy appearance and poor manners. I've just finished with my second difficult case in as many days, but I didn't want to let your contact go unanswered."

For privacy's sake, Lial didn't ask for more information, though he couldn't help but wonder what kind of patients had the man looking worse than he had after helping poor Aris. "I've long felt healers shouldn't waste time on needless pleasantries."

"Then you won't mind my asking rather abruptly about the reason for your communication?"

"I do not," Lial said with a wave of his hand. "Aris would like to request another session. He has been struggling of late and is uncertain of his control."

Tynan's eyebrows rose. "I'm surprised you're asking me after my error."

Though Lial wasn't particularly fond of the healer, he admired his blunt honesty. "Aris requested you, and my patient's comfort is more important than my own."

"That I understand," Tynan said. "I am more than willing to lend my aid."

"Will the head priest give you permission?"

From the twist of Tynan's lips, it was clear he'd correctly interpreted Lial's question: *Did you screw up too badly to be allowed?* But the priest merely nodded. "She understood the cause and has not forbidden me from travel."

"Do understand that I will not be lenient if you show such inattention around Kezari again."

"I believe Kezari is my potential soulbonded," Tynan said, his eyes level on Lial's through the mirror. "That was a shock considering our obvious differences, but I've had time to process that revelation. Regardless, I will be certain to consult with you before beginning a healing session. That lapse will not be repeated."

Lial didn't want to feel sympathy—when it came to healing, he'd long learned to be exacting in his expectations. But after dredging up his own past the night before, he couldn't seem to help himself. Soulbonds could be…difficult. He'd lost quite a few years of his life to the pain of a broken one. Perhaps he could give Tynan a bit of leeway.

"Consulting me will hopefully be sufficient." Lial paused, a new thought occurring to him. "Do you only possess the mind healing gift?"

Tynan's eyebrows rose. "No, but it is my strongest. I wouldn't have been able to repair Aris's bones the way you did, but I can knit minor to moderate wounds and speed the healing of set bones to some extent. Is there some other problem I need to know about?"

"We've had trouble here. A traitor the Myern is hunting down," Lial explained. Among other things, but he didn't want to mention the possible plague yet. "A week or two's aid with daily healing tasks would be much welcome while I deal with serious injuries."

"I will inquire with the high priest about the length of time I am permitted," Tynan answered, a healthy dose of surprise in his voice.

Lial nodded. "Thank you. Please let me know as soon as you can."

He'd dreaded the conversation, but as he disconnected the link, Lial felt...lighter. In truth, he should have recruited help much, much sooner instead of burying himself in work. Although he didn't think Tynan would be a suitable replacement after he relocated, the relief from this conversation prompted him to consider beginning that search soon.

But not now. He had a fertility potion to see enchanted.

22

Though the others left to take care of their own tasks, Lynia stayed at her table, re-reading the same books she'd already memorized in the vain hope that new information would leap out. Well, easy information, in any case. A couple of the history books gave more details about the downfall of Abuiarn, but none of them mentioned the method Bleyiak had used to cause it.

One book had discussed the outbreak of disease and the arrival of Emereh, but either none of the historians knew how Emereh had cured the illness or they weren't saying. The latter made less sense considering the horrible details they'd had no trouble listing. Madness from tainted energy—akin to what Kien's poison had caused—followed by chills, fever, and an increasingly wretched cough their bodies couldn't seem to heal. Then abrupt death.

After a couple of brutal weeks where most of the population was decimated, the healer had finally arrived to save those still alive. And that was the extent of the details—arrival, victory, abandonment of the colony. Surely, the person or people who'd given this account had known whether Emereh had used magic, potions, or some other method. Why wouldn't they have written this down in case the illness wasn't unique to Abuiarn? Had they even discovered the source of it?

No, there absolutely wasn't going to be an easy answer here.

There was only one thing of note that she kept returning to—Bleyiak hadn't caught the illness. In fact, none of the sources agreed on what had happened to the man. One said he'd been cut down by the guards after he'd released his spell, one claimed he'd taken over the throne, and the other said he'd escaped. None mentioned him dying a painful death due to the sickness he'd unleashed, and they probably would have if it had happened. That kind of cosmic justice wouldn't go unremarked.

So either he'd been cut down too soon to suffer the fate of the others, or he'd remained unaffected. But how? A spell or magical shield? A tincture? She knew little about the man beyond the facts given in the history books and the list of goods he'd authorized for the colony. She'd examined the list of herbs on his order, and while some of them might have been useful for thwarting an infection, it was impossible to know how they'd helped without a recipe.

With a groan, Lynia leaned her forehead against her palm.

And that was how Lyr found her a few moments later. "*Laiala?*"

Lynia straightened, lowering her arm to the table. "I'm fine. Just not making as much progress as I would like."

"I know the feeling." Lyr sat in the chair Selia had occupied earlier. "At the risk of bringing up bad memories…how well do you know Koranel?"

Her eyebrows drew together. "Not well enough to elicit any important memories, good or bad."

"But others around him…" Worry creased Lyr's eyes. "I have reason to suspect that Koranel was involved in past unpleasantness."

"I assume you're attempting to mention Telien's death without actually doing so?"

A smile ghosted across Lyr's face. "You know me too well. Yes, in a way. I have to determine whether Koranel was involved in the recent attack and in Norin's treachery. I don't yet know if it goes far enough back that Koranel was part of *Laial*'s death, but he refused to take a blood oath to prove his allegiance. I'd say it's possible he at least knew."

Naturally, the subject didn't improve her mood, but except for a twinge of pain, the deep grief that had haunted her so long wasn't evident today. Resolve filled her instead. If she could help bring someone to justice for her bonded's death, it would be a good thing, indeed. She didn't know a great deal about Koranel, but she would happily make the time to find out.

"I'll check the records from his recruitment as well as any commentary on his service," Lynia said.

"Are you sure?" Lyr frowned. "*Laial* surely wrote some of those, and I wouldn't—"

"Thank you, but I do not need to be shielded." She held her son's gaze until he nodded. "Would you avoid any work I had done, or would you celebrate it?"

Lyr had the grace to wince. "Good point."

"Personally, I hope there's something relevant in your father's notes," she said, her lips curling up. "That would be a perfect justice, don't you think? Especially if I'm the one to find it."

"It would." Though he returned her smile, Lyr rested his hand on hers and squeezed. "But I didn't come here to give you more work. Preventing this plague is the most pressing concern, and I'll be questioning Koranel regardless. I sought only your impressions of the man."

Lynia let out a soft laugh. "You truly can't resist trying to protect me, can you? You've always been my guardian, even when you were little. Remember when you used to insist on carrying your wooden sword when we walked to the village or through the woods? It's one of the things that makes you such a good Myern."

A hint of red tinged his cheeks. "I barely remember the wooden sword. Nor do I know what I would have done with it if we had been attacked."

"I'm certain you would have figured it out." She turned her palm up so she could grip her son's hand for a moment. Then she released him and pulled away. "Now go. It will take moments to find the records you need and skim them. I'll contact you telepathically when I'm finished so it takes less time."

Lyr stood. "Thank you. Though if you decide it is too much…"

She made a shooing motion with her hands. "Go plan your questioning or something. You'll have what you need in less than a mark."

"Yes, *Laiala*," Lyr answered with a laugh, his tone about as contrite as it had ever been when she'd chided him.

Ah, well. At least he generally listened, even if it seemed like he didn't.

By the time Lial descended the stairs to the workroom, Maddy had finished examining Caeleth. Lial gritted his teeth and did his best to listen patiently as she repeated her observations. Not that she was doing anything wrong. No, Lial was more interested in checking on the potion he had distilling than advising Maddy, but he wouldn't neglect her teaching for his own desires.

"It's interesting to see his healing rate slow instead of speed up,"

Maddy said. "Your augmentation only lasts for so long, I guess."

Lial nodded. "Yes. I will do another session once I've finished this tincture. I do hope I'll be able to allow Caeleth some time awake this evening. We've managed to get water into him in trickles, but I would like to try broth. That will be easier with his cooperation."

"He's healed enough for that?"

"Only broth," Lial said as he walked toward his workbench. "Even with accelerated healing, it will be several days before I test him on something solid."

Lial ducked down to study the clear flask half-full of a deep violet liquid. One more brief heating, and then the concoction should be ready for the settling stage—and Aris's contribution. After a quick mental check with Aris confirming the life mage's availability, Lial activated the heat spell beneath the flask and watched intently as it warmed. The moment before it began to bubble, he'd remove the heat.

"What are you making?" Maddy asked from beside him.

"A gift," Lial said, perhaps a little sharply. "Page three hundred and fifty-two of the potion book."

He was so focused on the potion that he wasn't sure Maddy had bothered to look it up until she spoke again. "Increased fertility? I'm surprised you aren't handing this out constantly considering how long elves go between children."

"It only increases the chance of conception by about five percent." Tiny swirls formed in the liquid, a precursor to boiling. "But some do ask for it regardless. I'm hoping Aris can increase the effectiveness."

"What…"

Maddy fell silent, but Lial didn't look up to see why. She could figure out the answer or not. His main concern was—there. He cut

off the heat just before the first bubble formed and shifted the flask to the curing spot. Conveniently, Aris chose that moment to enter the room.

The life mage kept his gaze averted from the bed as he strode over to Lial. "What would you have me do?"

"It's a simple task." Lial pointed at the flask. "Imbue as much life magic into the liquid as it can hold."

Aris frowned at the potion. "I'm still uncertain how this will work. Water is useful for life, but it isn't a living thing, even augmented with a plant's essence. My magic will surely disperse and fade without something to hold it."

"You created a sword that holds such power," Lial pointed out.

Aris shrugged. "In the heart of Earth's energy field while a seer and a god were building a portal. The sword was forged within. Besides, the sheath that holds it was given by the same god. It might leak magic otherwise."

"That's true." Lial returned his focus to the flask. "But I have an idea. If you'll indulge me?"

"It's your boon to waste," Aris said, wrapping his hand around the glass despite the doubt in his voice.

Lial was ready for the unique feel of Aris's magic this time, so he was able to ignore the echoes of verdant life that pulsed from the mage's hand. Instead, he turned his inner sight to how the power interacted with the potion—and as he'd hoped, the concoction practically vibrated in accord with the life magic. But Aris was also correct. As soon as he withdrew his magic, the resonance began to slip away.

Luckily, Lial had prepared for that.

As Aris dropped his hand, Lial surrounded the flask with his own power, the flash of blue so strong that Maddy let out a muffled

curse from somewhere behind him. Well, she would just have to close her eyes. He was focused on binding the life energy behind a wall of his own magic, a force similar to the one he used to keep bones together while they knit.

He'd experimented with creating commands inside other potions. The tincture used to heal cuts held an enchantment that carried the mixture first to the blood to aid clotting and then to the skin to assist in repair. But this…This would be spelled for a different purpose. His magic would have to bind the entire concoction together as it was processed into the bloodstream and directed to the womb.

By the time Lial completed the spell, his head spun and his stomach rumbled a harsh complaint. Had he eaten that day? For the life of him, he couldn't recall. But it didn't matter, because food could wait. He studied the potion for a moment and then smiled. It had worked.

He had a victory to enjoy.

"I…don't know what you did," Aris said slowly, "but it appears to have solved my worry. You realize that if it's effective, you could trade a sip of that potion for nearly anything, right?"

Lial took down a tray of vials and a funnel. "If I was interested in wealth, perhaps. First, I must determine if it works. I'll have a few doses to test, though I think it will only require one."

Aris rubbed at his temples. "I'm going to have to do this again. I just know it."

"Better than being constantly asked to attend people in their bedchambers, hmm?" Lial asked with a smirk.

"I suspect I'll find out," Aris muttered.

As Lial began to pour the potion into the vials in careful measures, Maddy sidled up to his other side to watch. Equal parts

worry and curiosity filled her tone when she spoke. "You said a few doses to test? You're going to experiment on people?"

"I should think not," Lial snapped, though he kept his gaze on his task until the last drop was secured in the final vial. "Every potion in that book has been carefully verified as safe by centuries of healers. To be included, fifty healers across Moranaia had to observe and report minute details on how the herbs interacted with those who ingested the potions. In fact, if you ask Lynia, there is surely a book detailing the specific research if you—"

"No, no," Maddy interrupted quickly. "Sorry. The way you phrased it made me wonder, but I should've known you wouldn't attempt something half-assed."

After sealing the final stopper, Lial finally glanced at Maddy. "Half an ass sounds like a serious problem requiring immediate healing."

Aris made a choked, coughing sound, and Maddy chuckled. "It means something that hasn't been thought out. As far as I know, there is no literal ass involved. Probably. Earth is weird, okay?"

"Good to know." Lial lifted a vial, and purple liquid sparked like a jewel as he rotated it in his fingers. "As for my statement about testing... I wasn't referring to a safety check. Neither the base potion nor the magics involved will cause harm, but it is impossible to know if the magic will actually aid in conception. Unless you were volunteering to try it with your mates?"

This time, it was Maddy who nearly choked. "Gods, no. I'm not ready to see how Fen would react to that. He's already worried about the whole *Felshreh* fertility thing. I'm hoping to give him a decade or two before we think about children."

"Alas," Lial said, replacing the vial in the tray. "We'll have to wait until Lynia decides she wants a child, then, unless someone else comes by seeking my help. I had the thought for her, but who knows if she'll ever be ready for that kind of relationship with anyone?"

Maddy grabbed his wrist as he began to turn. "Wait a minute. You went to all that effort, and you don't think she'll choose you? I thought maybe you were hoping for a child, too."

Lial sighed. "I've thought recently that it might be nice to have a family, but I have no intention of pressuring Lynia in such a way. When I give a gift, it is just that, provided with no expectations. I would have tried to do something like this for her and Telien had I known it bothered her."

"My gods." Maddy released him, but a broad smile stretched across her face. "You really are exceedingly nice beneath the grumpy."

Best not to give an answer to *that*.

Apparently, Aris decided to take pity on him. "Have you spoken to Tynan?"

"Yes," Lial said. "He sounded optimistic about being able to return, but he has to check with the head priest on timing. Though… don't you worry his presence might aggravate Kezari further? They are uneasy near each other."

"She will tolerate him for my sake." Aris glanced toward the bed and then quickly away. "She knows I worry about my reaction after seeing… I tried not to look at the surgery, but the blood… Even now, your patient makes me uneasy."

Miaran dae fe onai, Lial cursed. He should have found a way to take the potion to Aris instead of asking him to return here. The sight probably did feel like iron in the man's heart. "Forgive me for keeping you here, Aris. I wasn't thinking."

"No one forced me through the door," the life mage countered. "But I should go. Once Lyr questions his prisoners, I'll be leaving with Kezari and whatever scouts he assigns to search for the third traitor."

Lial lifted a brow. "Are you certain you're well enough for the task?"

"If taking a walk doesn't clear my mood, I will notify Lyr," Aris answered, his gaze clear enough that some of Lial's worry eased. "I give you my word."

"And I will hold you to it," Lial said with a sharp nod.

Only when the life mage had departed did Lial allow the deep, worried sigh to slip from his lips. The last thing he needed on top of a plague was an antsy dragon flying his traumatized patient over the edge of sanity. Lial wasn't a mind healer, so there was little he would be able to do but sedate Aris.

And for a mage of Aris's talent, that was no small endeavor.

23

A nger simmered in Lyr's stomach and heated his blood, but the look he focused on Koranel was colder than the icicle dangling from the tree limb outside the tiny, barred window. Just as potentially deadly, too. The *drec* had deceived them—the report Lynia had found proved that well enough. Koranel had transferred to Oria a couple of decades after his training, but Norin had elevated him to his second in command a few short months after he'd transferred back to Braelyn. Koranel's wife and children had remained at Oria despite his return.

Lyr ground his teeth together. He hadn't known Koranel had a family until reading that report—a family that Allafon could have used as leverage to keep Koranel loyal. If true, that meant Allafon had had two high-ranking officers, including Norin, planted in the army under Lyr's authority. And Norin would have been freer to act on his treachery if his second in command was part of the plot.

Frustration joined anger until it was all Lyr could do to remain visibly calm. What had his father been thinking to approve the promotion? He'd expressed reservations in his notes about Norin's choice, but he hadn't thought to question Koranel himself. And since that had happened long before Lyr became Myern, he hadn't known, either. What cause would he have had not to trust his father's decisions on such things?

A terrible oversight when it came to anything involving Norin.

"You're wasting your time," Koranel finally said, the first to break the tense silence.

"I have plenty at the moment." Lyr eased closer in the spare stone cell where the other man stood chained against the wall. "While you merely extend your misery."

Koranel snorted. "Or my life, depending on how I'm punished."

"Hmm." Lyr tapped his finger against the hilt of his sword. "A valid point. But I am more inclined to be lenient to the cooperative. Unless you've done something more horrible than I suspect?"

Something flickered in Koranel's eyes. "You should question Fenere. He'll speak more readily, I imagine. I have nothing to say."

"I've already spoken to Fenere," Lyr said. Not since they'd been hauled from his study and imprisoned, of course, but Koranel didn't need to know that. "I have learned more than enough to keep you bound here. If I'm incorrect, why won't you defend yourself?"

The other man pinched his lips together and turned his head away.

"Allafon is dead, as you well know." Lyr lifted a brow. "So it's curious that you haven't brought your family here. What is left of them after Morenial executed any traitors."

That last was a guess, but it hit the mark. Koranel's head jerked around, fury lighting his face as he strained against the chains. "If I had an iron blade, I would shove it into your heart for that. My daughter did not deserve death for serving in Allafon's guard."

So the man had lost a child. A twinge of sympathy filled him, but only for a moment. Loss didn't have to turn a person into a

traitor. "If Morenial judged her wrongly, why did you not come to me for redress?"

"As though you would have listened," Koranel spat. "After what Allafon did to you."

"Do I have a reputation for being unfair or unreasonable?"

Abruptly, Koranel slumped against the wall. "She didn't deserve death, but neither of us were…wholly innocent."

Lyr's nostrils flared. "What did you do?"

"Nothing." At Lyr's snarl, Koranel met his eyes. "Literally. Allafon wanted me to help Norin for the sake of my family, but I couldn't bear to. I just…didn't interfere. Norin threatened to tell Allafon about my inaction if I breathed a word, and by Lord Telien's death, my daughter was well-entrenched with the guard at Oria. She…believed in Allafon. Morenial killed her for her loyalty, but I could have talked her around. Korel promised to see her avenged if I stationed Fenere at the trainee's barracks and ignored his actions. I didn't know they were going to start attacking people."

Lyr gripped the hilt of his sword out of reflex, making Koranel flinch. "He's headed to Oria to attack Morenial?"

"I don't know." Koranel's eyes slid closed, and his muscles went lax as he lost the last of his fight. "I swear it. He has some kind of cloak like the ones Allafon had designed, but they don't work as well. That's the only other thing I know. Just…please don't harm my wife and son. They don't know I got mixed up in this. If you have any mercy, tell them I died in service."

Lyr studied the other man, weighing all the choices. Like many, it seemed Koranel had been caught in Allafon's web of abuse. Young Delbin had been exiled to Earth so Allafon couldn't blackmail him into using his magic to harm, only to return to find his brother Tenic had fallen to that fate. Even months after the rogue lord's death,

Lyr and Morenial were still finding families living in fear of a cruel variety of wicked punishments. If Koranel was to be believed, his was one of them.

Well, there was one good way to find out.

"Change your mind about the blood oath and help me find Korel," Lyr said, gaining Koranel's instant attention. "And I might not have to tell them anything."

Although it was still a few marks until dinner, the light was only a bare trickle through the window when Lynia returned to her room. She'd exhausted all of her books from the palace archives, including a couple of new ones Caraden had passed her way. She'd contacted a friend of Selia's at the Citadel for any of their sources, but that required yet another wait. Her research was crucial to their success, yet here she was, taking a break in her room before she screamed in frustration at her failure to find the answers.

It didn't matter that she knew such things took time—usually far, far more than a handful of days—and it hadn't even cheered her up to find the information so readily for Lyr. Not just because of the bittersweet nostalgia dredged up by reading Telien's boldly inscribed account, either. No. Time was running out on this plague. She couldn't explain the deep certainty in her gut about that, but she knew it was true.

And Lynia had little more than a handful of notes to aid in the fight. Despite all she'd read, she had yet to determine if their mystery infection was connected to Abuiarn at all. She might have abandoned that line of research if not for Ralan's guidance and Meli's runes—both suggested the illness of Abuiarn was relevant. But how? And what form would the infection take? Although she'd

decided that bacteria were less likely, she also couldn't be certain they faced a virus. She barely understood what a virus was.

Abuiarn's downfall gave no clues.

Lynia flopped down on the center of her bed with a sigh. Even the books from Earth were of limited use. She would need Lial with her to decode what many of them meant, if he even knew. She'd read the Moranaian healers' texts he'd suggested, and she understood them well enough. But there were so many foreign words and concepts in the Earth books that simply weren't in her English vocabulary. Not even Arlyn, who'd been born and raised speaking English on Earth, had been familiar with many of the concepts.

In annoyance, Lynia flung her arms wide, only to smack her left hand against something hard. Alarmed, she jerked upright, her gaze flying to the spot she'd hit. What in the world? It was a book. She absolutely would not have propped a book against her pillow. What if she'd rolled atop it or knocked it to the floor, causing damage?

She scooted over to grab the book, but the motion caused a small vial to roll across her bedspread in an arc until it settled near her hand. Her forehead furrowed. A potion? As a matter of fact, it looked like the book was the same one on potions she'd read in Lial's workshop. Had he come by her room to leave these for her?

Heat rushed through her at the thought of him entering her bedroom, and it wasn't caused by anger. No, this pooled decidedly lower, and the intensity of her desire wasn't helped by the memory of watching him sleep in this very bed. She'd never seen him so unguarded, but even so, he hadn't appeared soft. A sleeping warrior waiting to fight for life.

Swallowing uncomfortably at her thoughts, Lynia lifted the book, revealing a folded paper. Good, a note. Either it would explain the book and potion, or their lack of mention would reveal he'd

left one of the two behind on accident. The potion had most likely dropped from his pocket. Why would he give her something like that?

She set aside the book and unfolded the paper, smiling at the hurried slash of his handwriting.

Lyni- I've long had this book memorized, so I thought you might wish to study it since distilling interested you. The tincture you made was perfect, of course. Elan suggested I recruit you to help. Or was it Maddy? Time blurs.

Sighing, Lynia ran her finger across the smooth binding of the finely designed tome. Knowledge was the best of gifts.

The vial I left is yours as well. I hope you will receive this without feeling any obligation toward me, but I have been unable to forget the longing in your voice when you mentioned your fears about never having more children.

Her heart began to pound, and her gaze slid to the vial a finger's width from her hand. What had he done?

With Aris's aid, I augmented this fertility potion. It has life magic bound inside, and though I can't swear that it will work, my hope is that someday it will be of use. You need only go out and find a willing partner. When you have done so, drink this before you go to his bed, and it will increase your chances of conception.

Lynia jerked her hand away from the vial as though it was aflame, but the true fire surrounded her chest, a strange burning she couldn't define. Hope? Fear? Anger? Partially anger for certain. He gave her something like this and then told her to go find someone else to sleep with? Even after what they'd shared the night before, he'd dared to make a suggestion so…cold. Remote. She almost wadded up the paper and threw it instead of reading further.

But her curiosity refused to allow that.

I would be lying to say I hadn't once hoped you would choose me, but I never want you to think this was given for that reason. It is for your benefit alone. You deserve every happiness, and I would give up all chance of joy for myself for you

to have what you need. So take this potion and hold it until you should find the right person. I'll not leave Braelyn without offering you this hope. -Lial

Oh— And I do pray you'll wait until your back muscles have strengthened to use it. The weight of a child could cause trouble otherwise.

A drop of liquid splattered the side of her thumb, and she reached up to swipe the sudden tears from her cheeks. So much for cold and remote. Lial didn't *want* her to find someone else—he assumed she would. He'd offered her comfort and shared his secrets even as he anticipated rejection. And he couldn't resist worrying over her health despite it all.

Her gaze fell upon the vial once more. Gods, Lial really did love her. He'd said as much, but people said many things. This, though. He'd seen the secret core of her heart, her deepest desire, and brought it to life. What had it cost him to gain a life mage's help? He must have put a great deal of thought into the process despite all the other duties requiring his attention.

Lynia plucked the vial from the bedspread and settled it into the curve of her palm. Against her skin, the magic inside the potion practically vibrated through the glass. So much power. So much effort. Her throat closed around a well of emotion, and she curled her fingers around the vial, bringing her fist to her heart.

All this, and he was still planning to leave Braelyn. Because of her. *For* her.

Pain thumped beneath her fist with each heartbeat. She couldn't let him go, and it didn't have a thing to do with the people of Braelyn. He'd told her to find a willing partner, but she didn't want to increase her family with just anyone. She hadn't even remembered that deeply buried desire until she'd started evading thoughts of a relationship with Lial.

Lynia stood and marched over to her desk, opening the locked compartment with a touch of her magic. She kept her most precious

items here—things like the ring her mother had given her when she was a little girl, sentimental notes Telien had written to her over the centuries, and Telien's medallion, which she'd only stopped wearing a few years back—so many mementos close to her heart. She picked up the small wooden box carved with leaves and flowers that her grandfather had made for her and placed the vial inside, nestled against a strip of fabric from her grandmother's favorite dress.

She wasn't sure when or if she would decide to use Lial's gift, but something so precious and rare needed to be kept safe until she was confident. So she tucked the box back into the drawer and closed it, sealing the compartment with her power once more. While she wasn't willing to risk pregnancy with a plague on the horizon, she knew who to choose when the risk was negated.

Now she had to convince him to stay.

Lial couldn't deny that he was nervous, but he did his best not to show it. Based on the odd glances Maddy sent his way, he was probably failing, but he had to try. If she knew he'd exposed his heart so thoroughly in the note he'd left Lynia, Maddy would either tease him mercilessly or offer sympathy. He could do without either. As it was, he had to fight the urge to rush back to Lynia's room and reclaim what he'd left.

She would probably avoid him from the awkwardness of it all, but he'd done what was right. He had no regrets. And for that reason, he wouldn't take back the potion or the note, no matter how much her reaction stung. He'd meant what he'd said about her happiness being more important than his own. He was well-accustomed to living a numb, lonely life.

While he waited for one of the estate's helpers to bring a cup of broth, Lial ducked outside long enough to take food to the *camahr*. The small shelter he'd created a few years back was functioning properly—the magic melted the ice in a smooth arc around the wooden contraption, leaving a spot for the *camahr* to leave. But he had a feeling they hadn't. Why abandon a warm, comfortable home when ice coated the world?

Why, indeed.

Not that Lial had taken much action to leave his current home, aside from speaking to Lyr. But it was coming. No doubt after Lynia's reaction to receiving a fertility potion from the man she'd rejected, he would find all the impetus he needed to contact Dria. Most likely, he'd even be willing to petition Ralan if Dria said no.

Shaking his head at his own wry musings, Lial knelt in front of the shelter and replaced the empty bowl beneath it with one full of food. A small snout peeked out, and he thought he caught the gleam of eyes in the shadows. Was it going to come out into the open? Carefully, Lial gathered his cloak beneath him and sat on the edge of the ice. Then he waited.

Cold seeped into his bones until his teeth chattered, but it was worth the discomfort as the kits and their mother emerged. One kit lowered its glowing tail to the bowl, scanning the food, and Lial couldn't help but feel a wash of pride as the mother allowed them to eat instead of correcting the kit's technique. Last time, the little *camahr*'s magic had wavered. By winter's end, they would be ready to live on their own.

The food was almost gone when the clever kit's head rose, and its gaze met Lial's. Lial went still, even his breathing shallow to avoid startling the *camahr*. This was a new behavior. Had he begun to gain favor? Excitement made his heart race before reality reminded him of the impossibility of a link.

He should stop coming out here before the *camahr* became more attached. He would be leaving, after all, and if by some chance he transferred before the kit was old enough to leave its mother, his departure could cause the creature distress. So when it returned its attention to its food, Lial pushed himself to his feet and eased away, careful not to scare them.

Nothing on Moranaia deserved the pain of being left behind.

Lial returned to his workroom at the same time as the broth. Work. He could focus on work. He had Maddy take a small table to the bedside while he prepared to rouse Caeleth. After he expended the energy to carefully wake the mage and monitor him while he and Maddy helped Caeleth drink, Lial would likely be ready for dinner and sleep.

Probably not dreamless, but a man could hope.

24

By the time Lynia neared the healing tower, doubt had set in. Not about her feelings for Lial, of course. This was worry, and fear, and nerves all bundled into a knot in her abdomen. Had he changed his mind at last? He'd said he didn't want her to feel obligated, but perhaps he truly wanted to leave. *I would be lying to say I hadn't once hoped you would choose me.* Past tense. He might have given up on her after all her indecision.

Well, she wouldn't find the answer standing on the path in front of the tower, would she?

She'd barely knocked before his voice called out for her to enter. Taking a deep breath, she closed her trembling fingers over the door handle and entered. Unfortunately, it was immediately obvious that she'd chosen a bad time. The patient reclined semi-upright on the bed while Maddy held a cup to his lips. Lial sat on a stool beside the bed, blue glowing from the hands he held over the mage.

Grimacing, Lynia met Maddy's eyes over the patient's head. She gestured at the door behind her with an exaggerated motion and an apologetic shake of her head. Lial could come find her when he was done.

But she'd only managed to turn around when Lial snapped out a gruff, "Stay."

Her brows lowered in aggravation at his grumpy tone, but her feet refused to move. "I'm interrupting."

"No," Lial said. "Grab me a tincture of *nofa*, though. Please."

An herb used for stomach complaints, her memory supplied as she strode to the worktable and scanned the labels on the baskets. There. Lynia plucked out a green vial—not purple like the one she'd been gifted—and took it to Lial. The task occupied her well enough that she almost forgot to be nervous.

Until his fingers brushed against hers as he grabbed the potion. A hint of his magic tingled up her arm until she shivered, but thankfully, he was too focused to notice. Or so she thought until he spoke.

"Where is your cloak?"

Startled, Lynia glanced down, blushing to find that she'd left the main building in only her dress and hadn't even realized it. Had she really been in that much of a rush to get to him? Clearly so. At least the fabric was a thick winter weight, or not even her distraction would have saved her from freezing.

"I forgot it."

He cast her a brief, wry look. "You forgot your cloak. When it's cold enough to keep the ice on the ground from melting."

A lock of his hair slipped from the band holding it back, and Lial shrugged it from his cheek with his shoulder. Rather futilely, Lynia was amused to note, as the hair returned to its spot as soon as he uncorked the vial. Should she? She hesitated only a moment before tucking the errant lock behind his ear.

This time, he was the one who shivered, and the vial bobbed in his hand before he steadied it.

A muffled snort drew Lynia's attention back to Maddy, who now held the cup in front of Lial as she waited for him to add the tincture. Even their patient stared at Lynia with a drowsy, befuddled gaze, and her cheeks heated at the reminder of their audience. She couldn't even remember the poor man's name, and she was interrupting his healing.

Hah. She was the one usually chiding others for their manners.

"I'm sorry," Lynia said, meeting the mage's eyes. "It was rude of me not to introduce myself now that you are awake. My name is Callian Myernere i Lynia Dianore nai Braelyn."

"You don't look like a Myern's mother," the man mumbled. "Name's Caeleth."

Lynia blinked, uncertain how to take the comment. "I…"

"Myernere of our branch looks ten thousand. Maybe older," Caeleth offered, his words running together until she had to strain to understand. "Not young and beautiful like you."

That brought a pleased smile to her face, though the mage would surely be embarrassed when he was aware enough to remember the uncommonly blunt words. If he remembered. From the look on Lial's face as he dumped the tincture in the broth with more force than was strictly necessary, he might send Caeleth into another deep sleep sooner rather than later. The young man would probably think the whole thing was a dream.

Maddy chuckled. "Does he need the whole bottle?"

"Possibly," Lial grumbled, but he'd already placed the cork back in with the vial half full.

Awkward silence fell as Maddy put the cup to Caeleth's lips again. Lynia kept her eyes on the young Sidhe woman. "Where are your mates this evening?"

"Fen got bored and went with Aris and Kezari," Maddy said as she helped the mage drink. "Anna's working with Selia on water

magic stuff. Good thing since we're leaving tomorrow evening and—shit. Lial, we forgot about the blood you were going to study."

Caeleth jerked back with a sputter. "Blood?"

"Not yours," Maddy said, nudging the cup against his lips again. "Calm down. It's a healer thing. Research."

The mage didn't look convinced, but he started taking sips again.

"When will Fen return?" Lial asked.

"I don't know. They're tracking that Korel guy over to a place called Oria."

"That's where Kai is from," Lynia offered, though the truth was more complicated than that. Allafon, former lord of Oria, hadn't been Kai's real father, though he'd raised him, and his mother had been from another estate a few marks away from Braelyn. "Odd for Korel to be going there, although…"

She didn't say it aloud, but it lined up with the information she'd found for Lyr, at least if Korel and Koranel were working together.

"Although what?" Maddy asked as Lial gestured for her to remove the cup.

Poor Caeleth had fallen asleep.

"There has been plenty of trouble from there. Perhaps this is a remnant of Allafon's treachery," Lynia said, leaving out any other details.

Maddy appeared to accept that. She didn't ask any other questions as she and Lial put the broth and tincture on a side table and eased the pillows from beneath Caeleth so he could sleep more easily. Lynia gathered up the cup and vial while they worked, setting them on the worktable before turning back.

Lial used his magic on Caeleth again, but Lynia couldn't divine the specifics. She suspected he must have placed the mage into a deeper sleep based on the way the man's body went even more lax.

Then the blue light faded, and Lial spun to face her, his gaze full of questions and worry and hunger and—more than she dared guess, that was for sure.

"Thank you for staying," Lial said, his voice a soft contrast to the turmoil in his eyes. "Now I can ask you properly what you need."

"To speak to you." Lynia straightened her spine. "Alone."

Lial held her attention so thoroughly that Lynia barely noticed when Maddy slipped past them with a muttered, "My cue to go."

What was he thinking to look so upset? He had to have known she wouldn't let his gift and note pass without comment. Surely, he hadn't expected her to shrug and move on with her evening. But as the door clicked closed behind Maddy, he only stared at her.

"Unless you would prefer that I leave?" Lynia asked.

Lial scowled. "No."

"If you don't have time for a private—"

"Upstairs," he said, practically growling. "We can talk up there."

Gods, he sounded angry. He must have hoped to avoid an uncomfortable discussion.

But she wasn't leaving without talking this out.

"Fine," Lynia snapped, her own temper rising. "After you."

Lial should have realized she wouldn't avoid him, if for no other reason than it was the opposite of his expectations. He'd done something bold, and she'd come to tell him off for it. Well, why not? It would be the perfect end to a terrible week. No reason not to get it over with.

Resigned, he stomped up the staircase, Lynia following behind. At least she'd been kind enough to wait until no one else was around, though coming upstairs for privacy wasn't strictly necessary. Caeleth

was unconscious beneath the sleeping spell and wouldn't have heard what they said—or cared if he had. But if she wanted complete privacy, he would grant it.

In the center of the room, he spun to face her. "There. Alone."

"As alone as you ever get, I suppose," Lynia said, giving a quick glance over her shoulder at the spiral staircase. "I would not wish our words to travel downward to be overheard."

Lial huffed out an impatient sigh and activated the spell that closed the hatch over the staircase. The rough scrape of stone sliding on stone echoed around them for a moment until it sealed with a snap. He so rarely used the thing that it needed oiling again. Why bother when he rarely had personal guests? At least until recently.

Lynia stared at the hatch. "I didn't know that was there. What if someone comes into the tower needing help?"

"I have spells on the door that alert me." He threw his hands wide in a frustrated gesture. "Didn't you want privacy?"

She let out a long sigh, her shoulders slumping. "Yes. Sorry."

Was she…nervous? Unlikely. Lynia never had trouble telling him when he'd overstepped. "I appreciate you waiting until we were alone, but I'm not certain this argument is a memory I want in my personal sanctuary. For as long as it is mine, at any rate."

Her eyes narrowed. "What do you think I'm going to do?"

"Berate me, of course." Lial captured her gaze and refused to let go. "I'll save you time and say that I'm not sorry. Use the potion or not, but I won't regret the gift."

"Even if you see me carrying another man's child?"

Lial flinched. But he didn't yield. "Even so, if you are happy."

"And you'll just leave Braelyn." Her nostrils flared. "Walk away without a thought."

He studied her expression, full of an anger he didn't understand. Was she upset about the potion or not? "You know I will always think of you. Leaving won't change that."

Lynia closed her eyes and pinched the bridge of her nose. Then she surprised him by crossing the distance separating them, her furious steps sharp on the stone. She stopped so close he could make out the darker blue ring around her irises. Her hand darting up, she poked him hard in the chest.

"You're an idiot."

He frowned. "What?"

"I can't imagine why else you would make a fertility potion for the woman you profess to love and then send it with a note telling her to sleep with someone else. Did you really believe I would just shrug my shoulders and go find some random man in the mood to be a father? As though—"

"Lyni." He curled his hand around hers and pulled it against his chest to stop her from jabbing him again. "You said you might never be ready for a relationship, and I understand that. I wanted to give you something with no obligation."

"Which I appreciate. But after last night," she whispered. "The way you held me…"

His grip tightened slightly around her fingers. "What about it?"

"You can't leave." Lynia framed his cheek with her free hand. "After all of this, I couldn't bear for you to leave. I don't know how you could still intend to."

For several heartbeats, Lial couldn't think of a thing to say. Nothing. He could only stare into her eyes, searching the depths for the meaning behind her words. But there was too much there, and no small amount of it was more than he dared hope for.

"Kiss me," she murmured.

His heart pounded hard in his chest. "Lyni?"

With a frustrated growl, she rose on her tiptoes slightly and brushed her mouth against his. "Idiot."

"Ah, *clechtan*."

Years of control snapped in a single moment. He wrapped his other arm around her waist and tugged her against him, trapping their joined hands between them. Then he crushed her mouth beneath his. He nipped and savored, caressed and devoured. All of his frustrated desires found their way into that kiss.

I'll scare her. She'll leave.

Instead, she jerked her hand free and wrapped her arms around his neck until her body was molded to his. Lial groaned, bringing her hips tight against his without conscious command. There would be no doubt how much he wanted her.

Gods, he wanted to be inside her. Joined, though not just in body. Something he couldn't have. She might want him now, but she'd given no indication of anything else. And he should be happy to be with her in any way he could.

He wasn't.

Lial pulled his lips from hers. "Lyni… You're not thinking."

Annoyance flickered through her eyes. "Not a goal at the moment."

"Goal?" An uncomfortable worry flitted through his mind, refusing to be stifled. "Did you drink the potion?"

With a sudden glare, Lynia shoved herself away. "I wouldn't do that without talking to you first. Honestly, Lial. I'm not going to try to get pregnant when there might be a plague and especially not without the potential father's consent. By Arneen, I could just…"

She made an angry sound low in her throat and spun away, marching toward the closed-off staircase. Hurrying away from him.

Gods, she was right.

He was an idiot.

Her body burned with desire and anger, and for the life of her, Lynia couldn't decide if she wanted to kill Lial or shove him onto the bed—or the floor—and make love to him. He. Was. Maddening. Did he really think she would trap a man into fathering her child without his knowledge? Accidents were one thing, but fertility potions were hardly that.

His fingers wrapped around her wrist, forcing her to a halt, and the fire in her body leapt in treacherous response. Unfortunately, so did her fury. Lynia let him draw her around to face him, but not even the contrition on his face cooled her ire.

"I should have known better," he said.

"Yes."

"In truth, I can't imagine why…" A sharp breath whistled through his nose. "Why you want to be with me now. What changed?"

"I don't know," Lynia answered honestly. "It just happened. I suppose I finally stopped fighting myself."

Lial averted his eyes. "I'm uncertain I can handle a mere night with you."

So that was it.

Her temper eased at the soft confession. He thought this was a whim—and in a way, it was. She wanted to see what it was like to be held by him. Loved by him. But she suspected it wouldn't be for one night alone, even if she didn't know for certain what she hoped for beyond it. Did she have to?

"I have no intention of using you." Lynia shifted until she caught his gaze again. "Truly. No, I'm not ready to commit, but I'm no

longer denying the possibility of that happening. I want to find out what we can be together. Without promises or pressure or histories. Only us, discovering."

Lial frowned. "I am not a casual man, Lyni. With anything."

She nearly snorted at that understatement.

"Exploration is serious. Relationships are formed, not forced," Lynia said. This time, she was the one who gripped his wrist. "That's all I mean. I won't be with another until we decide where this goes."

Finally, a wry smile curved his lips. "You mean you're not willing to swear lifelong fidelity before we have sex?"

"Absolutely not." Lynia quirked her brows. "For all I know, you're terrible at it."

"Perhaps." He pulled her against him with a growl. "Though a healer *does* learn every part of a woman's body."

Gods of Arneen.

Lynia shoved against his chest, walking him backward until they reached the tangled mess of his bed. Well, it was about to get more disordered. She'd had enough of denying her attraction. She was ready to take.

He fell back on the bed, and she landed atop him with a soft *oof.* Certain of her actions now, Lynia tugged the band from his hair and fanned the flames of it across the sheets. Gods, she'd longed to pull that knot free so many times, but she hadn't let herself think about it. Now she could bury her hands in the mass while she devoured his mouth.

Lial tugged at the fabric of her dress, and she shifted absently, letting him draw it up her body as she kicked off her shoes. She certainly wasn't cold now. She could walk outside in the nude, and the ice would melt beneath her feet. Less fabric was a good thing. She sighed in relief when he tossed the dress away.

Abruptly, he flipped them over, rising above her in the soft glow of the mage lights. Lynia tried to draw his mouth back to hers, but he trailed his lips along her throat instead. Her breath hitched as he found each tender pulse point with unerring accuracy. Then his hand slid up her waist and closed around her breast, making her moan.

It didn't take long to realize that he hadn't been joking. He found her every sensitive spot and savored it. No caress wasted. His fingers slid unerringly to each crest and hollow of her body that gave pleasure, his mouth following behind, until she could barely remember her own name.

Tears gathered in her eyes at the focused reverence he showed her. If she hadn't known how he felt before, she would have now. And her body cried out for him.

Only him.

Frenzied, she pulled his tunic off, so quickly it almost tangled in his hair. With a huff of laughter, he helped her, then leaned back to shed his pants by himself. In haste, thank the gods. She sat up and slid her hands up the firm plane of his chest and down the defined muscles of his arms, formed not by fighting but by saving.

Unable to resist, she kissed a path across Lial's warm skin and trailed her fingers teasingly down his stomach until she could wrap her hand around the hard length of him. With a groan, he pushed her gently back to the bed and levered himself up on his elbows.

"You strain my control," he said, voice tight.

She smiled. "Good."

Lynia wrapped her legs around his hips and pulled him to her, no clearer invitation than that.

Which of course meant the stubborn man had to pause.

He braced himself above her with one hand, the other sliding along her hip and around to her spine. Lynia frowned in confusion

until the beautiful flow of his magic loosened the tension in the muscles beneath his hand. Gods, he couldn't even make love to her without worrying about her back.

Instead of the usual annoyance, a giddy warmth gathered in her chest. She reached for him, her fingers tangling in his hair as she brought his mouth down to hers for another kiss. And as his tongue danced with hers, Lial entered her in one sure stroke. She cried out, her back bowing. Perfect. How did he manage to find the exact—

Then he started to move, and she gave up on thinking at all.

25

Apparently, Lial had been wrong about the type of memories he would form with Lynia this day, though only time would tell if they would always bring joy or fade to bittersweet heartache. He gathered Lynia closer to his side and resolved to let the future figure that out for itself. For now, he could savor the feel of her soft skin against his and the way her pale hair tangled around his arm. He could close his eyes and let his heartbeat drift with hers as she slept.

Truly not an outcome he'd expected from the gift of a potion—one that hadn't even been used.

Not that he'd dared to imagine, outside of dreams, that he could be with her like this. He still couldn't quite fathom it. What had she said? That it had just happened? That she'd stopped fighting? There was comfort in knowing the attraction hadn't been as one-sided as he'd believed, but she'd made it clear that this was curiosity, not automatic commitment.

And he would give her everything.

She was right, though. The best relationships were formed rather than forced. Not even soulbonds always worked out, and not only because of death. Aris was proof enough of that. The man's potential soulbonded had held him captive and tortured him for years trying to coerce him into a bond. No soul link could ever cancel out such a vile betrayal.

In Lial's case, it was better to follow Lynia's lead. She'd had far less time to recover from Telien's death than Lial had had for Aralee's, and even after more than fourteen hundred years, he still felt the ache of it. Lynia deserved to process her loss at her own pace. If he tried to hold her too tightly, he would lose her, too.

Then he would truly be alone.

"What's wrong?" Lynia mumbled against his chest.

"Nothing."

She huffed. "Then why have you gone tense?"

Clechtan. She was right—his hold on her had tightened. Lial sighed and admitted the truth. "I told myself to savor the moment and then talked myself around to worrying."

Lynia wriggled around until she was draped more fully across his chest, her chin propped on her forearm as she stared at him. "I'm afraid I've been careless with you. I suppose you might regret—"

"No." He stroked his hand down her hair where it flowed across her back. "I would never regret this. You may purge that fear from your thoughts."

"Yet you're concerned I'll hurt you," she said, frowning.

Lial tugged gently at her hair. "I am not, for my pain would not be your fault. You've made your expectations clear. My emotions are my own to handle appropriately."

She tapped her finger against his chin. "Stubborn man. You know what I mean."

He studied her for a moment, trying to put his feelings into words without making a mess of it. "Don't we all fear hurt? Yes, that's part of my worry. But we both know that happiness isn't a

guaranteed eternal. I think that was at the heart of my musings. Of course, I was also considering how sound your reasoning is on the forming of relationships. I *do* plan to enjoy our exploration once I accept my good fortune. I'm not accustomed to such blessings, so you'll have to give me time to adapt."

Lynia smiled, and the lightness of her expression stole his breath. He hadn't seen her look so carefree in more years than he could count. If he could, he would ensure her life was always filled with such moments.

"That's good," she said. "But before I go exploring again, I need food. It has to be nearly dinner."

He glanced at the water clock on the wall near the bed. "So it is. We can request food here."

Her smile widened. "Afraid to face the family?"

"*Your* family will be insufferable," Lial grumbled, though in truth, he'd long thought of them as his family, too. "And that's not counting our guests. Gods help us if Fen is back. Maddy will be bad enough."

Lynia sat up, running her hand down his chest in a teasing stroke before springing to her feet. "You can glare them all into submission. Come on. I want to gather a change of clothes and a few other things if we're returning here after dinner. I imagine you'll need to stay close to Caeleth tonight."

It took him a moment to get moving, and not just because of her tormenting caress. She wanted to sleep here? With him? Lial scrubbed his hand across his face and forced himself from the bed before she caught sight of his chagrin. Of course, she meant with him. Gods, his brain was a muddled mess.

They were going to slay him at dinner.

After he'd picked his way along the icy trails for nearly a mark, Aris had believed he'd conquered the anxiety sparked by the sight of the mage's surgery. He'd been wrong. Unfortunately, he hadn't realized that until they'd begun their mission. Now with each wingbeat Kezari took through the frigid air, his muscles grew more tense, and his heartbeat increased its pace. Had it been too much to hope that his mind was healed enough to resume normal duties? He'd completed a difficult mission on Earth, by the gods. Why would searching for Korel throw him into such a state?

Maybe he could never be repaired.

"You are not broken, skizik," Kezari said softly into his mind.

"Easy for you to say."

"Yes," she agreed. *"We're connected. Very easy."*

Aris rolled his eyes at the back of her neck, the scales flashing gold in the light of the rising moon. *"Then why am I so near to losing control?"*

She hesitated. *"I cannot say."*

"Naturally."

"No. I cannot." Kezari banked to the right. She'd almost reached the next area of their search, and then there would be no time to ask. Fortunately, she continued without prompting. *"There's something odd surrounding your magic, but I can't access your power myself. I notice you are more upset after you've used it."*

His heart slammed against his ribs. Was there an anomaly in his magic? Some poison he'd picked up from when he'd helped on Earth? Quickly, he pulled his power forth, letting it flow through him. Millions of insects sprang to life in his mind, followed at once by every conceivable mammal and reptile within a few marks' flight of the area. He muted that information at once, shifting his focus to his own body.

He found nothing amiss.

"*I didn't say you,* skizik," Kezari muttered wryly. "*It felt more like…a sense? Like a daeri you can't quite smell. But you get a hint. A suggestion on the wind.*"

Great gods. Was she ever not hungry?

Kezari huffed. "*That was not the reason for the image.*"

Before he could respond, they reached the spot Inona had chosen to search next. She and Delbin had traveled through the local portal to meet Lord Morenial at Oria after scouring Braelyn's grounds with Fen. But since Fen was a stranger to their world, Lyr had not allowed him to join the search around Oria. A relief, to be honest. Aris liked Fen well enough, but he would have been one more person to keep an eye on as they tracked through the wilderness.

Aris flexed his power once more, narrowing his focus to larger mammals before his sight became overwhelmed. Almost at once, he found Inona, Delbin, and Koranel, along with three others he couldn't identify.

"*Are the people with you friends?*" he sent to Delbin, the only one save Ralan with strong enough telepathy to reach him in the air.

"*Yes. Lord Morenial and two of his scouts. We're sweeping to the southeast. Give us a direction if you sense something.*"

Aris made note of the unique essences of the other three so he wouldn't mistake them for enemies. Then he swept his senses outward, searching for someone who didn't belong. Their attacker might have a cloak to hide their energy signature from detection, but it wouldn't deter a life mage. Aris might not know *who* he'd found, but he could sense the presence of someone living. The others need only check to see who it was.

An exacting process. Find people in the woods, direct Delbin to the location, and wait to see if they discovered the intruder. Kezari

had to circle back twice since the others couldn't walk as quickly as she could fly. Five times, Aris sensed people below—a handful traveling between estates or visiting friends in another section of the woods, and one small group in an open camp. All visible, and none of them Korel.

Suddenly, Aris's hands started to shake, and he gripped the pommel of the small saddle keeping him steady. A wave of dizziness hit, forcing him to tighten his hold further. Kezari cast a concerned glance back at him, and her wingbeats slowed.

"Skizik?" she asked.

He closed his eyes and fought against a surge of nausea. Sharp fear coated his tongue, his very mind threatening to revolt from the all-too-familiar flavor. Why? Why? There was nothing here that should bring back the past. If his magic was trying to tell him something, then what?

A flicker of life filled his senses. "South," he whispered aloud.

Kezari seemed to hear him, her path shifting more south than east. Something was…wrong there. Aris squeezed his eyes together tightly and did his best to fight down his body's response long enough to focus. A person, he thought, their essence odd enough to give him pause. Could it be the cloak? He sent what information he could to Delbin before slumping forward to rest his cheek against the base of Kezari's neck.

There was something wretched about the person below—and they would have to find out what.

Although Aris and Kezari were missing from dinner, the table was as full as usual when Lynia and Lial entered—not quite late, but nearly. That meant, of course, that their arrival was unmistakably

noted by everyone. And though they'd both bathed, dressed, and straightened their hair, it was clear from the stifled grins and raised brows that they weren't fooling anyone.

Lynia smiled serenely and took her usual seat, nodding at Maddy who sat to her left while Lial took the open place at her right. Fen sat beside Maddy, then Anna after him. But that realization dampened some of the glow her time with Lial had brought. Last she'd heard, Fen had gone out with Aris and Kezari to hunt Caeleth's attacker. Had Korel been caught? Had something happened?

A point Lial made almost immediately.

"I'm surprised to see you here, Fen," Lial said. "Without the others on your mission."

Fen shrugged. "They shifted to Oria, and apparently there's some etiquette involved since I'm not a guest there."

"That's true," Lynia offered, her worry easing. His return hadn't been caused by another problem, then. "It would have taken far too much time to introduce you to Morenial, and it would be rude to send a foreign prince to his lands otherwise."

That drew a wince from Fen and a chuckle from Maddy. "Don't remind me."

Lynia relaxed as the focus shifted from her and Lial to the search for Korel. They could very well make it through this dinner unscathed by jokes and teasing if everyone remained preoccupied. Letting out a relieved sigh, she accepted the basket of bread from Lial, and the look he gave her when their hands brushed had heat searing through her.

"So," Fen said, an alarmingly casual tone to his voice. "What did you do this evening, Lial? It's been a while since Maddy returned from helping with Caeleth."

She could swear she heard a low growl from Lial, but his

expression was neutral when he glanced at Fen. "I was unaware you were so concerned with my activities. Very thoughtful of you."

Fen smirked. "I'm known as a thoughtful guy."

"Right," Maddy drawled, laughter dancing in her eyes.

Then she gave Lynia a quick, conspiratorial wink.

It seemed the young woman wouldn't tease them openly. Unfortunately, she was in the minority. On the other end of the table, Arlyn leaned toward her, ducking in front of Kai so she had a clear view.

"I stopped by the library to see if you needed help with research, but no one was there." Arlyn grinned. "I suppose you were working with Lial."

Beside Kai, Selia nodded. "Anna and I went by, too, with the same result. Very curious."

Poor Anna turned red, an interesting contrast to her blond hair, especially with the blue tinge near the roots. "Umm. Yes."

Lial had Iren and Eri to his right, a buffer from Cora, Ralan, and Meli. Probably a good thing with Lial's sharp tongue. He couldn't see Ralan's satisfied expression, one akin to Kezari's after she'd eaten the last slice of *daeri*, and chide the seer for his probable interference. But even if Ralan had been manipulating them in this direction, Lynia couldn't be angry at him.

Not after such pleasant results.

Though she'd been initially embarrassed by the pointed comments, Lynia decided she was too old to let it bother her. She was hardly in her first century of life. She'd had her share of lovers before meeting Telien, and if she and Lial didn't stay together, perhaps she would have plenty more. No shame in that. Besides, there was a certain delight in watching her son pretend not to notice the undercurrents of the conversation.

Especially when Meli spoke just after Lyr had taken a sip of wine. "I believe one of the books I helped Lynia find had an extensive section on anatomy. Perhaps that's what they were studying in the healing tower. Relevant, I imagine."

Lyr made a sound between a choke and a sputter, almost spitting out his wine before gaining control—at great cost, if the subsequent coughing was anything to go by. The others laughed, except the children, who looked up from their own conversation with befuddled expressions, and Lial, who lowered his head to rub circles around his temples. But Lynia couldn't help it—she joined the laughter.

Lial gave her a droll look, but his lips curved up slightly. *"I'm glad one of us is immune to teasing,"* he sent.

A shiver went through her at his mental voice and the emotion that rang through it, a tender counterpoint to his wry expression. *"We're both old enough to handle it, although you've been quieter than I expected."*

"Honestly?" Lial lifted his glass, hiding his wicked smirk from everyone but her. *"I'm too relaxed to formulate a properly scathing reply."*

Her heart pounding in her ears, Lynia cast her gaze down to her plate and focused on spearing a *nesel* before the heat of his words were reflected on her face. She might have found amusement in the teasing, but that didn't mean she wanted to encourage more of it. Her poor son deserved a break, if nothing else.

"Lady Lynia, I hope you remember what I told you about getting your work done," Eri said suddenly, catching Lynia's immediate attention.

At first, she thought the little girl had somehow joined the others in their joking despite her age, but there was nothing but earnest resolve on the child's face. Aside from Arlyn's quickly stifled cough and Selia's twitching lips, the comment drew little reaction—not even from Ralan, who stared thoughtfully down at his plate.

That didn't mean there wasn't more to her words than it seemed, however.

Lynia clearly hadn't studied enough today.

"I do, Eri," Lynia said. "Thank you."

Eri frowned. "I'm not sure what exactly you're supposed to do. You need to take books to the healing tower with Maddy and her mates, but my sight is blocked after you step through the door. I don't even see the same sleeping image. I…"

The little girl's words trailed off, and her pupils went wide and eerily fathomless. Her odd comment had finally drawn attention, but the blank shock on her face had Cora reaching for the child's arm. Not Ralan, though—he bore a more contained version of Eri's expression.

"Eri?" Cora asked.

The girl didn't move, not even when Iren patted her other shoulder. Lynia peered at Lial to gauge his reaction, but his expression as he watched Eri was more thoughtful than concerned. Likely not a physical ailment, then. She must be having another vision.

Suddenly, Ralan's hand slammed down on the table. "Fuck!"

"Isn't that usually my line?" Fen muttered beneath his breath before Maddy jabbed him in the side with her elbow.

Ralan didn't appear to notice. His focus went straight to Lyr. "Close down Braelyn and Oria. No one in or out. You'll have to send someone to Oria to retrieve Korel, though I'm not sure if it'll be dead or alive."

Lyr nodded, already standing. "I take it the futures shifted?"

"We should have sent Selia with Aris," Ralan said tightly.

Even Lynia heard Selia's gasp. "Aris?"

"He will be fine." Ralan slid around Cora's seat to stand behind Eri. As he settled a hand on his daughter's shoulder, he glanced at

Lial. "Summon Tynan immediately. Then whatever you're going to do with the blood Fen brought, complete it in the next couple of marks. Eri couldn't see that, but I did, since it involves the plague. You'll be needed at Oria after that."

"I should go with him," Kai said.

Ralan shook his head. "You are not prepared for what is to be found there."

"What is to be—"

"Later," Ralan snapped. "Megelien placed Eri in a trance when that wave hit. Once she wakes, I'll take her to our rooms and return to advise. The futures may shift further."

So that was why the child's face had gone so blank. Lynia might have relaxed, but in this case, knowledge did not bring solace. Not at all. If the goddess had stifled Eri's vision, there must have been an abrupt and terrible shift she wouldn't be able to handle. That was not good news.

As it was, poor Iren had heard more than he should have. Pale as the moons, he looked between Eri and his mother with wide eyes. "I could...I could sit with her. If that's okay, *Onaiala*? Then she wouldn't be alone while the adults handle...whatever is happening."

Though visibly shaken, Selia nodded. "Thank you, Iren. That is thoughtful."

Iren was eleven, five years older than Eri, and his growing maturity showed as he stared up at Ralan. "What can I tell her? I suppose I shouldn't mention a...a plague. Even though elves don't..."

"Tell her we're chasing the assassin, which is also true." Ralan hesitated. "I understand you bear some of your father's life magic. If you sense something off about any of us, prevent our entry. Including myself or Cora."

Lynia's chest tightened at the barely leashed panic on the boy's face as he gave his assent. He was far too young to bear such a command, but he would follow through. He'd used fire magic to defend Arlyn not long after he'd moved to Braelyn. As dearly as he cared for Eri, he would do no less for her.

Eri began to blink, and a confused whimper slipped through her lips. Ralan swept her up into his arms at once. "Hush, love. I'll take you to our rooms."

"*Onaiala*, too?" Eri mumbled.

Cora pushed away from the table with a questioning look, but Ralan shook his head. "I believe she is needed here. Iren wants to play, though."

"Oh," Eri whispered. "Good."

Without another word, Ralan strode from the room, Iren trotting behind.

Lyr speared his hands through his hair and sighed, the tired, resigned sound twisting Lynia's insides. "Meli, Arlyn, and Kai, you should join me."

"What about the rest of us?" Selia asked.

"To be honest, I'm not sure," Lyr answered. "Ralan didn't tell us what was about to happen, precisely. I would advise waiting here for his return while we close down the estate. Except for those helping Lial and my mother, of course."

As Lyr helped Meli to her feet, Lynia stood and did her best to shrug aside her shock. She'd sensed they were running out of time, and apparently, she'd been right. Now, she needed to gather her books and finish the research to the best of her ability.

At least they'd all had a brief moment of happiness.

26

Aris cursed when word came back from Delbin—a mental scan hadn't revealed anyone where Aris had indicated, and the scouts who'd observed the clearing reported it empty. Yet despite that, the person's twisted lifeforce—a sickening blight—remained unchanged to Aris's magic. If it wasn't Korel, it was someone else keeping themselves hidden from view. They would have to be confronted.

And since Aris was the only one who could sense them, he would have to do it—an unfortunate necessity.

"I hope you can land both quietly and close," Aris sent to Kezari, his mental voice trembling like his hands. Every moment spent near that perversion of nature strained his control until it threatened to snap. *"I need to finish this before their presence drives me mad."*

Kezari hummed her assent. *"Send me an image of what you see."*

Forming as clear a picture as he could, Aris pushed the visual into Kezari's mind, and she let out a hiss at the wretched, black and red throb of energy pulsating below. Sick and unnatural. He hadn't felt anything so wrong since—not since Perim, his potential soulbonded, had forced her presence on him. His whole body shuddered as pain sliced through him at the remembrance. His hands twitched on the saddle, the urge to press his palms against his temples and squeeze all thoughts of her from his brain almost overwhelming him.

But he resisted—at least he wasn't that far gone.

Kezari tightened her circles until they glided above the clearing, but it was so far down that the trees were specks dotting the landscape. If not for his magic, he wouldn't know where anyone was located—provided he could've sensed anything beyond the unholy beacon of madness that suffused his senses now.

"Hold on."

Aris obeyed the command out of instinct, and he was immediately glad he did. It was his only warning as Kezari rolled into a sharp dive. The wind screamed around him as she plunged toward the ground as though hunting a *daeri*, something he'd only made the mistake of being present for once. Aside from the blood, there was the awful shock when she slowed her descent.

No different this time.

Kezari's wings snapped wide, and she tilted to extend her back legs. Aris's already tender stomach lurched with the motion until he had to swallow bile. He wanted to ask what she was doing, but that would be a dangerous distraction during the tricky maneuver.

This was not how she typically landed.

They plunged between the trees without a sound, so fast he barely had time to process the sight. Aris's grip tightened on the saddle a heartbeat before they hit. The crunch-splat-yelp sound of impact echoed through the clearing and resounded against his darkest memories of torture, sending him abruptly to the edge of sanity.

A person, broken and bleeding.

"What have you done?" he gasped into Kezari's mind.

She curved her head around to look at him. *"I finished quickly. Enemy captured."*

"Or dead."

Anger welled up, though it wasn't entirely the dragon's fault. He should have anticipated that she would take him literally and act to help him. But this… Aris took several deep breaths through his nose, reminding himself that this was not the same.

Then the tinny scent of blood reached him, and he gagged.

Not mine. Not mine. I'm not injured, he repeated to himself, over and over until he could beat back the panic.

His body was whole. He wasn't hurt. No one was abusing him.

No one would dare with Kezari ready to eat them.

Eventually, Aris gained enough control over himself to slide down Kezari's back. Though still shaky, he drew his sword in a blaze of green light as soon as his feet touched the ground. The glow danced over the macabre sight of the person crushed into a broken heap beneath Kezari's talon. Oh, gods. His stomach lurched, and he sent out a desperate call to Delbin and more than one prayer to any deity who would listen.

I can do this, I can do this, I can do this.

The hilt of his sword bit into his palm as he eased closer to the person on the ground. Life magic flowed through him from the blade and blended with his own power, a steadying force. Until he scanned the man to see if he was alive. He was, if barely. That wasn't the problem. The sick, rancid energy pooling around him along with his blood?

Not good.

His magic rebelled at the tainted stuff, and he pulled his power back. That didn't stop him from vomiting in the grass. Pure perversion. Unnatural. Deadly. Even the thought of touching that

blood emptied his stomach again.

"Get away from him, Kezari," he whispered.

The others from their group appeared in that moment, the first three unfamiliar to Aris by sight. But not by magic, their essences the same as those he'd scanned before. Unfortunately, Kezari didn't have that advantage. Instead of moving away from their captive, she mantled her wings and whipped her head around to hiss at the newcomers.

The motion shifted her weight, and a terrible squelching sound had Aris turning his body away despite the danger. "They're friends. Allies," he told Kezari. "Stand down."

Only when Delbin and Inona shifted forward did Kezari lower her wings. *"Capture achieved,"* she broadcast to all.

"Holy hell," Delbin murmured, his gaze on the one spot Aris didn't dare to look.

Aris focused his eyes on Kezari's face. "Step back. Now."

She blinked at him. *"It is not wise to release one's prey until they are fully secured."*

"He's not in any condition to escape," Aris said. "And no one should touch him."

Slowly, Kezari eased her body away, and the gasps and blanched expressions of the others told him he didn't want to see what had been revealed.

"That's Korel," a man said, worry and anger lacing his tone. If Aris wasn't mistaken, it was Koranel, the former captain of the guard. "I was supposed to get information from him before he... *Miaran.* We need to know the extent of his plan. Hard to find out if he's dead."

"He isn't," Aris rasped. "Yet."

A man with long blond hair and features similar to Kai's stepped

forward. "I am Lord Morenial, the Dorn of Oria. Our healer is excellent, and she might be able to save him if we can get him there quickly."

A shudder trembled through Aris, shaking him to the bone, and his head spun. He brought his hand to his forehead, a useless attempt at calming the dizzy sensation. At this point, he had no clue if the nasty energy or the scene itself was to blame. Either way, he had to overcome. They didn't need the distraction of an out-of-control life mage. He couldn't be responsible for losing the information they needed by delaying Korel's treatment.

He forced his eyes to meet Morenial's. "Can you transport Korel without touching him?"

"I can fly him there," Kezari said.

Aris's heart pounded as he considered what that would mean—soaring through the sky with the smell of blood blown around them on the wind, the man's horrid energy wafting with it. Every moment would chip away at Aris's control, over himself and his magic. Rogue life energy could do terrible things, even alter people and animals, if not contained or immediately mitigated, and Kezari might be too occupied balancing her delicate cargo to properly shield him if he faltered.

Lord Morenial would have to go with Kezari.

There were so many things Aris didn't like about that, not least of which was being left alone. But it would be best. Already, his magic welled within him in counter to the perversion he could sense, and his hold on it could slip at any moment. He might be able to regain control by the time Kezari returned, provided they removed Korel from the area soon.

"You'll have to come back for me," Aris replied aloud. "I'll try to give him enough energy to survive the flight, but I won't be able

to tolerate prolonged proximity."

"I do not like this, skizik," Kezari complained.

Aris gave her the slightest nod. *"Nor do I, but we both know how close to the edge I am."*

She merely huffed in reply.

Unaware of their conversation, Lord Morenial eased closer. "What can we do to help?"

"Ideally, I'd need access to a waterproof cloak and someone who can levitate objects."

One of Morenial's men slung his cloak from his shoulders, and Inona stepped forward to help with levitation. It was easy enough to direct the scout to stretch the cloak out on the ground and explain to Inona what he wanted. Now, all they needed was for Aris to keep it together long enough to do his part.

"Kezari," Aris said. "You'll grab the bundle and fly toward Oria. Carry Morenial, if it doesn't break some dragon rule."

Her head lowered toward his, her teeth bared in a dragon's grimace. *"That is too far. We are not transport for bipeds, Aris. Only a skizik should ride—"*

"Please," Aris sent quietly. *"You'll need to know where to take Korel. And if there's any resistance, the lord of the estate can only help."*

Her annoyed snort curled heat around him, but she ceased arguing.

"I don't want to, but I will," she sent. And not just to him, considering the lord's wince.

There was no time for apologies. If they didn't hurry, their informant would be dead. Aris crept toward the heap of man as swiftly as he could manage without looking directly at the crumpled form. Then he pointed the sword toward Korel and forced through enough magic to flood the area with green light, so bright he had to

close his eyes until it faded.

Once he was done, Aris braved a scan with his power. The sick energy wasn't gone, but it was lessened, and Korel's pulse was slightly steadier. It was the best he could do against so many severe wounds. He gave Inona the signal and stepped back.

Then he made the mistake of opening his eyes.

Korel hovered in his line of sight as Inona shifted his body to the cloak. The light of Aris's sword coated the deep gashes in the man's side a sickly shade of green, and a memory flickered through his mind. Perim had once slashed him in just that spot. She'd allowed him to be warm that day, no numbness to dull the bite. The chamber had been flooded with light. Not quite green, but—

Aris dropped to his knees, the hilt of his sword slipping from his hand. Frantic, he shoved his palms to his eyes in a vain attempt to block the images. He could fight this. He would not be lost to the dark memories.

Gods, don't let me get lost.

Warmth washed around him. Kezari's breath. *"I'm here,* skizik. *I'm sorry. I didn't think of how this would affect you."*

"Go. Make the others run to Oria before I lose control."

She hissed. *"I will not leave you."*

Aris fought against the memories waiting to swallow him. *"You must. I refuse to cost us this information. Fly swiftly and return."*

A wash of dragon language filled his mind. All swear words, no doubt.

Then she did as he commanded. Voices swirled around him like the wind kicked up from Kezari's wings, but all of it blended and shifted around the memories of Perim's harsh commands. The hiss of the blade. And blood, endless blood.

Aris had no clue if the clearing was empty when his hold slipped

and his power exploded forth.

Lial perched on the edge of a stool while Maddy, Fen, and Anna sat across from him in the spare chairs they'd gathered into a loose circle near the stone operating table. Lynia had her books spread out along the workbench, her focus on her work rather than him or the vial of blood Fen drew from a thick pouch. Lial had to hope she found something if he didn't, because Ralan's reaction had been… unsettling.

Lial shoved the memory from his thoughts and reached out his hand. "If I may?"

"Be careful with it," Fen warned. "If something happens to the Seelie queen's blood…"

Blood was a powerful thing, a tool that could be used against its source. That the queen had granted it at all was a sign of trust.

"I am aware," Lial said, accepting the vial when Fen finally passed it over.

He ran his fingers over the warm, smooth glass before settling it in his palm. Then he closed his eyes and activated his magic, sending his awareness into the blood. The power of it hit him first, the strength of the ancient Seelie queen evident at once. That, Lial ignored. Instead, he focused on the composition of the blood. Namely, anything off.

It didn't take long.

Like a broken bone, the flecks of darkness stood out to his sight, but unlike the normal components of blood, he had no name for them. They reminded him of the specks in Naomh's body, but he hadn't been able to examine those this closely. Considering their suspicions of Meren's involvement, there was a high probability the

similarity was no coincidence.

A more detailed examination didn't help as much as Lial would have liked. What could the little intruders be? They weren't alive, but they might have been once. A hint of magic encased the tiny spheres, maintaining them along with the rest of the blood, but it wasn't the same as the preservation spell.

"I take it your magic is preventing the blood from decomposing," Lial said to Fen. "But there's also a different kind of energy surrounding the dark specks in the blood...magic that doesn't have the same resonance as yours. Remind me when this was collected?"

"It was part of what we drained from the queen while healing her." Fen exchanged confused glances with Maddy and Anna. "I made sure the sample contained the flecks we'd detected, but I didn't sense anything else."

"I thought I sensed energy similar to Meren's caustic water spell," Anna said. "But I assumed that was the speck itself."

Maddy shrugged. "At the time, I was too busy trying to keep control of my healing gift to notice that kind of detail."

Lial scanned the sample again, searching for more clues, but without breaking through the energy surrounding the flecks, there was little else to discover. Except that the queen had been low on essential nutrients, of course, but that was hardly relevant—or unusual, considering they'd had to feed her while unconscious. Many who woke from an improperly cast deep-sleep spell suffered the same affliction, and the healers there had no doubt hesitated to put her under as completely as they should have in case it made it difficult to detect a change in her symptoms.

"You said she was unable to wake," Lial mused. "If these flecks are capable of affecting consciousness, they must be able to cross

the blood-brain barrier."

Lynia spun partly around, one hand resting on a large book spread open on the workbench. "That sounds like something I would read in this text. I don't suppose you learned English from a human scientist? When I asked Arlyn earlier, she said much of this is technical language that she didn't understand."

After handing the vial back to Fen, Lial joined Lynia by the table. His hand found the curve of her waist as he leaned over to examine the book, and for a moment, he let himself relish the feel of her body brushing against his when she eased closer. But he couldn't enjoy it for long. He skimmed the text, and any hint of pleasure fled.

"Much of this is unfamiliar to me," Lial admitted, though one of the illustrations caught his attention. According to the label, it depicted a virus. "This reminds me of the structure of the flecks in the queen's blood."

It looked like an innocent ball of fluff, with patterns highlighted by different colors. But the patterns depicted on the page were different than the ones he'd seen in the blood sample. Lial slid the book closer, releasing Lynia so he could flip through the pages. There was a great deal about the structure of viruses and their methods of cell invasion that he could partially understand, especially with the diagrams and images. But these depictions were for humans, and it was difficult to tell if the terms were unfamiliar for that reason or because their healing methods were so different.

Maddy appeared at his left. "Maybe I can help? I've studied a little of this stuff."

"We don't have much time if Ralan's vision was accurate," Lial said. "But if the source of this plague is truly a virus, I need to understand how it works so I can direct my magic to dismantle it."

Lynia tapped her finger against her notebook. "That theory

matches some of the information that Meli found for me. Remember the account of Tebid Ored? If Bleyiak found out about the viruses they were researching in animals, he might have experimented with them. But I haven't found anything about that by our healers."

She was likely correct. According to Tebid Ored, the primary illness they'd studied had infected animals who had their own primitive magic systems. That would be a good base for creating a sickness to afflict elves. Of course, it wouldn't be the same thing depicted in the human books, but there could be enough similarity to provide some assistance.

"Maddy, would you mind helping Lynia find and copy descriptions of how viruses work and notate some of the language I'm unlikely to understand? Like…" Lial frowned down at the current page. "rDNA? Leukocytes? As much as you can identify yourself."

"Ugh. Definitions." Though the young woman's nose wrinkled at the suggestion, she nodded. "I'll do my best, but I've only studied this a little myself. Guess I should have taken biology class a little more seriously."

"Yes," Lial agreed, but he softened the word with a smile. Then he glanced at Lynia. "What about you, love? Do you mind doing this? I know there is little time, and you're already trying to research the source of the illness and its original treatment."

For some reason, Lynia's cheeks pinkened, but she opened her notebook to a new page and gestured for him to move back. "It's for the same cause. Of course, I'll do it."

"Both of you will need to relocate upstairs," Lial said.

Her eyebrows drew together. "Why?"

"Because I'm going to try to crack open the magic surrounding the potential virus in the queen's blood," he answered, his voice calmer than he felt. Hopefully. "I want you and Maddy shielded.

Fen, too, once he's helped me separate the blood into several vials."

"Fucking hell," Fen muttered behind him. "Crack open the magic? That is definitely going to damage the Seelie queen's blood."

As Maddy and Lynia rushed to gather books and head upstairs, Lial turned to face Fen. The young man had gone so pale he resembled his uncle Vek. "It will not. I plan to divide out a few tiny samples in case I need more than one, then remove the flecks and add them to a vial of my own blood."

A clatter sounded from the stairs, and his feet propelled him forward before he'd had time to process the cause. But he drew to a halt in the center of the room at the sight of Lynia picking up a book she must have dropped. Unusual for her. Then she turned her angry gaze his way, and he recognized the cause.

Worry.

"You will not experiment on yourself," Lynia said, one brow lifting regally.

"I didn't say I would, Lyni." He offered a slight smile, though it only heightened the anger in her eyes. "I won't put the possible virus into my own body, only into a blood sample."

She marched back across the room to face him. "You know very well that is not without risk. The spell placed on those dark specks could follow the energy signature in your blood directly back to you, which is why you won't risk trying this on the queen's sample. I may not be a healer, but I am not ignorant of such possibilities, either. I've certainly read enough healing texts of late. There were a great many pages on the things the unscrupulous could do to someone with their spilled blood."

Lial grimaced. "You're right, but I will do my best to shield against such an event. It must be done. Not only is there an immediate threat

here, but there's also Naomh. These specks of darkness resemble what I found in his blood. If I can determine what we're facing, virus or not, I'll be one step closer to helping him."

Biting at her lip, Lynia stared at him, and for that instant, the room seemed frozen, no word or breath breaking the silence. Then Lynia tugged him close with her free hand, her lips meeting his with quick intensity before she stepped back. Her eyes pierced his as she brushed her thumb along his cheek.

"Take care of yourself or else," she commanded before striding back toward the stairs.

The air left Lial's lungs in a whoosh. He couldn't decide if he should curse or thank the presence of this disease, for while it prevented him from sending the others away and carrying her upstairs, the problem had also brought them closer. But the sooner he eradicated the virus, the sooner he could enjoy his newfound good fortune, so he forced himself back to his worktable.

Time to find his focus.

27

Kezari's shoulders itched with the urge to shuck the foreign elf from her back.

There was nothing wrong with the man, or she would never have let him ride with her in the first place. But he wasn't Aris. She had no bond with this one, and his very presence in the saddle she'd formed for her *skizik* was an offense. If not for the nearly dead weight of the prey she shouldn't have captured, she would have turned back at once.

"There's a tower on the eastern edge of the estate, attached at the outer wall," Morenial shouted, as though she couldn't hear the squeak of a rodent in the grass far below if she wanted to. "That's where our healer resides."

Kezari replied in a quiet, calm mental voice in the hopes he would follow her lead. *"I will land just outside."*

"Thank you," the man yelled.

Her breath hissed out in a sigh, but it was carried away by the wind before it reached him. This was all her fault. If not for her foolish, hasty actions, she wouldn't be on this wretched mission without her *skizik*. How could she lament? She deserved this discomfort for the pain she'd caused Aris. As though summoned, another wave of his anguish surged along their bond, and her very wings ached to beat back to him at once.

She deserved far worse than itchy shoulders.

She should have known better than to attack Korel without speaking to Aris first. If it sounded practical to her, it would probably be a bad idea to the elves. Their traditions were strange and sometimes incomprehensible. Why not incapacitate an assassin immediately? They had two other captives to help find any other allies, didn't they?

Apparently, that was not sufficient.

A few choice curses rumbled up her throat as she circled the stone estate below. Awful place. Who had designed such a plain, blocky edifice? An ancestor of the man on her back, no doubt. If they escaped this disaster unscathed, she should offer her skill with stonework to help the place blend into the environment better. This obvious building would be easy raiding if her kind invaded the Moranaians again.

Kezari had no trouble finding the tower the elf had indicated. She descended carefully, mindful of her cargo. Korel, she held secure, but Morenial would no doubt fall off if she landed too roughly. Unlike Aris. He'd managed to stick to her even at his worst. As it was, her passenger squeezed her shoulders uncomfortably as she beat her wings to hover down to the clearing.

If I toss him, Aris will be displeased, she reminded herself.

She released the bundled man a moment before landing, satisfaction filling her at the thud of his body hitting the ground. Not hard enough to cause more damage, though from the way Morenial scrambled from her back as soon as her talons sank into the ground on each side of Korel, he didn't know that. As though

Solace

she would risk causing Aris more distress with carelessness. Didn't the foolish elf realize that crushing the man as she landed would be no better?

She spotted the elf reaching for Korel. *"Aris said not to touch him."*

Morenial drew his hand back with a frown. "Then how are we supposed to heal him?"

"You'll have to ask your healer," Kezari answered, extending her wings enough to test the air. The breeze was shifting, and a hint of moisture danced on the air. *"I must fly back before the rains hit. It will be ice higher in the atmosphere."*

Kezari didn't wait for assent. He might be some kind of nobility, but despite becoming a citizen of their people, their branching web of rankings still made little sense. Whatever rudeness she might be committing, she launched herself upward, using a hint of magic to assist her climb. Returning to Aris was all that mattered.

Almost grudgingly, Lynia set her notebook on the table and dropped the human-made textbook beside it. She hated being sent upstairs while Lial did his experiment, though she understood the reasoning. She and Maddy needed to analyze sources, and he needed to experiment on the Seelie queen's blood without distractions or concerns for their safety. Even Anna had decided to return to the guest tower rather than stay up here while they studied. Lynia was only surprised Lial hadn't hauled Caeleth up here, too.

"I don't know if I'm going to be as helpful as Lial is hoping," Maddy confessed as she sat beside Lynia. "Delbin should have thought to buy a medical dictionary."

Lynia opened the textbook to the page showing the contents—a pleasingly detailed list including relevant page numbers. "I wish it

had occurred to me, as well. I should have considered the differences between human medicine and elven healing."

"We'll just have to do our best." Maddy leaned over to scan the list. "Let's start here."

Following the line of Maddy's finger, Lynia flipped to the page beside the heading "Virus Structure." Simple enough to understand—until one attempted to read the information on the indicated page. DNA, RNA, capsid… So many words she'd never had cause to learn. Without a deadline, it would have been interesting, but now, she could only grind her teeth and mourn the lack of a dictionary. She tried to read it three times without much success while Maddy considered the text.

"Okay," Maddy began a few minutes later, "I know Lial wanted me to describe all of this with notations, but I'm not sure that's necessary. I mean, we can do that, but a quick description before… whatever is going to happen in an hour would probably be best."

Lynia grabbed a blank piece of paper from the table and slid it beside her notebook. "Good idea."

"The center of the virus has DNA or RNA. I don't think it matters which for Lial's purposes." Maddy ran her finger along a diagram as she spoke. "It's basically the building block of life. The genetic code that defines what something is. That will be coated by a kind of protein. Then there might be another layer of fat and protein called an envelope on top of that."

Though she didn't entirely comprehend, Lynia was able to understand more of the illustration. There was a good chance all of it would make sense to Lial since part of his gift was examining the inner workings of the body. She wrote down the description, then used her magic to copy the picture onto the paper.

"I wonder…" Lynia bit her lip. "It's a risk to disrupt Lial if he has started, but this description might be useful for what he's

doing now. He can try to identify these structures in the sample he's examining."

Maddy nodded. "Fen's not up here yet, so they're probably still separating the blood. Why don't you run that down, and I'll start working on something more detailed?"

Standing, Lynia gathered up the paper and rushed to the stairs. But her steps slowed as she descended, and at the base of the spiral, she halted entirely. To her left, Caeleth slept peacefully in his bed, and across the room to her right, Lial and Fen leaned over the worktable, a rack of tiny vials between them. She couldn't see the magic shielding their half of the room from the rest of the tower, but she could sense it, a low hum that tingled against her skin.

Hesitantly, Lynia sent her thoughts outward, hoping she could still connect with Lial through the shield. He angled his body slightly and glanced her way, his brow furrowing. But he answered.

"Lyni?"

She waved the paper. *"We have a simplified explanation that might help."*

"Hold it," Lial said to Fen before striding over to the invisible barrier and slipping through.

Her earlier worry returned, magnified by the exhaustion she could see in his eyes before he masked it. She would spare him from it if she could. "I was hoping this information might save you time during your experiment. We're going to write out something more detailed, and if we're lucky, we'll find more on how to destroy this if it turns out to be a virus. But this is a start. Maybe this will help you determine that for certain."

"Thank you." His lips tipped up as he took the paper. "If I hadn't just handled tainted blood, I would kiss you. Not until I check myself for contagion, though."

She surprised herself by chuckling. "Of course. I would expect nothing else."

"Is that a bad thing?"

Under different circumstances, she might have poked her finger against his regally lifted brow. "Not at all. Now…if we can't kiss, I suppose we should get back to work. For the good of the world and such."

"Alas," Lial said, lifting the paper. "Thank you again, love. Anything will help."

As had happened earlier, a flush of pleasure went through her at the endearment. He was free with the sentiment this evening, and she found that she enjoyed it. But she couldn't bring herself to repeat it until she was certain of the depth of her feelings. Lial didn't appear to expect her to speak in kind, for he returned to his work with a smile. Maybe he hadn't even noticed what he'd said.

Answers on that would have to wait, though. She had research to do.

Aris shivered so hard his upturned knees cracked against his forehead until he rested his arm between them. Cold wrapped around him from the icy ground below, rising to meet the chill in his heart. He'd defeated the memories, but he felt empty after the battle. Even his energy reserves were low due to the blast he'd released.

There was one good thing about the last part—the pool of Korel's blood had lost the sickly darkness that caused his stomach to roil. He'd used a precious bit of his energy to scan, but while there were broken fragments of something…off, the foul taste of perverted magic was gone. Another quick check revealed that even the remaining pieces were dissolving into nature.

At least something was going right.

He rocked his head against his forearm, savoring some hint of sensation. *I never should have come on this mission.* Months ago, Tynan had warned him that recovery took time and that mind healing was a tricky thing, unpredictable and never entirely complete. Doing this now, while Kezari was already restless, had been a terrible mistake. It had no doubt made her edgy enough to act hastily.

And she wanted to go hunt for other dragons on Earth. Earth, of all places. His heart thrummed at the challenge and adventure of it, but tonight's events shoveled doubt atop the eagerness in a heaping pile—much like the dung left by the giant *bersen* who hunted in the Maedi Mountains. What if he lost control on another planet?

Aris sensed Kezari's arrival before he heard her wingbeats, but he didn't glance up. Not even when her magic flared with her shift to elven form. *"Don't touch me,"* he sent.

A shock of hurt. Then, *"Why?"*

"You must have blood on you. It's tainted."

Warmth surrounded him as she approached. *"I cleansed my body with magic."*

He jerked upright at that. Kezari stood in front of him, no sign of the attack on her thin dress. "Where? When?" he asked aloud.

"As I shifted." Her brows drew together. "Scan me if you must."

"I'll need energy."

The ring of metal filled the air as he pulled his sword, followed by the hiss of the blade's power. There was little within him to meet it this time, but it gave him enough magic to search Kezari and the surrounding area for sickness. She was fine. Unfortunately, the place where she had landed bore the dark energy he'd already come to loathe.

As he stood, prepared to drain himself further to heal the land where the blood had fallen, a wave of power nearly knocked him

from his feet. Overhead, the sky lit to an alarming shade of green. Kezari frowned up at the sky, and a scowl twisted her lips.

"They put a shield over the area. I'll have to coast us low, or we'll be walking."

Aris frowned. "They?"

"It matches the energy of the shielding on Braelyn." Kezari's head tilted. "Curious. Something must have happened if Lyr sealed the region in like this."

He nearly laughed at that. Did he want to know what else had occurred aside from their failure of a mission? At this point, he didn't have the energy for that level of mirth. He needed to purge the dark magic and return to the others, if Kezari could fly them. Who knew when they'd make it back if she couldn't?

Lial took a deep breath to steady himself and lowered the tiny glass stem into a vial of the Seelie queen's blood. He would have to act fast to capture one of those little flakes without taking anything else, and he would have to be careful not to touch the tip of the thin pipette against the vial before he transferred it into the one with his own blood. The slightest mistake could contaminate the sample.

His magic glowed blue through the glass stem, tinging the blood purple. Carefully, he dipped the tip into the liquid and used his magic to gather one of the specks. Or tried to. His first few attempts were not ideal, the dark flecks fleeing like same-sided magnets. But he was patient, and soon he'd managed to pry one free and transfer it to the other vial.

With a quick twist, he sealed the first sample with a cork. Then he eased his magic away from the glass stem, allowing the potential virus to float free. If he'd been expecting something to happen

immediately, he would have been disappointed. Whatever force prevented the particle from dissolving appeared to keep it inert in his blood.

Fascinating.

What was the activation point? Something had to trigger it to cause illness. Frowning, Lial probed the fleck with his magic, tentatively at first. Power wrapped the darkness so tightly he couldn't discern the details of what hid beneath. If he had any hope of discovering its inner workings, he would have to crack through the spell containing it.

After a quick check of the shield protecting him from magical rebound, Lial pushed more healing magic around the tiny mass. It…hummed. But not audibly. The vibration trembled through his magic, growing in force until his teeth clenched, but he didn't relent. Instead, he increased his power, mimicking the way the energy in the body would intensify to eradicate foreign bacteria.

It didn't work the way he expected.

Oh, the outer shell of magic cracked and dissolved, revealing what was inside, but when the potential virus clarified to his inner sight, it wasn't entirely organic. As Lynia's note had mentioned, there was an outer casing—one made of more than fat and protein. There was magic woven into the mix, shielding the inner core of *inai*, the builders of life. DNA, human healers apparently called it, though how they'd found a way to see it without magic, he couldn't divine.

In truth, Lial hesitated to use the word *inai*. This truly was a virus, and there was no life in those. Nothing built. This was a parasite that used living cells to reproduce, leaving destruction in its wake. But it didn't latch onto any of the cells in the blood sample. Did it need to feast on the cells inside organs and tissue?

He shifted his focus to the blood's response. Magical beings had distinct immune systems, and Moranaian elves were particularly attuned to eliminating harmful bacteria. Their bodies detected viral invaders, but the primary response was to increase energy at the point of invasion, even if the elf in question was low on magic. That response was so strong he didn't know any healers who'd had time to study viruses.

With the blood in the vial shielded from his energy, the cells inside couldn't muster that type of response, so Lial added extra energy himself. Rather than dissolving, the outer layer of the virus absorbed the magic. Then it latched onto one of the helper cells and began to replicate.

What in Arneen?

Lial experimented with decreasing and increasing energy levels, observing the virus's response. This was different than the illness that had afflicted Fen, though the magic had a similar flavor. Had Kien been experimenting with this after poisoning Earth's energy fields, or was this alteration the Sidhe lord Meren's work? Probably the latter, since this sample had come from the Seelie queen.

Flooding Fen with healing energy had eliminated his mystery illness. Would this virus be destroyed if Lial increased the magic to higher levels? Certainly worth trying, but it would be the last experiment he could do if it worked. He didn't have time to take another speck from the other vial and free the virus from the spell encapsulating it. So he lessened the energy again, curious to see how low magic could go before replication ceased. The *inai* certainly appeared to flounder with less energy. How far could he take it?

Lial had just risked removing his energy from the sample completely when Ralan's voice broke through. *"Lyr is about to contact you. Answer promptly."*

Honestly, had Ralan thought he wouldn't answer when there was a possible emergency? *"I would not—"*

But of course, his annoying cousin was gone.

Only a breath later, Lyr's mind nudged against his, requesting mental speech. *"Yes?"* Lial sent sharply.

"Clechtan, Lial. I would ask what's fouled your mood if I had time. But I don't. You're needed at the healer's tower at Oria."

Before the last sentence was complete, Lial had already started checking the seals on the blood samples and securing them in a magically locked chest. *"What happened?"*

"According to Morenial, Aris nearly lost control, and Kezari swooped down on Korel, injuring him before they could get information." Lyr hesitated. *"Aris said something about Korel's blood being tainted, but the healer at Oria is attempting to save him anyway. She needs additional help."*

"You contacted Tynan?" Lial asked.

"The head priest gave Tynan leave to come, no limits. He should arrive as soon as he is finished with his current patient."

Before he left, Lial rushed over to check Caeleth—which reminded him. *"Put extra guards on this tower,"* he sent to Lyr. *"Ralan said we could have trouble from Caeleth's family if he is not guarded, as more harm might befall him."*

"Of course. Is Laiala still there?"

"Upstairs with Maddy. I assume she'll return to the library."

"Probably so. Be careful of the ice on your way over," Lyr added. *"And hurry."*

Lial gave his assent and then cut off the link. A quick scan of Caeleth's injury revealed no concerns, so Lial reinforced the sleeping spell before heading for the stairs. So much had changed in the brief time since he'd been called away for Naomh. Everything had shifted between him and Lynia, and Lyr's message or not, Lial

wouldn't neglect to apprise her of the situation this time.

Even by himself, he was no longer alone.

28

As the door closed downstairs, Lynia gathered up her notes. "While Lial heads to Oria, I'm going back to the library. With any luck, we'll have more books from the Citadel. I have to find the link I'm currently missing."

Maddy placed a marker in the textbook and closed it with a thud. "Maybe the historical information won't be necessary now that Lial has figured out what the illness is. There's probably a magical way to break a virus, and if anyone can figure it out from the information in this book, it's Lial. His ability to delve into the body is crazy strong, and we've already given him knowledge on the virus's structure."

"No." It was tempting to concede that point and cease searching, but Lynia never had been the type to give up on difficult-to-find facts. "Meli's runes pointed us toward Abuiarn and Rrelen for a reason. Considering the emphasis Ralan placed on my help, it's imprudent to neglect such clues."

"You're right." Maddy stood, and her hand knocked the book against the ring Lynia had noticed the other day. Smiling, the younger woman lifted the delicate metal band. "Fen was right. This is pretty. He's really hoping Lial will let him…"

When Maddy's voice trailed off, Lynia frowned. "Let him what?"

"Ah. Play with placing an enchantment on the stone," she answered, setting the ring carefully in the center of the table. "Fen has started learning new techniques from my father."

Lynia couldn't dismiss the odd look on the young woman's face. "Is there something I should know about the ring?"

"Of course not. At least, I don't think so. I only know what Fen told me," Maddy said, her words tumbling out quickly. "He said it was a random gift from a patient. Fen thought Lial should repurpose it since he's not a girl. Lial, that is. Not that Fen is a girl, either."

A gift from a patient. Lynia smiled, relieved despite herself. Notwithstanding Maddy's strange demeanor, the explanation had the reassuring feel of truth. She was well aware that Lial wouldn't have slept with her if he'd been in a relationship with someone else, but neither insecurity nor doubt befriended logic.

"Let's go," Lynia said. "Perhaps on the way, you can tell me why you're so nervous about a piece of jewelry."

With a wince, Maddy gathered the textbook against her chest and started toward the staircase. "It's not a long story. I was worried you would be upset about a woman's ring on your boyfriend's table. Sort of awkward."

"Boyfriend," Lynia said, testing the word. It was technically part of her mental English dictionary, but it was such a strange term. "Is it unusual for human women to have male friends outside of romantic relationships?"

Maddy's chuckle trailed up the stairs, but her answer didn't come until they'd both reached the bottom. "It depends on the culture, I guess, but that gets complicated. I don't think it's that odd for people in my area."

"What would you call a boy who is only a friend if the most logical term is taken?"

Maddy smiled. "Just 'friend.'"

"I see." Lynia didn't, exactly, but it wasn't her language to criticize. "Do you need to check on Caeleth before we go back to the library?"

The younger woman's gaze shifted to the bed, and she pursed her lips in thought. "Lial didn't ask me to. I don't want to mess up any spells he might have placed."

Lynia nodded. "I'll summon Elan to stay with him. I don't care if Lial doesn't like it."

"When it comes to dealing with Lial, you certainly have advantages I don't," Maddy said with another laugh.

"Perhaps if I annoy him, I'll be able to distract him again." Lynia kept her voice so mild, it took a moment for Maddy's eyes to widen. "It worked well this afternoon."

Maddy sucked in a breath. "I knew it!"

Lynia merely smiled. "Come on. Work never waits for gossip."

"They don't have to be mutually exclusive, either," the other woman muttered.

But she didn't protest when Lynia marched toward the door.

Lial hadn't been sure what he might find when he entered the healer's tower at Oria, but he definitely hadn't expected to see Alerielle, the ancient healer, kneeling beside a bench in the cramped entry room sewing a gash in Korel's side. Why hadn't she moved her patient to a more secure location? Fortunately, no one else was there except for Morenial, though he had to wedge himself between the bench and the corner to fit.

"Forgive my interference," Lial began, "But don't you have a storage room in the basement that would be a better place to treat someone infected with an unknown illness? We need to get him away from any possible contact with others in case he has the virus I just discovered."

Morenial straightened, concern pinching his brow. "Virus?"

"It's a possibility if Aris detected tainted blood." Lial frowned as the healer's hand wobbled. "Alerielle?"

Her head lowered, but he couldn't see her face. "I have someone down there already."

The whispered words drew a curse from Morenial. "You were to tell me at once about any injury, especially after this latest attack."

"My other patient is…not new." Alerielle tied off the thread on the wound she'd been sewing. "I do not have time to explain. Now that you are here, Lial, perhaps you can help me transport this patient to the upper level."

Uneasiness shivered through him, a sense that what she had to say would change more than he could guess. No use speculating, though. As the other healer stood, Lial skimmed his gaze across Korel, cataloguing his visible injuries. It was immediately clear why Alerielle had called for him. She was a skilled healer, but the number of wounds the man possessed would be difficult for anyone to take on alone, and that wasn't counting what Lial might find with his healing energy.

Together, they used magic to levitate Korel, guiding his body up a flight of stairs and into a small treatment room while Morenial guarded the entry. Lial knew very well this particular chamber wasn't where Alerielle did major healing work—it was generally empty, in fact. Those with minor ailments could wait here if she happened to be too busy to see to them at once, but most chose to remain downstairs in the entryway.

He'd observed Alerielle on more than one occasion, learning her techniques for stitching wounds since she was a master at it. They weren't exactly friends, but they'd compared notes too often for him to believe her actions in this situation were normal. At any other time, he would have challenged her to tell him the truth behind her strange behavior at once.

But not today.

Once Korel was settled on the bed—an unfortunate placement with so much blood to soak into the sheets—Alerielle pulled another needle and thread from the pouch secured on her belt. "I stopped the worst of the internal bleeding, but if you could repair his broken ribs while I close this other gash, I would be grateful."

"Of course," Lial answered, shifting to the other side of the bed at once.

It was strange not to be in charge, but he didn't mind deferring—until he did a deeper scan of the patient. Flecks of dark magic like the ones in the Seelie queen's blood filled the man's body, and the spell that had kept the virus inert inside those specks had been cracked open in quite a few places. Where he detected remnants of Alerielle's healing magic, the virus had escaped its magical containment, replicating in the spots she'd tried to repair. They reproduced sluggishly at the moment, but if he sent in his energy to repair Korel's ribs…

"Wait," Lial said. "You shouldn't be touching him."

Alerielle's brow lifted, but her hands didn't stop. "Impossible while stitching a wound."

"Didn't you sense the darkness in his blood?"

"Of course I did," she answered calmly. "It is unfamiliar. But these gashes require closing. I noticed that my magic did something to awaken the flecks, so I've used as little energy as possible."

Instinct warred with knowledge. He couldn't withhold healing, but he was uncertain exactly what type of magic had destroyed the spell keeping the virus inactive. Would any energy break that barrier? Healing magic specifically? The latter ran counter to his experience treating Fen, and magic hadn't worsened Naomh's condition, either. Even the sample he'd studied hadn't been broken open so easily despite the similarity of the virus inside. If he was wrong about the connection between those illnesses, did that mean they had multiple origin points for the plague?

A nightmare to contemplate later.

So what could he deduce from his admittedly limited experience with the virus? Earlier, adding energy to the sample had caused the *inai* to begin replicating. Taking over the blood. The more he'd added his magic, the more stringent the illness had become. Now, Alerielle claimed her magic had done something similar. They'd also used their power to levitate the man, but there was no sign the virus was active everywhere that type of energy had touched. That suggested healing magic might be the trigger for the virus.

His energy might do more harm than good.

For the first time in centuries, he couldn't decide what to do next.

"If healing magic activates this, then repairing his ribs with energy will release more infection into his blood, but we cannot leave him so broken," Lial muttered.

Alerielle tied off the thread and trimmed away the extra. "In all my many millennia, I have never seen a virus. Surely it isn't worse than the trauma that dragon caused."

In truth, Lial couldn't answer the implied question. This was something completely new, beyond the illness he'd purged from Fen or noted in Naomh. It wasn't even exactly the same as the darkness in the Seelie queen's blood, though that came close.

Could Korel have a version of the virus found in the queen? He was a Moranaian elf, not a Seelie Sidhe. How much of a difference would that make? There were too many unknown variables, and Lial had far too little time to discover them.

Lial rubbed the heel of his palm against his forehead. "I don't know."

He needed information.

He needed Lynia.

By the time Lynia reached the back entrance, she almost wished she'd stayed in the healing tower. The *sonal* had done their best to spread warning of the shield being raised over the estate and surrounding lands, but there was still an air of near-panic among the populace. She'd been stopped with questions by three of their household assistants, a gardener, and one of the mages who'd come to help reinforce the ridge. It wasn't that she minded offering reassurance—she simply needed to focus on solving the problem.

Even Maddy, who knew the cause of the shield, kept shooting uneasy glances at the greenish light gleaming above the bare tree branches. "How often is this used?"

Lynia opened the door and ducked inside before anyone else spotted her. "It's tested every century or so, but I'm not certain when it was last used for any kind of problem. Perhaps the attempted raid a few millennia ago in Lyr's grandfather's time."

"Someone tried to raid?" Maddy asked as she followed Lynia through the library door. "I didn't think you had that much turmoil here. Assassins aside. And I guess there was that thing with Kai's not-dad. Still."

"There haven't been any wars in at least ten millennia, if that's what you mean. But I'm not sure any society exists without some feuding from time to time. I can find you a book on the raid later, but you'll need to remind me. We have a virus to learn how to destroy."

Maddy gave a sharp nod. "Right."

After setting her notebook on the table, Lynia gathered several books from the stack from Earth and brought those over, too. She'd begun to understand more of the information while working with Maddy, even if much of the technical vocabulary was beyond her. At least now that she'd learned the basics of how viruses worked, she could hunt for information on how they could be killed.

Together, she and Maddy searched through the books, making note of any relevant information. They had to pause to puzzle out the meaning far too often, but after half a mark, Lynia found a helpful passage. The protein layer shielding the interior—that was what needed to be broken so the DNA inside could be destroyed.

"Do humans have methods for this?" Lynia asked.

Maddy frowned. "It depends on the virus. Some can be killed by washing well with soap. Externally, of course. A basic cleansing spell might take care of those. Some need chemical disinfectants or astringents. Otherwise, the immune system has to take care of it. Some viruses aren't destroyed at all."

Lynia tapped her pen lightly against her notebook. "I don't know what to suggest. I suppose I'll write all of this down and let Lial sort it out. I don't like that, though."

If she was supposed to be discovering crucial information as Ralan had prophesied, then why could she find nothing but trails to nowhere? She should be able to understand these concepts, as foreign as they were. She should be able to interpret everything and then provide the answers. Yet here she was, handing Lial a bunch of jumbled pieces to solve. It wasn't right.

"Why do you expect to have the knowledge of a trained healer?" Maddy asked. "I have the healing gift, but I don't understand most of this. Ralan didn't say you had to solve this single-handedly, did he?"

Lynia's shoulders slumped. "No."

Another voice echoed across the room. "Good, because I have books to add."

Surprised, Lynia glanced to the door where Selia had just entered, an armful of books balanced against her chest. "I thought you'd be helping with spellwork."

"Plenty of time for that." Selia placed the stack in front of Lynia. "In fact, I'm going to go check with Lyr now. But I contacted a friend and former classmate at the Citadel, and she remembered the same reference I did. She sent these to me."

Lynia read the topmost title. *On the Folly of Abuiarn: Or, A Study on the Dangers of Mixed Magic.* This was an old tome, and the inscription on the first page revealed it to be a copy of an even older version. A thrill went through her, and her fingers itched to skim through the delicate pages.

This was it—it had to be.

She barely managed to give her thanks to Selia before turning to the contents listing. Scanning the notations, she almost missed the page she was looking for. *Interlopers: The Increasing Problem with Galare*, 433. Her heart pounded as she turned to the right spot. Hadn't Cora wondered if Bleyiak might be Galaren?

As hope and nervousness fluttered in her belly, Lynia began to read.

Kai picked his way carefully along the path to the fairy pond, the sludge from the mages' last attempt to clear the ice sucking at his boots. Here and there, patches had already started to refreeze, and the farther he walked, the worse the problem became. Eventually, the cleared area disappeared altogether. He bent down to attach spikes to his boots so he could continue along the remote trail leading to the pond.

The call had hit him moments after the shield had gone up around the estate. No coincidence, surely. If Princess Nia had been uncertain about how to proceed, walling off the lands surrounding Braelyn would have prodded her into a decision. The question, of course, was the decision itself.

As he approached the fairies' land, a subtle glow filled the forest, the blue light blending with the greenish echoes of the shield high above. Kai had to narrow his eyes against the strength of it. What was going on? There was a constant barrier around the pond, one that couldn't always be crossed, but it rarely emitted such light.

Unfortunately, it didn't take long to solve the mystery once he'd reached the usual entry point. The shield around the fairies' land burned bright and solid, so thick Kai couldn't see through. Whatever the princess had to say, she wouldn't be delivering it to him inside her realm.

Or at least, not with him inside. The barrier wavered, opaque easing to nearly transparent, and the princess appeared on the other side. Though sympathy lined her expression, there was also a hard resolve there that told its own story—especially combined with the shield.

"Good evening, Princess Niesanelalli," Kai said, bowing slightly.

"Forgive the rudeness of this greeting," the princess replied, her voice echoing hollowly through the barrier. "We have decided to close our lands until this current danger has passed."

"Am I to assume your seers predicted something dire for your people?"

Princess Nia shook her head. "On the contrary. This virus has no ability to infect us, for it will not take hold in those who shift forms. But there could be other chaos to come. We will be of no aid, but we could sustain harm."

Other chaos? Kai scowled, uncertain if he wanted to ask. But he had to. "What else could there be?"

"It is the same trouble, in truth." Nia studied him for a long moment. "Every event ripples, each swell and dip spreading ever outward. Follow your past trouble to find future cares. If you do not address every grievance, Braelyn will see more bloodshed than it has in millennia. As will other places, but our seers have less care about examining them."

"I assume your healers will offer no help in this crisis," Kai said, mustering every bit of calm he could find. "Did you call me here only to deliver that warning?"

Her sad, regretful smile was answer enough, but she had the grace to confirm it. "I dared not send such a message broadly. I hope you will not hold a grudge against our people, but our healers have no knowledge of this affliction. We will wall ourselves off safely and provide no distraction."

It wasn't the answer he'd hoped for, but at least they wouldn't have to worry about sick fairies, too. "I will not speak for the Myern in this, but I do not believe he will hold enmity toward you or your people. On the contrary, he will no doubt appreciate the warning you have delivered."

"I hope you are correct," Princess Nia replied. "Myern Lyrnis is a good ally."

Although they bid an easy farewell, worry picked at Kai on the

way back to the estate like the tiny icicles that dropped from the branches above. Address every grievance. What did she mean by that? How far back did this go?

He had a feeling he wouldn't like the answer.

29

One of Korel's broken ribs slipped, slicing into an artery, and the decision was made.

"I don't know what the virus will do after this," Lial murmured, already directing his power to stop the bleeding. "Or if we'll catch it."

Suddenly, Korel began to convulse, and as his limbs flailed, Lial pinned the man's arms down and prayed to Bera he wasn't dooming himself in the process. But it had to be done. Each twitch and tremor did more damage to Korel's barely stabilized wounds. Lial poured magic recklessly into the area around the man's broken ribs to prevent more from slipping and to seal the damaged artery.

Alerielle shifted to Korel's head, and her eyes closed as she used her power to find and stop the cause of the convulsions. By the time his body was still once more, the elder healer's shoulders drooped with exhaustion, and the lines carved into her face stood out in stark relief in the shadowed light.

Her lips turned down. "This may not end well."

Lial nodded, though he wasn't willing to concede. Caeleth's injuries had been dire, too, but he'd survived. Not even the virus made the situation hopeless. So Lial closed out the world around himself and concentrated on the injuries at hand. First, he ensured the artery was repaired. Then he used his magic to reseat the ribs and start the bones mending. With no iron involved, it wasn't long until they were knit enough for him to move on to other fractures.

If Kezari had been there in that moment, Lial might have throttled her, even if it would see him eaten. What had she been thinking to dive on Korel like a raptor searching for its next meal? There were so many breaks, tears, and bruises it would take ages to find and heal them all despite the presence of two full healers.

Lial sighed and shrugged away the sweat from his brow with his upper arm. His muscles trembled from the effort he'd expended, but there would be more. So much more. Because as soon as the life-threatening injuries had been stabilized, he checked again for the virus.

It was everywhere.

Eating away at the lungs beneath the ribs Lial had repaired. Replicating in the organs. Attacking the brain. If this could be killed by pouring in energy like the other versions Lial had treated, then it had to require immense levels of magic. The rib area alone had taken a great deal of power to repair, but the virus hadn't been phased.

"I don't know what to do," Lial confessed, the words burning his throat.

When she glanced up, Alerielle's hand still hovered over the concussion she'd healed on Korel's head. "Nor do I, save this."

"Do you see how the flecks of darkness have spread?" he asked. "Examine them. They have their own *inai* but do not create life."

As soon as she checked for herself, her eyes widened. "Bera bless us. I have no experience with such a thing."

For a moment, Lial allowed the bleak despair to wash over him, growing like the disease he didn't know how to cure. He'd trained for everything he'd believed possible, but he hadn't trained for this. Now, everything relied on the fractured, incomplete knowledge they'd managed to gather before disaster hit. It wasn't enough.

Gods be with him, he had to make it enough—no matter the cost.

"I'm going to see if more healing energy will help," Lial said quietly. "I'll be drained after. Why don't you let me check you for the virus while I am able, and then you can warn the others?"

Alerielle straightened, her shoulders shoving back with a snap. "I think not. I've lived over ten thousand years, young one, but I am hardly feeble. I will help."

"I don't know how this is transmitted. Every moment we linger here brings us greater risk."

"So be it." The other healer's lips thinned. "Though I do ask this. If I should succumb, save my other patient. She has suffered enough."

His blood chilled with the same foreboding he'd experienced earlier. "Who?"

She averted her gaze. "Lady Elerie."

Lial blinked. Then blinked again. He couldn't have heard her correctly. The only Lady Elerie he knew was Kai's mother, dead for more than five hundred years. Allafon had pushed her down the stairs not long after Kai's birth.

"When I realized I couldn't repair her wounds, I placed her into the dreaming," Alerielle whispered. "Then I hid her until Allafon was defeated."

Great gods. She was serious. "Is that why you've been seeking spine healing techniques?"

"Yes."

Lial shook his head to clear it, but the confession still rang in his ears. Though it sounded impossible, it wasn't. He'd seen others

who'd remained in a dreaming state for longer. But for Alerielle to have hidden this from Lady Elerie's sons… There was no telling how they would handle this news. Especially Kai, who'd never had a chance to meet his mother.

"I would not have distracted you with this now," the healer said. "But someone needed to know in case of disaster."

"Indeed," Lial agreed.

He wasn't exactly safe from harm. Despite Ralan's assurance that Lial was unlikely to die, there was a chance he wouldn't escape this healing session unscathed. The prince hadn't Seen Kezari's actions, after all. The futures might have changed for the worse. With that in mind, Lial connected with Delbin, the closest strong telepath he trusted, and passed along the information about Elerie.

Then Lial took a deep breath and got to work.

A Galaren healer—Bleyiak had been a Galaren healer.

The discovery brought a wide grin to Lynia's face in spite of the serious nature of her research. She couldn't help it. She'd had so little to go on that each revelation was its own miracle. Maddy stared at her in confusion, but Lynia didn't explain, lifting her pen to take more notes from *On the Folly of Abuiarn: Or, A Study on the Dangers of Mixed Magic* instead.

Much like Moranaia itself, the colonies of the time had taken in fae from other realms, and political turmoil in Galare had caused an influx on Abuiarn. Bleyiak had come from a noble family, a younger son who'd played at becoming a healer though his ambitions reached higher. He'd wanted power, and Abuiarn had provided the opportunity.

Until it hadn't.

Before the incident with the princess, Bleyiak had met and befriended other newcomers. Tebid Ored, for one. It was unclear how close the two men had been, but Bleyiak must have at least heard the account of Rrelen. This book made no allusions to the meaning behind its title—the reckless blending of a virus from a little-explored colony and the magic used by Galarens had indeed brought folly.

"This is phenomenal. In a horrible way," Lynia said, explaining what she'd learned to Maddy. "Although I have to wonder if he actually released the virus into the energy field. Another book said that 'the Source heaved as it absorbed, and its touch brought perversion instead of renewal.' That sounds more like the poisoned energy Kien used, which harmed mental channels and prevented magic use instead of sickening the body like a disease."

Maddy pinched her lower lip between her fingers for a moment as she listened. "I have to wonder if it's both. Release the two methods at the same time and you have total chaos."

"I wouldn't like to find out." Lynia shuddered. "I suspect the *onraiee* of the time didn't want to, either, as details are sparse on the actual mechanics of the spell or spells used."

"What about treatment?"

"Also annoyingly sparse." After flipping back to the proper page, Lynia skimmed the short passage again. "This mentions the arrival of Healer Emereh, who was summoned by Tebid Ored."

Maddy's brows rose. "Now, isn't that interesting?"

"Very." Lynia ran her finger along the next line. "As is this. 'Emereh devised a treatment to cure the affliction, but many died before it was shared. When the rest were cured, so few remained that the survivors followed Emereh to his home realm.' If I had time, I would search for the descendants of those survivors to see if any

stories remain. Maybe one of *them* wrote down the actual treatment. Although I suppose I may still find it in the last book Selia brought."

"Here's hoping."

Lynia lifted the final tome, the rough leather binding catching against her fingers. The book must have once been quite expensive. Though ancient, the paper still held enough crispness to suggest fine quality, and based on the flecks glinting yellow in the creases of the embossed title, the letters had once been filled with gold foil. Were she to make a copy of this one, she would never be able to bring herself to do a simple transfer to a plain book. This deserved to have a duplicate crafted, gold and all.

The Wayfarer's Trial. A curious title for an account of Abuiarn's fall. An outsider's perspective, perhaps? Lynia searched the cover and the opening pages for the name of the *onraiee* who'd written the work, but she found nothing. An anonymous traveler, then. Well. Whoever it was, Lynia could only pray their adventure had been useful.

Recklessly, Lial drew in magic from the world around him, using a fair amount of his stores to convert the energy to his use. Then he concentrated the power on the worst spot in Korel's lungs. With luck, the virus would react the way Fen's affliction had and die off. Even as Lial repaired the cells already damaged, he monitored the disease's progression.

Viral replication increased at first, and he almost cut off the energy flow. Could this version of the illness be destroyed by healing magic, a force of creation? Lial's very breath slowed as he watched— and prayed he wasn't making a terrible mistake. He added more energy, as much as he could spare.

And waited.

Just before he pulled back, the virus slowed its reproduction enough for hope to build beneath the surface of his worry like the first bubble preparing to boil. Alerielle joined her power to his, then, and some of the shells surrounding the invader's core began to break down, the *inai* within dying beneath the force of their magic. This could work. If they could sweep enough energy through, it would absolutely work.

But bubbles were made to be broken.

They'd only managed to clear one section of Korel's lungs when Alerielle's energy gave out. Panting, the ancient healer braced her hand against the bed, her head dipped low. Normally, Lial would have checked on her, but he was too busy fighting the exhaustion that blew through him in a dizzying rush. He blinked against the urge to close his eyes for a moment's rest.

He did his best to pull in extra power, but the task needed more magic than his body could convert from the natural world. Really, it would take more energy than he possessed at the best of times, and he was far too worn out for that. But he couldn't give up. Though he might faint from energy loss, it would be worth it to try.

"Stop," Alerielle said, her voice rough and strained.

With a shake of his head, denying her command, Lial let his eyes close—not to sleep. It would make it easier to block out the world and suspend thought. To simply be. Then he sent his awareness into his patient.

The bits of virus they'd killed hadn't revived, but the infection hadn't been stopped, either. Outside the small area where they'd overwhelmed the virus, replication had accelerated. *Miaran.* Their power might have destroyed some, but the rest had soaked up the ambient power to fuel reproduction, and thus greater destruction.

There were more dark flecks in Korel's blood than when they'd begun.

Lung function decreased, and the man began to cough violently in a vain attempt to purge the invader. Lial hesitated. If he tried to clear the lungs, it would feed the virus. But if he didn't… He did another scan of Korel and cursed. The damage had spread so quickly while they fought the virus in one spot that there were now countless things to repair. Every organ was headed toward catastrophic failure, and the only tool Lial had—magic—would make it worse.

With his natural ability to regenerate rendered moot by the strength of the virus, Korel would die a terrible death.

Lial jerked back, his gaze flying to Alerielle. She sat straight now, and although pale and worn, her eyes gleamed with knowledge. She'd recognized before he had that it was over, yet even now he struggled to give voice to what they both knew.

He'd failed.

"I have a potion that will ease his suffering," Alerielle said softly.

Lial's stomach lurched, and his hands shook as he wiped his damp palms across his knees. She wasn't talking about pain relief. He had similar potions in his own collection, but he had never had cause to dispense them. Either he'd saved his patients, or they'd died too quickly to require such a thing.

The tincture did ease pain and relax the body, but it also took time to work. It wasn't designed for something like this; it was to aid the elderly in their last days. How long would the virus ravage Korel's body, prolonging a miserable experience and allowing the virus time to spread? It had already reached the nervous system, and soon—

Korel's body jerked, a cry slipping from his lips as the affected nerves fired. A death like this would be akin to torture.

"Magic would be faster," Lial whispered, though everything within him rebelled.

Alerielle studied him for a moment before nodding.

The usual flare of his power was a dull, cloudy blue as it surrounded Korel—this time not to heal. Lial's nails dug into his palms with the urge to pull his magic back, and it didn't matter that the man was a traitor. Even if Korel were to be executed in a few marks' time, Lial still would have healed him.

Lial brought life. It was his calling.

He'd been tasked with preventing this plague, but he was the one taking the first victim.

The weak thread of Alerielle's power joined his. "I'll help," she whispered.

Lial couldn't answer. He could barely handle the feel of his own skin as he grasped Korel's damaged, stuttering heart with his magic while Alerielle took control of the man's mind. Was it murder to bring relief to the almost dead? Lial's head said no, but his soul might never accept it.

He exchanged one last glance with Alerielle, waiting for her assent. Then together, they brought Korel permanent ease.

A state Lial might never find again.

30

Excitement coursed through Lynia's veins as she turned the page to find exactly what she needed—a recipe. If she'd been able, she would have kissed the unknown archivist who'd pulled this book to send to Selia, for although there was no *onraiee* attributed to the work, it hadn't taken Lynia long to figure out the source. This was Emereh's own journal. Emereh, who hadn't been a Moranaian healer at all, at least not exclusively. He'd traveled between realms, studying as much as he'd lent aid.

She skimmed the list of ingredients he'd used in his potion, and each one picked at her memory until realization crashed across her in an avalanche. *Almost all of these things were ordered by Bleyiak.* Not all, but enough that she had to wonder if the man had devised a cure in advance for the very disease he'd unleashed. Quickly, she scribbled the theory in her notebook before pushing the thought aside. She could research the *dree*'s intentions once the crisis was past.

For now, she had a potion to concoct—but it would work best with Lial's help.

"I have something," Lynia said to Maddy. "But I want to see if

Lyr has news of when Lial might return before I go to the healing tower. Do you think Anna would be willing to purify water again?"

Maddy's brows creased in thought. "Probably. I can check. But what did you find?"

Lynia smiled. "The recipe for the potion Emereh used to cure the original virus."

That certainly served to brighten Maddy's expression. The younger woman stood, closing the book she'd been studying. "Then I'm almost certain she will help. You check with Lord Lyr, and I'll check with Anna."

With a quick surge of power, Lynia copied the recipe in her notebook, sealing the ingredients in her memory. But she grabbed *The Wayfarer's Trial* and her notebook anyway before heading for the library door. The faster they could proceed, the better. If she was lucky, she could already have the components prepared and ready for use before Lial returned from treating Korel.

There was no need to knock on the study door this time. It opened not long before she reached it, and Kai strode out, a frown on his face. "If you need to speak to Lyr, you should probably hurry. We were interrupted three times during a simple report."

"Did something else happen?" Lynia asked.

Kai's expression darkened further. "The fairies have refused to help. They only provided one helpful bit of knowledge, aside from telling us to get our shit together. According to the princess, natural shapeshifters are immune."

"Good news for Kezari, if not the rest of us," Lynia muttered. She settled her books against her chest. "Is Lial back? He will want to know."

"We haven't heard anything from Oria yet." Kai ran his fingers through his hair. "Another worry, that. I'm trying not to think about why Ralan didn't want me to go."

Lynia gave his upper arm a quick, comforting squeeze despite the knot of fear his words created in her stomach. No word from Oria was… "Better not to speculate," she said, as much for herself as Kai.

"I *do* have enough to fret over otherwise. I haven't heard from Caolte about my father's health, either. Arlyn says no news is good news, but…"

"I understand." With her own concern for Lial, she more than comprehended. "Let us hope it is good, indeed."

As Kai hurried off, Lynia took a deep breath and entered the study to find Lyr pacing behind his desk. Alone. "Where is everyone?"

Lyr pivoted to face her at the question.

"Meli is speaking with the head of the household's assistants, and Arlyn and Kera are filling in some of the senior scouts on the current crisis," he answered, rubbing at his brow. "I've been answering anxious mirror calls and monitoring the shielding. Cora and Selia went to check on their children, but gods know what Ralan is doing. He has kept himself scarce since heralding upheaval. As usual."

Once again, exhaustion lined her son's face, and it twisted Lynia's heart to see it. Her fingers tightened on the edge of her books as she stopped near the edge of his desk. At least she had a possible solution for the crisis, provided it worked—and she was able to create it.

"I have a potion recipe that might help," Lynia said. "But I need Lial here for optimal effect. Kai said you hadn't heard anything from Oria?"

Lyr crossed his arms. "I haven't."

"*Clechtan*," Lynia cursed. "I'll have to get started without him. I wanted to warn you of a possible request, though. If he doesn't have

all of these ingredients on hand in the healing tower, I'll need you to find them for me quickly."

Her son nodded. "Let me know."

Before Lynia could leave, the mirror chimed, and Lyr groaned—a sound that only deepened when he identified the source. "It's from the Rekel of the Taian branch. Caeleth's father, no doubt. Could you tell me how Caeleth is doing when you reach the healing tower?"

"Of course," Lynia replied. She'd seen the Rekel's temper firsthand, though it had been a few centuries. "I'll go now."

Avoiding conversations like that was one thing she didn't miss about being Myerna. One thing out of many.

Delbin's hands clenched into fists, but he couldn't say the motion was borne of anger. The chaos coursing through him was more complicated than that. Why had Lial chosen him, of all people, to share that revelation with? Now he was forced to wait in the tiny entry room with Moren, withholding information the other man would surely want to know.

Wasn't that a fine twist of fate? For years, Moren had known that Delbin's brother had fallen to Allafon's influence, but he'd never sent word while Delbin was living on Earth. Even now, they hadn't spoken about how Moren hadn't brought Delbin home after Allafon's death. They'd been too focused on the search for Korel for that confrontation. Ironic that Delbin had learned a secret that might even be more extreme.

"I suppose I deserve the disdain in your eyes," Moren said softly from his place by the stairs. "I am sorry about your brother."

Well, damn. Delbin's irritation didn't fade, but guilt was happy to join the party. How was he supposed to keep from telling the

man that his mother was alive when he was being sympathetic? Then again, how *did* a person reveal that someone's mother hadn't died five hundred years ago? That wasn't covered in one of Lynia's etiquette books.

Probably. Those things were surprisingly thorough.

"Now might not be the best time to discuss such things," Delbin hedged, because if they fell too far down the family discussion rabbit hole, there was no way *hey, your mom's unconscious in the basement* wouldn't slip out.

The door opened, and Aris stumbled through, Kezari in elven form close on his heels. The poor guy looked like hell, his face gaunt and his eyes heavy with grief. And though usually unbothered by much of what happened around Braelyn, Kezari was by no means neutral now. She kept casting guilty looks at Aris and then trying to hide her concern, only to glance over again. At least she seemed to realize she'd messed up.

Aris headed toward the narrow bench against the other wall, only to halt halfway there. Yeah, Delbin hadn't wanted to sit in the blood still pooling on the wood, either. But when Aris turned to Moren, it wasn't just disgust on his face—it was fear and revulsion.

"The healer didn't cleanse the spot?" Aris asked harshly.

Moren shook his head. "When Lial arrived, they took Korel upstairs. They're trying to save him now."

Kezari stopped beside Aris, her hand settling on his shoulder. "You are too drained for this."

"Everyone in this room is at risk," Aris said. Ripples of fear coursed down Delbin's back at the mage's stark tone. "The only dark energy I sense in this chamber is on that bench, but that doesn't mean it will stay that way."

"*Skizik—*"

Aris drew his sword with a hiss, green light flickering around the blade. "I stopped having a choice the moment you squished Korel's body into the ground like a waterskin. I don't know why his blood was filled with obscene magic, but it should never have been spilled."

"I am sorry," Kezari said. Her hand dropped to her side, and she stepped back, though Aris didn't appear to notice. "I thought only of you."

"I know," Aris muttered.

Delbin couldn't help but feel sympathy for the dragon, no matter how badly she'd fucked up. He knew what it was like to have a different way of looking at the world. After all, he'd been voluntarily exiled to Earth a hundred years ago at the young age of sixteen and had lived there until recently. He might be Moranaian, but he didn't always think like one.

If Aris felt any of that same sympathy for Kezari, he didn't show it. His focus was on the blood staining the bench and pooling on the floor. The life mage staggered over, his steps uneven, until he was close enough to direct his energy into the blood with a flash that made Delbin cover his eyes.

When the light faded, Delbin blinked to clear his vision, only to see Kezari supporting Aris with her arm around his waist. Together, the two stumbled over to the thin slice of wall beside the door. Gray beneath the warm tan of his skin, Aris leaned against the stone. Then his body went limp, and only Kezari's strength kept him from falling. The dragon woman lowered him carefully until he slumped against the wall.

"Great, now there are three unconscious people in the tower," Delbin said under his breath. "We'll never get Lial out of here."

"What did you say?"

Delbin froze at the harsh question. Dammit. Now he'd done it. Hiding a wince, he turned his head slowly until he met Moren's gaze. "Forgive me, Lord Morenial. I did not intend to speak aloud."

Maybe the extra courtesy would throw the man off. Or not. Moren's eyes bore into him like a tent stake into the ground. "Why would there be three patients in the tower? What do *you* know that Alerielle has kept from *me*? And I recommend you answer carefully. You may receive your missions from Lord Lyr, but you are still a citizen of this estate and therefore under my command."

Delbin wasn't entirely certain whether that was true, but it was a moot point. Lial hadn't sworn him to secrecy, but even if he had, Moren was the highest-ranking person in the room. He thought. Even Lial might technically be lower in rank, though Moren wasn't likely to make *that* challenge.

"I know more than I would like," Delbin replied. With a sigh, he pinched the back of his neck to relieve the sudden tension. "Look, Lial told me… He said…"

Moren straightened, a scowl crossing his face. "Told you what?"

Honest to the gods. There really wasn't a good way to say this. He should have requested to go back to Earth to help with the outpost instead of getting involved in hunting down Korel. "Your healer told him that Lady Elerie is the patient in the basement. She has been in the dreaming until Alerielle could heal her."

For a moment, the words didn't seem to register, but that phase didn't last long. Moren rushed forward, slamming Delbin against the wall. Delbin swallowed nervously at the way the other man's forearm dug into his collarbone just shy of his throat, but he didn't attempt to fight back. Only the truth would get him out of this, and he'd already told it.

"That is foul," Moren snarled. "I made mistakes with your family while I tried to help so many, but none of those errors warrant a lie like that."

Delbin forced his muscles to go lax, resisting the urge to shove the other man away. "This isn't something I made up. I'm only repeating what Lial said."

"He's telling the truth."

The thin, frail voice of Oria's healer reverberated through the room like thunder. Moren's eyes bulged, and the color leached from his face. Abruptly, he stepped back, releasing Delbin so quickly he almost stumbled. Then Moren spun to face Alerielle.

"That is impossible."

The healer leaned against the wall at the base of the stairs, but even with that support, she swayed slightly. "No. When I realized her spine was shattered beyond my ability to repair, I placed her into the dreaming and hid her away. I only brought her here when Allafon was truly dead."

"Then who did my father burn upon the funeral pyre?" Moren advanced on the woman until he was near enough to throttle her the same way he had Delbin. "She was dead. I…I saw her. Didn't you say Kai's crying was because babies could sense the loss of that bond?"

Holy shit. They'd had an actual funeral pyre? Delbin considered the possibilities and winced. At this point, he couldn't summon any of his previous anger for Moren. Delbin might have had a lot of things go wrong in life, but it wasn't as bad as this.

"I lied," Alerielle said, softly but without a hint of regret. "You weren't the only one with allies in this place. A little illusion goes a long way."

Moren's gaze swung from the outer door to the basement stairs, then back again. Indecision, doubt, grief—the emotions shifting

across the man's face were enough to bring pain to Delbin's heart. He was half-surprised the man hadn't immediately bolted to the basement to see his mother, but that was probably the scariest action of all.

Until Moren descended those steps, the truth was a nebulous thing. A theory to be examined. But there could be no denial once he verified Alerielle's claim, and that would change everything he thought he knew about the last five hundred years. Delbin wouldn't exactly be eager to find out the truth, either.

Lial leaned against the table where Alerielle stored her potions and fought the urge to sweep everything to the floor and stomp on it for good measure. None of those vials or bottles had helped them. Useless, as his power had been useless. Could any herb defeat a virus like that? His lack of knowledge had his fingers tightening until the wood bit into his skin.

Finally, he gained enough control to shove away from the table and face the body once more. He'd seen death, of course, but he'd never delivered it. He'd never stopped another's heart, in mercy or in anger. Shame singed his throat and burned through his veins until he scanned his blood out of reflex. No sign of the virus in him, though it was what he deserved after veritable murder.

But what else could he have done? It wasn't just a matter of Korel's agony. There were thousands of people living in and around Oria, and he had no idea how the virus might spread to them. Forcing Korel to suffer a prolonged death would have increased the risk to everyone else. Yet he couldn't stop berating himself for not thinking of another solution anyway.

Lial almost speared his hand through his hair, but he hesitated. He'd cleaned away the blood, but... Holding out his hands, Lial

stared at his palms. Could there be germs on his skin he couldn't see? Would his magic detect the virus outside of his body? He already wanted to scrub himself clean in the hottest water he could find, and he hadn't even figured out what to do with Korel's body yet.

If heat didn't kill the virus, then burning the body might release it into the air. But would burial taint the ground and spread the contagion? There was no protocol for this. He didn't even know what to do about the blood-soaked linens where Korel had been placed. Or the bench downstairs, for that matter.

The bench they'd carelessly left in a room that anyone could enter.

At that thought, he cursed. Had Alerielle realized the same thing? She'd left to update Moren some time ago, but she still hadn't returned. Perhaps someone else had already fallen ill? *Miaran.* Lial ran a cleansing spell along his body again and hurried from the room.

When he reached the base of the stairs, Lial drew to a sudden halt. Moren was nowhere in sight, Delbin slumped against the wall to the right, and Aris was crumpled up beside the door, Kezari and Alerielle kneeling on each side. Green glimmered around the sword stretched on the ground beside Aris's leg, and the flickering light painted the bottom of the healer's robe in eerie blotches.

"What happened?" Lial demanded, forcing himself into motion.

"It is merely low energy," Alerielle explained as Lial reached Aris's feet. "I don't see anything like the poison we found in Korel's body. You should scan, as well."

Lial did, and as Alerielle said, there was no sign of the virus. "How did he come to be drained?"

Kezari straightened, and from the hint of scales flickering across her skin, she was more upset than her soft tone suggested. "He lost

control. I had to carry Korel and Moren here, leaving Aris in the forest. Seeing those injuries…"

One of the life mage's memories flashed through Lial's mind, and he grimaced in sympathy. "He has been unconscious for that long?"

"No." Kezari's gaze shifted to the bench. "He purified the room. Some darkness in Korel's blood affected Aris greatly. In fact, his response to Korel's proximity was what caused me to strike when I shouldn't have. A flood of life magic destroys the bad energy but at great cost."

Life magic destroyed the virus? Lial had known it would work on poisoned energy, since Aris had been the one to heal Fen after Kien's spell had backfired. But the trick hadn't been tested on the virus beneath the magic encasing it.

Curious, Lial strode to the bench, stopping just short of touching the blood. He closed his eyes and stretched out his senses, searching the spilled blood for any hint of disease. Clear, except…there—a few fractured remnants, too damaged to replicate. Any hint of the spell holding it together was gone.

Now he just needed to understand why.

31

Though the night was quiet and calm, two warriors flanked the door to the healing tower. They nodded at Lynia and gestured her through when she reached them. Apparently, Lyr had commanded the guard to be more visible in Lial's absence. It made her more comfortable, actually, with the potential for more assailants out there somewhere. There hadn't been any indication that others were involved besides Korel and Fenere, but nothing said there weren't, either.

The air was cool and still in the workroom, the lights turned low. With Lyr's request in mind, Lynia set her books on the table near the baskets of potions and headed to the bed on the other side of the room. She increased the glow slightly with a hint of magic and bent down to study Caeleth's face, uncertain what she was looking for. What could she say about the young man's condition? That he was breathing? Rekel Osni wasn't likely to be amused by the observation.

Caeleth's coloring appeared fine; in fact, he had a hint more pink to his cheeks than earlier. His chest rose and fell steadily. She lowered the blanket to his waist to examine the bandages and found the fabric clean, no sign of blood. Good. Gently, she tucked the bedding around his arms once more. The cool of the room was refreshing, but it verged on cold. No need risking the man shivering his stitches loose.

"He's sleeping and healing normally, as far as I can tell," Lynia sent to Lyr. *"I'll let you know if Maddy detects anything different when she gets here."*

"Thank you, Laiala. I appreciate your help."

The exhaustion and frustration weighing down her son's inner voice made Lynia want to march back to the study and rebuke Lord Osni into the next millennium, but Lyr wouldn't appreciate the gesture. Nor would it help, in truth. Relations between the nine highest-ranked nobles—three from each branch—could be fraught at the best of times. Lord Osni was second down the Taian branch and Lyr third down Callian, which meant that Lyr was technically lower in rank. But being on the Callian branch, Lyr was in no way under Lord Osni's authority.

Not that the odious Rekel Osni was likely to acknowledge that fact.

With a huff of annoyance, Lynia returned to the workbench and opened her notebook. There wasn't much she could do about annoying nobles, but she could relieve some of her son's stress by starting the potion. Not to mention the help it might provide for her... Lover? What *should* she call Lial now?

Boyfriend, Maddy would have said, but that term didn't seem adequate. Lynia pondered that as she skimmed the list of ingredients and gathered vials and bottles from the shelves. Lial was her friend, and perhaps he could be called her lover, which usually implied the type of relationship that lasted more than a single day.

Both accurate—neither enough.

Her hands stilled around a jar of powdered herbs as emotion poured through her at the memory of their afternoon together. He'd

touched her like the world began and ended in her skin, and she'd felt it. Such love. It resonated in her heart even now, but the source… it was no longer him. The thrum of this came from her own soul.

She loved him.

Fear shook her hands until she settled the glass container carefully on top of the table and twined her fingers together. This wasn't supposed to happen, especially not now. His life was in peril as he worked to cure a deadly plague. What if he died? What if she'd fallen for another man who ended up leaving her, however unwittingly?

She should never have let herself do such a thing.

There was nothing wrong with love. Of course, there wasn't. But couldn't her heart have waited a few months longer? This cursed plague had drawn them together, and now she risked yet more suffering. Annoyance sparked against fear until she let out a grumbled "*miaran*" worthy of Lial himself.

Lynia was still muttering a long string of curse words when Maddy entered, her mates following behind.

Fen whistled low as they approached. "Those particular expressions didn't make it over when I was spell-given your language. I *knew* there had to be more colorful phrases."

Cheeks heating, Lynia snatched another bottle from the shelf and set it beside the others with a sharp *clack*. "Forgive my discourtesy. I would not typically speak so freely around someone I do not know well."

"I'm the last one you should apologize to when it comes to language," Fen said with a shrug. "Honestly, I'm inspired."

Maddy shoved into him with her shoulder. "I thought you wanted to help."

"I do," Fen protested.

"Really?" Lynia asked, shooting him a quick glance. "I don't suppose you're a strong telepath like Delbin?"

Grimacing, Fen shook his head. "Nope."

"Being bonded with Lial would be useful right now," Lynia grumbled absently. Her attention was on lining up the bottles and vials in the recipe's order to make sure she hadn't missed anything. "I would love to be able to ask him if he's returning soon. As it is, I'll have to rely on Ralan to get the word out if he Sees that Lial is supposed to be here."

Maddy stepped up to the workbench. "Isn't Ralan close enough to ask?"

"He isn't in my range, and Lyr doesn't know where he is. A terrible time for him to disappear."

"We probably don't want to know why." After grabbing a large flask of water, Maddy gestured Anna closer. "Will you check this, love?"

Anna gave Maddy a quick kiss on the cheek before taking the flask from her mate's hand. "Sure."

"Is there *anything* I can do?" Fen asked.

Lynia paused to consider the question, but not even another skim over the recipe revealed any tasks that would fit the young man's talents. These components were all herbal, nothing for an earth or blood mage to alter. Although…her gaze slid to the books she'd grabbed. He wasn't a healer like Maddy, but he was from Earth. He might find something useful in the texts.

"Why don't you go upstairs and take more notes on anything in the textbook that might be useful? Especially if it relates to destroying a virus."

Though his nose wrinkled like she'd asked him to drink old blood, Fen dutifully retrieved the book and started toward the stairs.

"Probably won't do much good, but I'll give it a shot," he said before beginning the climb.

There was a fair chance he was right, but another perspective couldn't hurt. If nothing else, Fen would have something useful to do while staying near his mates. Better he be cursing human scientists upstairs than causing a distraction in the middle of potion creation. Even without Lial's magic, Lynia hoped to have a sample produced soon.

If only it could have been done yesterday.

Unfortunately for Lial, a conscious Aris brought little clarity.

It didn't help that the life mage's mental state was precarious, though not nearly as bad as it had once been. Lial had sent Delbin outside to wait with Inona and Koranel before daring to question Aris, but Lial couldn't risk asking too many questions lest the mage lose control again. Still, he'd hoped for more than "I'm not sure how my magic works against the illness. I merely react."

They were both clearly missing something.

"What are you sensing that affects you so deeply?" Lial asked carefully.

Aris tipped his head back against the wall. "I don't… It's… It's just wrongness. Perversion. Something obscene is wrapped around the bundle you call a virus. But it takes a lot of power to nullify it, and I don't know if my magic would work against it while it's inside a living person. Not without altering that person in a noticeable and maybe detrimental way."

Lial rocked back on his heels. That was a possibility he hadn't considered but should have. With enough knowledge and power, life mages could change or even create species. Would attempting to

destroy the spell encasing the virus cause another problem instead? Messing with the body's systems was a perilous action.

"I don't know how to proceed," Lial admitted, the words burning his throat like a rancid potion. "I'm not even certain what to do with Korel's body."

Alerielle shifted closer. "The room is stone. If we seal it, a powerful mage could immolate everything inside, and a strong earth mage could prevent damage to the stone. Then the three of us could check for remnants."

"I could do both."

The voice held such a low rumble that Lial almost didn't recognize it as Kezari's. In fact, he'd forgotten the dragon woman's presence entirely. She'd settled in the darkened corner near the staircase and gone as still as any predator. But when she stepped forward, her demeanor held no hint of the confident hunter. He'd never seen her look so abashed.

"I've cleared caves to create a new den using such a method, and few fires burn hotter than dragon flame." Kezari's gaze shifted toward the ceiling. "There is little else I can do to ease the burden of my mistake."

Lial almost felt sorry for her—until he remembered the ruin she'd left of Korel's body. Her mistake *was* a burden. The virus might never have been activated if they hadn't been forced to use so much healing magic, a catalyst. Only her clear repentance held his tongue, though he couldn't deny that the size of her teeth and claws when shifted to her true form held a certain amount of influence.

"If you are sure you can maintain the integrity of the stone, Kezari," Lial said, "Then yes."

Kezari gave a sharp nod. "I can."

Aris shoved away from the wall. "Perhaps I should—"

"No, *skizik*," Kezari interrupted softly. "I can do this. Rest."

As soon as the dragon disappeared up the stairs, Aris slumped. But he didn't follow. Lial spared a moment's regret for the strain between the two, but there was nothing he could do for it. Not now. There was far too much to deal with, and he had far too little energy. Gods help them if there was another emergency before he could rest.

"I don't suppose you want to tell me about Elerie's condition," Lial said to Alerielle.

The other healer sucked in an audible breath, her eyes darkening with sadness. "I've attempted to repair her spine multiple times through the years, but I am not strong in that technique. I've tried some of your methods. Unfortunately, I believe it might require multiple healers working together after so long."

Lial scowled, though he wasn't surprised. Everything was slower during a dreaming state, including healing, but after five and a half centuries, the bones would have fused. Alerielle had to have known that before seeking his help. Too bad she hadn't come to him for advice sooner. He'd been at Braelyn for over four hundred years, so there'd certainly been ample time. And what about the previous healer? An adept enough man, as far as Lial knew.

"Why didn't you carry her to Braelyn's healer?"

"He wasn't trustworthy." Alerielle's lips pursed. "Which is no doubt why Myern Telien replaced him. I suspected the former healer was sympathetic to Allafon, and that I could not risk."

"I see." And he supposed he did. He, too, would go to such extremes to save a patient. "I would like to examine her after we are certain we are free of illness and there is no more risk of plague."

Alerielle nodded. "Perhaps while we wait for your dragon friend to finish, you can check me."

Lial couldn't withhold the deep sigh. His energy might be low, but this couldn't wait. He couldn't return to Braelyn without knowing for sure. "Very well."

Dizziness spun through him like the flames no doubt roaring upstairs, but he held his power steady. A quick examination, and then hopefully he could rest. As if there was any chance of that happening.

If it wouldn't have confused the others, he might have laughed.

Fen shoved the book away with a frustrated curse. He was decently educated despite his years on the streets, and he'd spent many quiet hours taking online courses to ensure it was so. Apparently, he should have added a few classes on medical terminology because not even acing biology helped him with this. Had Delbin picked the densest text possible?

"Probably ordered the cheapest one he could find on the internet," Fen grumbled, giving the book another push for good measure.

He was so annoyed that he almost missed the soft ping of metal hitting stone. Frowning, Fen peered beneath the table. Light from the nearby mage globe glinted against the delicate ring he'd admired earlier. Damn. He must have knocked it off while shifting the book. He stretched his hand out until he could grasp it and then straightened.

It truly was a fine piece. Fen had just started working with Maddy's father, a renowned Sidhe jeweler who'd set up shop on Earth with Maddy's human mother, so he had greater appreciation for the ring than he would have a month ago. Lial really should have enchantments placed on it if he decided to gift this to Lynia. Shayan had created rings for Fen, Maddy, and Anna that had proved more than useful.

I would love to be able to ask him if he's returning soon.

The memory of Lynia's muttered wish clicked against the thought of the spells in his own ring, and Fen smiled. He might not be able to pull anything useful from that textbook, but he could play around with a telepathy mod. Of course, he would need Lial's presence to activate the magic fully, but he could get started. If the healer objected, Fen could always remove what he'd added.

Besides, he wasn't exactly an ask-for-permission kind of guy.

Ralan stood on the border between Braelyn and Oria and waited.

Later, when the crisis was over and peace resumed—if it did— he would have a long talk with Delbin about the value of keeping his damned mouth shut. How had the whelp survived for a century amongst humans? A true mystery if he couldn't guard a secret longer than a few minutes. If it would have helped, Ralan would have ordered Delbin's ass out here to the middle of the wilderness in the icy cold. Morenial, the Dorn of Oria, wasn't likely to stop his approach for anyone short of the crown prince, though.

Too bad Ralan hadn't Seen Elerie's return sooner. Before tonight, he'd only caught a few brief glimpses of her a decade or two from now, but he hadn't known her identity. After tonight's visions, especially the potential futures stemming from Morenial speaking with Kai, he'd grown all-too-familiar with the lady's name.

Why had Delbin taken the least probable future and opened his mouth?

There were so many possible disasters that could land on them from this night when it should have been under control. At the

beginning of the evening, Lynia and Lial had been nearing their needed discoveries, Koranel's deception had been uncovered before he fell under the control of the Sidhe lord Meren, and Korel was about to be captured. Crises nearly averted.

Then Aris's control slipped, and Kezari made a foolish, hasty choice. The lack of futures Ralan could See for Korel—except those involving being burned or buried—meant he'd likely succumbed to the virus he'd carried in his blood, which also meant said virus had been activated. And in carrying Korel to the healer, the secret of Elerie had been revealed too soon.

Thanks for the help, Delbin.

Ralan had to clear the scowl from his face as Morenial appeared on the path. Ralan was angry, but not at the Dorn of Oria. Who wouldn't be in turmoil after a revelation like this about one's own mother? But although he could sympathize, Ralan stepped from the shadows without hesitation and cast a mage globe above his head, leaving no doubts as to his identity.

Morenial drew to an abrupt halt, surprise filling his expression. "Prince Ralan?"

"You will not speak to Kai tonight. Nor tomorrow."

The other man's lips turned down. "He should be there when I... Never mind. It is too much to explain."

"I've Seen more than enough futures about it, believe me," Ralan replied wryly. "How do you think I knew to stop you?"

"My mother—" Morenial's words choked off.

"Kai cannot know this yet," Ralan insisted. "And your presence could expose him to more than distress. There's a chance you are or will be infected. I cannot tell the origin point. I suggest you seal yourself away from others."

The color leached from the man's face. *"Miaran."*

"Exactly." Ralan didn't bother mentioning that he'd put himself at risk to stop this. If Morenial couldn't infer that for himself, telling him wouldn't do any good. "I trust this doesn't need to be an order?"

"It does not." Morenial tapped his chest twice and bowed. "I will return home and isolate myself at once."

"See to it."

Even after the man disappeared, Ralan stood in the cold, huddling beneath his cloak. Well. Nothing to do now but head back to the healer's tower and wait outside in the ice until Lial returned and examined him, perhaps hours from now. If his brief contact with Morenial had led to infection, Ralan needed to know before returning to his family even if it took all night.

And if it did, Cora was going to be pissed.

32

By the time Lial stepped through the gate from Oria to Braelyn, his shoulders were as tense as the boulder currently inhabiting his gut. They'd found no sign of the virus after Kezari had immolated everything, but they had encountered Morenial on their way to the portal. Ralan had warned the Dorn of possible contagion—unfortunately, Ralan had been right.

Everything within Lial told him to heal Moren immediately, but he had to ignore instinct. There was minimal virus in the elf's blood, and from what Lial had observed before jerking his energy free, it hadn't been activated. How much had Korel borne inside of himself for it to have been so pervasive in his body? It hardly seemed accidental that a traitor had wandered the area like a biological entrapment spell, just waiting for a healer to release that mess into the wild.

"You're sure we're okay?" Delbin asked as they paused in the entryway. "I was in the same room as Moren."

Lial's gaze skimmed along the group that had accompanied him, but he didn't have the energy to examine them a second time. Not with magic. He'd barely managed at Oria, but he hadn't been willing to allow anyone to return to Braelyn without doing so, even if he couldn't bring himself to rely upon the results. Thankfully, Delbin, Inona, Koranel, Kezari, and Aris all appeared to be free of disease.

"I'm as certain as I can be, though you should remain in your rooms as much as possible." Lial sighed. "I'm uneasy with the fact that neither I nor Alerielle showed sign of infection despite working so closely beside Korel."

Inona nudged Koranel. "At least this one shouldn't be exposing anyone after returning to his cell."

The former captain stared at the ground, his expression bleak, and guilt added more weight to the stone in Lial's abdomen. Koranel had messed up, but he'd been willing to rectify that mistake. Now there was no way for him to obtain the information Lyr had demanded he acquire from Korel. What Lyr would do with him now was anyone's guess.

Yet another cost of Lial's failure.

"Go ahead and take him there," Lial said.

Inona raised a brow, a slight smile tipping one side of her mouth. "Are you the Myern now? We are supposed to report back to Lord Lyr."

"No, but I am in charge of keeping the Myern healthy." Lial pinned her with his gaze. "I will not allow any of us near him until I am certain we haven't missed some trace of this illness. Isolate yourselves, or I'll find you each rooms of your own in the holding tower. I'll chain you up myself if I have to."

Beside Inona, Aris sucked in a harsh breath as the color leached from his skin. "That's…"

"*Miaran,*" Lial cursed, frustrated at himself for his careless mistake. The last thing the life mage needed was a reminder of his captivity. "Not you, Aris. Isolating yourself from Selia and Iren will be sufficient, just in case."

Aris gave a jerky nod. "Have you heard from Tynan?"

"According to Lyr, Tynan should be arriving soon. He may be here already," Lial replied. "I'll ask when I report in."

Inona scowled, though Delbin shot her a warning glance. "I thought you said not to report."

Lial speared his hand through his hair and tugged. "I *said* not to go physically near him. Use telepathy. Send a note. I don't care, so long as you do as I command. I cannot tell you how little I care about rank in this regard."

The scout's lips tightened, but she inclined her head in assent. In truth, he understood her hesitation—she was trained to report back without fail, but he hadn't been joking about hauling her to the prison himself if he had to. The way that virus had torn through Korel's body… Lial barely kept from shuddering.

"Go," Lial said. "I need to talk to Lynia. Hopefully, she has found some answers in her research."

Not that he would be able to get physically close to her any more than he could Lyr. A cruel twist of fate, that. After all this time, they'd finally come together, and now he would have to stay away. If he were like Fen, Lial might have said the gods were assholes. But no. A healer dared not court irreverence.

Not with a profession that so often required the benevolence of Bera.

There. That was all she could do.

Lynia's eyes slid closed, but she couldn't decide if it was in relief or exhaustion. Maybe it was both. With every herb she'd measured,

tension had wound tighter inside her until her shoulders ached and her fingers stung from pinching the measuring spoons. Even so, she was fairly confident she'd done it. The potion bubbled away merrily under the influence of the heating spell.

"Thank you," Lynia said to Maddy and Anna, who stared over her shoulders at the potion. "Your help was invaluable."

"I can't believe I might have contributed to the cure for the elven plague," Anna said. "I hope I purified the water right. Is there some kind of safety test for these things?"

Smiling, Lynia turned to face them. "We'll have to ask Lial."

"I hope he gets back soon." Maddy cast an uneasy glance toward Caeleth. "I scanned our patient without finding anything wrong, and Elan said Caeleth was fine when he checked. But…I still worry. He hasn't been fighting the sleeping spell like he did at first."

"It *is* the middle of the night," Lynia countered, although she had to admit that the mage's quiet bothered her, too.

"Speaking of which…" Maddy tipped her head toward Anna, who slumped on the stool next to the workbench. "We should probably get some sleep. We're supposed to go home tomorrow if we're cleared to leave. I guess that's another reason to hope the potion works."

Anna sighed. "Yeah. I don't exactly love my job at the restaurant, but I don't want to lose it, either."

Fen chose that moment to bounce down the stairs, books tucked under his arm and a sly grin curving his lips. Lynia's eyebrow rose at the latter. If there was reason to be amused, she didn't know it. Naturally, he didn't bother to explain. He set the books on the workbench and curled his arm around Anna, who softened against him.

"Did I hear someone say sleep?" Fen asked.

Maddy rolled her eyes. "You know you heard every word. But yes. I did."

"Did you find anything useful in the books?" Lynia asked.

Oddly, there was more satisfaction than remorse in his expression as he answered. "I'm sorry, but no. I didn't. I'm not very good at that kind of stuff."

Lynia didn't believe that for a moment. Oh, the text was challenging enough, that she knew. It was his excuse she didn't accept. He'd delivered the words with all the authenticity of a low-level *omree* claiming he'd sung for the king. It might have happened, but not the way one was led to think.

No need to question him on the matter, though. They were all too tired for that. "Thank you for trying."

After the three bid their goodbyes and departed, Lynia returned to Caeleth's side. Maybe it was normal for a patient to remain under Lial's sleep spell for so long? She frowned down at the man. He appeared a little flushed, but his breathing was steady. Perhaps she had tucked the blanket around him too tightly.

Lynia eased the blanket beneath his arms but was careful not to expose the bandage. There. Surely, Lial would return soon, and he could verify that all was well. If nothing else, Elan intended to return every mark, so if Caeleth needed the ambient temperature adjusted, the other healer could do it. She might find it pleasantly cool, but she wasn't covered in blankets.

Her son's energy brushed against hers, and Lynia opened the connection immediately, the mage forgotten. *"Yes?"*

"Lial just returned." Lyr hesitated, though a hint of his somber mood filtered through. *"The healing did not go well, and reporting to me didn't help. If he's in a foul mood when he returns to the tower, well… I thought you should know so you won't take it personally. Go easy on him."*

She nearly rolled her eyes like Maddy. *"I would hardly be cruel."*

"Of course you wouldn't," Lyr hurried to say. *"But with all the tension between you of late…"*

"I care for Lial." She loved him, in truth, but she wasn't going to tell her son that before the man in question. *"I appreciate the warning, though I can't imagine offering harsh words. I would always comfort him if he'd let me."*

"I'll leave you to discover that for yourself," Lyr replied, a touch of disquiet in his tone.

No doubt he didn't want to think about the forms comfort could take.

As they ended the link, Lynia settled into one of the chairs they'd gathered while examining the Seelie queen's blood. That had only been five or six marks ago, but it felt like a century. A never-ending night. Another six or so marks until sunrise with so much left that could fill it.

She could only pray for no more disasters.

Despite the cold, Lial had paced around the clearing in front of the estate as he'd given his report telepathically to Lyr. A painful accounting, that, especially after Lyr's surprised *"You* failed to save him?" His friend had apologized profusely for the insensitive comment, but the wound those words had carved remained. Lial had failed in his first challenge against the plague when so many relied upon his success. That was undeniable.

He might falter yet again if he didn't rest, and there was no help forthcoming. Lyr had also told him that Tynan was delayed until the next morning. A strange turn of events when Lial wished for the mind healer's presence instead of the opposite, but having more aid would have relieved a little worry. If Aris's control deteriorated further…

Better not to contemplate that—like so many other things of late.

Finally, his feet carried him toward the healing tower, but he couldn't bear to go in. Lyr had told him Lynia was there, working on some kind of potion she'd discovered. She would want to know what had happened, but Lial had no clue if he could tell her. She respected him as a healer, not a killer. And like the horrible memories he'd accidentally gleaned from Aris, this darkness was more terrible than she deserved to encounter.

She shared her dream of Telien, his conscience whispered. *And let you comfort her.*

That was a loss they both understood, though. Lynia had never had to stop a beating heart with her magic. The sick stain of that… Shuddering, Lial walked around the perimeter of the tower until he reached the *camahr* den. The food he'd left was gone, and the water was getting low. He melted ice into the bowl for them before settling onto his favorite rock.

Miaran, it was cold. Lial curled his arms around his upturned knees, tucking the cloak around himself until only his face was free. Of course, he *could* take his foolish ass inside if he wasn't so afraid. Not of Lynia or the illness he potentially carried, though the latter was bad enough. He feared a different kind of exposure—his true self revealed, his darker edges clear to her sight. How could he stand her rejection once she saw the layers of pain he so often bore?

The first blackened edge might have been burned into him by the sharp agony of Aralee's loss, but every subsequent mark had been worn into his soul, little valleys carved from the endless torrents of difficult healing sessions.

Every terrible story shared in confidence. Every error. Every death.

His failures piled on top of each other until…

"You know, out of about fifteen strands, you moped out here for a solid fourteen."

Lial jolted, then muttered a curse. "*Clechtan*, Ralan. What are you doing behind my tower in the middle of the night? Do I even want to know?"

"Probably not." When Ralan's voice didn't move closer, Lial turned to stare at him at the edge of the tree line. "I was waiting for you. After meeting with Morenial, I need you to scan me for infection. I didn't see any dire strands about that, but we both know I don't always get a clear picture of things involving myself."

Instead of leaping to his feet, Lial slumped, what strength he had left evaporating at the thought of more work. "I don't know if I have the energy. Truly, I do not."

"I'm sorry," Ralan said, and he sounded like he meant it. He paused for a moment before switching to mental communication. *"I would not have taken the risk knowing what you would have to deal with, but tonight's discovery could not be shared with Kai. I don't even want to mention Elerie aloud lest one of the guards should overhear. Besides, you're more than aware what this revelation will do to Kai. Had I allowed Morenial to proceed, there's a high chance that Kai and Arlyn would have gone to find the truth about his mother immediately, and she would have lost the babe. In fact, all three might have… Well, I suppose you can guess what I don't wish to say."*

Indeed. Lial understood exactly what he meant. Kai never would have stood by waiting for a safer time, and Arlyn wouldn't have allowed him to go alone. They likely would have been infected in the process, all before anyone realized the scope of the danger. He'd only scanned Morenial for the virus because of Ralan's warning.

Lial shivered. This was one bit of Ralan's interference they could all appreciate.

"I'm surprised you told me," Lial sent back.

"Normally, I wouldn't." Ralan held his gaze. *"But I'm well aware of the strain I'm adding to your resources. You deserve to know the reason, and nothing is harmed by you having the knowledge."*

Lial thought back to his previous conversation with his cousin, and the grudging respect he had for Ralan grew. The prince might sound dismissive more often than not, but there was more consideration behind his demeanor than most gave him credit for. Including Lial, prior to tonight.

Shoving to his feet in spite of the ache spearing through his muscles, Lial let out a deep breath and tried to stretch out the cramps. He was exhausted enough that his hands shook slightly where he gripped his cloak closed, but the weakness was hidden beneath the fabric. Even so, he'd been worse. He could do a simple scan, couldn't he?

Pain sliced through his mind as he extended his magic toward Ralan, but Lial shoved the inconvenience aside. He had to be thorough. And so he ran his magic through his cousin, searching every cell of his body—at least to the best of his ability. Only when he returned to himself did he realize that he was swaying on his feet.

"You're fine, I believe," Lial said through lips gone dry.

Ralan frowned. "You believe?"

"Unless there are markers of disease that I am unable to recognize," Lial clarified. He blinked, only to find Ralan gripping his arms. "You move fast."

"No," his cousin said tightly. "You didn't realize that you were about to black out."

Lial stared at Ralan. "What?"

"I'll give you energy the way I did when Lynia was injured."

It took a moment—and an infusion of magic from his cousin—for Lial's muddled brain to recall what Ralan was talking about. Lynia's fall, when he'd had to heal her spine. He wouldn't have succeeded if Ralan and Eri hadn't contributed magic, theirs being easier to process because of their blood connection. It seemed this time the gift would help Lial rather than his beloved.

"Normally, I would complain about your pushiness," Lial said. "But not tonight. Thank you."

"You're welcome." Ralan peered at him for a moment longer before releasing his arms. "Go sleep. And don't be stubborn about letting Lynia comfort you."

A smile ghosted across Lial's face, but he let the comment pass. No use asking if it was advice or prophecy. Anyone who knew him could guess at his possible stubbornness without need of the latter. "No promises."

"No surprise," Ralan muttered.

Shaking his head, Lial turned away and started walking, though he tossed a pleasant enough "Good night, Ralan" over his shoulder. He was too tired to debate the matter with his cousin; they were both obstinate enough to spend the rest of the night in the endeavor. Ralan appeared to agree, as he let out a chuckle before heading in the opposite direction.

A flash of light at the base of the tower caught Lial's eye, and he slowed to study the hole where the *camahr* lived. But the light didn't repeat again. Probably one of the kits getting restless in its sleep. Sighing, Lial forced himself back into motion. No use delaying any longer. He still wasn't certain what he would tell Lynia, but he couldn't stay out in the cold all night.

He would just have to let his heart lead.

33

For the third time since she'd spoken to Lyr, Lynia resisted the urge to contact Lial. Where was he? Her foot tapped an impatient beat against the stone, an odd counterpoint to the soothing sound of the bubbling potion. But she couldn't help it. He'd already reported to her son, and the walk from the main building to the tower could have been completed ten times already. Had he fallen on a stray patch of ice? Had he come upon someone in need of healing? What?

Lynia stood, gripping her elbows as she began to pace the room. Truly, waiting was torture. She should contact him, but part of her feared being rebuffed. Lyr had said the healing at Oria hadn't gone well, so Lial likely wanted time alone. But iron's burn, the man also claimed to want a relationship, and that meant she deserved at least a brief mental message that he'd returned safely.

Didn't it?

Drooping a little, Lynia rubbed at her eyes and grabbed hold of her errant emotions. What was wrong with her? She wasn't usually this quick to worry, and she'd never been so insecure about Telien. Of course, that had been different. Being bonded meant less ability to hide one's emotions, so while they'd had disagreements, she'd always been able to feel his love. No guesswork there.

She would never have that assurance with Lial.

Well, maybe it was uncertainty, but exhaustion couldn't help. It had been a long night after a seemingly eternal day, and she had used more magic than usual. She should return to her room and get some sleep. Everything was as well as it could be, and Lial was fine— probably brooding. If she left him a note about the potion along with the recipe, he could take a look and add energy if he had any to spare. It needed another seven marks' time of brewing regardless, so she might as well rest. Maybe then he would be ready to talk.

She'd just pulled a piece of paper from the stack so she could spell-copy the recipe when the door creaked open. Startled, Lynia glanced over, only to freeze at the sight of Lial standing in the entrance. The light from the mage globes cast the shadows beneath his eyes into stark relief—even the lines of his cheekbones were carved sharp, the hollows of his cheeks more pronounced than usual.

Over the centuries she'd spent at Braelyn with its many warriors, she'd seen more than a few looking exhausted and heartsore. But this… Lynia needed no bond to feel the weight of his grief. It settled on her shoulders much the way it bent down his, and she wanted to cry from the injustice of it all.

Lial stepped inside, closing the door behind him. Then he halted, and her heart thrummed at the conflict on his face. "Lynia."

There was a wealth of emotion in that whisper, and it broke something loose inside her. Shoving away from the workbench, Lynia darted over and threw her arms around him before he could say another word. But he didn't relax—if anything, he grew more tense.

Worry threaded through the pain she felt on his behalf until she pulled back. "Do you want me to leave?"

"No." His jaw clenched, and he let out a harsh breath. "No, but you should. It isn't safe to touch me. Had I realized what you were going to do, I would have warned you away."

Her brow furrowed. "Why?"

"I didn't find signs of the virus in myself, but I…" His voice trailed off, and he averted his gaze. "If I'm wrong and you catch this illness, I won't be able to save you."

Lynia ran her finger along his firm jaw. "You would."

He jerked free of her hold with an abruptness that drew a gasp from her lips. What had she said? Then she noted the stark pain on his face and winced. Lyr had mentioned that the healing hadn't gone well, but that must have been an understatement. She'd never seen Lial look so agonized or defeated in all the centuries he'd been at Braelyn.

"What happened?" she asked softly.

Lial's nostrils flared. "We killed him. That's what."

In the silence that followed the echo of his words, Lial went pale, and he rubbed at his arms as if cold. Lynia certainly felt chilled. What could he mean by that? He was no murderer; of that she was sure. Did he mean that he and Alerielle had failed to save Korel?

"I wasn't even certain I could tell you of my shame," Lial murmured before slinging his cloak from his shoulders and spinning away to hang it by the door.

He didn't turn back to face her.

"You can't save everyone," Lynia ventured, worried that she shouldn't speak at all.

"No." Lial braced his hand against the wall. "I am aware. But I didn't misspeak. We failed so badly at stopping the virus that

Alerielle and I had to kill him. It was a mercy. It prevented the illness from spreading. I used my magic to stop his heart, Lyni. What kind of healer…?"

Understanding poured through her, along with a fair amount of horror. No wonder he was struggling. He'd remarked more than once that he wasn't sure if he could ever harm another with his magic, only to be forced into that very thing. And it *was* horrible, as death always was. Unfortunately, it was also necessary at times. There was no ideal world—not in any dimension.

"You shouldn't—"

He swung around, and the torment on his face cut off her words. It shattered her heart. He couldn't keep this pain inside. All too well, she knew the cost of holding in such strong feelings. So when he strode toward the stairs, she grabbed his wrist, tugging him back around.

"You shouldn't blame yourself for what had to be done," Lynia said firmly. At the doubt in his eyes, she gripped his face in her hands. "You. Are. Not. A. God. You aren't Bera, Goddess of death and healing. You're one person."

Lial's eyes pinched closed. "Ralan said I could stop this plague."

"No, he didn't." Lynia gently shook him until he looked at her. "He said *we* could stop it. And there was no promise that nothing would be lost in the process."

"I may never feel clean again, Lynia," he whispered.

She took his hand and pulled him toward the stairs. "Come on. I'll help."

Together, they climbed the steps to the upper bathing chamber, and together, they undressed. Lynia waited patiently while he activated the spells to release and heat the water from the wall, an unusual modification that Lial had requested after Lyr brought the idea back from Earth. A shower, it was called.

Not her favorite, but she stepped beneath the spray with Lial. And once he'd scrubbed himself practically raw, she gathered him close and let the water wash away both their tears.

For a blessed moment, Lial felt as hollow as the pipe that had drained the water away beneath his feet. Washed clean, no thought or emotion to remind him of past or present. Then Lynia ran a drying spell over his body and through his hair before handing him a loose robe, and love flooded through him once more. No one took care of him, not usually. But she did.

"Thank you," he murmured.

Lynia smiled slightly as she dried herself, turning her hair from dark yellow to nearly white in the process. Unable to resist, he twined a silky strand around his finger. He craved her, but he didn't deserve the kiss he wanted to take. She'd given more than enough for one night.

"Let's go to your bedchamber," she said. "You can tell me what happened if you're ready. Or just sleep, which you obviously need."

His brows drew together. "Ralan gave me enough energy that I'm no longer wavering on my feet. I didn't think it was that obvious."

Her smile widened as she tugged her hair free and wrapped herself in another loose robe. "Alas, I know you too well. You've gone well past overworked, beyond 'took on more than you should,' and straight into the realm of 'why haven't you collapsed?' Though I suppose in this case, the answer is Ralan."

Lial shook his head. No hiding anything from her. "Will you stay with me? It's selfish. I should scan you for illness and let you go, but I…"

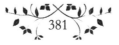

"Why?" She surprised him by laughing. "Honestly, Lial. I hugged you. We just showered together. If I'm going to catch the virus from you, I've surely done so. Going back to my room now would only risk spreading it. I suppose I'll have to be quarantined with you."

He couldn't hold back a growl. "How can you be so casual about this?"

"Because I don't think you missed anything." Lynia leaned close, brushing her lips against his for good measure. "You said Ralan gave you energy, which means he must have gotten close. Did he tell you anything about me?"

Lial blinked at the shift in topic, but the answer to her question clarified her reason for asking. Ralan had grabbed his arms and told him to accept comfort from Lynia. Would he have done either of those things if he thought Lial was infected? Ralan must have Seen a reasonably clear future to be so confident in his actions.

"He said I shouldn't be stubborn about letting you comfort me," Lial admitted. Sighing, he took Lynia's hand. "Don't tell him I took his advice."

She chuckled. "I'll endeavor not to."

They walked hand in hand to the stairs, but he was forced to release her so they could descend. He focused on the warmth that her fingers had left on his rather than the self-recrimination waiting to swamp him. Though the shower had brought some relief, the pain wasn't gone. He knew from experience that it hovered, ready to attack as soon as his guard was down. No one escaped working through grief.

But he could do his best to be distracted from it.

As soon as they'd both stepped from the stairs into his room, Lial activated the spell to close off this chamber from the workroom

below. Dizziness rolled through him from the use of that simple magic, and he pinched his eyes closed until the sensation passed. *Miaran.* He'd really done it this time. He had to rest. If anyone else got sick or injured, he would be unable to help.

Lynia's arm curled around his waist, and he opened his eyes to meet hers. "Get in bed."

Despite everything, he grinned. "I've longed to hear those words from you many times."

"No offense, love, but I don't think you're in any condition to take advantage," she teased.

He barely heard most of what she said. His heart had locked on "love" and set its beat to the meaning. It was a simple endearment, one that she couldn't mean literally. She was too uncertain of him and their relationship. She'd wanted to explore possibilities, not commit. Exhaustion was making him hallucinate.

Lial pulled away and shrugged out of his robe, tossing it on a chair before crawling under the covers. A line between her brows, Lynia stared at him for a moment before circling to the other side and slipping out of her own robe. She slid in beside him and nestled herself against his side before she spoke again.

"Why did your expression close up a moment ago?" she asked softly. "A memory?"

He wrapped his arm around her waist. "No. Only…I wish you would beware your endearments. My heart is weak and greedy."

"What do…" Her voice trailed off. Then she propped herself up on his chest and met his eyes. "Because I said 'love'? What if I meant it?"

As soon as her meaning hit, Lial shifted, rolling until he rose above her. His arm muscles shook with the strain, but he barely noticed. His hair fell like a curtain around them until all he could

see was her face. Her beloved face, more serious than her light tone would have suggested.

"Be careful," Lial said with a growl. "Or I might decide to keep you."

Smiling, she ran her hands up his arms and gently squeezed his shoulders. "Is that right? And what would you do with me?"

Lial gave her lower lip a quick nibble. Almost retribution for her teasing, but really a pleasure for them both. "Tell me the truth, Lyni."

"I'm not sure I know it." She brushed her lips against his, and their breaths mingled. There was a vulnerability in her expression that had him kissing her once more, hoping to spare her—both of them—from what she didn't want to say, but she pulled away. "No, Lial. No evasion. I shouldn't have asked that when I haven't decided for myself."

He sighed. "And I shouldn't have pressed."

"You should have." Lynia cupped his cheek, and the spark in her eyes made his heart pound. "I think I'm falling in love with you, but this is so…different. I'm used to the certainty of a bond. This is like falling in truth. I have no idea what I'll find at the bottom."

"You'll find me. You know I'll always catch you."

Her expression softened. "Is that so?"

"Of course." Lial flipped them over again, surprising a laugh out of her as she sprawled across his chest. Gods, he loved making her laugh, a sound heard too rarely. "See? I can even be your bed while we sleep."

Lynia's hand trailed down his side and over his waist. He sucked in a sharp breath. "Didn't you say I'm in no condition—"

Her fingers wrapped around him, cutting off his words, and she chuckled again. "I suppose I was wrong. Though if you prefer to sleep now…"

"No," Lial managed. "Perhaps I have *some* energy left."

With a wicked grin, Lynia sat up to straddle his waist. "Good."

Gods' blessings. If it wouldn't mean admitting he'd followed his cousin's advice, he might have considered sending Ralan a gift. Then thought fled as Lynia took him in, her body moving over his. She was all he could see or feel. Everything.

And as they exploded together, he could forget that the world wasn't perfect.

Lynia woke to the insistent internal pinging of her alarm spell. Grumbling, she shifted against her oddly warm bed and then froze when she realized that she was pressed against skin, not fabric. Lial. Lazy contentment filled her before it reached her lips in a slow smile. She'd fallen asleep sprawled across him.

Carefully, she lifted her head to find that she'd had her face snuggled in the vee where Lial's neck met his shoulder. He still slept, and she gave herself a moment to savor the relaxed peace of his expression in the gentle glow of the dawn light slipping through the window. But she couldn't tarry. She'd directed the alarm spell to wake her a mark before her potion was supposed to be complete.

Lynia disentangled herself as slowly as she could, though she expected him to wake at any moment. He was a light sleeper, ready to come to the rescue at the slightest sound. But although he stirred, a frown marring his brow until she tucked the blanket over him to ease the chill of her absence, he remained asleep.

He truly had drained himself of magic last night.

Her footsteps fell silently as she tiptoed to the wardrobe holding Lial's clothes. She had no change of clothing, and she was loath to don the dress she'd left upstairs in the bathing chamber. She might

know spells to remove wrinkles, but she didn't know a thing about clearing away bad memories. She would never forget the look on Lial's face as he'd flung his own clothes at the wall and stepped into the spray.

Shoving the image to the back of her mind, Lynia opened the wardrobe and peered inside. His pants wouldn't fit, nor would his healing robes—both would be too long. Maybe a tunic? It would be rather short, but it would have to do. If Maddy stopped by, Lynia would have to beg her help in retrieving something from her room. For now, she grabbed one of the longer brown tunics and pulled it over her head before rolling up the sleeves. Then she dug out a long strip of fabric to use as a belt.

Absolutely anyone who stopped by would know she'd spent the night, but she couldn't find it in herself to care.

"That looks far better on you than me," Lial said, his voice a sleepy growl that sent a shiver of pleasure down her spine.

Even so, she stiffened in embarrassment before spinning to face him. "I forgot to stop by my room. I hope you don't mind."

Lial sat up, shoving at his sleep-tangled hair. "I don't. But why are you up?"

"The potion is almost ready."

"Potion?" A line formed between his eyebrows, and she had to resist the urge to kiss it. "I don't know what you mean."

Of course, he didn't. He'd been in so much pain the night before that she'd forgotten to mention her own discovery. "I found a recipe created by the healer Emereh in a journal Selia had sent over from the Citadel. According to the text, it's what he used to treat those with the illness in Abuiarn."

Lial sprang from the bed, not seeming to notice his nakedness. *Gods, he's well-built.*

386

She shook the thought aside as he reached her, but she had to train her eyes on his to do so. Then the strange expression on his face caught her attention. Hope, sure. But there was also guilt and pain in the mix. Why would the idea of a potion be a source of unhappiness?

"I wish I'd known yesterday," he whispered.

Oh. *Oh.* Lynia gave him a quick, soft kiss. "I'm sorry my gift isn't strong enough to reach you from here. But would Korel have survived his other injuries long enough to wait for the tincture to be distilled?"

"No, he wouldn't have," Lial grumbled. "That doesn't stop me from hoping for a different outcome. I'm not sure I'll ever forgive myself for what I had to do."

Lynia studied him for a moment, trying to think of something to say. Something to help him see. Then she knew. "I suppose you're upset at the king for killing Kien."

Lial scowled. "What?"

"I imagine Kai shouldn't have killed Allafon, either." She settled her hand against Lial's chest. "And if anyone should do the same to Meren while trying to capture him, that would be a terrible wrong."

Lial's expression only grew darker. "I know what you're trying to say. They are warriors."

"Healers are, too, in their way. You're merely on the other side of the battle." She tapped her fingers against his skin. "I never thought you considered warriors to be murderers, but I guess you must."

"Lyni, that's—"

"Nothing more than the truth," Lynia insisted. "Killing Allafon and Kien might have saved hundreds or thousands of lives. So did killing Korel."

Lial tugged his hair away from his face with an impatient swipe. "It doesn't feel the same. We don't really know what might have

happened if Korel had gone free. The virus appeared to be inert in his blood, still locked behind the containment spell. I don't think it would have been activated if we hadn't used healing magic on him."

"You had to, so that's irrelevant."

"That supposition, yes." Lial huffed. "But there's also the fact that neither I nor Alerielle appear to have been infected despite our close proximity during treatment. If I'd had some other method, he might have been saved without harming others. Maybe it was convenience for myself and not the salvation of others."

"Would Korel have lived until the potion's completion?" Lynia asked. "Could you have stopped the virus's progression for so many marks?"

Lial's jaw clenched, and for a moment, she thought he wouldn't answer. "No. It was eating through him like fire consumes the plains. Once the virus reached his nervous system, I'm not sure anything would have stopped his agony. Attempting to use magic would have fed the virus, and it would have required deadly amounts of potion to numb the pain."

"So it was mercy, too," she pointed out.

"Even so… I should have done better."

Lynia wanted to kick him, but then he would have insisted on using energy to check her toes for injury. Annoying man. "You're upset that you didn't kill yourself trying, aren't you?"

Shock covered his face before it was replaced by guilt. "Perhaps I am."

"Well, don't," she snapped. "Kill yourself during a healing, that is. No one should ask that of you."

Lial winced. "I suppose nearing that line has become a habit."

"A habit you need to be well rid of, especially if you hope to have a relationship with me." She pushed lightly against his chest.

"Think on whether you can do that. I've already lost Telien. If you plan to throw your life on everyone's funeral pyre, we should end this now. There's no stopping the unexpected, but this is far from that."

He covered her hand with his. "I should have considered that."

"Yes," she said tightly.

"I'm not used to having anyone to worry about but myself." Lial's sigh brushed her lips, a sad substitute for a kiss. "I've been alone for a long time."

Lynia smiled. "Sounds like a change is in order."

"Perhaps I could take on a few more assistants and another master healer," Lial conceded. "Assuming we all survive this."

Lynia's thoughts flicked back to the potion brewing below, and she peered around him at the water clock. "*Clechtan.* I've lost a quarter mark. Get dressed and meet me below. Then we'll see if we've found a bit of good fortune."

There were no guarantees with this potion, but Lynia didn't let herself consider that. Instead, she gave Lial a quick kiss and hurried toward the stairs, trusting he would follow. If the concoction did fail, it wouldn't be for lack of attention.

34

Lial smoothed his tunic and slipped his feet into a pair of low boots. The rumble of his stomach reminded him of the bread he'd stashed in the small box on the far edge of the table. It might be a little stale, but it shouldn't be moldy. He grabbed a clean plate from the nearby shelf and set it on the table—only then noticing the piece of paper with a scrawl of unfamiliar handwriting, the gold ring on top.

Frowning, Lial slid the paper from beneath the ring and scanned the note. Then he read it twice more to make sure he'd read the written English properly. Which he had, of course. He'd spent enough time around Fen that even the slang took only a moment to grasp.

Don't be pissed, but I added an enchantment to the ring. Maddy's father Shayan taught me. If you and Lynia link mentally while the magic is activated, it should allow for a stronger telepathic bond. If she's wearing it, anyway. I can undo it if you had something else in mind.

P.S.: Don't screw this up. Seriously, put a ring on it.

Well, mostly grasp. Put a ring on it? Lynia was hardly an object. But if there was some other translation, Lial wasn't going to ask. Fen taunted him enough without revealing that lack of knowledge.

Though the lad could be thoughtful, Lial had to admit. Smiling, he tucked the ring in his pocket and retrieved the bread. It was good enough for a quick snack, so he placed it and a carving knife on the plate. He and Lynia would welcome something better when food arrived from the main estate, but at least they wouldn't be starving.

Unfortunately, the mirror chimed before he could carry it down. Grumbling beneath his breath, he stomped over to activate the charm, but he was careful to keep his expression neutral. Few people contacted him through this direct link, so it generally meant business.

Tynan's image filled the screen, and Lial just managed to hold back a frown. "Good morning, Priest-Healer Tynan. I confess you have caught me off guard."

"Good morning." Tynan rubbed his chin. "Forgive my haste in asking, but were you not warned of my intention to contact you? My superior spoke with Lord Lyrnis last night."

Iron curse it. Lial had completely forgotten that Tynan was supposed to report to him this morning. "I'm afraid we had an emergency that took my attention. Were you apprised of the situation?"

"The illness? Yes. I should have considered that would have occupied your thoughts." Tynan's expression grew somber. "I had a crisis here that delayed me, but I wanted to confirm with you that I can arrive within three marks' time if it is still convenient. The Myern left it to your discretion."

Would it be fine? Lial had no clue, considering how much chaos the last few days had brought. But as he'd thought the night before, having another healer around wouldn't hurt, and it would make Lynia feel better until he could find more permanent assistants. "That should suffice, so long as you're willing to take the risk."

"I am. A priest of Bera is always prepared to step into danger to help others," Tynan said, his voice firm enough that Lial couldn't doubt his sincerity. "How is Aris this morning? If I need to hasten…"

Lial's mind went blank at a sudden realization—he had no clue how Aris fared. Nor Caeleth or any of his other patients. None. Gods. What kind of healer left his two most crucial patients unmonitored? Heat climbed up the back of his neck and spilled across his face until Tynan's eyebrows shot up.

"Is something wrong?" Tynan asked.

"No," Lial snapped. "There's a potion that needs my immediate attention. I will see you in three marks' time."

The younger healer's lips twitched. "Very well. Until then."

Lial cut off the connection without another word. No use wasting time on pleasantries since Tynan already knew his brusque nature. Instead, he grabbed the plate and hurried toward the stairs while sending out a mental call to Aris. He received a sleepy—but calm—reply that eased some of his tension. But not all. The life mage could have had a breakdown strong enough to level half the estate, and Lial would have slept through it.

He'd been too busy indulging himself, first in self-recrimination and then in Lynia's presence. He might have needed the sleep, but he should have returned to work as soon as he'd woken rather than lay there admiring Lynia as she'd nabbed his clothes from the wardrobe. His first thought had been to coax her back to bed. How could he have forgotten the lives that relied upon him?

Sounds like a change is in order.

Lynia was right about that. But while he recognized the need for more helpers, those extra healers weren't here yet. Not even Tynan would arrive for another three marks. Lial would do well to focus on the task at hand.

The potion had turned the palest shade of purple, much like the sky as the sun set in winter. Lynia tilted her head, hoping to see a slight shift in color at the motion, but nothing happened. According to the recipe, the completed concoction would take on a bluish tinge if one shifted perspective, almost like a prism effect. Then it would cure to a violet blue.

At least there would still be time for Lial to add energy.

His footsteps sounded on the stairs, and she turned to smile at him. But the curve of her lips flattened at the stern expression on his face—one that barely softened when he reached her. Though he carried a plate of bread, he hardly appeared to notice it as he frowned down at her. What had happened in the few moments since she'd left him to get dressed?

"Lial?"

"I forgot about Aris," he muttered, and she noticed then the angry flush tinging his cheeks. "And Caeleth."

Well, that explained it. "Elan was leaving as I came down. He visited Caeleth every mark. I'm certain he would have notified you if there was a problem."

"A pale bit of solace, that." Despite his words, his expression softened, and he glanced down at the plate he held. "I brought us food. My usual meal won't arrive for another mark or two, but I keep extra on hand because of my odd schedule. If Elan was just here, we have a moment to eat it."

At the reminder of food, Lynia's stomach grumbled. She laughed softly and shifted to one of the chairs from last night's discussion. Lial took the seat beside her before cutting the bread in half.

"Would you like for me to slice it into smaller pieces?"

Lynia shook her head. "Don't bother. I'll need to eat it quickly so I can check the potion."

After he handed over her half of the bread, they ate in silence. A comfortable one, for the most part, although she could have sworn a hint of nerves were in the glances Lial kept casting her way. Was he bothered by something? Perhaps he didn't like her using the workbench.

"I hope you aren't annoyed that I started the potion," Lynia said as soon as she'd swallowed the last bite. "You weren't here to ask."

His brow lowered. "Of course, I don't. Why would you think so?"

"You keep giving me strange looks."

"Ah." Lial shoved an errant strand of hair away from his face and brushed his palms against his pants. Then he carried the plate to a tall table beside the workbench before finally turning to answer. "It has nothing to do with that."

Lynia stood, but he didn't move closer. Instead, he slipped his hands into his pockets and stared at her. What was wrong with him? "I can leave if you prefer," she said.

He let out a laugh laced with no small amount of self-deprecation. "How do we always end up like this, Lyni? No, I don't want you to go. The truth is, I found a gift left by Fen, and I'm not certain what I should do with it."

This involved Fen? Her eyebrow hooked in question, and Lial released an audible sigh. His eyes locked on hers intently as he approached. Then he drew his hands from his pockets. It took her a moment to break her gaze from his long enough to peek at the hand he'd lifted between them, but when she did, she nearly gasped. In his fingers, a ring gleamed in the morning light. It was the same one she'd seen on the table. What was he doing?

"I didn't think that was a gift from Fen."

"The ring itself isn't." Lial took her right hand in his, their fingers linking loosely. "He added an enchantment that strengthens mental telepathy."

"So that's what he did instead of researching last night," Lynia mumbled.

"It seems so."

Well, she had mentioned wishing she could talk to Lial. It just hadn't occurred to her that Fen might take that literally—provided it was supposed to be hers at all. If Lial didn't know what he wanted to do with the gift, that might mean he hadn't decided who to give it to. It would be a terrible presumption to claim it unwarranted.

Lynia swallowed down a sudden burst of nerves. "What are you uncertain about, then?"

"Whether the intended recipient will be willing to take it." His fingers tightened against hers. "Before the enchantment, I'd thought to offer this to you as a show of my commitment, but I feared you weren't ready for such a thing. Now there's an added link, though it isn't something as permanent as a bond."

Their eyes met, and she couldn't look away from the solemn pool of blue, so full of emotion she could barely fathom the depths. She wanted to pull him close, but fear held her back. What did he want? What was she willing to give?

She cleared her throat. "What are you asking me?"

"I ask nothing *of* you." One corner of his mouth tipped up. "It is an oath from me. A promise that I will love you forever, even if we should ultimately part. The spell Fen added is only a bonus."

Her heart swelled until she feared it would shatter, and her eyes tingled with moisture. How could such a stubborn, contrary man hold such unexpected sweetness? She lowered her forehead to his chest as she struggled between past fear and future hope. Yes, she loved him. But to say it risked so much.

The warmth of his lips brushed against the top of her head. "If you are not ready to accept that, I understand," he murmured. "Truly, I expect nothing in return."

Lynia tipped her head back and brought her mouth to his. "I would wear it proudly. But with me so unsure of the future, are you certain you want me to have it?"

"Completely," he replied at once.

She pulled back a little so that she could meet his eyes once more. "Then yes. I'll accept the ring."

She hadn't realized the depth of his tension until his shoulders sagged in relief. Then he lifted her right hand, their fingers still twined, and shifted his grip to her palm so he could slide the ring over her finger. Emotion rose up, filling her throat, but she couldn't untangle any of it. At the moment, she didn't want to.

"If you'll link with the spell and then me, we can activate Fen's gift," Lial said softly.

Lynia reached for the enchantment within, connecting easily. "Solid work."

When Lial's energy brushed against hers, she opened without hesitation. *"So it is,"* he whispered into her mind.

The magic surged, firming the link, and their feelings spilled between them with no need of words. And for a moment, she wanted nothing more than to hold him.

So she did.

Lynia curled her arms around his waist and settled her cheek against his chest, the steady pounding of his heart a comfort she hadn't realized she needed. Then he enfolded her in his arms, one hand splaying low on her hip and the other curving up her back.

Almost absently, he caressed circles across the base of her neck until she shivered.

"I wish we could stay this way all morning," Lial murmured.

"As do I." She wanted to savor the moment, but the image of the bubbling potion broke into her thoughts. There could be no true savoring with so much left undone. "Unfortunately, the potion will be ready soon, and it will be ruined if I miss the curing stage."

His sigh tickled her ear, but she felt him nod. "Let's see it, then."

Still, he held her for a few heartbeats longer before loosening his hold. Lynia kissed him and stepped back, trying to ignore the way her lips tingled as she crossed over to the workbench. She wanted to forget about potions and plagues and drag Lial upstairs, all the worlds be damned. The only thing that stopped her was the sure knowledge that it would destroy them both.

Neither of them would be able to live with such an abdication of duty.

Lial rested his hand lightly against her side as he bent down to examine the potion. Then he skimmed the recipe beside it. "This looks perfect. Well done."

"I thought it might help if you add healing magic."

The color washed from his cheeks. "No."

"Why not?" Lynia asked, taken aback by the sudden snap in his tone.

"The way my healing magic fed the virus…" Lial dropped his hand from her waist and turned his back on the potion as though avoiding temptation. "I'm afraid my power could bring disaster. It might accelerate the sickness in everyone who drinks it."

Oh.

For a moment, that *oh* was all she could think. The impact of such a thing… A shudder went through her, and she had to resist the urge to tug Lial away as though his proximity might contaminate the mixture. If he hadn't made that discovery last night, they very well could have created that disaster.

"I hate to say that what happened with Korel is a good thing. But." At Lial's angry, startled glance, she rested her hand on his shoulder. "We wouldn't have known otherwise."

Lial flinched. Gods, she shouldn't have said that. He wasn't ready to hear any such thing. He was a brooder—really, they both were. She wouldn't appreciate such an observation if she were in his place, either.

"I should do a healing session with Caeleth," Lial said softly. "Food should be arriving soon, and I've contacted Maddy, who will help me feed Caeleth. You can finish the potion yourself, correct? I assumed that you would."

She wanted to groan at the way he'd closed himself off, but she understood it. He'd been so broken the night before, and although he acted more like himself today, that pain wasn't gone. Even in the tender moments, it waited beneath the surface. She might prefer he confide in her, but only when he was ready.

Besides, she could see herself in another role in addition to confidant, one she could fill beyond this crisis. They could work together here. If she mastered distilling, she could take care of that task while he healed the more seriously injured. As a bonus, she could send away the annoying few who wouldn't take care of small cuts and scrapes on their own.

"Of course. See to Caeleth."

Despite his turn in mood, Lial leaned down to give her a quick kiss before striding away, and she smiled. Then she remembered that

Maddy would be arriving soon to help, and a new realization had her wincing instead. She'd planned to see if Maddy would retrieve her clothes, but the young healer wouldn't have time for that now.

Lynia was going to have to ask Arlyn or one of the other ladies, but her friendship with most of them was fairly new. Though the same could be said of Maddy, the younger woman was less inclined to jest at her expense. Considering how much the others had teased her at dinner the other night, she might be better off putting on her cloak and heading for her room herself. Then she wouldn't have to hear endless jokes about spending the night with Lial.

Not that it should concern them. Nor should she be embarrassed by it—and she wasn't. But she'd never been good at handling the teasing of friends. Lynia could shrug off or rebuke an enemy's taunts, but her tongue froze at a well-intentioned joke. No matter how many centuries she lived, she never learned the trick of it.

Better to focus on the potion awaiting her attention.

Her mood nearly as sour as Lial's now, Lynia snatched the recipe from the workbench and scanned the directions again. Had she missed anything related to healing magic? There was no mention of a healer adding energy. Or not. But why would Lial's power have affected the virus in the first place? Resting her chin on her hand, she lowered the paper to the table as she considered the question.

He'd said the virus was protected by magic in the outer... envelope, it was called. Lynia opened her notebook and flipped through the pages until she found the sections Maddy had highlighted on viral structure. She hadn't taken the time to spell-copy these pictures—that was a more exacting process—but she'd started to understand the descriptions better.

Somewhat.

The answer had to be in the way viruses worked. If Meren had altered the virus Bleyiak had used on Abuiarn, what changes might he have made? Were they specific to Moranaian elves, or would the same thing happen to Naomh if Lial attempted to heal him? Lynia grabbed her pen and started scrawling down the questions. Lial might have some of the answers, especially when it came to Naomh.

She was so intent on her thoughts that she almost missed the shift in light as the potion finished. Fortunately, she caught it in time to remove the flask from the heat and shift it over to the curing station. According to the recipe, it would need to set for three marks before the herbal concoction reached full potency.

Nothing to do now but wait.

35

Lial stared down at the mage in the bed, almost hesitant to scan him. Gods, what had last night done to him? He rarely paused before attending to his duties. Now, he found himself peering at Caeleth with his eyes instead of using magic. Why? Was it fear, or was there a reason for his odd reticence? If Elan had reported nothing amiss, the latter seemed unlikely.

Even so.

The mage's cheeks had a pink tinge as though he'd been out in the cold or wind. But of course, the man had ventured into neither. Frowning, Lial pressed his wrist to Caeleth's forehead, and the heat of the man's skin set Lial's heart to pounding. That wasn't normal.

He lowered the blanket to check the mage's wound. The bandage appeared to be fine, but that meant little with a fever present. Sure enough, as soon as Lial removed the dressing and examined the injury, cold dread filled him. Where before the gash had been healing cleanly, today the scab had taken on a yellowish tinge, and the skin around the wound was an angry red.

An infection.

As always, Lial had scanned for bacteria during the initial healing. The gut in particular could be tricky that way, although elven bodies generally purged errant bacteria without a healer's aid. Most wounds that festered this way had done so because of iron fragments caught in the body, as Lyr's injury had once done.

Lial needed to scan the gash with his magic, but once again, he hesitated. A small shiver slipped down his spine like fingers mapping vertebrae, and he stiffened against the sensation. No. This wouldn't be like last night, no matter what he had to do to ensure it. He clenched his jaw and extended his magic in a quick, almost defiant scan. The truth took only a moment to find.

It wasn't iron to blame—it was the virus.

Out of reflex, Lial took a step back as he withdrew his magic, but it was a futile gesture. He'd already been exposed. As had Lynia, Elan, and gods knew how many others. Maddy, Fen, and Anna had all been here the night before. Even the guards outside the door might be at risk. But how long had Caeleth been infected? Who had given him the illness? It made no sense.

He spun around to ask Lynia if anyone had stopped by, but the words locked in his throat. She perched on the stool beside his workbench where she could hunch over her notebook. Though he couldn't see her face, he could imagine it—forehead furrowed, her teeth worrying at her lower lip as her eyes skimmed the page. How could he tell her they were both at risk? If anything happened to her, it would be his fault.

Just like Aralee.

All of his years of study, reduced to nothing. Gods. He should have left her alone. If he hadn't been a selfish *drec*, he would have withheld his feelings instead of declaring himself with a ring. He should have kept their interactions to research alone, and she would

be safe in the library, not sitting across the room from likely death—a death he would be helpless to stop.

The thought of her writhing in pain as the virus tore through her body, damaging everything in its path, had him shaking like a scout who'd stayed in the cold too long. *Miaran.* He'd made it his life's work to learn every healing method he could after Aralee's death, but none of them had helped save Korel. Quite the opposite. What if he was soon faced with the same choice he'd been forced to make last night?

He could never stop Lynia's heart. Never.

Lial pinched his eyes closed and forced himself to take a breath. Then another. If he let his thoughts keep going in that direction, he would go mad. They weren't there yet, and they might never be. Not even Caeleth was lost yet. After all, there had to be a solution, or Ralan wouldn't have tasked them to find it. The amount of virus in the young mage was far, far less than Korel had borne. If no one used healing magic on him, they might yet save him.

"Lial?"

His eyes snapped open, and he held up a hand before Lynia thought to approach. "Stay over there."

Her lips turned down. "What's wrong?"

"Caeleth has the virus." Lial walked to the center of the room, away from the mage, before daring to use his magic to scan himself. As before, he found no trace of illness. "I don't understand how this is transmitting, but we're both at risk. Even though I haven't found it in myself, I…"

Lynia's eyes went wide. "You can't be sure. But how could Caeleth be ill?"

"I don't know that either." Lial flung his arms wide, frustration welling within him. "Did anyone enter while I was gone? Did you notice anything amiss?"

"No one new entered in my presence." Lynia stood, but she didn't approach. "As for anything amiss… He seemed well enough when I checked on him for Lyr last night. He had color in his cheeks, though he did seem warmer than I would have expected for the coolness of the room."

So the fever had already been present, though Elan hadn't seemed to note it. His negligence was a problem that needed addressing, but it wasn't exactly a surprise, since fever wasn't something elves tended to experience. A young healer of Elan's skill level wouldn't have thought to check, which was both a blessing and a curse. If the other man's healing magic was stronger, his examinations would have increased the virus's fervor.

Nor had Lial's healing link alerted him to the oddity—a lapse he would have to rectify in the future.

"The only person we've known to have it is Korel," Lial mused. "But if Caeleth was building a fever yesterday, that means the sickness was affecting him last night before I returned, so I couldn't have unwittingly carried it from Oria."

Lynia's gaze flicked to the door. "I've seen guards at the door, except when I came to ask you about the fertility potion." She gasped. "Oh, no. Being with me… Did I distract you so much that…?"

He shook his head. "I have spells set on the door to alert me to anyone's entry. Only Elan is spelled to enter without disturbance."

They stared at one another for a moment, countless questions heavy in the air. Then Lynia straightened her spine, and a determined glint entered her eyes. Settling her hand on her notebook, she tipped up her chin.

"Let's get to work, then. This potion has a couple of marks to cure before we can test it. It's time to put together what we know."

"I shouldn't—"

"I've been around Caeleth as much as you have," she snapped. "Don't be an idiot. The faster we find answers, the better. For everyone."

Everything in him screamed to protect her. To send her as far from this danger as he could. But Lynia was right. No one would be safe if they couldn't discover the best way to proceed. So he notified Lyr of the latest problem, directed Maddy to stay in her rooms, summoned Elan, and then he and Lynia settled in to work, piecing together all that they'd discovered to find the connections—and the cure.

Or so they hoped.

Koranel let the guards half-carry him into the holding room where Fenere was chained, though he was more than capable of walking. If he could complete this mission, he would be free, and so he gave it his best effort, moaning softly and double-layering the glamour that made him appear battered. He needed the other man's commiseration if he hoped for cooperation.

The guards chained Koranel against the wall to Fenere's left. Koranel groaned and slumped against the stone, letting his head loll as though he were exhausted. One of the guards kicked him in the leg with a bit more force than necessary, but Koranel could hardly blame the man. After all, he had betrayed the Myern by not revealing Norin's and Allafon's disloyalty, and no matter that Koranel had been trying to protect his family.

Even receiving a pardon wouldn't erase his complicity.

Once they were alone, Koranel had to resist the urge to speak. He wanted to ask Fenere all the questions he would have demanded of Korel—things he should have started asking decades ago when

Allafon sent him to Braelyn to work with Norin. How far did this conspiracy go? Who else was involved?

What were their reasons?

Koranel didn't have anything against other types of fae or even humans. Millennia ago, they'd shared an ancestor before branching into their current forms, and all were still similar enough to allow cross-breeding. What did it matter if more of their distant cousins came to Braelyn? Unfortunately, Allafon had hated humans in particular. He'd threatened to kill Koranel's wife and children if he didn't help bring down "that human-loving Telien and his miserable family."

In the end, the why was incomprehensible.

"They've tortured you worse than me," Fenere said.

The *drec* even sounded sympathetic.

"I was in charge," Koranel said, putting a raspy growl into his voice as though he'd been screaming. "They didn't believe I knew nothing."

Fenere smirked. "Ironically, they did believe me, though the opposite is true."

Koranel rested his head against the wall. "Don't tell me. I'd rather not have something to torture out of me."

As he'd hoped, Fenere's eyes narrowed on his face as he processed what Koranel hadn't said—Fenere would be up next. "Why'd they put you in here with me?"

Koranel shrugged, rattling the chains with a harsh clack. "Guess they're taking you to isolation next. Glad to see the end of that room."

Fenere's throat worked, and his gaze darted toward the door as though the guards were about to march through. "This is Korel's fault. You think they've caught him?"

"No one brought him to where I was held," Koranel said. True, if not the whole story. "He doesn't seem the type to come back to help us."

It didn't take much to loosen Fenere's tongue—only time and fear of pain. Koranel could see the moment everything clicked in the other man's mind, shifting his plans. "Korel wanted me to stab that mage. While the man was unconscious, Korel was going to feed him some of his blood for some spell. The mage wouldn't have spotted me if I hadn't slipped on a loose stone. I barely managed to get the knife in him before he pulled down part of the ledge. Good thing you trained me to move fast in a disaster, eh? And I still got a few bruises on my back from getting pelted."

Sloppy. No wonder the man hadn't advanced far in rank. Koranel sent this new information to the Myern, but Fenere wasn't done.

"I don't know why Korel let that Seelie lord put some kind of trap in his blood. You think he actually made the mage drink it? I wasn't going to stick around to find out, but I feel bad for the mage if he did."

Koranel barely noted the end of Fenere's words, too caught up by the beginning. A trap in the blood? That didn't sound good.

"You think feeding the mage blood was some kind of trick?" Koranel asked carefully, trying to gain more information without showing too much interest.

The chains rattled with Fenere's shrug. "I don't know for sure how it works. Korel thought it would take longer for anyone to notice the trap that way, but he didn't give me details. I didn't want to know. Sounds too much like gross *Felshreh* stuff."

Koranel sent the new information to Lord Lyrnis, but he needn't have bothered connecting telepathically. Only moments passed before Fenere called out for the guards, claiming that Koranel

had confessed to having more knowledge of the attack. Koranel continued his act, moaning and pleading with the guards who carried him out, all the way until the cell doors closed.

Let Fenere feel a moment's triumph—his downfall would surely come soon enough.

Maddy paced around the spacious living room, only the view outside the windows making it clear that their guest suite was suspended in a tree. She'd never been afraid of heights, but she found herself giving those windows wide berth on each pass. Unlike Fen, of course, who was leaning against the edge of the open door leading to the balcony, his back to the view. He was too busy watching her.

"What's the deal?" he asked.

Anna frowned over her shoulder at him. "She wants to be helping Lial, idiot."

Fen huffed. "I get that, but… Elven plague. We don't even know if we already have it."

"Exactly," Maddy said. "We're staying away for safety, but we might be infected already. So why not help?"

Fen pushed away from the railing and strode back into the room, closing the outer door behind him. "If this shit circles back to Kien… Dammit, I suppose I should try to find out, even if it doesn't make sense. It might not be related to the stuff we found in the Seelie queen. We haven't had a chance to talk to Lial about how the virus worked with Korel."

"Then let's go." Maddy halted in the center of the room, her gaze going from Fen to Anna. "Unless you both want to stay here? I can help alone. It's just…Lial said Caeleth has a fever. What do elves know about treating that sort of thing? He might be way more experienced at energy healing, but not with this. Especially since he said healing magic makes it worse."

Anna stood, a determined glint in her eyes. "I'm with you. How about I grab a pitcher of water and make sure it's purified? We can use water and a washcloth to cool him down since they probably don't have fever-reducing medicine."

"I'm probably going to be useless, but I'll go, too." Fen smiled wryly. "Better than being bored, right?"

Relief lightened Maddy's steps as they crossed toward the front door. It was scary to head into danger, but everything within her told her it was the right decision. Hadn't Ralan told Lial that Caeleth needed to be guarded? They'd kept him safe from another physical attack, but perhaps that hadn't been what the prince meant. There was no way she was going to sit on the sidelines and watch disaster unfold. Not when she could help.

Lynia tapped her finger against the notebook. "I think bloodborne makes the most sense."

For a moment, Lial's brows lowered as though he would argue, but he read the passage she indicated without a word. Then he gave a hesitant shrug. "Perhaps. I am always careful to cleanse blood from my hands, and I have no cuts or scrapes where a virus might enter. But how did Morenial become ill?"

"He rode atop Kezari while they carried Korel to Oria, correct?" When he nodded again, she smiled grimly. "That could be it. She would have been covered in blood, and some might have blown on the wind."

Lial's sudden pallor stood out against the red of his hair like parchment dipped in blood. An unfortunate comparison that had

her hiding a wince. "Blown on the wind? It's a good thing Oria is under containment. We'll have to check anyone who might have been in range. Perhaps even downwind."

No need to hide the wince this time. "I didn't consider that."

"Let me contact Lyr."

While Lial did that, Lynia scrawled a few notes about their conclusions into her notebook. This situation could be bad, but if this virus tracked with the ones in the human textbooks, it could have been far worse. Bloodborne wasn't airborne, which meant that being in the same room as someone infected wouldn't transmit it. They would only need to isolate the ill and do their best to find a treatment.

But one thing bothered her—if it was bloodborne, how had Bleyiak spread the disease through Abuiarn? Actually, it was a good question no matter how it was transmitted. Was it somehow related to the magic of the place? Bleyiak was said to have been from Galare, and the fae there had to bind with the location's energy in order to use it. What had Cora said? That a Galaren might be able to inject a spell into the core of a planet's energy?

What else could they do with such a link?

On a whim, Lynia reached out to Cora. Though she sensed a moment's confusion, the other woman answered quickly enough. *"Is something wrong? Ralan and Eri are here, so I know they are well."*

Hmm. If this conversation was important, Ralan hadn't seen fit to tell his bonded. *"I've discovered that Bleyiak was said to be from Galare. You may not wish to tell me this, of course, but I'm wondering…Are there spells that join a linked Galaren by blood to a place?"*

"Blood?" Cora asked, shock and repulsion in her voice.

"We believe that's how this virus is transmitted, but I don't understand how that could have been the case on Abuiarn," Lynia said. *"When we last*

spoke, you mentioned that a Galaren could fracture or inject spells into the energy field of the place where they were linked, correct? Now I'm wondering if that spell might have involved tainted blood. Any ideas?"

"That's…" Cora paused. *"I don't know. How could he have had a blood link to everyone? That passage you read before…it sounded more like a surge of magic into anyone who was connected to Abuiarn's energy. Shove a spell or a power blast through. Activate something else."*

Activate. The word sparked in Lynia's brain like a mage globe springing to life, and she was a couple of lines into her notes before she realized that she hadn't disconnected from Cora. But it made sense now. Bleyiak hadn't sent the *poison* into the populace through the fracture—he'd activated it, just as Lial's healing magic had triggered the virus in Korel. He must have found a way to see them infected.

"Sorry, Cora."

A pause, followed by a hint of amusement. *"No problem. And Ralan says good job."*

Normally, Lynia might have paused over a compliment like that from a seer, but she merely sent her thanks and disconnected. She had to tell Lial about this. But when she glanced his way, his eyes were distant as though he still spoke with Lyr. Had something else happened?

Just as she was beginning to worry, Lial blinked a couple of times before meeting her gaze. "Well. Lyr had Koranel get information from Fenere. It seems Korel slipped up behind Fenere and fed Caeleth infected blood while he was pinned by the rockfall. That's probably why it took so long to show up. Korel's body was inundated with the virus, but it needed to establish itself in Caeleth. It had to work through his digestive system before crossing into the bloodstream."

"And why it reached the wound in his stomach, perhaps?"

Lial inclined his head. "Possibly so. You were right, as much as I hate the truth. It's a good thing I was too distracted to do a healing session on Caeleth last night. The virus is reproducing very slowly in the absence of a healer's magic."

The door opened, and Elan slipped in, worry lining the young healer's face. Those lines deepened when Lial jerked to his feet. Poor Elan. Under other circumstances, Lynia would have slipped from the room to avoid witnessing the chiding sure to come, but she didn't want to leave in case the potion showed signs of curing early.

"Elan," Lial said. "Why didn't you alert me to Caeleth's increased temperature?"

The other healer frowned. "I'm afraid I don't know what you mean."

She gave the young man a sympathetic look as Lial gestured for him to follow to the bed, but she otherwise focused on her work as Lial pointed out the varied signs of the mage's illness. Really, the poor healer hadn't done much worse than the rest of them. Most of this was a mystery to their people, after all.

"Don't be too tough on him," Lynia sent.

"I will not be. However, fevers are an irregularity he must learn to note despite their rarity. This cannot go without correction."

"I'll simply say this." She smiled down at her notebook for the annoyance she was about to cause. *"None of us have done perfectly in this, including you. I didn't consider his increased warmth to be a problem, either."*

Lial didn't respond, but she noticed that his tone softened. Little did Elan know how much he owed her.

As the two began to make note of symptoms and discuss options, Lynia observed the potion. It had turned from purple to

more of a violet color, which meant it was nearing completion. According to the recipe, the potion would be a blue violet when finished, and there would be no alteration in color no matter which angle she looked. She tilted her head, changing the way the light streamed through the flask, and the liquid shifted a deeper blue. Still not done. She sighed and returned to her notes.

She'd forgotten to ask Lial what had happened with Lord Naomh during treatment, a hole she needed to fill. If the Sidhe lord hadn't worsened with energy use, then it might be a different illness entirely. She grimaced at the very thought. The absolute last thing they needed was an extra disease floating around.

It could be another strain of the same thing, but there was no connection between the two that she was aware of. Naomh had grown sick after Meren's attack. What link could Korel have to that? Her hand tightened around her pen. There were missing facts here, and if there was one thing she hated, it was research she hadn't managed to gather yet.

A sudden commotion erupted across the room. Lynia turned toward the source of the thudding sound, and her heart slammed at the sight of Caeleth thrashing in the bed. Cursing, Lial bent to steady the man, Elan reaching to grab the mage's other arm. Lynia stood, thinking to help, but then she hesitated. What did she know about a situation like this?

As she considered her options, the door opened, and Maddy, Anna, and Fen all slipped through. Lynia's eyebrows rose. "I thought you were told to stay away."

"Fen has made me a terrible listener," Maddy quipped.

"I imagine so," Lynia said, though she suspected Fen had merely heightened the woman's natural inclinations. "But I'm afraid you've come in at a bad time."

Maddy looked over at the bed, and her eyes went wide. Without a word, she grabbed a pitcher and stack of fabric from Anna and darted across the room. What was she doing? Lynia peered after her, but her actions didn't become much clearer as she dipped a square of cloth into the water and began to brush it across Caeleth's forehead.

"Damn, he's burning up," Maddy said. "We have to get this fever down."

"You are not supposed to be here," Lial growled. "If you haven't been infected already, you're at risk of such now."

Maddy shrugged. "Yeah, well. The guy's having a seizure from his high temperature. Elves aren't exactly known for their skill with fever reduction, so I thought you might need help. Looks like I was right."

"Point taken."

Lynia gestured toward the workbench, and Fen and Anna followed her without a word. Out of reflex, she checked the potion, and the bright, blue-violet hue made her gasp. Forgetting the others, she bent down, tilting her head to see if the color changed. It didn't.

It was ready.

She pulled out a container of vials and a wooden holder and shoved a basket of stoppers into Fen's hands. "Close them after I pour. Anna can place them in the holder."

He might have nodded, but she wasn't concerned with whether he was happy with the task. He and Anna were available, and she needed to get this done. Lynia didn't know what would happen if the potion was left on the curing station, nor had she learned how to adjust the spells controlling the distilling device. Though a delay might not hurt, they didn't have another ten marks to wait for another batch if she was wrong. Caeleth needed help now.

Determined, Lynia lifted the flask and started to pour.

Standing in the private alcove in his bedroom, Lyr settled his hand gently against Eradisel. Instantly, her peace filled him until his knotted shoulders eased and his heartbeat slowed to normal. Dawn had brought more problems than expected as many had awakened to the shield blocking them inside Braelyn's lands. If he'd thought he'd had a deluge of panicked questions in the first few marks after the shield's activation, he'd been mistaken.

He had to announce what was happening, and he needed the sacred tree's power to do it.

After so many years communing with the tree, Lyr only needed to send an image of what he wanted before he received her assent. He closed his eyes and connected to the deepest level of the estate's shield, the one that showed where every person was located. Then with Eradisel's help, he expanded outward to the greater land shields until he could find every person under his command.

His body shuddered with the effort, but he pushed his exhaustion aside and opened a light mental connection. As swiftly and clearly as he could, Lyr explained the situation, though the surges of fear strained his concentration. He couldn't blame them. Disease was an unknown enemy here, and they were trapped inside with it.

"We cannot risk carrying this outside of these lands," Lyr sent. *"Though few are known to have been infected at all. I know this is a difficult and frightening event, but I am relying on you to protect the rest of Moranaia from calamity. Remain in your homes and know that you will be cared for. Above all, obey the commands of Lial and any other healers in this regard. I will coordinate aid under the guidance of his expertise."*

As soon as Lyr ended the link, he slumped into the seat he kept in the alcove. Though his hand fell from Eradisel's trunk, her energy continued to flow through him, along with wordless encouragement. He did his best to send his thanks, but with telepathy being far from his strongest gift, his head ached beneath the strain of communicating mentally once more.

He wanted to fling himself across the bed and sleep, but that wasn't an option. Not even the briefest nap. With an exhausted huff, Lyr pushed himself to his feet. There were many terrified people under his command, a responsibility too heavy to allow his own ease. If that message hadn't sufficed, he would be in his study, ready to help as needed.

Of course, he didn't expect that need to find him in the form of Kai shoving his bedroom door open with a bang. "Caolte contacted me. He said you weren't at your mirror."

Lyr groaned. "Not good, I'm guessing?"

"No." Kai ran his fingers through his hair, panic twisting his face. "Naomh has grown worse, but it's more than that."

"More?"

Kai's nostrils flared. "Now Caolte's sick."

Miaran.

36

Lial couldn't relax even after Caeleth's seizure stopped. The fever still raged, and there was no guarantee his body wouldn't react again at any moment. They had to find a way to lower the mage's temperature. Quickly, Lial searched his memories for what he'd learned on the condition, though it would be little. There were a few rare occasions where gut bacteria made it into the bloodstream and caused a fever before the patient was healed. The only other parallel was what happened sometimes after childbirth or a pregnancy loss.

In usual circumstances, he would simply go in with his magic and heal the cause, erasing the increased temperature with it. Currently not an option. Maddy's technique of wiping cool water across the man's head and chest appeared to help. But for how long? Until the virus was gone, the fever would only return.

He tugged the blanket off, leaving only a sheet covering Caeleth's lower body. Then he connected with the cooling spell on the room and lowered the temperature slightly. Too much would be a shock to the man's body—that much Lial knew. But something else teased at his memory, close enough to be frustrating but not to clarify.

"Do you have herbs for this?" Maddy asked. "Fever-reducing medicine?"

Ah! Lial smiled as Maddy's question shoved the errant memory forward. Women took a special potion after miscarriage or birth that prevented complications. Many pregnant women kept a dose on hand in case there wasn't a healer nearby. And one of those herbs prevented fever.

"*Tobahn*," Lynia said.

Lial lifted his brows. "Yes. I was just recalling that very one."

"It was on Bleyiak's import list, so I looked it up." Lynia lifted a vial, but it wasn't from his baskets. "I have the new potion complete, if you want to try it on Caeleth. I'll hunt for a distillation of *tobahn* while you consider it."

It was a risky thing, trying a potion he hadn't personally seen tested. A concoction vaguely mentioned in an ancient book? But what choice did they have? The man had shifted from flushed to a sallow white, and a brief glance at his wound revealed the reason— the barely healed flesh had torn open once more. Traces of blood welled in the yellowed scabs and trailed down his side.

"How is it administered?" Lial asked.

"Orally." Lynia marched across the room with a determined stride, though her hold on the vial was gentle. "There was no mention of any other method. I don't know if it would be effective to pour on the wound."

Lial took the vial and lifted it, peering through the glass to the liquid within. He probed it with his magic as deeply as he dared, and he didn't find any components that would cause harm if applied topically. That didn't mean there weren't any, though. How much time did they have? He flashed his magic across the mage for the briefest of scans.

The virus had accelerated its reproduction in the couple of marks since his last examination. If he didn't act, the man would be nearly as sick as Korel by nightfall. It was time to trust Lynia's research and Ralan's prophecy. Either they would defeat this plague together, or they would all be overrun.

Decided, Lial removed the stopper from the vial, tipped Caeleth's head back, and poured a sip between his lips. "How much?"

"Half a vial now and the rest in another mark."

Lial nodded and eased more of the potion between the mage's lips. Then again and again until half was gone. It was surprisingly difficult not to upend the entire thing into the man's mouth for good measure, but he knew well enough that more was not always a boon.

After replacing the stopper, Lial slipped the vial into his pocket and studied the wound. He needed to do a deeper examination with magic. Had any of the interior stitches burst, or was the damage on the outside only? More injury to the man's organs could be a disaster in this situation, releasing toxins and bacteria into an already ravaged body. He didn't dare risk using his healing magic, though.

Miaran.

"I'm going to have to reopen this wound," he murmured.

Lynia, who had just returned with the *tobahn* tincture, let out a gasp. "You'll be… But the blood…"

It was a risk to come in contact with the infected blood, that was certain. Unfortunately, he didn't have much choice. "Did the book say how long that potion takes to work?"

"Several marks beyond the second dose to work fully," Lynia whispered, her gaze locked on the trail of blood on Caeleth's side. "But I'm guessing he can't wait that long."

Lial sighed. "No."

"Do you not have *any* protective gear?" Maddy demanded from her spot at the head of the bed. "Seriously, nothing? No gloves or masks? Safety glasses?"

Lial frowned at her. "With cleansing spells, why would we develop something else? After thousands upon thousands of years, no one has considered the possibility of a plague. Even Abuiarn is an anomaly, one few remember."

"Then it's something to think about." Maddy's eyes narrowed on her own hand as she dipped the cloth back in the water. "Crap. I'm contacting his sweat here. *I* should be wearing protective gloves."

After ordering Elan to retrieve the pouch containing his surgical tools, Lial took the second vial of *tobahn* from Lynia and dispensed a single sip to Caeleth. With luck, it would successfully treat the fever alongside the other potion, but he was uncomfortably aware of how uncertain all of this was. Including his own safety.

Lial met Lynia's eyes. "I will do my best to keep myself protected."

Though her expression was somber, she nodded. "Thank you."

He took the kit from Elan and checked to ensure the tools he would need were all there. Normally, he would shift his patient to the stone table, but the less Caeleth was moved, the better. The bedding would already need to be burned, after all.

Before he could proceed, Lyr's mind brushed against his. Lial sat back in his chair, gritting his teeth even as he opened communication. *"What? I'm about to do surgery."*

"Caolte is sick, too."

Lyr didn't need to say anything more to have Lial cursing aloud, drawing more than one concerned glance. *"Same as Naomh?"*

"Not yet as bad. And Naomh has gotten worse." Dread slipped through Lyr's mental tone. *"Dare I ask who you're doing surgery on?"*

Not just dread—pain lined the edges of their link. *"Why do I sense pain? Are you injured?"*

"I sent out a mental call to everyone outside the healing tower, and now my head hurts. That's all," Lyr explained. *"Now answer the question."*

"Caeleth. I have to re-stitch his wound." Without magic, too. Lial did a quick mental search of his herbs for anything that would reduce such extreme pain. Something he had never had to consider before. *"Lynia created a potion we're testing against the virus."*

"Well, we need to test it on Naomh. He's apparently near death."

Lial stood, his chair scraping against the floor with the force. *"Near death?"*

"So I'm told." Lyr paused. *"What do you advise?"*

"I don't know. Let me think. I'll contact you when I decide."

With little choice, Lial braved a scan of Caeleth's wound with his magic. So many of the internal stitches had shredded that he let out a weary sigh. Staying here and leaving Naomh and Caolte to their fate would earn him no friends—it might even lose him one in Kai. But this had to be repaired. The nastiness spilling from the mage's stomach would kill him before even the virus could.

"What is it?" Lynia asked.

"Your son contacted me. Caolte is now ill, and Naomh has worsened." Avoiding the others' surprised glances, Lial hurried over to the shelf of potions and grabbed three. "However, if I leave here, Caeleth will die."

He couldn't forget Ralan's warning, one he'd thought because of the assassin. *Caeleth's death could cause decades of trouble for Lyr. Maybe centuries. Caeleth needs to be guarded.* But it hadn't been an attack they'd needed to shield against. It was this.

Maddy lowered the cloth into the pitcher and met his eyes. "I can help. Maybe if Lynia tells me what to do, I can administer the new potion?"

"I'll go with you," Lynia said to the younger woman. "I created the concoction, and my age will earn me respect where they might doubt you. No offense intended, of course."

"None taken," Maddy said. Then she shook her head. "It's a smart idea. I've had run-ins with these two Sidhe lords before. They aren't enemies, but I wouldn't call them friends, either."

Fen and Anna joined them, getting close enough that Lial tensed. There were far too many in the room with a deadly virus for his comfort. "I'm not certain about this plan. You aren't ready to heal something like this, Maddy. And Lynia…"

"I do hope you aren't about to utter some drivel about me needing your protection."

As he spread his pouch of tools across the bed beside Caeleth, Lial exhaled through his nose and tried to shake off his nerves. Wordlessly, he handed the vials to Elan and ran a cleansing spell over his hands and the patient's stomach. He could only hope it wouldn't trigger the virus to replicate.

"Lyni, you know the reason for my fear. It's similar to your own." Her lips tightened, and his hands burned with the need to grip hers. But he couldn't. "I'm trying not to let that rule me anymore. I love you, but I don't control you."

"Is that supposed to be agreement?" someone muttered.

Lial was too busy staring at Lynia to care who.

Her eyes gleamed wetly, but she only nodded. "We need to do this. Shield yourself, too."

He didn't have to ask what she meant—the full import was clear. They were both taking risks. Lial caressed her with his gaze, letting

the weight of his emotions reside in full view. Then he bent over Caeleth, and remembering Maddy's earlier words, he placed a thin shield of energy between his face and the surgery site. Probably not ample by human standards, but it was the best he could do on short notice.

"Would you tell Lyr the plan? Elan and I will do our best to save Caeleth." Lial nodded at Elan, who administered the first vial. It would work rapidly thanks to the magic imbued within—a blessing and a curse if the magic caused the virus to spread. Another risk he had no choice but to take. "And tell him to send Tynan to Aris once he arrives."

"Of course," Lynia said. "I'll have a vial sent to Morenial, too."

He didn't have time to curse himself for forgetting yet another patient. The task at hand could no longer wait. "Thank you. If you need me while you're gone, test the ring. For you, I will answer. No one else."

Then he selected his sharpest knife and thought through each step of the coming surgery—each angle and possible outcome. He barely noticed when the others left.

Eri sat on her window seat, her cheek resting on her upturned knees as she stared out the glass at the early morning light. Across the room, Iren was fast asleep, curled up in the armchair he'd claimed when they returned from dinner. She'd pretended to be all right so he wouldn't worry, but she had a feeling he knew.

Her father had returned from helping Lord Lyr in the middle of the night, not too many marks before dawn, but Eri hadn't gone out there. For some reason, she didn't want her father's comfort. Or maybe she didn't want him to lie to her anymore.

He thought she wouldn't guess that something was terribly wrong, even though it was obvious. Whatever it was, it had to be the reason her Sight was blocked. Unless the goddess was upset with her. Eri nibbled on her lower lip and tried not to think about that. Not being able to See well was bad enough.

Her father hadn't even noticed how bothered she was by her messed up Sight. She hadn't minded the missing pieces at first, assuming there was some grown-up reason for the blank strands around Lial. Then she'd stopped seeing Lynia's future, too. She'd barely had a chance to nudge the two together.

Yep. Something was wrong. She was young, not stupid.

But maybe the problem was within her. She'd made so many mistakes, and now people were afraid of her. Was it because she'd accidentally gotten Iren hurt by leading him into that cave? Or helping him rearrange stuff in the tower where his father needed to stay? She might have been so bad that even the goddess wanted her to stop Seeing the futures so much. And Iren. He'd acted strange around her since they'd come back from dinner.

Eri pinched her eyes tighter and reached for the strands. There were a lot, so many futures it took her a moment to orient herself. But at the same time…holes. Too many holes, the threads completely invisible. She could see a lot of variations of herself, her family, her baby sister…then nothing.

Her heart pounded as she searched for Iren's strands. So much missing, and the rest scrambled. And she couldn't find a why. Why couldn't she find a why? Random images of his parents flickered through and then disappeared. Were they all going to die or something?

She heard the door open, but she didn't open her eyes. She could feel her father's energy without looking, and she didn't want to hear him tell her to stop Looking. How could she ignore this? It was her destiny to Look and to plan. She couldn't even remember when she'd first known it.

It just...was.

Her father lifted her from the seat and then settled down with her in his lap. "Eri."

"Don't bother," she whispered, though she couldn't resist tucking her head against his neck. "I know you're going to lie."

He sighed against her hair. "I'm not."

"Fine. Are we going to die?" she challenged.

He stayed silent so long that she slumped in resignation. But then he surprised her by answering. "I don't think so, but it isn't impossible."

Eri sat up straight so she could meet his eyes. "Why can't I See?"

"I think you know," he answered.

"The goddess said there were some things a child shouldn't experience in a vision." She nibbled on her lower lip. "I thought maybe it was adult stuff at first, but..."

Her father tucked her hair away from her face with a sad smile. "I'm sorry, Eri. I wanted to guard you, but I can feel your distress from the other room. The truth is, there's an illness out there. A virus that can hurt our kind. The potential number of dead...that's what the goddess doesn't want you to experience."

"I have known of bad stuff before without witnessing it," Eri said. "Lady Megelien blurs my Sight. I didn't actually See you sort of die even though I knew."

"The scope of this could be great, beloved." He kissed her forehead. "But it isn't your fault, and you haven't been bad. Perhaps we should start working together instead of against each other, hmm?"

Eri smiled at that. "Okay."

"Good," he said. "Then I'll give you a mission. Keep Iren here. We need his father to get his next healing session without interruption. Think you can do that?"

She wrapped her arms around his neck and hugged. "You know it."

37

After grabbing the last three potions from the rack, Lynia headed straight to her rooms, no hesitation in her stride. Behind her, Maddy and her mates trailed, but Lynia didn't ask why. She left them waiting while she sent one of the vials to Morenial and then connected with Lyr and updated him on the latest happenings, including their current plan. While she expected him to protest out of his usual protectiveness, he didn't argue.

"I'll send two of the elite guard with you," he insisted. Not a surprise. *"Naomh and Caolte are our allies now, but if either of them should die…"*

She smiled as she strapped a knife to her thigh and tugged on a pair of pants with a slit in the pocket so she could draw the blade free. After shrugging into a short, long-sleeved tunic, she wrapped a belt holding another knife around her waist. Lynia had learned more than one trick for self-protection since being attacked.

But even so, she wasn't a warrior. *"If they are willing to take the risk, I would welcome their aid. There are no guarantees this potion will work for anyone."*

"I will ensure that they understand." Weariness and worry filled her son's tone, making her heart ache. *"Kai is going to assist Inona in*

helping you through so he can keep his distance. She has agreed to accompany you, too."

"Thank you." Lynia attached a hard leather pouch to her belt and stuck the vials of potion inside before heading to the door. *"Have them meet me at the portal. I'm going there now."*

She could feel, then, how much Lyr didn't want her to do this. His frustration was like a humming spell in the back of his mind, fighting to be free. But he didn't say a word about it. *"I love you, Laiala. Be safe."*

"I love you, too, tieln."

Lynia let her feelings slip across their mental link before they disconnected. If she'd learned one thing in her long life, it was the importance of telling others how she felt. She'd rarely said the words with Telien, taking their link for granted. Why repeat what the other knew? But sometimes, the words were their own reward. A purposeful thought rather than background noise.

She closed her bedroom door behind her and froze as a memory hit. *I love you, but I don't control you.* Lial had said the words, but had she answered in kind? She searched her mind but couldn't remember amidst the chaos and worry. And yes, fear. She'd hinted that she might the night before, but she hadn't granted him any certainty. Now, she was heading into danger. Hardly a war, of course, but not a casual journey.

Maddy straightened from the wall where she'd leaned beside her mates. "Lynia?"

"I wish I could contact Lial, but I don't want to distract him right now." He would undoubtedly want to hear about her feelings, though not during major surgery. "I'll have to tell him what I forgot later."

"Hey, maybe the ring will work across dimensions," Fen said as he and Anna approached. "Glad to see Lial took my advice."

Why did Lynia have the feeling she didn't want to know more? Not that she would hurt Fen's feelings by saying so. "I regret to report that he didn't share the source of his inspiration."

"Worry about it later, Fen," Maddy said, sending her mate a cross look. "We need to go."

Lynia started down the hallway, trusting the others to keep pace. "Are Fen and Anna accompanying us to the portal?"

"They are coming with us," the young woman countered.

"Really?" Lynia lifted a brow. "I do not recall agreeing to such a thing."

"Think about it." Although Maddy's voice held a hard edge, there was a pleading light in her eyes. "The three of us purged a similar darkness from the Seelie queen before anyone knew what it was. Maybe Meren infected Naomh with the same thing. If the potion doesn't work on this version, we might be able to pull it from his blood the same way."

Lynia considered that as they descended the spiral staircase and exited through the front doors. Cold wrapped around them, and she pulled up the hood of her cloak without breaking stride. An unspoken question replayed in her mind with each step—was it worth the risk of exposure? They'd already been too close to Caeleth in the healing tower.

But Maddy's argument was sound. They'd found a solution for a similar illness using a different method. Except... "Why didn't you attempt this on Caeleth?"

"The virus in him is actively reproducing, but the one inside the Seelie queen was inert. After what we've learned here, I sort of wonder what Meren planned to do to activate it."

"If Naomh and Caolte are sick, doesn't that mean their version isn't inert?" Lynia asked.

"Maybe." The younger woman shrugged. "If there's a chance it isn't, we might as well have the three of us there together so no one has to travel back and forth."

"The risk…"

"We're all willing to take it," Anna said softly, and the other two nodded.

Lynia turned down the path to the portal. "Fine. Let's see what we can do."

As soon as the patient's heart rate slowed to an even pace, Lial pricked the man's skin with a needle to check if he was numb. A clumsy method, but it worked. Caeleth showed no reaction, which meant Lial needed to act fast. The potion would wear off within a mark, and subsequent doses wouldn't be as effective.

Lial handed Elan the half-empty vial of Lynia's potion. "Watch the time and give him the rest if I'm still stitching."

He didn't wait for an answer, knowing his assistant would obey without question. Instead, Lial lifted his knife and made the incision through the partially healed skin beneath the stitches. Blood pooled and ran until he had no choice but to use a hint of magic to close off the relevant veins—but only for a moment. He grabbed clamps from his pouch to use where he could, minimizing the energy required.

He didn't bother scanning for the virus. He couldn't focus on it, not with the wrecked mess of organs he had to repair. He kept his thoughts on the rise and fall of needle and thread and the steady pulse of the patient under his care. He'd failed once with Korel, and he might do so again.

But it wouldn't be for lack of trying.

The gallbladder would have to go, as would a portion of stomach and intestine. The shredded stitches had created so many new tears that it would take marks to fix, if it was possible at all. Without the threat of the virus, he might have attempted it, but it wouldn't be worthwhile now. The patient would survive well enough with the alterations.

A sour smell hit his nose, and he used the lightest burst of magic to clear the toxins leaking from the patient's gut. Then he did his best to stitch and repair faster. Sweat dampened his tunic and beaded lightly at his temples, but he didn't dare brush at his face. The unpleasant smell of infection wafting from the wound hadn't entirely disappeared.

Caeleth's body began to tremble, and Lial risked a glance at the man's face. He'd gone even paler, and a sheen of sweat covered his skin. The virus? The fever? Lial couldn't pull his hands away to check.

"Is his temperature elevated?" he asked Elan.

His assistant rested his wrist against the mage's forehead. "No. His temperature is normal now."

Perhaps Lynia's potion was working. Anxious to find out, Lial finally scanned his patient for the virus. Lessened—but only in parts of the body. Replication hadn't halted in the wound, no doubt because of the magic he'd been forced to use. The fever must be breaking because of the *tobahn*.

"How long until the next dose?"

"A quarter mark."

Then it would take time to start working. *Miaran.* He needed to stop the patient's trembling, but more magic would undo current progress. Not to mention increase the amount of virus in the gut. Should he risk washing the wound with more of the new tincture? It would either accelerate healing or cause some unknown disaster.

Which was the greater risk?

As Lial ended his scan, he detected a trace of another danger—gut bacteria entering the bloodstream. Gods. Well, that solved the question of greater risk. He was going to have to use more magic to solve that. Immediately.

"Pour a couple of drops of that into the wound," Lial said.

Elan didn't hesitate. He too seemed to realize there wasn't much choice. Hurriedly, Lial used his magic to spread the concoction as he sent his energy after the bacteria. None of his stitching and tinctures would matter if the bacteria weren't purged.

It took only moments, but everywhere his magic touched, the virus reproduced in a frenzy. Lial withdrew his power and did his best to stitch while fighting the urge to scan and monitor. They couldn't have much time left with the numbing potion, but it would be difficult to tell without magic.

How did human healers manage without scanning?

He barely noticed when Elan administered the rest of Lynia's potion. This repair work was too intricate, and he had to pause periodically to remove tissue. But finally, he was almost through, just the outer skin left to stitch. The sour smell was nearly gone, but detecting it at all was a touch worrying. He had to hope all of this wouldn't be for nothing.

"If there are any drops left in the vial, upend them."

Elan held the vial upside down, and the last remnant rolled down the glass to land in the cut with a wet plop. Lial resumed stitching, hoping to seal as much inside as he could. It might not work, but it didn't appear to hurt. At this point, they needed whatever aid they could find.

Abruptly, Caeleth's trembling increased, and the mage let out a harsh groan.

"More *tobahn*," Lial said.

As Elan complied, Lial focused on his task. But the sharp flinch of his patient beneath him caught him by surprise and the needle rolled, piercing the side of his finger as he pulled it through Caeleth's skin. Lial cursed and ran a cleansing spell over his hands at once, knowing it might not be enough.

He couldn't think about that now. He had a patient to stabilize.

Lynia had never seen an underhill realm so denuded of life. She'd visited a few on diplomatic missions with Telien, and even the ones artfully designed to simulate winter hadn't been so lacking in life. There was no carefully arranged snow with its winter greenery. Instead, the trees were bare, the leaves brown and decaying on the forest floor. The trail was lined with dead flowers, and the path itself hadn't been cleared.

If Caolte now held the energy of this realm, he must be more ill than she'd imagined.

"Wow," Maddy said. "Are we in the right place?"

"Kai assured me that we were," Inona answered, though she frowned at the trees with equal confusion. "Otherwise, I would be asking the same."

Pehnen, one of Lynia's bodyguards, moved forward to take the lead, the other guard trailing behind. Pehnen and Orit had watched over her frequently over the centuries, so she hadn't been surprised when they'd agreed to this risk. She'd already thanked them, but she still sent Pehnen a grateful smile as he passed by.

So far, they'd only encountered a single warrior guarding the gate, and he'd stayed as far away as he could while confirming their purpose. The lack of visible protection made her as uneasy as the

mission itself. The Seelie didn't tend to post their guards in the treetops the way Moranaians did, so one could assume they were at a minimum crew.

After a short walk, a large house emerged from the too-quiet forest. Two guards stood beside the front door, but there was no other sign of life despite the size of the place. Though it was worrisome, Lynia kept her expression smooth as they halted a short distance away. The warrior on the left took a step forward.

"I am Callian Myernere i Lynia Dianore nai Braelyn, here on behalf of my son, Myern Lyrnis Dianore, and our healer, Sebarah Lial Caran." Lynia met the guard's gaze. "I and my companions are here at the behest of Lord Caolte a Nuall."

The warrior bowed. "Yes, milady. If you would follow me?"

That had gone better than she'd expected. The Seelie Sidhe could be quite formal—and fierce with it. Technically speaking, neither Lynia nor the others had been invited here. Under different circumstances, the switch in people would not have gone unnoted. Was the situation that desperate?

Pehnen followed the guard in first, Lynia just behind. They crossed a huge entryway with a sweeping staircase and descended more stairs than she'd anticipated. What kind of place was this? The building could have housed hundreds, but they saw no one except the guard who led them. A lonely place if she'd ever seen one.

Once they reached a massive ballroom deep underground, the guard bid them to wait and left. Lynia examined the elaborate walls and intricately inlaid floor, her gaze eventually resting on the broken spot in the ceiling where one of the elaborate, hanging mage globes was missing. Frowning, she examined the floor beneath and spotted the gouge.

This must have been the room where Kai had fought with Naomh. He'd mentioned one of the globes crashing down from a surge of Naomh's magic. If memory served, Kai and Arlyn had emerged here from a series of underground rooms. Whoever had designed this place had taken the idea of the underhill a bit too seriously if there were layers deeper than this.

A door opened at the far end, and Caolte appeared. His flame-red hair lacked the spark of fire she'd noted on the few times she'd seen him. Their introduction at the autumn festival had been brief, but that hint of flame was too noteworthy to go unremarked. Combined with his sallow skin, she had no trouble believing that he was ill.

"Lyr warned me of your arrival," Caolte said in a low, rough voice. "But he made no mention of so many companions."

So Lyr had notified the Seelie of the change in plans while they were traveling through the Veil. That explained their easy entry. "Princess Maddy brings her mates, Prince Fen and Princess Anna."

Beside her, Maddy let out a sigh, but the sound was too light to carry far. Lynia had to hold back a smile. As much as the three young fae didn't like their new status, it would carry undeniable weight here. And no small amount of added safety.

"I see you've all advanced to royalty since our last meeting," Caolte said. "Can't offer congratulations about that misfortune."

Fen laughed. "Got that right. Listen, I know there was some tension between you and my uncle when I was sick, and I couldn't begin to guess whether you're feuding with my mother. But I have no argument with you or Naomh. My mates and I have helped others with a similar illness, so we thought we'd see what we could do here, too. No strings attached."

In a less formal—hah—situation, Lynia would have rubbed at the bridge of her nose. But even if Fen had no desire to stick to niceties, she wouldn't abandon them. "Please forgive our presumption. If you prefer, only Maddy and I will advance."

Caolte waved his hand. "All of you may come. Even the bodyguards. At this point, I don't care who sees the tunnels."

Though Lynia wasn't sure she liked the sound of that, she motioned the group forward. From what she'd heard from Arlyn and Kai, the descent would be interesting, if nothing else.

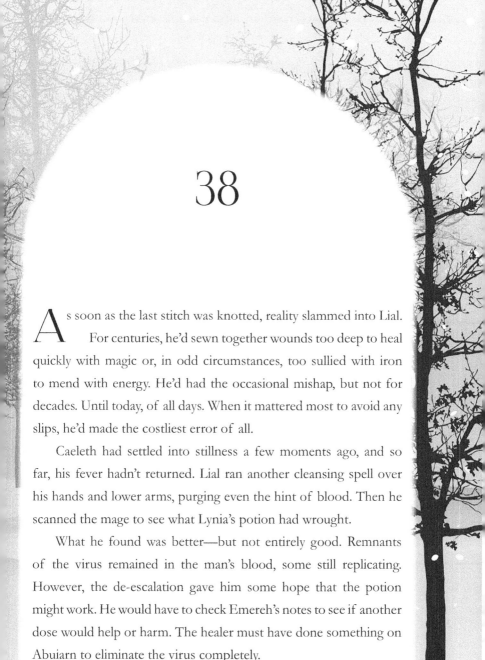

38

As soon as the last stitch was knotted, reality slammed into Lial. For centuries, he'd sewn together wounds too deep to heal quickly with magic or, in odd circumstances, too sullied with iron to mend with energy. He'd had the occasional mishap, but not for decades. Until today, of all days. When it mattered most to avoid any slips, he'd made the costliest error of all.

Caeleth had settled into stillness a few moments ago, and so far, his fever hadn't returned. Lial ran another cleansing spell over his hands and lower arms, purging even the hint of blood. Then he scanned the mage to see what Lynia's potion had wrought.

What he found was better—but not entirely good. Remnants of the virus remained in the man's blood, some still replicating. However, the de-escalation gave him some hope that the potion might work. He would have to check Emereh's notes to see if another dose would help or harm. The healer must have done something on Abuiarn to eliminate the virus completely.

Lial strode toward the workbench, but he stopped in the middle of the room. He could check all the notes he wanted, but he couldn't avoid the one thing he didn't want to face. Had he been infected? He lifted his hand, staring at the finger where the needle had pierced. There was no sign of a scab, no mark to reveal his doom.

Perhaps he would be safe.

His deep exhale caressed his skin, its warmth an echo of his healing energy as he sent his magic into himself. But though his lungs found new oxygen, his heart found the opposite of hope. Such a few tiny flecks of darkness to steal so much.

"Elan," Lial said roughly. "I have to check something. Then I'll need you to render me unconscious."

"Pardon me?"

Lial glanced over his shoulder. "I'm infected. The needle caught my skin."

The younger healer's eyes widened. "But why do I need to...?"

Though Lial clenched his hand out of reflex, the motion would do nothing to stop the poison now in his blood. "Healing energy speeds the virus's spread. A type of magic I happen to be filled with. After I'm unconscious, my energy will need to be drained. Too bad I'm not allergic to iron, as that would do it."

"Why don't you take the new potion?" Elan asked.

Lial closed the distance to his workbench and stared at the empty vial rack. "I believe Lynia took the rest with her. We'll need to buy time to create more."

Emotion roiled within him like the liquid in a distilling flask. He'd promised Lynia he would be careful, only to ruin it all. Yet again, he could only curse himself for letting his love for her be free. *If you plan to throw your life on everyone's funeral pyre, we should end this now,* she'd said. Though that hadn't been his intention the result would be the same. She deserved far better than this agony.

His gaze landed on the large, ancient book opened beside the distilling apparatus. *The Wayfarer's Trial*, the journal of Emereh.

Without stopping to think, Lial's hands reached for the flask, and he began following the instructions out of rote. He'd made so many different tinctures over the years that it took little time. Unfortunately, it took seven marks just to distill, then two to three more to cure.

Ten marks to keep the virus from eating him alive.

Before heading upstairs, Lial placed a marker in the book and flipped to the beginning. He'd never met a journal-keeping healer who didn't notate their methods within the introductory section of the text, usually behind a long discussion about why they were keeping the notes in the first place. If there was anything they were missing about this cure, it would be there.

Under the circumstances, it was a good thing he knew what he was looking for.

They ended up in a small room, one so cramped Lynia's shoulder brushed against Maddy's as they circled the low stone slab in the middle of the dirt floor. Vines and leaves withered around Naomh where he lay atop the rock, and his breathing was so shallow she feared he might already be dead. Then a cough shook his body, disabusing her of that notion.

"I developed a similar cough this morning," Caolte said quietly. "Though mine is less frequent and not so deep."

So far, Lynia hadn't seen Caolte cough, but she didn't doubt his word. "Could you have been infected from the same original source?"

Caolte shook his head. "Lial found no illness in me before."

Maddy nudged her shoulder gently and took a step back. Although Lynia didn't know the reason, she followed her lead, as did

Fen and Anna. "If this is airborne, we're all at risk," Maddy said. "We need some way to contain the germs."

"Germs?" Caolte asked, frowning.

"The virus." Maddy retreated toward the door, and they all followed her back out into the hallway. "It can be shed through breath, especially if there's coughing or sneezing."

"I have never heard of such a thing," Caolte said, but he created more space between them despite the doubt in his words. "Did Lial sicken from his last visit?"

"I don't think so," Maddy replied.

Lynia could answer that, at least. Lial had scanned himself enough that he would have known, and he'd not avoided her the way he'd tried to after Korel's death. "No, he wasn't."

Caolte's eyes narrowed. "Then it makes no sense."

Fen took a step forward, the impatience in his expression making Lynia hold her breath. "Then how do you explain your illness?" Fen snapped. "Have you been making out with your brother? There aren't too many other ways to catch something."

"If you weren't here on a mission of aid—"

"Enough," Lynia said firmly, employing her most stringent *behave* tone. "We are here to offer what we can, but none of us are Lial. We're doing our best. That being said, these three are from Earth where viruses are common, whereas elves and fae know little about such things. I'm inclined to trust their analysis in this, and arguing will only waste precious time."

The fight left Caolte's demeanor. He coughed against his arm before rubbing his palm against his forehead with an exhausted sigh. "You're correct. I can take young Fen to task at a later date. I suppose the question now is one of risk. If Maddy is correct, it is not safe for any of you to be in the room."

"Do you have any thick scarves?" Anna asked, apparently surprising Fen enough that he stopped glaring at Caolte.

"Oh, that's good thinking." Maddy lifted the edge of her cloak. "We could cover our mouths and noses with our cloaks, but that would get annoying after a while. I mean, it isn't a perfect solution, but it would lessen our chances of infection."

Lynia stared at the young healer. "That would stop a virus? Why haven't you suggested such a thing sooner?"

"Because the illness on Moranaia doesn't act the same. No one is coughing there or anything." An apology flashed in Maddy's eyes. "It wouldn't do much good against something in the blood unless you're performing surgery or something. Blood doesn't float in the air."

Caolte flicked his fingers toward the stairs. "I sent out a call for scarves. In the meantime, what do you suggest? Naomh worsens by the hour."

"How about I scan you?" Maddy asked. "I'd like to see if your virus is similar to others we have treated."

At Caolte's nod, the young healer covered her lower face with the edge of her cloak and moved closer to the man, though she stayed out of touching range. As the moments passed, the healer's expression remained the same, her brow wrinkled in concentration.

An unusual sort of restlessness flitted through Lynia's gut and settled beneath her breastbone with a twist. Foreboding. It was the same pressure that had led her to hurry on the potion, the sensation so strong she wondered if she had a hint of the seer's gift. She'd had the same disconnected anxiety for days before Telien's death.

Was this mission about to go wrong?

Maddy shifted, awareness of her surroundings returning to her gaze. "This is like a weird hybrid of our two problems, and that sucks."

Perhaps that explained what was behind Lynia's uneasiness. Between Caolte's confusion, Anna's resigned sigh, and Fen's harsh expletive, the news wasn't pleasing to anyone. Yet that didn't seem right, either. What was the problem? Was there something else they were missing?

"It's sort of like the darkness we removed from the Seelie…I mean, from our previous patient's blood, but this is more active," Maddy mused. "It doesn't react to healing energy, though. I don't know if the potion will do anything to stop it or not."

"You have a potion?" Caolte asked.

Lynia opened the pouch at her waist and pulled a vial free. "Yes. We developed this from a healer's notes on a similar disease that almost wiped out one of our colonies several millennia ago."

"I see." Caolte stared at the vial for a long moment. "Have you tested it?"

Though she wanted to prevaricate, Lynia wouldn't. "Not fully. We gave it to someone before I left, and we witnessed no poor reactions. But I also don't know if it helped."

The other man continued to study the vial with an expression so intense she expected the fire to return to his hair. Apparently, he was too exhausted, for no spark appeared by the time he finally gave a sharp nod. Meeting her gaze, he held out his hand.

"I will try it," Caolte said. "If it works, we can risk the mixture on Naomh. I would rather be the one to suffer if we're wrong."

There was more family drama here than she could begin to guess at, and she had no intention of trying. If Caolte wanted to risk himself for his brother, she wouldn't stop him. She didn't know the half-Seelie's age, but she suspected he was far older than she was. More than old enough to make his own choices without being questioned by a stranger.

Lynia crossed the space between them and settled the vial in his hand, then backed away. "Drink half now. The rest you'll take in a mark. Or hour, I suppose you'd say."

He uncorked the vial and tossed back half without a moment's hesitation. Aside from a slight grimace at the taste, he showed no reaction. She couldn't say she would have been as bold. The thought of using a potion gleaned from an ancient book made her apprehensive if she stopped to consider it—so she did her best not to.

"When will I feel the effects?"

"I have no idea," Lynia answered. "Maddy?"

"I'll check him again in a bit to see if the potion is starting to kill the virus." Maddy crossed her arms. "I guess it was a waste for Fen and Anna to come, because that's all I know to do. We can't pull this out of the blood if it has already taken root in the lungs."

Anna wrapped her arm around Maddy's waist. "It was a good thought."

If only it had been so easy. Lynia fought the urge to pace up and down the long corridor stretching behind her. She wanted to be back on Moranaia already, not standing here staring at a sick half-Seelie lord. Part of her had hoped Maddy's other idea might have been possible. The triad could have pulled the virus from Naomh's blood, and they'd already be on their way.

Lynia glanced over her shoulder, spotting her bodyguards and Inona standing guard at the far end of the corridor. Everything within her longed to rejoin them and begin the journey back to Moranaia. The wait was going to be intolerably long.

Especially since the dread in her heart hadn't eased.

An odd awareness tingled over her skin, and the ring on her right hand warmed until she studied the pale yellow stone with a

frown. This ring connected her to Lial, which meant… Her heart pounding, she poured energy into the stone to activate the link. The metal heated until the ring was almost uncomfortable to wear, but it was worth it when the mental connection snapped firm.

"Lynia. I dare not use much magic, but I had to speak to you."

She pressed her hand against her breastbone, the warmth from the ring settling above her heart. *"What's wrong?"*

"I'm infected. The needle slipped." Very little emotion crossed with his words at this distance, but she still caught the hint of self-recrimination. *"I'm sorry. Elan is going to render me unconscious while the next batch of potion brews. There's more information on the potions in the introductory chapter of the book, but I don't have time to describe. I love you."*

"I love you, too," she answered automatically.

Before it was too late.

"Take care of yourself, beloved," Lial sent.

Then he disconnected the link, so abruptly her other hand clenched around the ring as though she could pull him back through that fragile connection. Hot tears tracked down her face, but they did nothing to wash away her resolve. Sick Seelie lords or no, she was going back to Moranaia. Now.

She never should have left.

39

Lial shouldn't have used the energy required to contact Lynia over such an immense distance, but a quick scan revealed no sign that communication magic had increased the virus's spread. His own innate healing powers, on the other hand… He took a deep breath through his nose and exhaled slowly through his mouth. Then again. A small calming effort for a massive, terrifying problem.

He had no idea if he would ever wake again.

Nevertheless, Lial stretched out on the bed and did his best to remain composed as a pale Elan hovered over him. If he had more time, Lial would contact Ralan and yell at him for the inaccuracy of his prophecy. Unless, of course, it had been a lie all along that Lial had little risk in all of this. There were no guarantees with his cousin.

It was far better to place his trust in Lynia. She would find the page he'd marked in *The Wayfarer's Trial* and use the information to perfect the potion. He could allow himself no other thought as he settled against the pillow.

"Do it," he muttered.

"But what if Caeleth worsens?" Elan asked in a low, frantic

voice. "What if you develop a fever or other sign of illness? I don't have the power or training to save either of you."

Lial sighed. He couldn't even have a quick, easy rest when he was possibly dying, could he? "Use the *tobahn*. It isn't perfect, but we have few options. Otherwise, listen to Lynia when she returns."

"But—"

"Would you *please* knock me out?" Lial snapped, his patience gone. "It's the chance you've surely been waiting for."

That only drew the barest smile from the young healer. "Not like this. But very well."

Lial closed his eyes and opened his shielding to allow Elan access. Then he pictured Lynia's face until he slipped into darkness.

The mists swirled in the portal behind her as Lynia followed Inona through, her bodyguards close on her heels. Maddy had scanned them before they left and found no signs of virus, but Lynia still ordered the portal guardians to step away as she paused in the clearing in front of the broad, stone arch.

"You should head back," she said to Inona. "I trust you can sufficiently guard our guests if events go poorly there? Though Maddy, Fen, and Anna seem a formidable triad on their own."

"I believe so, Lady Lynia," Inona answered.

Lynia gave her a strained smile. "Thank you."

The scout hurried back through the portal, closing it behind her until the view of the mists faded into the forest behind the stone arch. Lynia turned to her bodyguards. "You'll need to isolate yourselves near the healing tower. I'll not risk Maddy being wrong about this infection."

After receiving their assent, Lynia strode from the clearing, her cloak snapping around her legs with each hurried step. She trusted them to follow, for her thoughts were too focused on the problem at hand to put much worry behind their obedience. Lial was counting on her to find the answer to his illness.

There's more information on the potions in the introductory chapter, he'd said. What had he meant by that? She'd skimmed that chapter for mention of Abuiarn, but there'd been nothing about the colony there. Though Emereh had spent a solid twenty pages on how and why he'd chosen his research subjects and treatment methods, nothing had stuck out to her. Clearly, that had not been the case for Lial.

As she walked, Lynia tapped her fingers against her thumb in a restless gesture. She needed those pages in front of her now. Why hadn't she taken the time to spell copy the entire book instead of the recipe alone? She could have reviewed the introduction from memory if she had. The lack left her feeling oddly bereft.

As she neared the estate, Lynia connected with Lyr. *"I've returned early. The others remained to help Lord Naomh, but I cannot leave Lial to die."*

Surprise filtered through. *"How did you know?"*

"A gift from Fen." At the wash of confusion, she shook her head, though Lyr couldn't see. *"He made a ring to augment telepathy. But Lial couldn't hold the link long enough to give me many details. Something about a needle slipping?"*

"I received little more from him personally, but Elan contacted me. Caeleth began to convulse near the end of the surgery, causing Lial to poke himself with the bloody needle." Lyr hesitated. *"Should I have Elan send any resources you might need to the library? I'm not sure that being in the healing tower is wise."*

Lynia glared at the path beneath her feet. *"Your concern is noted, but I'm ignoring it."*

"*I suspected you might,*" Lyr said. "*Laiala…*"

"*I know.*" The healing tower came into view, and she hurried her steps until she was almost at a run. "*I might lose him. We all might. That would be a terrible loss, not just for me but for the entire estate. I'll do my best to prevent that on all our accounts.*"

"*Do you think you can?*"

A small voice inside whispered its uncertainty, but she stifled it ruthlessly. "*I must.*"

Lyr sent her a wave of love. "*Let me know if I can help.*"

After agreeing, Lynia ended their link and swung through the tower door. On the right side of the room, Elan slumped in a chair beside the bed, but he shot to his feet at her entrance. "Lady Lynia?"

"I'm here to help." She cast a glance at the bed. Blood-stained sheets rose and fell with Caeleth's breaths, and red colored the edge of the sheet beneath him, too. "Shouldn't you change his bedding?"

Elan's nose wrinkled. "Ideally, yes, but I'm not certain if I should in this case. I'm…waiting for Lial."

He didn't say that he was relying on her to ensure that Lial would be alive to direct him, but Lynia felt the words all the same. "I'll do what I can."

The book was in the same spot she'd left it, but a small scrap of paper jutted out from the top. A note from Lial? Hopeful, Lynia opened the book, but the paper was blank. Though her heart dropped, she skimmed the dense lines of text for the purpose of the marker. It couldn't be an accident.

The first page held several paragraphs arguing the merits of energy versus herbal-based healing. Then Emereh launched into the reasoning behind his travels, key among them the acquisition of new experiences. A bit of a repeat, if she recalled from her first scan of this chapter. She'd moved on quickly after reading twenty pages of similar exposition.

When she spotted the relevant line of text, her breath hissed out in frustration. It was only a few paragraphs from the ending of this section, a quick thought easily missed. *For instance, I learned from Tebid Ored on Rrelen that one could combine life magic with healing magic in a single mixture to amplify its effects. This advancement led me to add my gift for life energy into each tincture, unless otherwise noted.*

Lynia's face went hot. She was no novice researcher, but she'd been in such a rush that she'd neglected to examine this section thoroughly. She'd skimmed for "potions," not similar words like "tinctures," and she hadn't had a chance to study the text again for more detail. Though she probably wouldn't have made the same mistake if she'd had ample time, the error still burned.

Quickly, she connected with her son again. *"Did Tynan arrive? Is he with Aris?"*

"Yes," Lyr answered warily. *"Why?"*

"I need a life mage, and I need one now." Lynia glanced at the new flask bubbling in the distillation device, waiting for an infusion of energy. The batch started by Lial—four precious doses that meant so much. *"I hope Tynan has helped Aris enough that he'll be able to lend aid. My work requires both of them, and as soon as possible."*

"I'll speak to them," Lyr answered before disconnecting.

Lynia paced back and forth in front of the workbench and let her thoughts clatter and combine. A healer using a method from Rrelen, where the virus had supposedly originated. Life magic, the essence of life itself. Hadn't Lial said the fertility potion had been augmented by Aris?

And from what he'd told her of Korel's illness and death, Aris was capable of nullifying the virus in spilled blood. Possibly more

if his power was increased in some way. If he had more energy, he might be capable of eliminating it from someone infected, but that wouldn't be practical for an outbreak.

They had to perfect the potion.

Unfortunately, the mixture took several marks to distill and only created enough for four full doses. How had Emereh managed to save a colony at that rate? She would need to do a closer read to find out if she'd missed directions on increasing the batch size. In the meantime, though… What could she do to help Lial?

Her gaze landed on a small basket with a thin vial just visible over the top. That looked similar to the one Lial had given her, and the color of the liquid inside was right. She stooped to examine the card attached to the top and smiled at the contained scrawl of Lial's writing—it wanted to be messy, but he would never allow ambiguity here.

There were only five vials in the basket, the rest of the batch of fertility potions he'd made for her. Was the life magic inside bound to this mixture alone, or would it help in other ways, too? Could it stave off the infection a little while they waited? Of course, there was also the matter of safety. If it was designed to aid in conception inside the uterus, would it cause damage to those without said organ?

Lyr's presence returned. *"According to Tynan, it will be half a mark more at least."*

"I see." Lynia wanted to demand Aris help them at once, but he couldn't be forced. Such an order would be the opposite of helpful for all of them. *"Tell them to come when they are able."*

After their telepathic link ended, Lynia frowned at the basket of vials. Then she glanced over her shoulder at the young healer beside the bed. "Elan? I have a few questions."

His was not a job that could be rushed—a fact Tynan had learned the hard way, the most recent in this very room. Today, he'd had the foresight to ask Selia to accompany them. The last time he'd attempted to work with Aris, Tynan had almost been overcome by the life mage's powerful magic.

A novice's mistake, but one he wouldn't repeat. Fortunately, Selia had been able to help, since the couple's son, Iren, remained with his friend Eri to comfort her. Tynan had had little to do with the girl, but he gathered the child was a powerful seer whose current lack of foresight caused her distress. Though he disliked hearing of her suffering, he couldn't deny the benefit Iren's absence brought.

The nearly empty room echoed Aris's harsh breaths as he worked through the meditation Tynan had assigned. Carefully, he examined the life mage's channels, searching for the trigger that had returned the man to his traumatized state. A regression, but not entirely. At least they wouldn't have to repeat the more wrenching form of healing required last time.

Tynan tapped his fingers softly against his knee, the motion practiced enough to make no sound. He was young for the job, but he'd helped thousands through such meditations already. He'd had to find ways to dispel his own restlessness during the process, especially when the outside world held other important tasks.

Like saving the estate's recalcitrant healer.

If he could speed this work by reaching in and rearranging the mental pathways created by trauma, he would. Oh, that was partially what he did during intense healings, but the brain was a tricky organ. Trauma layered in so many ways and in so many places that magic could never really replace the work required of the patient. Some pain couldn't be erased, only rerouted.

"I was cut there," Aris murmured.

"Where?" Tynan asked, though he didn't really need to know. At least not beyond offering aid. The patient's revelation was the important part.

"In the same spot as Caeleth." Despite the warmth of the room, Aris shivered. Energy hummed on the air, and Selia, in her place against the far wall, lifted a crystal to absorb it. "Not as deep, but the blood... I thought she might allow my intestines to spill free, but she only drained my blood until I was weak."

Aris had already theorized to Tynan that witnessing the surgery had likely been to blame, but working through the memory aloud would help. Tynan increased his magic, easing the stress lining Aris's brow but leaving him in control of how he experienced the memories. Actively rerouting this together would help more than the forceful method a true emergency required.

The life mage let out a long breath. "Caeleth isn't me. Nor was Korel. Those weren't my injuries."

Tynan had no clue who Korel might be, but it wasn't important. "That is true."

In just that way, Tynan talked Aris through, prodding and suggesting as the moment required. All the time, his magic drained in a steady stream to the other man. A balm to ease healing, one he gave freely despite his exhaustion. It was far preferable to a full connection, which required him to experience the memories along with the patient.

As he had with the woman who'd delayed his arrival until today.

Tynan shoved that thought—and its accompanying images—down deep. He had to help Aris be fit enough to save Lial. He owed the other healer, for although Lial had berated him for healing Aris without proper preparation, that criticism had been warranted. Lial would have been within his rights to report the matter to Tynan's superior, but he hadn't.

Time to prove he was capable.

40

Lynia's breathing hitched as she climbed the stairs up to Lial's room. Her fingers tightened around the vial until she forced herself to relax lest she break the glass. Gods, she didn't want to see him like this. But he'd stayed with her through more than one injury, and she found she could do no less for him, no matter how it hurt. Until Aris arrived to work on the potion, she would offer comfort.

And the fertility potion. Elan had concluded that it would have no effect on Lial since it was not the blend designed to increase male fertility and nothing within the mixture would cause harm. There was every chance that the life magic imbued into the tincture would do no good, either, but she had to try something. Elan had drained as much magic as he could from Lial, but the younger healer had no ability to block his magic's regeneration.

As soon as her head rose above the line of the floor, a strange blue light caught her eye. Had Elan left a mage globe on in the middle of the day? But by the time she was halfway across the room, the source became clear—and had her halting a few paces from the bed.

At the foot of the bed, a small *camahr* curled, the light on its tail glowing softly where it rested against the top of Lial's leg. The creature lifted its head and pinned her with its gaze, clearly taking her measure. Lynia held still and let it. She didn't bother to ask how it had gotten into the room, for the *camahr* were sly creatures.

This one had clearly chosen Lial.

The *camahr* stood, stretching its long, lithe body before turning a circle to curl up once more. Dismissing her, it settled its long snout against its paws, the fine fur around its toes fluffing out like feathers against the coverlet. No one knew how the *camahr* judged ally from enemy, much less chose a companion, but this one appeared to find her acceptable. She hoped.

Her steps slower, Lynia advanced, but the *camahr* ignored her. Mostly. Its long ears twitched as though listening to her motions, and the light on the tip of its tail pulsed from time to time. She was so intent on ensuring the creature didn't take exception to her presence that she was beside the bed before she truly glanced at Lial.

Then she did, and a strangled cry slipped from her lips.

It wasn't that he looked a great deal different than he had during normal sleep, at least on the surface. His expression wasn't pained, and his breathing was slow and steady. Elan must have tucked the blanket around Lial's arms, since both were beneath the bedding. The scene was too neat and perfect, no twitch or restless motion to break the stillness. He would have looked much the same stretched out upon the litter heading toward his funeral pyre.

She squeezed her eyes closed and bit her lower lip until she nearly drew blood. But lingering on her own pain delayed her goal—to offer comfort, not require it. Stiffening her spine, Lynia tucked the vial into her pocket as she peered around the room, finally spotting a chair to drag over. Her back twinged, and she rubbed it absently as she sat at Lial's side. He would be annoyed at her for exerting herself like that. No doubt, he would be running healing magic through the muscles and fussing if he could.

She twisted her fingers together in her lap in a futile effort to regain control of her wayward emotions, but she couldn't keep her hands still for long. With a broken sigh, she tucked a strand of his hair, red like the blood that had injured him, behind his ear and traced her gaze over his face. The skin beneath her fingertips didn't feel hot the way Caeleth's had, so that was something, but the shadows under his eyes were darker than she was used to.

How many times had she waited much like this as Lial healed someone she loved? Wringing her hands at their bedside, useless to help. Only a few months ago, she'd had to do that very thing as Lyr fought for life after being attacked and left for dead. There was no shame in it, of course, since healing was beyond her talents. But she had knowledge of this virus and an idea that might help. She didn't have to sit here doing nothing.

Not this time.

Lynia's hands went cold and damp as she withdrew the vial from her pocket and uncorked it. Then she paused, considering. Would he instinctively swallow? Should she lift him? She slipped her hand through his hair and settled her palm against the base of his skull, tipping his head forward before settling the glass against his lips. It took quite a few tries, but little by little, she got the concoction into him.

The *camahr* lifted its head as she settled Lial back against the pillow, but although the glow from its tail intensified, she didn't detect any threat from the creature. Could it be contributing magic in some way? If so, it wasn't a type that she could identify. She watched the *camahr* for several drips, but it rested its head atop its paws again with no further action.

Lynia returned her attention to Lial. She wasn't certain what she should be looking for, but best she could tell, there was no change in him after the potion. She had no power to scan for the virus, no way to know how deeply it spread. All she could do was sit and wait.

And pray.

Standing in a creepy ass hallway deep underneath a Seelie lord's palace wasn't Fen's idea of a good time.

How long were they going to wait here for the damned potion to work? Periodically, Maddy scanned Caolte to observe the virus's reaction, but otherwise, they were apparently going to stare at each other all night. He and Anna finally shifted to lean against the wall since no one offered them a chair.

When an hour had passed, Inona returned, escorted by one of the Seelie guards. This time, instead of waiting at the far end of the hallway, she joined them. The scout's assessing gaze took in all of them, and he had no doubt she made note of everything, right down to his boredom.

"Is it working?" Inona finally asked.

Maddy narrowed her eyes on Caolte for a second before nodding. "Yeah. It's almost time for the second dose, too. It doesn't appear to have affected him otherwise. No obvious side effects."

Inona frowned. "What do you mean?"

"Some treatments can cause a reaction in the body," Maddy explained. "It's fairly common with human medicines. Like…a salve to heal bruises causing someone to break out in a rash."

Caolte's hands flew up, and Fen's lips twitched as the guy stared at his skin as though a rash would appear at any moment. "Relax, man. What's a rash if it means surviving the plague?"

"Would such a reaction remain a mere rash?" Caolte asked, one eyebrow lifting.

"Most of the time," Maddy said cheerfully. "We won't think about any other options."

Caolte scowled. "I am uncertain—"

"Time to take the rest." Maddy's lips firmed into a stern line. "You said you were willing to test this for your brother's sake, right?"

She had the guy there. Grinning, Fen watched as the half-Unseelie lord downed the rest of the vial and then glared down at the tiny swirl of violet remaining in the bottom. Apparently, all the talk of side effects had lessened the man's drive to be helpful.

"What about the tiny bit left?"

Maddy shrugged. "I don't know. Get what you can, I guess."

As they waited for Caolte to deem the potion safe enough for Naomh, Fen started to consider locking himself in one of the dungeon cells just for something to do. Or wandering the weird, abandoned rooms they'd traveled through. Surely the dead-end staircases and hallways had been illusions. For all he knew, they had a television and game system hidden behind a mirage spell.

Okay, probably not, but a guy could dream.

When Maddy scanned Caolte again, Fen decided to see if he could spot the virus like darkness in the man's blood. While he did catch a few hints, that wasn't what stood out the most. No, there was something else. A flavor he'd tasted before. He'd been working with Vek on identifying family connections and tracing them, but that wasn't quite this. Maybe.

"Are you related to the Unseelie royal family?" Fen asked.

A spark of flame flickered in Caolte's hair, and the man slammed a shield between them with a fierce glare. "Keep your powers to yourself, whelp."

Whelp? Really? Fen laughed. "That's a little antiquated, don't you think? You could have just said no. Or yes. I don't give a damn. Honestly, I don't know a quarter of the people I'm related to."

"My Unseelie family is not up for discussion," Caolte snapped.

"Whatever," Fen answered. He didn't need to ask any more questions. From the way the guy reacted, it was obvious they had some connection, however faint, but Caolte was sensitive about it. "I don't need more annoying relatives, anyway."

Anna curled her arm around Fen's, and the pointed look she gave him had his mouth pinching closed. That was definitely her *you're making things worse, so shut the fuck up* expression, and he had to admit she was usually right. So he kept his attention away from the cranky Unseelie bastard as the wait continued.

And. Continued.

Lynia couldn't help but smile at the look on Elan's face when he spied the *camahr* stretched along Lial's calves. The creature must have arrived between the time he'd sent Lial to sleep and her return. But although fear widened the young healer's eyes, he approached the head of the bed with less reserve than she might have expected. Well. He couldn't be lacking in bravery to work with Lial at his crankiest.

"Did the *camahr* arrive with you?" Elan asked as she scooted her chair down to make room.

"No." Lynia studied the furry, gray creature. Tiny white specks dotted its pelt, and the thick hair on its paws was the color of snow. "I don't know how it got here."

The healer's lips thinned. "I hope it doesn't cause harm. It doesn't seem safe to have a wild creature in the same room as a patient, even if Lial has been feeding the beasts for a while."

"Do you dislike them?" she asked, eyebrows rising.

"They are fine for those who aren't sick," Elan explained. He flicked a glance toward the *camahr*. "And once solidly bonded, they are excellent companions. They've been known to offer support to the blind, for example. But a wild *camahr*? They are unpredictable."

Out of some strange impulse, Lynia stretched her hand toward the creature. It lifted its head, its ears swiveling toward her as her fingers neared its face. She paused to let the *camahr* sniff her skin, and when it showed no hostility, she dared to touch the bridge of its long snout. The creature let out a rumble-huff and lowered its head back to the coverlet where it nuzzled Lial's leg.

"I think the *camahr* has made its choice clear," Lynia murmured. "Lial certainly tried long enough to tempt one."

A wave of grief closed her throat at that. He'd fed and protected this kit's mother through at least one other litter, patiently hoping one might find him worthy. And now that one had, Lial might never wake to see it. What kind of horrible world allowed an injustice like that? It wasn't right.

Her eyes burned with tears, and she pressed her palms against her eyelids in a futile attempt to hold back the pain. She had to do this. She couldn't break down now, not when Lial needed her. She sucked in a deep breath and lowered her hands, though she let the tears flow silently as she stared at the man she loved.

"I wish I had the ability to scan him," Elan said quietly. "I can't reach a detailed enough level to find this virus."

Lynia sniffled. "I'm not sure knowing would help. We can't do anything but wait until Aris arrives."

She rested her hand against Lial's lower arm, hating the cloth between their skin. She wanted to be curled against him, offering comfort, but he would have fussed at her for touching him at all. To

her, it was worth the risk of infection. If it wouldn't have disturbed his rest, she would have pulled his hand from beneath the blankets just to hold it.

The muscle beneath her fingers twitched, and Lynia leaned closer, peering at his face. Was he grimacing? Lial's nose twitched. Then his lips. Could he be dreaming in this state, or was he somehow waking?

"Is something wrong?" she asked Elan.

The healer frowned for a moment before letting out a curse. "He's fighting free of my spell. Gods. I knew I wouldn't be strong enough to hold him unconscious, and his magic is beginning to surge. We need a stronger healer."

Lynia rarely used the spell that connected her to everyone on the estate, especially since Lyr had become Myern, but she didn't hesitate after Lial's arm spasmed beneath her hand. They needed help. Within a few heartbeats, she found Tynan walking with Aris on the far edge of the main estate, and she requested a connection with Tynan with such force that he would surely realize the urgency at once.

"Lady Lynia?"

"We need another healer at the tower," she said at once. *"Now."*

Through the estate link, she could sense his approach quickening before he answered. *"What's wrong?"*

With her heart pounding in her ears, she told him everything. Every sensation she could describe and every observation Elan relayed. The less time wasted, the better.

Lial floated in a dark gray haze, his awareness flickering like the pale blue light pulsing at the edge of his sight. A dull pain nagged at

him, but he couldn't define the source. Instinctively, he summoned his magic to scan for the cause of his discomfort, but the action caused a new spear of pain through his head.

At least he didn't have to wonder about the location of that agony.

Before he could try again, he sensed Lynia's presence. *"Rest, love,"* she whispered into his mind.

"I ache," he tried to send back.

Lial had no clue if he succeeded, but Lynia's spirit surrounded his mind like a lullaby, and he let himself sink into the comfort of her essence. *"No need to use your magic. I'm watching over you,"* she said. *"Sleep."*

With a soft sigh, he let himself drift.

41

Lynia found the link with Lial surprisingly easy to maintain even when she was distracted by the sounds of Tynan's arrival down below. At first, she'd considered whether the strength of their connection might be due to the ring, but its spell was inactive. Yet it was as though they'd spoken on this level before, deep and quiet. Why was this so familiar? Memory tickled the edges of her mind, but when the other healer entered the room, the thought slipped away.

She studied Tynan with a critical eye as he came to a halt beside the bed. "Are you a powerful enough healer to scan for illness?" she asked.

He settled his hand against his hip, just above one of the flowers embroidered down the side of his robe. She'd forgotten he was a priest of Bera, the Goddess of Healing, and she tried to take that as a sign that her prayers from before had been answered. Even if his expression *was* a touch more smug than she would generally associate with a priest of such a benevolent deity.

"I am, though mind healing is my greater talent," Tynan replied. "Elan showed me the vial of tainted blood, and I think I can identify anything similar in Lial's body. The trick will be doing so without utilizing much magic."

Lynia nodded. "Especially since you'll need to use magic to send him into a deeper sleep. I was able to calm him enough to keep him from using his power on himself out of instinct, but he still hovers near full awareness. He said he aches."

A frown creased the healer-priest's brow, and he impatiently flicked away a strand of his short, white hair as he bent over Lial. The strand returned almost immediately to its previous spot, but Tynan didn't appear to notice, his eyes slipping closed as he stretched out his hands. As with Lial's magic, a glow lit the air, this one green instead of blue.

At the foot of the bed, the *camahr* sat up on its haunches, and its eyes trained with unblinking intensity on Tynan. The priest ignored the creature, unlike Elan, and eventually the *camahr*'s hackles lowered as though it had discerned the other man's good intentions. Fascinating. If not for the crisis at hand, she would have hunted down a book on the animals. She'd never heard of such a young kit becoming so protective.

Lynia shivered as a tickle of awareness distracted her. Lial was waking. She leaned forward, reaching out to calm him, but before she could make contact, the priest detected the problem. With abrupt certainty, he sent Lial into a deep sleep, one that strained the link she had formed. Though she didn't want to, Lynia pulled her awareness back, leaving only the slightest connection.

Better that than inadvertently disturbing him.

It was only a moment before the healer's gaze returned to her, the green glow of his magic winking out. "I do not believe the virus has concentrated in any one spot, but it has spread throughout his bloodstream. No doubt the cause of the ache."

Her eyes burned, but she held these tears back. "How bad is it?"

"Not as dire as I suspected, but serious enough." Tynan knitted his brows. "I detected a hint of life magic, which I believe has held the virus back. But not enough. We need to drain his energy. It isn't an easy task under the best of circumstances, usually requiring cooperation from the patient for any chance of success. Not to mention that, unlike mages, we healers haven't found a handy way to store power taken from another when it *can* be managed."

"Could Selia do this?" Lynia asked. "She sealed Aris's life energy into crystals."

The priest shook his head. "The two types of energy are different, though you wouldn't think so considering how healing is linked to life. But…there's a fathomless connection in the energy linking all living things, a unifying factor that allows life mages to give energy to anyone. Healing techniques have many similarities, but the power behind them is as unique as the individual. Very personal. Aside from life mages, only blood relatives can share energy easily with a healer."

Before Lial, Lynia hadn't spent a great deal of time around healers. Now, though, she'd not only experienced Lial's method of healing firsthand, but she'd seen how Maddy's and Tynan's contrasted with it. None of the three had the same feel. While all magic users had a hint of uniqueness, she hadn't encountered such a strong difference in other fields.

"How did Elan drain Lial's power earlier?" she asked.

Tynan's gaze turned down to the patient in question. "Lial was able to lower his shields while still conscious and was already somewhat depleted. When I spoke to Elan downstairs, he said he was able to convert a little of Lial's magic to use on Caeleth, but not much. Unfortunately, Lial regenerates faster than Elan can absorb,

and I fear I won't fare much better. It's no wonder he is able to serve an entire huge estate on his own. I would stay drained much longer."

She hadn't realized that Lial regained energy faster than usual, but it made sense. Of course, that meant one of his greatest strengths had become his greatest weakness. With each moment that passed, his power rebounded, providing fuel for the virus that would ravage him. What else could they do until the potion was complete?

"You said a blood relative could share energy," she pondered aloud. "But could they absorb and dispel—"

"I'll do it."

At the imperious voice, Lynia flinched in surprise, but the shock lasted only a heartbeat. She should have known that Ralan would intervene. But when she glanced toward the top of the stairs and the prince who had emerged from below, another unexpected sight met her gaze—Meli came to a halt beside him. In her hands, a clear crystal globe gleamed in the midday light.

"Or more accurately, we will," Ralan said, gesturing toward Meli.

"You risk much to come here." Lynia couldn't help but think of Lyr as she stared at Meli. If his soulbonded became infected, they could both be lost. "We aren't certain this is only bloodborne."

Usually shy Meli lifted her chin almost defiantly. "Lial saved Lyr's life, probably more times than I've heard. I will not let him die without trying to help."

Lynia's throat clogged with tears, and she nodded.

"Kai gave me this." Meli raised the globe a touch higher. "A crystal he earned acting as guide. Arlyn wanted to offer her steel sword, but Lyr mentioned that Lial isn't allergic to the iron. Too bad we couldn't have drained his power by placing it beside him."

On any given day, Lial probably thought his actions mattered little, but this was evidence to the contrary. That they would all come

together like this… Lynia took a deep breath, stuffing her emotions down as best she could. Then she rose to her feet, prepared to shift out of their way.

"Where should I move?" she asked.

Ralan shrugged. "You needn't go far. We're keeping our distance as much as possible." His gaze caught on the *camahr* as he and Meli approached. "Ah, good. I was hoping the kit would choose him."

Lynia might have asked anyone else what they meant—but not Ralan. Instead, she inclined her head in acknowledgement and concentrated on sliding her chair nearer to the head of the bed. She could remain close, but she wouldn't be in the way of the energy transfer. Provided the two could make it work.

"Even with a blood connection, drawing out a person's magic is a difficult task," Tynan said, voicing the doubts she tried not to consider. "And I am uncertain how Lady Meli might be of aid."

"I'm a Diviner," Meli said softly. "I don't have much magic, but I can channel it. I've been working with Selia on ways to use that skill beyond my runes."

Lynia's brows rose. "Really? I thought a Diviner helped discover paths. The way to a lost object or person. That sort of thing."

"Directing energy is its own sort of path-making." Meli smiled. "So I've discovered."

Lynia's skin prickled with nerves as Ralan ordered Tynan to go below and then moved to a spot a couple of arms' lengths from the bed, Meli to his left. This wasn't a natural exchange. For good reason. If it could commonly be done, then wars and conflicts would become a true power struggle.

As Ralan's eyes slipped closed, hers did the same. She found the dormant connection to Lial and prepared herself to soothe him if the process became too terrible. She owed him much, herself. Like

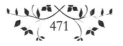

Lyr, Kai, and so many others, Lial had saved her. Not just after her fall in the library, either. He'd kept her from going insane from grief after the abrupt shattering of her bond.

At once, the memory she'd tried to grasp earlier came clear.

When Lial had held her beside Eradisel, she'd recalled how he'd spoken into her thoughts during those dark and terrible days after Telien's death, but she hadn't considered the extent of the connection that might have formed. But it was clear now. The quiet link between them, the deep whispers into the subconscious—it must have been built in those countless marks of time.

She couldn't remember much of what he'd said, but it hadn't mattered. From mundane descriptions of the weather to reminders of the life she would leave behind, he'd clearly told her anything to keep her from falling into the darkness. She could do the same for him.

The ring he'd given her might augment their range, but their connection needed no help with its depth—a boon she wouldn't hesitate to use.

Moment by moment, the pain crept higher. Slowly. So slowly his awareness of it faded for a time as a familiar surge of energy sent him back into darkness. But the blissful night didn't last for long. The relentless ache drew him ever closer to a light he didn't want to see.

He had to find the cause. If he was injured, he could repair the wound. As he'd always done, aside from the pain of losing Aralee. But he didn't have another bond to break. This couldn't be the same.

It wasn't from Lynia. She'd whispered to him earlier, and if he tried, he could sense her presence. What had she said? Not to heal

himself? Impossible. The instinct to draw upon his power stung nearly as sharply as the pain in his blood. How could he ignore what was integral to himself?

He reached for his magic, but before he could connect, his body seized. No. Froze.

"You will not."

Ralan. The *drec*. Gods, he hated when his cousin broke into his thoughts without permission. *"Leave me alone."*

"I need to drain your energy," Ralan said. *"If you want to survive."*

Panic beat his heart against his ribs in a sudden surge. *"I never thought our arguments would lead to this treachery, cousin."*

"No treachery." Ralan's mental voice was maddeningly calm. Had he lost his sanity like his brother Kien? *"And no, I have not. I'll yell at you for that insult later, when you're not so far gone. It's the virus, remember? The illness you caught from Caeleth? Healing magic strengthens it."*

Lial's memory returned in a rush, but it didn't ease the panic clawing at his very nerves. He hadn't felt this terrified since he'd almost failed to save Lynia. *"I opened my shields for Elan to do this. What happened? I shouldn't be conscious."*

"You're too strong for him to keep you under." A hint of dark humor entered Ralan's tone. *"Don't worry. I'll have no trouble. But you're regenerating faster than poor Elan can handle. I'll have an easier time of it since we're related."*

Despite everything, Lial hesitated. He and Ralan had never been friends, but they hadn't been enemies, either. There was no reason for his cousin to lead him astray. But. This was his power. The very heart of him. Elan never could have pulled enough for true harm, but Ralan? If he'd discovered a way to leech power, nothing would stop him if he wanted to take control of Lial's mind and drain him to nothing.

"You might not believe this," Ralan said. *"But I have great love and respect for you, even if I don't always like you. I will do my best to make certain you live."*

If his cousin had pretended unswerving amity, Lial would have fought. *Even if I don't always like you.* That, though, described their cantankerous relationship well enough that he found himself relaxing against the mattress. He didn't always like Ralan, either, but he would fight hard to save him if their positions were reversed. Such was the odd way of family.

"I will do my best to cooperate." A wave of dizziness swelled, threatening to muddle his thoughts once more. *"Take control of my mind if you must. But* only *if you must."*

There was a fair chance this was going to hurt. A *Felshreh* could take another's energy without pain, but Ralan was hardly that, at least not close enough on the family tree to matter. That ancestor was entirely too far back. Too bad. Would've been handy. Except it would require a blood transfer, which would spread the disease. How did a *Felshreh* process any viruses they might encounter in human blood? Though this was clearly different since it could affect fae. And Fen had been infected with a similar—

"Focus," Ralan snapped. *"Send me what you can. Then I'll take over."*

Right. The transfer.

Lial reached for his power, but he had to stop almost at once. *"Can't. The urge to heal myself…"*

Ralan's deep mental sigh was his only answer.

Then the true pain began.

42

Though the energy itself wasn't visible, there was no doubt when the transfer began. Lial's shoulder twitched violently beneath her fingers. Then his muscles tensed like rock, and a moan vibrated from low in his throat. Shock and pain leaked through their mental link until she considered whether she should keep the connection open.

Of course, she would. She kept her hand steady on his shoulder in case he could sense her reassurance.

Lynia barely noticed the light flaring in the globe between Meli's hands. Instead of considering that, she delved deep, brushing her thoughts against Lial's. Lightly at first. Then farther, until his pain became her own. If there was one thing she understood, it was mental anguish.

"Relax, my love," she whispered, gentling her mental voice. *"If you can. Help send your power instead of fighting the draw."*

She didn't expect him to answer, but he did. *"I'm trying. It's unnatural."*

Perhaps she could distract him from it? *"I believe I've decided what to do about our relationship."*

His breath hissed out. *"Lyni. Now? I cannot bear more than this."*

Did he think she was going to reject him? Idiot. *"I hardly intend to work so hard to save you, only to let you slip away from me later. Grumpy you may be, but you're my grump."*

Lial relaxed a little at that. *"Be careful. The more I care, the more protective I can be. I annoy everyone I love."*

"Meli is here, you know. Channeling your power into a crystal donated by Kai." Lynia swallowed back a surge of tears. *"Aris is below, ready to offer assistance. All people you have helped. They give back out of love. Don't underestimate yourself."*

"Even so—"

"Did you know there's a camahr *draped across your legs?"*

There was a moment of stunned silence. *"What?"*

"It was here when I came in," Lynia explained. *"No one is certain how it got in, but it appears to have chosen you."*

Pain still lingered around the edges of their connection, but it was somehow more distant, like a tone they'd grown accustomed to hearing. Perhaps it was a reflection of Lial's distraction or a sign that her methods were working. But he wouldn't process this latest news for long. What else could she say to keep his focus?

"I wonder where we should live," Lynia finally mused. *"This place isn't very private, even with the ability to seal off the stairs. If we have children… You did say you would be willing to give me children, didn't you?"*

"Truly, Lyni, you must work on your timing. It is not an opportune moment for me to think about those possibilities," he answered, his mental voice gruff with annoyance. *"But yes. I would be happy to have as many children as we may. You're correct that this is not the place to raise them, however. Even if I move to your room in the main building, it will grow quickly crowded there."*

Another voice broke into their conversation. *"I have an idea about that."*

"Ralan…" Lial began.

"A healer's enclave linking Braelyn and the lands of the new palace would be an excellent thing to have," Ralan said calmly. Unperturbed as ever. *"It will need a lead healer, and a researcher would not go amiss, either. As we have learned."*

Lynia had to admit the idea intrigued her, but she couldn't tell what Lial thought based on his snarled answer. *"Get out of my thoughts, cousin. This is a private conversation."*

A light laugh sounded. *"Think on it."*

While Lial stewed, their connection growing murky with his distraction, Lynia considered what Ralan had said. The idea held many possibilities—but also questions. A healer's enclave between the two lands meant that it could fall under the dominion of either. Would that leave Lial under the direct command of the palace once more? Considering his past, he would not be fond of that result. Of course, the enclave could end up under Lyr's control. It might even end up as its own sub-branch like Oria.

"I'm not sure I trust my cousin's intentions in this regard," Lial said, the mental link returning to focus. *"But I suppose I'll have to live to consider it. You'll think on it, too?"*

"Of course."

His pain began to ebb, at least where Lynia could detect it. A moment later, the light around Meli flickered, drawing her attention. The globe swirled with blue, and a soft glow emanated from it, the flickers settling into a steady throb. It was beautiful. Mesmerizing. Lynia had to pull her gaze away from the draw of Lial's soothing power.

"I believe Ralan is going to send you into a deep sleep soon," Lynia sent. *"But if you should wake, call for me. I'll hear."*

His reply was slow and sluggish, no doubt because of the energy loss. *"I will. I love you."*

"I love you, too," Lynia replied, no hesitation this time. And never again. *"I'll be just downstairs, working on the potion."*

Lial gave the barest nod, and she couldn't resist stroking her hand through his hair in a comforting sweep. Then as Ralan forced him under, Lynia stood, a new determination filling her. They had a few marks before the new batch was done, and she wouldn't waste them.

She approached Ralan and Meli, who stared down into the blue crystal globe in wonder. Too much wonder, truthfully. "Meli?"

"It's beautiful," the other woman whispered. "So much peace…"

Clechtan. There *was* a peaceful aura surrounding the stone, a type of soothing wonder she had only felt in healing sessions—which Lial's patients hated to leave. Would Meli get caught up in this magic the way she did her runes? They might have considered such a possibility if time hadn't been so short.

"May I?" Lynia asked, although she was tempted to tug the stone free without warning. But that could have terrible results if the spell channeling Lial's energy hadn't been closed.

Meli blinked a few times before jerking her gaze to Lynia. "Oh. Ah…sure."

Lynia braced herself, but she still wasn't prepared for the impact of the energy that hit her as she took the smooth, warm stone from the other woman's hands. For a moment, she could only stand there, frozen by the embrace of Lial's energy as it resonated against every memory—good and bad—that she had of him.

The dark days after Telien's death, the pain barely relieved by the comfort of Lial's magic as he spoke into her mind. Those precious minutes after her fall, when she'd been so close to slipping away, and the agony that followed before his magic slipped in to numb her injuries. Those were undoubtedly the bad, despite the soft moments within them.

But there had been times not owned by pain. The shallow cut he'd wasted time healing after she'd stopped to pluck a late summer flower. The countless sessions he'd done on her spine as she regained strength, speeding the process when he didn't have to. Even the night before, when her back had twinged while they'd made love, and he'd soothed her pain even amidst his own pleasure.

So many moments of giving.

Well. She wasn't going to save him by soaking up this pale remnant of him, was she? The sphere was amazing, but it couldn't compare to Lial himself. Resolute, Lynia marched over to the cabinet and opened the door. He'd used silk to insulate the steel sword Arlyn had brought from Earth. Surely that wasn't the only piece— Yes, there. She claimed a silk scarf and wrapped it around the globe before settling the bundle into a leather satchel in the base of the cabinet.

"Would you see if Selia has a better way to insulate this kind of object? I don't know what Lial will do with this when he's healed, but there has to be a more elegant solution than a sack." She glanced at Ralan and Meli as she closed the cabinet. "I have work to do."

Meli nodded. "Something more secure is certainly needed. If an artifact of such power is discovered, I can't imagine it would be good. Especially if it is as uncommon as Tynan claims."

"Thank you, Meli," Lynia said. "That will be a great help. Now truly, you both should leave. Isolate yourselves until Lial is well enough to check you or Maddy returns to verify. Tynan is still learning to detect this virus, and I would not see any others put at risk."

"As you command." Ralan flashed her a quick smile. "I do hope you and Lial will consider running the healer's enclave. You would both be perfect for the task."

Lynia wasn't positive that he meant the statement as a compliment, at least not entirely, but she didn't care. To her mind, it was no bad thing to be assertive with a cause. And when it came to fending off unreasonable demands or reminding people of their proper course, she had no qualms about issuing directives.

It was a relief after the two decades she'd spent in the fog of mourning. For the first time in years, she felt like herself—and it was glorious.

Standing just outside the open door, Maddy fought the urge to adjust the fabric of the far-too-thin scarf tighter around her nose and mouth. Not that it was completely useless. But anything short of a hazmat suit would make her feel exposed. She'd wrapped the thing twice around her face and fiddled with it enough that Caolte had grown visibly impatient at the delay.

The positioning was as good as it was going to get.

Caolte rounded the stone slab holding Naomh and knelt at his brother's side. It couldn't have been more than half an hour since Caolte had taken the second dose, but that had been sufficient for him to risk giving the potion to Naomh. Maddy had opted to scan from the doorway while Fen and Anna sat farther down the hallway. Inona insisted on remaining at her side, seemingly unbothered by her own scarf.

Stifling, annoying fabric. Why did the things that were best for you have to be the most uncomfortable? Medicine? Disgusting flavor. Exam gowns? Itchy with a side of embarrassment. Even the hazmat suit would have been a bitch to wear. But if the scarf prevented her from breathing in the virus, she would suffer through it.

After tipping half the vial into Naomh's nearly lifeless mouth, Caolte sank back on his heels and sighed. "I'm not certain how much this will help. It's almost as though he has given up, his body resigned to death. That he stays at all is probably for me."

Maddy scanned the Sidhe lord, though it was too soon for true change. It wasn't that the virus had grown a great deal worse. It hadn't. Yet his condition had declined. His breathing was slower and raspier, his muscles more lax. She had a suspicion that Caolte was right. Naomh was giving up.

"But why?" Maddy asked.

"He has never been the same since losing Elerie." A muscle twitched in Caolte's cheek. "I wish I'd encouraged him to go after her when she didn't return. If either of us had had an inkling that she carried Kai... Well, there is nothing to do about that now, is there? Even I can't bring back the dead."

Inona shifted restlessly beside Maddy. "But Elerie isn't—"

As Maddy turned a startled glance on the scout at her hastily ended statement, Caolte shot to his feet and rushed around the slab holding his brother. "What do you know of Elerie?" he demanded.

Inona didn't flinch at the powerful lord's approach, but her eyes flashed with chagrin over the folds of her scarf. "You'll want to speak with Lial when he is healed. This is...knowledge I should not have."

If it had to do with Kai's mother, Maddy couldn't imagine how... But wait. Delbin was Inona's boyfriend. Delbin, who was from Oria the same as Kai. Hadn't Delbin been on the mission to capture Korel, which had ended at the healer's tower in Oria? Suddenly, Maddy wished she'd gone with Lial to try to heal the guy. It had clearly been a more interesting trip than anyone had said.

"I don't care where you gained the information," Caolte snapped, the red of his hair flashing. "If it will save my brother..."

Inona stared steadily at the man. "You would have to swear not to tell Kai."

Caolte frowned. "A difficult oath when this concerns his mother."

"He'll be told, but not now," Inona said. "Ralan's orders."

The half-Unseelie lord's expression turned more considering. "I see. How about if I give my word to withhold this knowledge from him for a month? Any longer I cannot promise. He is my nephew, after all."

An entire negotiation seemed to happen in the looks that passed between the two, but whatever Inona saw must have satisfied her. Finally, she nodded. But she didn't speak until Caolte had given his word.

"Elerie is alive," Inona said softly. "She's been kept in a deep sleep after Allafon pushed her down the stairs, but now that he's dead, Alerielle wants Lial to help heal her."

Oh, damn. Maddy definitely hadn't seen that one coming.

Considering Caolte looked like Inona had punched him, he hadn't, either.

43

"How is he doing?" Lynia asked as she studied Caeleth for any clues. The young mage appeared healthier to her eyes, his color more normal, but she had missed the signs of illness once before. "It's been a while since Lial gave him Emereh's potion. Did it work?"

Beside her, Aris shook his head. "Yes and no. The virus is almost gone, but I can still detect the stain of it. Unfortunately, I can't seem to eradicate it. I might be able to manage the task if I risk flooding him with life magic, but I don't know how much power I will need to add to this potion. Not that I'm certain of success there, either."

"I hope you find your confidence." Lynia propped her fist against her hip and gave Aris a stern glance. "We can't let Lial die, nor any of the others afflicted."

From his place near the foot of the bed, Tynan spoke. "Why do you have doubts?"

"I provided energy for a fertility potion," Aris answered, no hint on his face that he knew she'd been the intended recipient. "But the power faded from the mixture quickly without Lial's intervention.

He used some kind of spell to trap my life magic inside. He's not here to do that this time."

"Do you know if there are any vials left?" Tynan asked.

Aris shook his head. "I have no idea what Lial might have done with them."

"I do," she said. "I gave one to Lial in case the life magic would help. What do you have in mind?"

"I'll see if I can study the spell used to imbue it." Tynan's expression turned sheepish. "I am no expert at potions, but I have more skills as a healer than my earlier visit here might suggest."

Aris appeared puzzled for a moment before wincing at the memory of his difficult healing. For her part, Lynia didn't bother to stifle her own aggravation at the reminder. She'd been the one to help Lial back to his rooms after Tynan had forgotten to warn him that Aris's mind healing was about to begin and to disconnect the healer link. Lial had suffered terribly for that lapse in judgement.

Now wasn't the time to chide him, though.

"Come," Lynia said, leading the way to the workbench. She took the proper vial from a basket and handed it to Tynan. "You two work on this while I study the book for anything I might have missed. Ways to speed up production or double the amounts, for one."

As Tynan and Aris settled into chairs, Lynia's focus shifted to *The Wayfarer's Trial*. She couldn't tell them how to imbue the life energy and hold it there, but there was every chance her research could provide the answer. The question was where to look within the text. This book wasn't as neatly indexed as many others, no doubt because it had been written during Emereh's travels. Even the introductory chapter was more a description of what he planned to do, not what he'd done. Any changes would be notated where they'd occurred.

Gods help her if the alterations had been slow and rarely remarked.

She started by flipping through each section, pausing to read the notes on any potions or recipes the healer had written down. She made it halfway to the section on Abuiarn before she found the first note about a change in methodology—he'd excluded life magic for that case. The next two made no mention of differences.

Then she reached the chapter written during Emereh's travels on Rrelen. She'd intended to examine this sooner but hadn't had time. This was the place where the virus had first been studied. If there was vital information they hadn't yet discovered, it was no doubt here.

Lynia had just reached the description of Emereh's first meeting with Tebid Ored when Tynan tapped her shoulder. "Excuse me, Lady Lynia," he said. "We're going to attempt to enchant the remedy for Lial."

The scrap of paper trembled in her hand as she marked her spot in the book before gathering it to her chest. Suddenly, she didn't want to give up her space. What if they messed up Emereh's potion so much that it needed to be mixed again? That would add more marks of time to their already strained limit. But if Caeleth was anything to go by, the tincture wouldn't fully work without imbuing it with Aris's life magic.

A look of understanding crossed Tynan's face. "I give my word that I will stop if there's a risk of ruining the new batch of the potion, but I truly think I can reproduce the trick."

Lynia searched for composure as she swept up her notebook and backed away. "Of course."

Then she could only watch as the other two worked their magic.

Maddy had been surprised by the news that Kai's mother still lived, but Caolte vacillated between shock and anger. He paced around his brother's sleeping chamber in frenetic laps, his boots thudding against the dirt floor like rage muffled. Now and then, the man paused to shove his hand through his sparking hair until she worried he would burn himself. The guy had to be immune to his own magic, for she caught no hint of a singe each time he lowered his hand.

"I don't know what to do," Caolte muttered, so low it could have been to himself. "If I tell him right away, he'll storm Moranaia as soon as he can walk. Too soon for his health for certain. But it could motivate him to reach for life. Even with the medicine, I fear…"

With a shake of his head, Caolte resumed pacing.

Maddy sensed Fen sidling up behind her a moment before his arm went around her waist and he settled his chin on her shoulder. "Fun times," he whispered.

"Shush," she hissed. "It's a bad time for snarky commentary."

"Sorry. Does not compute."

With a huff, Maddy nudged her elbow back into his stomach, but he only chuckled in her ear. "Do you need something?"

"I was only checking on the situation," Fen answered, his tone turning serious. "I think his color might be a little better."

Maddy glanced between the two sick lords. "Which one?"

Fen was silent for a moment. "I think both, but hard to tell about the unconscious one. Caolte's got fire in his hair again. That's something."

He was right about that. If the half-Unseelie lord could conjure fire in his aggravation, his energy levels had to be returning. The air wafting from the room was warmer, too. And when Caolte paced back her way, she noticed that the circles beneath his eyes were starting to fade. A quick scan revealed what those signs implied—the virus had lessened significantly.

She turned her attention to Naomh. He was still ridiculously pale, but there could have been a hint more warmth to the tone. His breathing appeared to be smoother, too. As she had with Caolte, Maddy used her magic to check. It was difficult to tell at first because his illness was so much more advanced, but…

Yes! The potion was working.

She'd tried hard not to consider whether Lynia had found a way to help Lial, but knowing they'd found some success here, she could no longer avoid thinking about it. What if she could assist in some way?

Besides, she wasn't capable of healing anyone here. Aside from confirming that the potion was making a difference, there wasn't anything else she, or the three of them, could do. It wasn't like the Seelie queen, and she wasn't Lial. Maddy consulted telepathically with Fen and Anna, and at their agreement, Inona.

All concurred. It was time to return to Moranaia.

"The potion is working," Maddy said to Caolte, who drew to an abrupt halt. "I can't tell you what to do about your other dilemma, but I can confirm that."

"What?"

"Look at your brother."

After peering at Naomh for a moment, Caolte crossed his arms. "He is not healed."

"I said *is* working, not *worked*," Maddy replied. "Give him his next dose on time, and he should continue to improve, just like you have. There is nothing else for us to do."

"What do you mean by that?"

A single spark rose toward the ceiling, and the warmth increased perceptibly. But she was undaunted. "What I said. We need to go."

Caolte's spine snapped taut, and the glare he sent her would have quailed a woman who hadn't been kidnapped by a madman and stood trial in the Seelie court—on two different occasions, no less. Fen's arm tensed around her waist as the other man advanced, but Maddy merely laughed.

"Don't try to intimidate me." Maddy smiled. "What's the point? You would be far better served to let me return to Moranaia to help Lial, the person who actually has the training to do more than scan for sickness. If your brother worsens again, contact Lord Lyr. Our mission here is complete."

Though his nostrils flared in anger, Caolte halted, his hand going back through his sparking hair. "There is truth to what you say, though I do not like it."

"Sorry," Maddy said. And she was. She knew what it was like to worry over family. "Give me another decade or two of training, and I'd be of more use."

Caolte let out a long sigh, heavy enough to carry across the space. "Forgive my ill humor. I do thank you for your aid. Once you exit this hallway, one of my warriors will escort you to the surface. I'll remain with Naomh."

Fen relaxed behind her, and her own muscles loosened.

Okay. Maybe she had been a little nervous.

Lynia leaned against the headboard of Lial's bed with *The Wayfarer's Trial* open across her lap. Though the *camahr* had eyed her when she'd climbed onto the mattress, the creature had settled quickly, and a strange sort of peace had surrounded them all. Lial breathed steadily beside her, a calm-seeming sleep, and she tried to think of his current condition as only that—a nap he would awaken from soon.

She'd watched Aris and Tynan until they were satisfied with their modifications to Emereh's potion. Then she'd returned upstairs with her research, anxious to be near Lial. Elan had come up to check on them once, but the young healer had retreated to the top floor to take a nap while he could. Tynan and Aris kept watch over Caeleth.

With a heavy sigh, Lynia forced her gaze back to the book. It was difficult reading, and not because of the text's age or complexity. The things they'd studied on Rrelen... She shivered. Thankfully, the worst accounts were second or third hand since Emereh either hadn't yet arrived on the colony or hadn't been willing to participate in those experiments himself. Like torturing animals.

I cannot adequately express to you the depravity of some of the mages here. Tebid was correct to leave in disgust. I begin to regret my decision to visit this horrible colony myself, and I do hope my report to the queen will have some impact on the laws that govern it. In the best of cases, this land will be emptied of all inhabitants and the worst offenders imprisoned or executed.

I suppose I do not regret this sojourn, however, if for one reason: my ability to help heal some of the wrong committed. I have returned several animals to their original states with my life magic, and now I must confront the unusual illness revealed by the perversion of the virus endemic to one such pitiful creature. While all life mages may make alterations to living beings, those changes must fall within the Natural Order. The changes made to both the creature and the illness pervert that order terribly.

How so? Since the animals bearing the highest amount of the virus also possessed natural resistance to attack spells, a pair of mages from the land of Gale had hoped to use the virus to strengthen their magical protections in a similar way. The mages twisted the virus into a spell and then found a way to insert that poisonous energy into their workroom's magical shielding. They didn't consider how those shields linked to the world's energy fields, nor did they care when it became obvious. They craved only power.

489

I have never seen the like. The virus-like spell broke free from their shielding and spoiled the local energy source before it could be contained. Then that pair tried to draw in the tainted magic to make themselves invulnerable, but it altered their mental channels and rendered them insane. Ample life magic cleansed that wicked well, and I was able to purify the local energy before Rrelen as a whole was affected. The mages were beyond saving, and their death was no loss. A sad thing for a healer to say, but it is truth.

However, this newest horror presents some challenge. The same virus has recently been altered by another healer, if one could call him such. At first, I attended this bit of research, curious to see how the virus acted within the unfortunate animal. But Qene went forth with a mad plan while I was absent: inserting this virus into his assistant.

The speed at which she died was appalling. Our kind are not prone to such diseases, and the structure of the virus that destroyed her is a mystery barely discerned. I thought this would be enough to dissuade Qene from future experimentation, but that was a foolish assumption. He continued unbeknownst to me, which brings me to my current problem.

There are now multiple ways this virus invades the body. One offshoot lives readily in water, especially mist or the vapor expelled from living beings. As mentioned earlier, one type becomes a form of poison to any energy it touches, and one is transmitted through the blood. Can I create a concoction that defeats all forms? With enough power, any decent life mage should be able to repair energy fields, but the rest… I'll need my healer's skills to confront the other.

Lynia rubbed her eyes, stinging from the strain of reading in the dwindling light. A quick glance at the nearby water clock showed that it was three marks until sunset, but between the clouds that had gathered and the sun falling behind the treetops, the light coming through the window had grown dim. She activated the mage globe beside the bed and inspected Lial to see if the glow had disturbed him. Only when she was assured that he slept soundly did she return to her book.

Truth be told, she barely understood half of the experiments Emereh detailed as he sought a cure. He spoke of a huge variety of healing magics, herbs, and potions, so many ending in failure over the span of what had to be months. How had he persevered for so long? But eventually, he listed the final potion, the same recipe he'd repeated in the section about Abuiarn.

Exactly the same—all that reading and no extra information that would help her improve the mixture.

More insight into the situation, though. There was a good chance the energy poison deployed by Kien had been related to the virus, especially if Meren had used Kien's spell as a base. They had no way of knowing if Meren or Kien had read *The Wayfarer's Trial* or some other account. Meren could have attempted to recreate both the airborne and bloodborne variants—or they might have been an accident. Either way, it sounded like the potion would treat both if they could master it.

Clink.

Lynia's gaze flew to the window, and a groan burst from her lips as one *clink* and then another sounded. Ice. Was there supposed to be another ice storm today? Gods help them if they had to handle case after case of careless injury on top of Lial being incapacitated and both he and Caeleth infected, besides. Tynan might be more skilled than she assumed, but he'd also indicated he wouldn't be able to handle being the sole healer of an estate this size. Unfortunately, he was the only one they currently had.

Carefully, she eased from the bed, tucking the book beneath her arm and stealing a glance at Lial. His chest rose and fell steadily, but the slight crease of his brow and downturned lips gave her cause to worry. Just how quickly did his energy regenerate? Ralan and Meli hadn't reappeared, so surely, it wasn't that dire.

Yet.

Lynia padded across the room as silently as she could and followed the curve of the stairs down. As she reached the base, the door to the healing tower opened, and Maddy slipped in before closing it behind her. In that brief glimpse, the situation became clear—they were definitely in for an ice storm. The sky held the purple tinge of frost, and the scent that blew in on the breeze was unmistakable after the centuries she'd lived at Braelyn.

"I didn't expect you back so soon," Lynia said as Tynan stood from the chair beside Caeleth's bed. She wasn't certain where Aris had gone. "What happened with Lord Caolte? And Lord Naomh. I hope nothing dire."

Maddy's smile held as much exhaustion as relief. "The potion appeared to be working well on Lord Caolte, and there was a little progress for his brother. There wasn't anything else I could do, though. I figured I would be more use here than I would be staring at two Sidhe lords in a freaky basement."

Despite the situation, the young woman's words surprised a chuckle out of Lynia. "Their home is certainly…fascinating. What about your mates?"

"Quarantining in our guest tower," Maddy said. "I checked us all for the virus and didn't find it, but I don't know how long it would take to build up enough for magic to easily detect it. Besides, Anna wanted to call the outpost to see if Vek or Dria would talk to her boss. We were supposed to go back to Earth around now, and she was scheduled to be at work tomorrow."

Tynan stepped forward until he stood beside Lynia. "You are in training as a healer?"

"Ahh…" Maddy began, a look of uncertainty crossing her face as her focus shifted to the priest.

Lynia's face went hot at her lack of manners. Introductions should have been the first thing she performed when Maddy arrived, but she was so distracted that she'd forgotten. Now poor Maddy was stuck trying to figure out why a stranger was asking her such a question.

Hastily, Lynia moved between the two. "Forgive me, Maddy. I forgot that you weren't here for Tynan's last visit. Allow me to present Callian ay'tor Beronai pel asebarah i Tynan Fessen nai Calai. And Tynan, I present to you…"

Lynia's mind went blank, and the heat in her face became a wildfire. Gods. If she'd ever been formally introduced to Maddy, she couldn't remember her full name. Was she no longer capable of basic etiquette? Ah, the smug look Lyr would give her if he knew of this!

"Maddy a Shayan a Clairen of the Cairdai," Maddy filled in with a smile. "A clan of the Seelie Sidhe, if you are unfamiliar."

"I am, I'm afraid," Tynan replied.

That title was too simple, though, wasn't it? Lynia frowned. "What about the Unseelie court, Maddy? Shouldn't that rank be included now that you're mated?"

"Crap," the young woman muttered. "Truth be told, I forgot how to pronounce it. I guess you should just add 'princess' to the front of my name and call it a day."

"Very well, Princess Maddy." Lips twitching, Tynan tapped his chest and gave a slight bow. "And if you're as unfamiliar with Moranaian titles as I am of Seelie, it might help to hear that I am a priest of the Goddess Bera and a mind healer. I was first summoned here for the latter."

A curious gleam entered Maddy's eyes, but Lynia wasn't certain of the cause. Though Maddy's surprised "A priest?" provided some

hint. Arlyn had been confused during Tynan's first visit when Lynia and Selia had speculated on the attraction between him and Kezari. Apparently, some priests on Earth were required to be celibate.

Tynan frowned. "Yes. Is that unusual among the Seelie? I had not thought so."

"Of course not," Maddy said with a shake of her head. "I...ah. I didn't expect the roles to be combined, I suppose. I didn't mean to be rude."

Lynia stepped in to smooth over the moment. "A difference in culture, I suppose. It would be a pleasure to compare the two later, but I'm concerned about the weather. Is it as bad out there as it seems, Maddy?"

Grimacing, Maddy nodded. "Getting colder by the moment, and there's more cloud than clear sky. Inona received warning of a storm as we approached the guest tower. So...I'm guessing that means we're going to have a lot of incoming accidents soon. Fabulous timing, right?"

Lynia didn't dare wonder if there was anything else this month could bring, though she dearly wanted to. There was too much work already to dare the gods in such a fashion. Instead, she focused on preparation. If they split the potions into smaller vials, they could at least provide easy relief for scrapes and bruises.

Without Lial, they would need every bit of help they could muster.

44

When the first knock cracked against the door, Lynia grabbed her basket and sidled outside, pressing her back against the wood as she studied their first patient. The cold wrapped around her every breath like the cloak she'd shrugged around her shoulders, and her lungs stung from the sharpness of it. At least, she hoped it was the cold and not a sign that she'd caught the virus from Caolte or Naomh. She did trust Maddy's and Tynan's scans, but not even that was certain. They'd even had the guards retreat to the trees for safety's sake.

"Lady Lynia?" the scout before her asked, confusion in her tone.

"Is your injury dire?" Lynia demanded. She had no energy for coddling. "Or would a tincture suffice?"

The woman's eyes widened, and she blinked. Then her shoulders lifted in a shrug. "I had hoped Lial might heal this scrape on my ankle. Though it should knit together on its own, my duties will be more—"

"So a tincture would suffice." Lynia gritted her teeth against her impatience. It wasn't the scout's fault that Lial had spent decades healing every tiny injury he came across. "Lial is ill, struck by the disease he has been trying to cure for everyone's safety. Our first priority is his recovery."

The distant chatter of birdsong resounded loudly in the sudden silence.

"Lial is…" The scout's mouth worked, but no other words emerged.

"Yes." Lynia dug around in her basket and selected a vial containing a single dose of the appropriate potion. "Use this. Then bind the wound and tell your superior if you need someone to replace you at your station. My son is aware of the situation and is no doubt prepared for this very possibility."

Or so she hoped. He was an excellent Myern, better than his father at the job if she were honest. Still, it might not go amiss to send him a warning of her directive. As the scout accepted the vial with a somber nod, Lynia connected with Lyr just long enough to update him.

"What if something bad happens?" the woman asked, clutching the vial to her chest with an anxious frown. "Falls happen during ice storms, especially early on. My sister broke her wrist in just that way a few decades back."

Lynia smiled softly to put the scout at ease. "We have a healer-priest here to help Elan, and there's also Lial's new trainee, Maddy. However, their energy must be reserved for difficult cases like broken bones. In the meantime, I'll stand ready to hand out tinctures until supplies run out. If you could pass the word along to your fellow scouts, I would be grateful."

The woman inclined her head. "Of course, Myernere. Thank you for explaining. And prayers to Bera for Lial's quick healing. I can't think of a scout or warrior on this estate he hasn't helped at least once."

"I'm certain he will appreciate your prayers."

Gods above, but Lynia hoped he would survive to find out about those prayers.

As afternoon tilted toward evening, the gratitude he wouldn't have expected poured in. The third time she went outside to dispense a tincture, she found a stone altar set up against the side of the tower wall, a candle burning merrily despite the ice pelting around them. She traced the hint of magic surrounding the flame to a nearby tree, where a scout perched while keeping guard.

By the time Emereh's potion was nearing completion, the other side of the altar was covered in bundles of herbs, a few pieces of jewelry, and gold coins. More herbs were stacked against the base until she could barely discern the shape of the altar. All still dry, thanks to a friend of Caeleth's. The mage had cast a shield over the doorway and altar, preventing the ice from landing on both the offerings and anyone who dispensed tinctures.

Elan and Maddy took over answering the door, and whether it was a blessing from Bera or the fact that most had remained indoors after Lyr had activated the shield, Tynan only had one broken bone to mend. Outside the tower, of course. Although none of the healers nor Aris had sensed the virus in the air, they'd deemed it better not to bring others into the healing tower.

At least she had fewer distractions while she continued her research.

Mostly.

"It is difficult to believe that a healer cured an entire colony with four doses," Tynan muttered beside Lynia as she lined up the vials she would need. "Are you certain there were no directions for increasing the amount?"

Eyebrows raised, Lynia sent the healer a sidelong glance. "I

assure you both my reading and research skills are excellent. When I find such directions, you will know."

Tynan flushed. "Forgive me if I hinted otherwise. I only wondered because you are not a healer."

"There are many things one can comprehend without actually doing them." Lynia tipped her head to the side and let out a relieved sigh when the potion appeared to be the correct color. "In this case, I've had to learn the art of potion-making quickly, but I haven't had time to study everything about this one. I'm currently searching through nearly a thousand pages of notes written by a traveling healer millennia ago, all concerning a colony that no longer existed when my grandparents were born. There's only so much a researcher can do."

"Ahh…"

If he hadn't annoyed her so badly, Lynia might have taken pity on him after hearing the uncertain tone of his voice, but she let the sound hang in the air and focused on her work. Ever so carefully, she poured an equal measure of the potion into each vial. Only four doses.

Hopefully, they only needed one.

Once again, the unknowing darkness gave way.

There was no drifting this time, no nagging awareness of distant pain. This agony was sharp, needles rending his veins rather than repairing them. Lial reached for his magic, but it kept slipping from his grasp. His reserves were dangerously low. Why were they low? He had to scan himself before it was too late.

Panic tightened his throat, and he sucked in a strangled breath. But before he lost all sense, Lynia's presence surrounded him, her energy calming him instantly. If she was here, it couldn't be too terrible, could it? She wouldn't allow him to suffer.

"I'm sorry for waking you, love," she whispered into his mind. *"Can you drink the potion if Tynan lifts you a little?"*

Potion? What potion? And why was the mind-healer there? His muddled memories slipped back into the darkness where his consciousness had been. Then a wave of pain swept through him, and for a moment, it was all he could do to breathe. Whatever the potion might be, it was clear he needed it desperately.

"I will try," he attempted to send back, though he wasn't certain he'd properly connected until his body shifted position.

His head swam so badly he didn't dare open his eyes. His stomach roiled enough as it was without risking that—a poor state with a potion to drink. Lial set his attention to calming his insides, his focus on stifling the rising bile. He only just managed it when he felt cool glass against his lower lip.

A rush of liquid, and life itself might have flowed into him. What was that brush of gold and green and glory? He followed the cold trail down his throat and into his stomach, where it washed away the nausea that had plagued him.

But still there was pain. Only when the darkness swallowed him again was there reprieve.

Once again, Lynia sat at Lial's side with *The Wayfarer's Trial* in her lap. But this time held a different kind of agony. If she'd thought she couldn't stop checking on him before… Well, she'd been wrong. It took all her willpower not to stare at him incessantly. Would the potion work? What if she'd mixed a component wrong? An error could ruin everything, and she didn't want to miss a single sign of something going bad.

Never had precision in her research been quite so literally life

or death. Had it been less vital, the challenge might have exhilarated her, but she couldn't shake free of the fear. How did Lial bear such a burden day after day? Perhaps his work wasn't always so dire as a plague, but he held life in his hands regardless.

Lynia snapped her attention back to the page in front of her. Emereh had moved on from Abuiarn, and she might have ceased reading except for one thing—the references. Every time she considered skipping to another section, there was a tantalizing "unlike the challenge of healing the people of Abuiarn" or the like to draw her in.

In spite of her absorption, she almost missed the information she was searching for. It was a small aside, one that didn't mention the colony by name at all. *Fortunately, I'll be leaving for Ikilse on the morrow. I denuded my supply of ilni on my previous mission, and if I must undertake a similar task, I'll be stuck without the means to hasten the speed of distillation. Though it is to be hoped that I never need a potion with such urgency again.*

Snatching her notebook from the blanket at her hip, Lynia copied the words over, careful to highlight *Ikilse* and *ilni*. It would take more research to discover how the herb—if it was an herb— could be used to diminish distillation time, but it was a start. With any luck, Lial might know.

If the potion worked.

Her gaze slid to Lial once more. His chest rose and fell steadily, and when Tynan had arrived to help with the second dose half a mark ago, he'd reported a marked decrease in the virus. Added to some promising news about Caeleth, who'd had the remnants of the virus wiped out by a single dose of the new potion, Lial's seeming improvement held a flicker of hope steady in Lynia's heart.

But she was afraid to encourage that spark to flame. Something could still go wrong. Lial's innate healing magic was rising again, and that might interfere. Lynia nibbled on her lip. Should she ask Ralan and Meli to return? She hadn't summoned them in the first place, so surely if they were needed, they would reappear. Ralan almost certainly wouldn't pass up the chance to save the day.

Abruptly, the *camahr* stood from Lial's legs and padded up his body to sit on his chest. The light on the tip of its tail brightened until Lynia squinted against the blinding blue, but otherwise, she didn't dare move. What was the creature doing? Worry pinched her heart, but before it could grow into fear, the light winked out, and the *camahr* jumped down. The little kit walked away with a smooth, rolling swagger, no hint of hurry to its movement.

She blinked, and the *camahr* was gone.

Why had it left? Was its departure a good sign or a bad omen? As Lynia examined Lial for any hint of distress, she sent a call out for Tynan, but he and Maddy were working on a dislocated shoulder and Elan was feeding Caeleth. Had their luck run out, then? If Lial had worsened, it would be a bit of time before she knew. The shoulder apparently wouldn't take long to fix, but it was a delay nonetheless. What if that cost them all?

Though she hesitated to do so, Lynia finally reached out to Selia to ask if Aris would help with his life magic. The life mage had experienced enough trauma that she hesitated to contact him directly—for his sake, not hers. Unexpected mental communication with a woman he didn't know well might be uncomfortable, and the last thing she wanted to do was cause him more pain.

Lynia hadn't heard the details of his torture, but she didn't need to. She'd seen Lial in the aftermath of experiencing the memories. That was enough. It felt like a blessing when Aris sent word through Selia that he would hurry over.

Hesitantly, she placed her hand on Lial's chest. Until he was

deemed recovered, there was a risk in touching him, despite their theory that the virus here was bloodborne. Lack of knowledge did not equal safety—one didn't have to see the monster stalking through the dark to suffer the bite of its claws, after all. But she needed to feel for herself that his breathing was as regular as it seemed.

Heartbeat steady. No hint of struggle in the rise and fall of his breath.

"Lyni." The dry rasp of his whisper caught her flickering hope and fanned it to fire, the heat of it only intensifying with his next words. "What are you doing? You shouldn't risk yourself by being so close."

If he had the wherewithal to nag her, he was certainly improving.

Lynia met his eyes, and the shadows of worry caught at her heart. "When the *camahr* left, I grew concerned that you were worsening." Then a new fear hit. "What drew you from rest? Tynan put you under rather deeply after your last dose."

A ghost of a smile crossed his lips. "Healers are difficult to keep unconscious. We know how to unravel the spell, and we often do so unintentionally. But it wasn't pain that made me stir this time. Truthfully, I'm not certain what drew me to the surface. A blue light?"

"The *camahr*," Lynia said softly.

"If anyone but you made that claim, I doubt I would believe it." Lial's eyes drifted closed, and a quiet sigh slipped from his lips. "Gods, I'm tired."

Her throat tightened. "I hope the others hurry," she rasped.

One eye slitted open. "Why?"

"To scan you." Lynia resisted the urge to run her hands along his body in a useless attempt to check him for illness. It wasn't as though she would glean any insight. "If you are recovered, you shouldn't be so weak, right?"

"Not necessarily," Lial answered. "But I think I can summon enough energy to scan for myself."

Lynia shook her head. "You shouldn't…"

She let the words trail away when she felt his magic pass beneath her hand where it still rested against his chest. Of course he hadn't been able to resist. What had she expected? Had she the ability to scan herself, she wouldn't have had the restraint, either. Very little would be able to stop Lial.

The frustrated huff of his breath made her heart leap. "What's wrong?"

"Only a few remnants of the virus remain, and those are no longer replicating." Deep furrows formed around Lial's mouth as his lips turned down. "But the damage left behind is…extensive."

She drew back, her spine stiffening so much her muscles ached their protest. "Damage?"

His intensifying frown did nothing to ease her worry. "Relax, Lyni. I don't have the energy to heal your back right now. If the muscles spasm—"

"Truly, I cannot believe you are fussing at me about an old injury after what you just learned." Nevertheless, Lynia closed her eyes for a moment and forced her muscles to relax before she continued. "You are being rather casual about damage you called extensive."

Lial's shoulder lifted slightly, rustling the bedding. "It is healable. Though nearly every organ sustained some injury, rest and a few healing sessions should be enough for a full recovery."

The words should have eased her heart, but they didn't. Lynia couldn't manage to release the apprehension that had held her prisoner since she'd first learned of his infection. Could they trust this potion? She weighed the facts in her mind—the success at

Abuiarn, Caeleth's recovery, and Lial's own scan—but fear refused to give way to reason.

"I don't want to lose you," she whispered. And suddenly, she understood why. "I lost Telien so unexpectedly and in an unnatural way. I can't seem to process hope."

"Ah, beloved." Slowly, Lial freed his arm from the covers. Then he surprised her by settling his hand against her hip, and that small motion brought her more comfort than anything. If he believed the virus still posed a threat, he wouldn't touch her. "I never prevaricate about matters of health, as many an unhappy patient can attest. You included."

Lynia found herself chuckling, and some of her tension dissolved. If not all of the worry. "True enough."

His lips curled upward. "Besides, I well remember what you said when you gave me solace. When a woman offers her love and bids you to father her children, it would be a terrible insult to die. I will recover, though it might take a few days."

Her cheeks heated. "Didn't we also need to decide where to live?"

"I suppose so," he murmured. "But not now. At the moment, I care only about resting here with you."

Lynia shifted her books to the side table and then slipped beneath Lial's arm to settle against him. The steady thrum of his heart under her ear soothed the remainder of her tension until finally, she allowed the bone-deep fear to release. Faith was never easy to grasp or maintain.

But it was time.

45

Lial drifted in and out of sleep for an indeterminate amount of time before a voice cut through the peace. "It actually worked."

He cracked his eyelids open, though it almost wasn't worth the effort. It was Tynan, and the man would no doubt be smug about having assisted. But Lial had to admit there was no hint of that emotion on the other's healer's face as he studied Lial. Relief and happiness, but no self-satisfaction.

"We did it," Tynan said to Aris, on his right. "The magic portion, at least."

Lynia straightened to a sitting position, her pale hair tumbling around her. "I was unaware you had such strenuous doubts about that outcome."

Tynan winced. "I did say the results weren't guaranteed."

"Yes, but—"

"Don't fret, Lyni," Lial said before she could tear into Tynan. "Healers are an odd bunch when it comes to predictions. Some things are better left unsaid."

A hint of surprise sparked in Tynan's gaze. "Thank you. Yes. I didn't want to offer false hope or false fear. Forgive me if my moment of pride caused alarm."

Amusement flickered through him at the others' expressions. Tynan, eyes still wide after Lial's defense. Aris's hint of a smile at the interplay. And Lynia, her eyes narrowing in anger once more. Lial chuckled, a sense of contentment easing his tight muscles at the experience. He'd feared more than once that he wouldn't live to see something so normal again.

"Might I ask what caused such uncertainty?" Lial asked.

"Ah," Tynan began, his gaze sliding briefly to Lynia. "Apparently, the healer who created the potion was also a life mage and imbued his concoctions with that energy. Aris and I had to improvise something similar. I used your work on the fertility potion as a reference since you have a method to prevent the life magic from dispersing before use."

"Glad to see the potion is already coming in handy, if not the way I'd intended." Lial did a quick scan of himself, then blinked against the surge of dizziness the use of his magic triggered. "I don't believe there are active remnants of the virus remaining, but my strength is…diminished."

Lynia rubbed his shoulder. "You should let yourself rest."

"Sorry, love. It's difficult to fight against habit." Lial slid his hand back to her hip and tried not to worry about the effort it took. "In any case, it seems I owe you all thanks."

"Not quite yet. There is more work to be done." In one sudden motion, Aris drew his sword, and a surge of life magic pulsed through the room as green flared around the blade. "With the virus inactive, I should be able to purge anything that remains. I don't sense the perversion surrounding the vile construct, but nevertheless, safety demands it. I've already done the same for Caeleth, and it doesn't risk using enough energy to alter you in any way."

Lial studied the other man for a moment as he considered the offer. As he'd learned when Aris had provided energy during Caeleth's surgery, life magic was a heady thing. But it was also a rare gift. Such mages were wary of others' requests even without the kind of terrible experience Aris had suffered—too many would be happy to misuse such potent power.

"What's wrong?" Lynia asked.

"I admit I worry about being swept away. A healer sensing the heartbeat of life…"

Lynia took his hand between hers and squeezed. "Then focus on me."

Nodding, Lial closed his eyes and reached mentally for Lynia. It took a mere breath for them to link, their connection stronger than it had ever been. They might not have a soulbond, but they were nearly as close.

"I need to find a ring for you now," Lynia whispered into his mind. *"Perhaps I can get Fen to concoct something for me."*

The thrill of that statement dulled the shock of Aris's magic flooding his veins. *"You truly weren't jesting."*

"Jest—" Her hands tightened around his. *"We were talking about children and living situations. Do you truly believe I joke about such things?"*

Life magic surged, and Lial sucked in a breath. He had to force his thoughts away from the beckoning pull of life. What had she asked? If he thought she'd jested about her feelings? *"No,"* he answered gruffly. *"But I can't resist needling you."*

"I would think you'd had enough of needles," Lynia grumbled.

With that sobering reminder, Lial shook his hand loose so he could twine their fingers together. Energy arced between them, but he did his best to ignore it. *"I promise I was not intentionally careless. You're right that I should be more mindful. And as much as I hesitate to participate*

in one of Ralan's plans, his idea has merit. A healing enclave on the edge of the estate would allow me to see serious patients in the area while having enough assistance to keep me from becoming overwhelmed. How do you feel about doing research there?"

Her hesitation felt thoughtful, not upset, and her mental voice was vaguely happy when she finally replied. *"I find I like the idea. I'm not particularly useful here."*

His mind rebelled at her words, but before he could counter them, another, stronger wave of power washed through his body. Lial gasped from the force. Life glimmered at the edges of his vision, clouding his thoughts. How did Aris resist diving into the flow and merging with it?

So beautiful.

Then Lynia jostled his hand, bringing him back to their discussion—and the protest he couldn't deny. It hurt his heart that she believed herself to be useless. Even now, she was helping more than she knew.

"That's not true, Lyni."

"I am not maligning myself. It is true," Lynia insisted. *"Lyr had the estate handled even before Arlyn and Meli arrived. Now, he has an heir to train and a new Myerna to help with his duties. Except for the odd bit of research, I have had little to do. For a while after Telien's death, that was what I needed. But not anymore. I tire of being 'the Myern's mother who hands out history books.'"*

He almost protested again out of reflex, but when he considered her words more deeply, he was able to see the truth in them. She had been treated in just such a way of late. Why hadn't he noticed her discontent? Had he been too caught up in her recent injury to see the greater picture? Obviously so. He should have guessed—the quiet types like Lynia always hid their unhappiness for as long as they were able.

Ralan's offer would provide satisfaction in more than one way, then. Lynia had shown great skill at distillation, and with a proper healer's library, she would be a huge asset to the enclave. One they would likely need, if Ralan's involvement was anything to go by. Better not to think about that, though.

"We should do it," Lial finally replied.

The life magic began to ease, and he wanted to cry out at the loss. His hand jerked with the urge to reach out as though he could hold the energy close, but Lynia's grip tightened again, anchoring him. He forced himself to relax. To let that beautiful power go.

This time, Lial spoke aloud, centering himself in his own body—and away from the tempting life energy "Are you willing to be in charge of the research library? I'll have enough to do finding healers to staff the enclave, not to mention a replacement here."

"I would enjoy working on the library. But aren't you still going to see patients?" Lynia asked. "It shouldn't be that far."

Now that the green light had faded, Lial cracked his eyelids open so he could connect with Lynia's gaze. "Yes, but considering training emergencies, storms, and such, it's important to have someone immediately available."

As though summoned by his words, Maddy's head poked up from the stairs. "We have a shattered scapula down here. Or whatever you call it. Shoulder blade?"

With a sigh, Tynan shook his head. "I'm beginning to regret revealing that I can heal more than minds. Please, rest. I can't wait to hand your estate back to you. I don't even want to think about whatever enclave you're discussing."

Lial narrowed his gaze on the man's back as he hastened toward the stairs. He'd formed a poor impression of Tynan after his slip during Aris's healing, but that opinion had perhaps been hasty. If the

man was capable of deconstructing the method Lial had used in the fertility potion and applying it to something new, he was obviously talented. He could also heal broken bones, it seemed. And having a mind healer available was hardly a bad thing.

"You're still considering relocating?" Aris asked. "If you're thinking of asking Tynan to replace you here, I doubt he would agree. He's a priest. Most prefer to live close to their order."

"His parting words weren't encouraging, either," Lynia said.

Lial merely smiled. The idea might go nowhere, but he couldn't shake the thought that he'd already found his replacement.

Tynan just didn't know it yet.

Lial only lasted a handful of marks before exhaustion gave way to impatience. It wasn't quite the middle of the night, but the tower had fallen into silence. Lynia slept against his side, and for a time, he contented himself with running his fingers through her hair where it draped across his chest. That didn't occupy him for long, though.

He did a deeper scan of himself than he'd dared before. Tentatively at first, but once it was clear that the virus was completely gone, he searched each vein and organ and catalogued every hint of damage he discovered. Not comforting, in truth. He could have ingested fire laced with poison for all the trauma his body had endured. His body would heal naturally, but it would take weeks without help.

He had sufficient energy now to do a healing session on himself. It would drain him enough that he would be useless to anyone else, but for the first time in years, he didn't hesitate to dismiss all those faceless others. He couldn't neglect his own health, not after something like this.

Besides, the longer he was ill, the more Lynia would worry. He couldn't have that.

Oddly, healing himself took far more concentration than working on another, and by the time he'd completed the session, he was tired enough to drift in and out of sleep for a while. But it didn't take long for his restless energy to return. He stared up at the ceiling, trying to determine why he couldn't stay asleep.

Lial glanced at the water clock, and his brows rose. It was only a couple of marks past dinnertime, though it had seemed so much later. No wonder. He rarely went to bed so early even when he was exhausted, and he'd been unconscious a great deal of the day. His mind was searching for normalcy.

Whispers wound their way up the stairs, catching his attention. Was Tynan still here? Elan or Maddy? Lial searched the tower with his magic and detected Tynan's and Maddy's energy below. And Lyr's. Frowning, Lial jostled Lynia awake. As soon as she sat up, blinking at him in confusion, Lial eased himself out of bed.

"What's going on?" she asked, her sleep-roughened voice tempting him to crawl back in beside her.

"I sense Lyr below," Lial answered. "I'm going downstairs."

Lynia scowled. "He can come up here. You're recovering."

"I need to move, anyway," Lial said.

"But—"

"Would you help me on the stairs?" He wasn't fond of pleading, but he might consider it in this case. If he had to stare at the ceiling until dawn, he would go mad. "I have to ease my restlessness. Maybe then, I'll be tired enough to go back to sleep."

Though she muttered beneath her breath, Lynia stood and brushed the wrinkles from her rumpled clothes. Then she walked around the bed to his side, her eyebrow rising as she waited for

him to move. And he would. In a moment. His leg muscles simply needed to adjust.

Lynia crossed her arms. "Get back in bed."

Shaking his head, Lial took a tentative step forward. Then another. It wasn't too bad if he kept his gaze locked on a set point to prevent dizziness from creeping in. He'd healed people when he'd felt only slightly less bad. He could do this.

With Lynia's steadying hold on his arm, he finally reached the small, triangular landing where the spiral staircase paused on his floor. Panting, he leaned against the center column and peered down. There hadn't always been so many steps, had there? He was considering the merits of plopping down at the top for a rest when he heard the door open below. *Clechtan.* Who was leaving?

"Wait!" he called.

Maddy appeared at the base of the stairs. "What the hell are you doing?"

"That's what I asked," Lynia complained.

Lial attempted to smile, but he suspected it was more a grimace. "I sensed Lyr below. Has something else happened?"

"By the gods." Lyr's voice drifted up the stairs, though Lial couldn't see him. "Go sit down before you collapse. I'll come up."

He'd wanted to rid himself of his restless energy, and that goal was more than accomplished. Without a word, he faced the table and set a new task—reaching a chair without tumbling on his ass. Not a single person here would let him forget it if he ended up comatose on his own bedroom floor.

He released his hold on the column and wavered on his feet. Lynia tightened her hold on his arm to help him regain his balance, and he gave her a grateful, if weak, smile before he started to walk.

Lial didn't glance toward the stairs again until she'd helped him into a seat, which was thankfully angled out enough that he could lean against the table. He expected to find Lyr grinning at him from the top of the steps, but as with Tynan, there was no hint of smugness on his friend's face. An unusual occurrence, since Lial honestly deserved it. He'd given Lyr enough grief about overdoing it while recovering from injuries, after all.

"I wasn't trying to wake you," Lyr said, his gaze shifting momentarily to Lynia, who'd sat at the table across from Lial.

"You didn't," Lial replied. "My body might be tired, but my mind wouldn't let me rest."

"Were Tynan and Aris correct?" Lyr strode forward before stopping to hover at the edge of the table like a *camahr* mother at mealtime. "Are you healed?"

"Yes." Though technically true, it didn't precisely feel like it at the moment. "The virus is gone, at least. Full recovery will take more time. Is that why you're here, then? No new disaster?"

"I wanted to verify that Maddy and her mates will be able to travel back to Earth, and I'd heard rumors of the offerings piling up outside." Lyr did grin, then. "I had to see that for myself."

Offerings? Lial gave Lynia a questioning glance, but her answering smile didn't clarify matters. He blinked up at Lyr. "What do you mean?"

"Based on the amount of gold, jewels, flowers, and herbs outside the front door, I'd say you're more beloved than you know. Good thing Maddy moved to the guest tower. You might need the upper room to store it all. The attic would no doubt overflow."

Lial shifted uncomfortably in his seat. Lyr had to be overstating things. He didn't doubt that he was appreciated, but beloved? That defied all reason. Honestly, the jokes about his ill humor were

practically legendary. Who would leave gifts for someone with his reputation?

"Don't you have work to do?" Lial managed to grumble around the lump in his throat. "Panicked citizens? Afflicted Sidhe bond-relatives?"

"If you mean Naomh and Caolte, I'm happy to report that your potion has been of some benefit. I spoke with Caolte about a mark ago, and he said there has been improvement."

Lial rubbed at his temples. "Send Inona with the new versions."

"I already have." Lyr smiled. "Tynan suggested I do so. I also had one sent to Morenial over at Oria."

There was a place Lial wasn't in the mood to consider. His failure to heal Korel was far too fresh in his mind, not to mention the fact that this treachery had begun at that estate with Allafon in the first place. His jaw clenched against a scowl. At least Lyr would be the one to deal with tracking down all involved in the latest plot.

"What of our traitors?" Lynia asked, echoing his thoughts. "Have you made a decision about Fenere and Koranel?"

Lyr's jaw clenched. "Koranel has agreed to continue to appear friendly to the Sidhe lord Meren. If possible, he'll infiltrate Meren's inner circle and give us information."

Or perhaps it wasn't a boon that Lyr was the one dealing with this. Infiltrating the Sidhe lord's camp? There was an almost certain chance Lial would have another crisis to heal because of that, especially with Koranel involved. The man had already turned traitor once.

"You would trust him after what he did?" Lial snapped.

"I trust the blood bond." Lyr shrugged. "Otherwise, we shall see. Fenere will be exiled, likely to one of the abandoned colonies. At this point, I don't care which."

"No," Lynia protested. Lial frowned at her sudden pallor, but the cause was quickly explained. "This plague came from Rrelen and was used on Abuiarn, and it is possibly the basis for Kien's poison. I haven't had time to research where Kien was exiled before he escaped to Earth. For all we know, he learned the trick in one of those places. It would be wise to consider future locations most carefully. I would rather not deal with another forgotten horror."

Lyr grimaced. "Indeed not."

A new wave of exhaustion swirled through Lial until he considered settling his head atop the table for a nap. He could no longer deny what he would tell any patient of his—he needed more sleep. Followed by another healing session and yet more sleep. If he remained in this seat any longer, they'd have to haul him to his bed.

Lial stood, wavering on his feet. "I think I'm ready to rest now."

He barely remembered bidding Lyr farewell or settling beneath the covers. Everything was well-handled, no crisis awaiting him and him alone. As soon as Lynia nestled against him, he let himself drift to sleep.

Lial was making her crazy.

Only five marks past dawn, and already, Lynia was contemplating murder—and they'd slept through the first mark of that. Though his body was still weak, his magical energy had recovered, which made keeping him abed a nightmare. Every time she turned around, he was at the table taking notes from *The Wayfarer's Trial* or pacing the floor like a caged *camahr* instead of lying in bed with the book she'd brought him.

According to Tynan, multiple healing sessions throughout the night had repaired much of the damage to Lial's organs, but such an

unprecedented attack on the body had drained his physical reserves. Vitamins and minerals? Depleted. Innate cell repair? Sluggish. Magic could only do so much against that. He would need all of his energy to regenerate.

But as usual, Lial had to push himself. She'd finally fled downstairs for a few moments of peace before she throttled him.

Maddy and her mates had been allowed to return home, so Lynia didn't even have Maddy to commiserate with. A week ago, she wouldn't have expected to miss the trio, but she did. Tynan was nice enough, but he didn't have the same openness as the young fae from Earth. Now, she was a little lonely. But at least she'd been able to make a special request of Fen.

Stifling an inexplicable sense of frustration, she stopped at the table beside the workbench. Lial would have to sit still to eat, right? *Sure.* With a snort, Lynia lifted the tray of food and headed toward the stairs. She smiled at Caeleth and Tynan, who was helping the young mage eat his breakfast, but she didn't pause to chat. Time to see what trouble Lial was getting into—risking himself in some way, no doubt.

Her hands tightened around the breakfast tray as she navigated the spiral stairs to his room, but she almost threw the entire thing to the floor when she spotted Lial standing before his mirror and speaking to someone through the link. Why was he using that much magic so soon? Lynia sucked a breath in through her nose and did her best to settle the tray on the table without slamming it. She wanted to march over there, grab the tail of his glorious hair, and drag him back to the bed at once. Not for fun, either.

"Thank you," Lial said. Obviously not to her, for if he could hear her thoughts… "Any equipment you could send would be greatly appreciated. I hope to distribute as much of this potion as possible in case our containment spell failed to stop all infections."

When Lial closed the link a few moments later, Lynia approached. Now that the mirror had returned to casting a reflection, he caught sight of her and turned. The lines of strain around his mouth in no way eased her temper.

"What would you say to me if I was doing this much work so soon after a major illness?" she asked sweetly.

His lips twitched. "No doubt something terrible."

Lynia grabbed his wrist and tugged, drawing him toward the table. "Did you really need to expend your energy like that? Your body needs that power to heal. I'm sure Lyr would be willing to contact other estates for distilling equipment since he's already hunting down more of the *ilni* mentioned in Emereh's research."

"I'm not so bad as all of that," Lial said, though he sat and took his food from the tray without complaint. "I should be able to return to my duties by this evening, tomorrow at the latest, which I'm certain Tynan and Elan will appreciate. Not to mention Caeleth. I'm sure he's growing impatient with confinement, and Tynan is not as good at regeneration magic."

"He seemed content enough eating breakfast."

"But he will have to remain immobile after that," Lial argued. "He risks tearing his stitches when he moves until I can speed the healing on his abdomen. That'll be slow enough already if all the bleeding during the second surgery didn't flush out the rest of the iron."

Logically, his words made sense. He had important duties awaiting his attention, like Caeleth's healing. Lynia knew that. But she also knew Lial. As soon as he was well enough to work, he would overdo it again. She was not going to sit through another vigil, waiting to see if he would survive. At least not any time soon.

"Perhaps I am selfish, but I want you to be in good health for me," she finally admitted over her last bite of bread. "I want to be

517

with you without worrying that you'll regress. Not to mention that you're a terrible patient. Do remember that next time you complain about someone who won't take your advice."

Lial chuckled softly at the last, but his expression quickly sobered. When he ran his finger gently across the back of her hand, she shivered. "Perhaps I could use more time abed, Lyni. But I'm unaccustomed to indolence, you know. I might do better if you rested with me."

Her body went hot, but she shook her head. "You need more sleep."

"I assure you that is not what I need most."

"You almost died yesterday," Lynia argued, doing her best to ignore the fire in his gaze. "As a healer, you should know better than anyone that you have to save all of your energy for recovery. I'm annoyed enough that I found you using the mirror before you'd even had breakfast."

Lial made a show of grabbing an extra slice of bread from the tray, and she rolled her eyes at him for the effort. "Ample nourishment should help more than anything, Lyni. And comfort. Closeness. Drifting in that dark place between life and death…"

Some of her annoyance eased, if not the concern. "I slept at your side all night."

"And that was precisely what I needed. Then."

Lynia huffed. "Gods. Did I mention that you're a terrible patient?"

"I'm the worst," he agreed without a hint of shame. "I ache for you, love. I want to seal the words spoken in darkness with our bodies now that I've returned to the light. I promise I am healthy enough for that."

When Lial stood, she did, too, but they didn't touch. Instead,

he held her gaze, his feelings shining clearly in his eyes—love and hope and longing. A desire only she could quench. Heat prickled her skin, and her breathing went quick and shallow. It would be foolishness to do this, wouldn't it? But after all the fear and near-loss, the temptation was great.

Lynia eased closer and wrapped her arms around his waist, settling her cheek against his chest. His heart beat steadily beneath her ear, the same lullaby that had soothed her to sleep the night before. He was alive, and that hadn't been a certainty less than a day ago.

Maybe he was right—maybe they needed to be together.

"I can't believe I am considering this," Lynia muttered into his tunic.

Lial kissed the top of her head. "You're more than welcome to take the lead again if you're worried for me."

She leaned back. "And then you'll try to use your magic on my back, won't you?"

"Maybe." His hands slid along her spine in one long caress, his thumbs working out the slight ache she'd barely noticed when she first woke. "A fine test of my abilities, I'd say."

He cupped her bottom and drew her against his hardness, leaving no doubt about his readiness in that regard. There was no trembling in his hold, no sign of weakness in the muscles beneath her hand. She searched his face for any hint of strain and discovered only desire.

Safe. It truly was safe. The danger was passed.

It seemed she would get to keep him after all.

Her worry crumbled, and she sagged against him. "I've been afraid to accept that the worst was all over. That you wouldn't regress or just…"

"Die suddenly, like Telien," Lial said softly.

Lynia nodded. "I'm sorry."

"Don't be." He brushed his lips against hers. "Though you should know I'm too stubborn to die that easily, especially now that I have you. I've only waited twenty years."

"Is that all?" Lynia slid her fingers into the bundle of hair at the base of his head and tugged his mouth to hers for a longer, more satisfying kiss. Then she smiled against his lips. "It seems I'll have to commission *you* a fabulous ring. Clearly, you deserve it."

"I only need you, Lyni," he said.

Her hesitation gone, she let him lead her toward the bed.

The healer knew best, after all.

Epilogue

Two weeks later

Lynia trailed her fingers up Lial's side and smiled when he shivered. It was barely sunrise, but he'd wanted to awaken early so he could return to the healing tower before the storm hit. It hadn't taken as much coaxing as she'd feared to convince him to join her in her room for most of the nights, especially since Tynan hadn't yet departed.

The healer-priest hadn't agreed to stay, but she had a feeling Lial was wearing him down.

"I must go soon," Lial said, even as he tucked her closer against his side. "But if you want to make love again—"

"That wasn't what I had in mind. Not that the idea doesn't have merit." Lynia levered herself upright. Lial didn't seem to notice when she reached for the small box on the side table, his focus on her nakedness. There was some benefit to attempting to surprise a man before getting dressed. "Hold out your hand."

Though he quirked an eyebrow, he sat up to do as she asked. Her heart fluttered as she placed the square wooden box atop his hand and waited. What would he think of her gift? He would never hurt her feelings on purpose, but that didn't mean it wouldn't be obvious if he was unhappy. That would hurt as much as an intentional slight.

"What is this?" he asked.

She huffed out an impatient breath. "Open it and see."

More slowly than strictly necessary, Lial lifted the lid and peered inside. For a moment, she could only study the forest scene intricately carved into the wooden top, too nervous to check the look on his face. But she couldn't stand the suspense for more than a heartbeat. Unfortunately, his expression was blank.

Dratted man.

"You'll need to use some words here, Lyni," he said softly, his gaze lifting to hers. "There's too much for me to interpret."

Lynia snatched the box from his hand and lifted out the ring, holding it up between them. The small vial still inside clicked gently against the wood as she settled the box in her lap. "I don't want our relationship to be casual. Not that it is, but…I want you to marry me. You've already given me a ring, so I had one made for you. Fen had it sent through the outpost portal."

"I thought you were joking about that," Lial said, his voice awed. "Are you certain about this? I would like nothing more than to wed, but there is plenty of time."

She smiled sadly. "Is there? I think it's clear that not even our long-lived kind are guaranteed a single day. And didn't you see the other thing I included?"

He glanced down, and his eyebrows rose. "The fertility potion."

"We don't have to use it now, but I don't want to wait too long." Lynia worried the little vial with the tip of her finger. "The shortness of time and such."

Lial stared at her for so long that she began to reconsider her definition of eternity, but a slow smile finally curved his lips. "Yes."

It wasn't an opportune time to throttle him, and yet...

"To which request?" she asked with all the patience she could gather.

His grin widened. "Both, of course."

Finally, Lial took the ring and slid it onto his right ring finger. Unlike hers, the band had no stone, but the silver was engraved with tiny leaves. And the magic imbued inside was different. "According to Fen, you can alter the shape. Stretch it into a bracelet or necklace if you need it out of the way for surgery. Among other things, if you'd like to read the note."

He didn't appear to be interested in those other things. Lial gave her a long, sweet kiss before lifting the vial from the box. "We may need to wait until tonight for this. Come to the healing tower with me in case we get iced in."

Lynia laughed. "I'm not certain I'm at a good point in my cycle for best effect, though I'm happy to join you regardless."

Lial settled his hand low on her abdomen. "May I check?"

Lynia nodded, her hands knotted in the sheets. What if he found a problem? The potion would be a waste, and they would both be disappointed. Not even the peaceful swell of his healing magic eased her fear—and his sudden pallor certainly didn't.

"We'll...not need this at the moment," he finally murmured, placing the vial back into the box.

Her heart dropped. "Something is wrong."

"You misunderstand." His wide eyes found hers. "We... You..."

Gods. Would she have to shake the words free? "*Miaran*, Lial. You're a healer. You should have plenty of experience delivering bad news by now."

"That's not…" He pressed his palm between his eyes before dropping his hand with a sigh. "Lyni, you're already pregnant. With, ah…two."

It took so long for the first part to sink in that she almost missed the second. "What? You must be mistaken."

Annoyance replaced some of the shock in his eyes. "I assure you I am more than capable of such a simple examination, my love."

Of course he was. She knew that. Even so, it took several heartbeats before she could fathom the reality. She'd wanted to have children soon, but she hadn't expected it to be so fast. Or… numerous. "Will they be identical, do you think?"

"No." Smiling, Lial closed the box and settled it on the table. Her thoughts were still a muddled mess when he drew her into his arms. "They are fraternal. Conceived just after my illness, considering their developmental stage."

"Twins are such a rarity," she whispered against his neck.

His breath rustled her hair. "Typically. But you were beside me when Aris flooded me with life magic to eradicate the last of the virus. I should have considered that."

That reminded her of the fertility potion, and a new thought crossed her mind. Even though he'd been the one to take the tincture designed to increase her fertility, she'd gotten pregnant anyway. As laughter shook her body, Lial drew back with a concerned frown. Eventually, she wiped her eyes and grinned.

"Maybe it's my fault," she said, stifling another chuckle. "I did give you that fertility potion out of desperation. Elan said it shouldn't affect men, but…"

His frown only deepened. "You would have had to release two eggs for—"

Lynia pressed her fingers against his mouth. "Just enjoy the irony, love."

His expression softened, and he lowered his mouth for another kiss. But it wasn't long before the sharp crack of ice against the window drew them apart. Lynia glared at the glass, but it did nothing to change the weather.

"You should stay here," Lial said. "I don't want to risk you walking on the ice. This will be difficult enough on your back without a fall."

"Lial?" At his quirked brow, she smiled. "Shut up."

In the end, he helped her pack.

Though the ice was nearly as thick as his hand, Lial lowered himself to the ground behind the healing tower. There were fewer injuries now that the season was settling in, and he'd ordered Tynan to keep watch while he slipped out to check on the *camahr*. With their bowls filled, there was nothing for him to do but wait and see if any of them emerged.

It was difficult to credit the accounts he'd heard of being guarded by a *camahr* kit, but no one had reason to lie. Lynia certainly wouldn't. But if one of the creatures had chosen him as a companion, why had it left? Had it only been drawn to the impure magic used in the virus? They did use their tails to check for tainted food. Why not bad energy?

Gods, he hoped he didn't have to untangle the full mystery of the virus. He would much rather produce the counter potion and allow others to track down Meren and his tangled plot. A few decades ago, the challenge might have interested him, but not now. He would not risk further injury. If he got himself hurt before their wedding, Lynia would kill him.

Not to mention impending fatherhood. He could still barely fathom the weight of it. And though he'd delivered many babies over the centuries, the thought of doing so with his own had ice layering his gut like the ground beneath him. He knew all too well the things that could go wrong.

Best not to dwell on those.

At least he had an idea to help handle the virus and any potion distribution, provided he could…ease Tynan into the role. It would be a risk, since the plan involved Kezari, and Tynan was nothing if not distracted around her. Nevertheless, it was something to discuss with Lyr. Their immediate outbreak might be over, but there would no doubt be trouble in other realms.

He had plenty to occupy his thoughts here. Alerielle had inquired about his willingness to help with Kai's mother, and that was a mess he couldn't ignore. It was bad enough that Naomh's stab wound wasn't mending even though the potion had eliminated the virus. Those two things would take a great deal of energy to solve on their own.

Of course, he apparently had a crystal full of his own energy in a sealed chest in his room, so there was that. It was too rare to be used casually, but it could prove vital if the virus resurged or shifted. His cousin had done something useful after all, despite his failure to read the futures clearly. Though Ralan *had* been guilt-ridden enough to promise him an elaborate family suite in the healer's enclave.

Which he would need. Gods.

Movement at the base of the tower caught his eye. A snout. One of the kits peeked out at him. Then its mother appeared, nudging the kit fully from the hole with a grumbled *rrowl*. Slowly, the young *camahr* approached, its silvery fur gleaming in the afternoon light.

He blinked, and the kit jumped in his lap.

Emowa, he heard.

The kit's name?

"Oh, good," a cheerful voice called from the tree line. "You didn't give up."

Lial almost winced, but he caught himself in time. He would not hurt the child's feelings again, especially since her warning had been a boon. All of her warnings were, no matter how little one wanted to hear them.

"Thank you, Eri," he simply said.

"I'm glad you didn't give up on Lynia, either. I was hoping."

With a grin and a wave, the little girl darted away, somehow managing to fly across the ice despite the spikes attached to her shoes. He kept his eye on her until she was out of sight, but she showed no sign of slipping. A trick of youth or the foresight of a seer? He was happy not to know.

"Are you coming with me, Emowa?" he whispered, feeling more than a little foolish.

At least until the *camahr* climbed down from his lap and stared at him in expectation.

Apparently so.

His new companion followed him around the base of the tower and through the door, where it found a spot beneath his workbench to curl up. He would have to commission bedding, but the kit seemed content enough at the moment. Unlike Tynan, who frowned in disapproval.

Too bad.

Lial headed for the stairs where Lynia waited above.

Now, the last thing he had to worry about was being alone.

Character List and Dictionary

Characters

Allafon: Previous Lord of Oria, an estate under Lyr's command. He betrayed Lyr and was eventually brought to justice after Arlyn's arrival.

Anna: Mate to Maddy and Fen. Anna once believed herself to be human, but after the barrier fell, allowing magic to return to Earth, her fae blood began to awaken. Ann is a descendant of the Gwragedd Annwn, Welsh fae.

Aralee: Lial's previous beloved

Aris: Selia's husband and Iren's father. Aris is a life mage who can connect with the essence of living things and manipulate them. Once presumed dead, he returned to his family after the dragon Kezari rescued him and was instrumental in destroying the barrier.

Arlyn: Half-blood daughter of Lyr and his potential soulbonded, Aimee, who he met on Earth. Arlyn traveled to Moranaia after her mother's death to confront her elven father and quickly bonded with Kai. After helping Lyr and Kai defeat Allafon, Arlyn decided to stay on Moranaia and train as her father's heir.

Caolte: Brother of Naomh and Meren. Caolte was born of an affair between his father and an Unseelie woman, making it difficult for him to fit in with either faction. Caolte is sworn to protect his brother, Naomh.

Cora: Ralan's soulbonded. Originally from Galare, Cora fled to Earth after a failed betrothal put her in danger. To pull power from an environment, Cora must bond with that particular place. When Ralan was almost killed defeating Kien, Cora saved him by linking to Moranaia.

Delbin: A young elf exiled to Earth one hundred years prior in order to escape Allafon's machinations. Now that Allafon is dead, Delbin is able to return to Moranaia. He is often sent on missions requiring knowledge of modern Earth.

Dria: Youngest child of King Alianar and Enielle. Dria was sent early to the Citadel, the place where the highest-ranking mages train for battle. At 317, Dria is one of the youngest to complete her training and take her place within a mage troop.

Elan: A lower-level healer who acts as Lial's assistant.

Eri: Daughter of Prince Ralan and a human woman. After nearly dying from energy poisoning, her father brought her to Moranaia from Earth to be healed.

Fen: Mate to Anna and Maddy. Son of Ara and a human man. Fen was abandoned on Earth, where he got involved with Kien's group of outcasts. To atone for working with Kien, Fen helps repair the damage he'd once contributed to creating.

Fenere: One of three bodyguards assigned by the previous captain, Norin, to protect Arlyn after she first arrived.

Inona: A Moranaian scout most frequently assigned to check on exiles banished to Earth. After finding Delbin, she is often sent on missions to Earth with him.

Kezari: A dragon from the distant Isle of Dragons on Moranaia. Kezari rescued Aris from captivity and returned with him to Braelyn to fix a problem she detected with Earth's energy.

Kien: Son of King Alianar and Enielle. Power-hungry and determined to someday claim the throne, Kien plotted to kill his brother Ralan, a seer, first. When he was ultimately discovered, Kien was banished to a distant planet but managed to escape to Earth. He finally made his way back to Moranaia and was killed by the king.

Koranel: Current captain of Lyr's army, next in command after Lyr

Korel: One of three bodyguards assigned by the previous captain, Norin, to protect Arlyn after she first arrived. Of the three, he was the only one banished by Lyr for failing to stop an attempt on Arlyn's life.

Leral: One of three bodyguards assigned by the previous captain, Norin, to protect Arlyn after she first arrived.

Lial: The primary healer at Braelyn, Lyr's estate. Lial is renowned for being both highly skilled and easily annoyed.

Lynia: Lyr's mother. A researcher whose magic lies in books and knowledge. Lynia was almost killed during Allafon's attempted coup, but Lial saved her.

Lyr: Lord of Braelyn. Son of Lynia and soulbonded of Meli. Forced to leave his first potential soulbonded on Earth to find his father's murderer, Lyr expected neither a future mate nor children. But after Arlyn's arrival and the subsequent upheaval, Lyr has learned to stop expecting anything—unless it is unusual. Now he lives with his daughter, Arlyn, his new bonded, Meli, and an odd assortment of people he never thought could coexist on a single estate.

Maddy: Mate to Fen and Anna. Maddy lives in Chattanooga, Tennessee and is currently buying her friend Cora's shop, The Magic Touch, after Cora moved to Moranaia. Maddy is half Seelie Sidhe and half human. Maddy helps any fae who need to integrate with humans.

Meli: Lyr's soulbonded. One of the rare Ljósálfar (Norse elves), Meli guided her king's ambassador to Moranaia to ask for help with the energy poisoning affecting their realm. She ultimately bonds with Lyr and remains on Moranaia.

Meren: Brother of Naomh and Caolte. Meren is the oldest of the brothers but diverges sharply in ideology. Believing that the Seelie Sidhe should leave their underground realms and reclaim the surface, Meren will do whatever he deems necessary to achieve his goals.

Naomh: Brother of Meren and Caolte. Kai's father. Naomh once worked with Kien in a misguided attempt to keep his people from returning to the surface. Now, he tries to stop Meren from causing further trouble.

Norin: Previous captain of Lyr's army who secretly worked for Allafon. He attempted to capture Lynia and was killed in the process.

Ralan: Son of King Alianar and Enielle. Eri's father. Soulbonded to Cora. Now that Kien has been defeated, Ralan is helping establish a secondary palace to monitor the new gate Aris and Kezari created to Earth.

Telien: Lynia's soulbonded and Lyr's father. Killed by Norin at the command of Allafon.

Tynan: Mind healer and priest of Bera. He temporarily traveled to Braelyn to help Aris with his trauma.

Common Terms

Bera: Goddess of the afterlife, protection, and healing

Braelyn: Lyr's estate

camahr: An animal on Moranaia that is somewhat between a fox and cat in shape and disposition. It can use the tip of its tail to detect impurities.

clechtan: A Moranaian curse word similar to 'damn'

cofol: A type of wolfdog used in hunting

daeri: deer

drec: A Moranaian insult. Someone who defiles nature or the natural order.

elnaia: Moranaian word for grandmother

Eradisel: One of the nine sacred trees, symbol of Dorenal

Felshreh: Unseelie word for blood elf

Gwragedd Annwn: Welsh water fae, said to inhabit lakes.

inai: DNA / builders of life

laial: More formal Moranaian word for father

laiala: More formal Moranaian word for mother

Meyanen: God of love and relationships

mialn: Beloved (used for mate or lover)

miaran: Iron (literal). Used commonly as an expletive

miaran de fe onai: Expletive phrase meaning "iron in the heart"

onaial: Moranaian word for Dad

onaiala: Moranaian word for Mom

onraiee: Author / writer / creator

peresten: Elvensteel

ruya: Seelie curse word meaning corrupted / to corrupt

tieln: Beloved (used with a child, sibling, or parent)

Made in the USA
Coppell, TX
07 June 2021